Outstanding praise for E⟨

"Confounding twists and seismi⟨ ⟩ meticulously crafted, diabolically plotted mystery. Structured to max-imize suspense, the tale unfolds in seven parts, each with its own nuanced first-person-present narrator and unique voice. Every new section delivers a kaleidoscopic turn, reframing all that came before and keeping readers perennially off-kilter. A devilishly clever delight." —*Kirkus Reviews* (starred review)

"In this excellent small-town spine-tingler, Hill (*The Secrets We Share*) shuffles through multiple perspectives to examine the murder of a restaurant owner. As soon as readers think they've found a safe landing place for their sympathies, Hill detonates one of the series of game-changing twists he's planted throughout the narrative. Fans of Riley Sager will want to check this out." —*Publishers Weekly* (starred review)

"Praised by critics as dark, complex with great character development, this standalone thriller is both provocative and engag-ing. Highly recommended for thriller fans." —*Mystery Tribune*

And outstanding praise for *The Secrets We Share*

"Shari Lapena meets Ruth Ware. A compulsively readable domestic thriller." —Charlie Donlea, *USA Today* bestselling author of *Twenty Years Later*

"A bold, ambitious novel with a big, multigenerational story line, a busload of characters, and a smart balance between mystery and suspense. . . . For fans of Robert Bryndza and Karin Slaughter." —*First Clue* (starred review)

"Hill keeps the clock ticking and the twists coming right up to the shocking conclusion. Suburban thriller fans will be well satisfied." —*Publishers Weekly*

"This suspenseful story will have readers careening from one erro-neous conclusion to the next." —*Library Journal* (starred review)

"Full of whiplash twists and dark family secrets, Edwin Hill's new standalone is clever and chilling. Be advised to not trust anyone." —Peter Swanson, bestselling author of *A Talent for Murder*

Books by Edwin Hill

LITTLE COMFORT

THE MISSING ONES

WATCH HER

THE SECRETS WE SHARE

WHO TO BELIEVE

Published by Kensington Publishing Corp.

WHO TO BELIEVE

EDWIN HILL

KENSINGTON
PUBLISHING CORP.

www.kensingtonbooks.com

KENSINGTON BOOKS are published by
Kensington Publishing Corp.
900 Third Avenue
New York, NY 10022

ISBN: 978-1-4967-4242-1 (ebook)

ISBN: 978-1-4967-4241-4

First Kensington Hardcover Printing: February 2024
First Kensington Trade Paperback Printing: January 2025

10 9 8 7 6 5 4 3 2 1

Printed in the United States of America

To Shawn

September 14. From the online Monreith Dispatch

Laurel Thibodeau, 36, was found dead early Sunday morning in her house on Linden Lane. Her husband, Simon Thibodeau, 38, alerted the Monreith Police Department after he returned from catering an event in Rhode Island and discovered her body. Laurel Thibodeau was last seen late Saturday evening leaving the Firefly Bistro, which she owned with her husband. As of Sunday evening, according to Police Chief Max Barbosa, crime scene investigators have begun processing evidence. He assures the public more information will be forthcoming. "The state police will be managing the case with the full cooperation of this department. We encourage anyone with information to come forward while we explore every possible angle."

While Barbosa did not reveal the cause of death, sources within the Monreith Police Department report Laurel Thibodeau had been asphyxiated with a plastic bag. Foul play is suspected.

PART I

The Shrink

CHAPTER 1
Farley

"I'm frightened," Alice Stone says.

She sits across from me as she has every Friday afternoon for the past eight months. Her voice is so soft I can barely make out her words. She averts her eyes in a way that tells me she has something to confess, a secret to share. I let her statement hang between us, offering her the space to fill in the rest of her story. She doesn't speak. Instead, she runs her hand through Harper's fur. The pit bull mix sighs and rests her brindled snout on Alice's foot.

Usually, Alice presents as a pleaser, an eager client who's more concerned with whether I like her than sharing a truth. She chats from the moment she arrives for her session, filling every silence as she runs through fights with her husband, Damian, or struggles with her son, Noah, providing commentary and analysis on her own meandering thoughts. Despite all the chatter, I suspect Alice Stone has spent a lifetime masking her true nature. We all have a hidden self, a shadow side we try to keep private, but my job is to help her peek out from behind that mask, and today, forty minutes into her session, is the closest we've ever gotten.

I rest my chin, rough with afternoon scruff, on my palm. "You're frightened," I say, mirroring her words, my voice soft, too.

Alice perches on the edge of her chair as though she's ready to bolt from the room. Autumn light filters through the slats in the blinds and across her smooth skin. A curtain of dark hair cascades over her shoulders. I'd have to be blind not to notice how stunning she is, even in this moment of vulnerability. Or maybe *because* of that vulnerability. If I know one thing about myself—Dr. Farley Drake, MD—it's that I have a savior complex.

"We're all frightened," Alice says. "We'd be fools not to be. I *knew* Laurel."

Laurel Thibodeau.

Most sessions I've had this week have eventually come back to the brutal murder. Laurel—along with her husband, Simon—owned a local bistro, one with warm lighting and an easy menu of steak frites and pub burgers. Nearly everyone in town knew the couple, or at least they believed they did. Last Saturday—or Sunday morning, to be accurate—Simon Thibodeau returned home, supposedly from catering a wedding, to find his wife bound and gagged in their bed. She'd been suffocated by the plastic bag tied at her neck.

In the ensuing days, state detectives have descended on this tiny coastal town, digging for secrets and turning rumor into truth, especially when it comes to husband Simon. The Thibodeaus had money problems Simon tried to hide from the cops: maxed-out credit cards, a secret second mortgage. And Simon had not been catering a wedding as he'd claimed. Instead, he'd gone to the Mohegan Sun in nearby Connecticut and lost twenty grand at the blackjack tables. Lucky for him, his every move at the casino had been caught on tape, although the gossips' latest whispers have Simon putting a hit out on his wife because of the two-million-dollar life insurance policy the couple had bought six months earlier, the one Simon had kept paying premiums on even as he let his other bills lapse into collection. Most of my clients have already tried and convicted him.

But there's more to the story.

Laurel, the victim, had her own secrets. She volunteered at the local Unitarian church, driving older parishioners to various appointments during the week. She also had sticky fingers, especially when it came to jewelry and cash. The police discovered a stockpile of missing items in the Thibodeaus' garage, along with an online auction site that has since been disabled. My guess is that Laurel was trying to keep the Thibodeaus afloat as Simon gambled away their earnings and put them further into debt. Supposedly, Laurel was even threatened a few weeks ago by a thug who Simon owed money to.

Each of these details has come to me in sessions throughout the week, enough that I could probably solve the murder myself. As a small-town therapist, I have a unique view of this community's factions and alliances through my roster of interconnected clients. Pieces of this puzzle present themselves, allowing me to gather them and fit them together. Maybe someone else had a hand in the murder, like that person Simon owed money to. Maybe there's a different killer out there who's been setting Simon up from the start.

Maybe the killer has sat in this very room.

I focus on Alice Stone. Frightened or not, I suspect she could kill under the right circumstances. But then, most of us could. "A death like this one leaves a bruise on a community," I say. "It will take time to heal."

"Believe me, I know," Alice says. "Damian hunts monsters. Now it's like the monster has come to us."

Alice is a financial planner who works with customers all over the country. She spends her days meeting with them online. Her husband, Damian, is a documentary filmmaker who focuses on true crime. Before moving here to Monreith in Massachusetts last winter, they'd lived in northern Maine so Damian could document a small community of French speakers, ostensibly to record part of the French diaspora. After a local priest named Jean-Marc died, though, Damian discovered dozens of victims of sexual abuse whose stories he told in the film. The result, *Acadian Autumn*, has been making the rounds on the festival circuit and, according to Alice, getting some buzz. "Though not what we'd hoped for," she'd confessed to me a few weeks earlier. Now the Stones are staying at a friend's farmhouse while Damian works on his latest project. When he finishes, they'll take off for new horizons.

"What are people saying to you about the murder?" Alice asks me.

"You tell me," I say, deflecting the question back to her. "What *are* people saying?"

"That Simon will be charged with obstruction of justice, at the very least. He's been lying from the start."

"Who's saying that?"

"People."

I can guess who these "people" might be: Max Barbosa, the chief of police, who lives next door to me. I can see his back deck from my kitchen. I watch him out there in the morning drinking coffee and going through his morning workout, his prematurely white hair still sticking up before he changes into his starched uniform, puts on his public mask, and oversees law and order in this town. I've also watched Alice join him once in a while in the afternoons, one foot on the rail, drinking beer from a can while they play cribbage.

I like to observe my clients in the wild, especially when they're doing things they don't want known. It allows me to understand another side of them, the side they conceal in this office. It's unorthodox, maybe worse, but it works. With Alice, it's hard to miss the way she touches her neck when she's with

Max, the way she shoves his arm while they play cards, or the way she lingers as she's parting. But that's the kind of data I keep to myself, at least until Alice opts to bring it into this room.

"Do you think Simon will be charged?" I ask. "It's been a week since the murder. What are they waiting for?"

I am curious, for a number of reasons. I'm testing to see if Alice will betray any of Max's confidences, but mostly I wonder if she'll present new pieces of the puzzle. I have my own hidden self. Maybe I want to be an amateur sleuth more than I care to admit.

"I like Simon," Alice says. "And I really like going to Firefly. I hope it doesn't close. God, did that make me sound shallow?"

There's no judgment in this room.

"I almost invited Simon to the party tonight," Alice continues, "but I couldn't quite bring myself to do it. I doubt he has many other invitations these days."

I lean forward and tent my hands. Tonight is Alice's birthday, and she's having a gathering at the farmhouse. Like any small-town therapist, I run into clients socially. It can't be avoided. Usually, I leave it to the client to decide whether to disclose our relationship, and then I maintain a professional distance. Lately, though, Alice and I have gone a step too far and become friends. Tonight, I'll be at her party as a guest where she'll call me Farley instead of Dr. Drake, and it's a line I really shouldn't have allowed us to cross. "We've talked about a transition to a new therapist," I say.

Alice waves a dismissive hand. "I haven't had the time to find one."

"Still," I say.

"I'll take care of it this week," she says. "I promise. And I'm making ratatouille. You'll love it."

The first time I went to the farmhouse, Alice made a tagine

that tasted of nothing but carbon and salt. She's a terrible cook.

"You mentioned being frightened," I say. "What were you circling?"

Her gaze sharpens as she scans the room for one of the many clocks. Beside her, Harper sits up, as though sensing Alice's need to escape.

"No one's keeping you here," I say. "You can take off whenever you want. But there are only five minutes until the end of our time together. Three hundred seconds. Why not get your money's worth?"

Alice rests her bag on her lap, forming a barrier between us. "I shouldn't have said anything to you. I knew you'd latch onto this like a . . . like a . . ." She lowers her voice. "Like a pit bull."

I allow myself a laugh. "That's my job. And from where I sit, Harper has a strong sense of self."

"Then you haven't seen her during a thunderstorm."

"She's aware," I say. "That's good. Thunder frightens her. What frightens you?"

Alice settles into her chair for the first time this afternoon. Her shoulders relax, and she crosses one shoe over the other. This is how she normally presents, and I worry we may have moved beyond the potential breakthrough.

"Sometimes," she says, "I make things up in these sessions because I can't think of anything to say. I mean, what do I have to complain about? I didn't find my husband with a plastic bag over his head."

Somehow, I doubt she'd be upset if she did, but that's a topic for another session. "You're hardly the first client to make something up," I say. "But we'll end at 3:50 whether you answer my question or not. You have 180 seconds left. And feeling frightened is normal. Let's get to the source."

"Do you pull everything you say out of a bag of random platitudes?"

"What would you like me to say instead?"

"How about something real? Why not ask what you want to ask? When I say I'm frightened, who would you guess I'm talking about? What do you think I mean, Dr. Drake?"

I wait to answer, and I can't help it, but the edges of my mouth begin to twitch into a grin.

"I know what you're going to ask," Alice says. "Don't you dare!"

"What do *you* want it to mean when you say you're frightened?"

Alice plants her feet on the floor. She snaps the leash onto Harper's collar, who stands and wags her thin tail.

I open my hands. "I can't do the work for you."

"It's stupid. I mean, admitting it will make me sound small and self-involved. Especially when we were just talking about someone getting murdered."

"There isn't much I haven't heard already."

"Fine. I turned forty today. That's a big deal, right? We're having a party, and I took care of nearly every single detail. I mean, I did my own cooking! But Damian needs to remember the cake. And it better be carrot. *With* raisins."

"Does he know that?"

"We've been married for almost twenty years. Shouldn't he know my favorite kind of cake?"

"I meant does he know you want him to get the cake?"

"I'm supposed to remind him to get a cake for his wife's milestone birthday? Is that something else I should be responsible for? Maybe I *should* get a new therapist. A woman. Someone who would understand."

This may be the most honesty Alice Stone has ever shown. "For the record," I say, "I love carrot cake. And you don't sound idiotic to me." I scratch Harper behind the ears as the clock ticks over to 3:50. "That's time. We'll pick up next week."

"Not if I find a new therapist."

She won't. But I'll keep pushing.

Alice doesn't move. "Please don't mention any of this to Damian."

I learned to keep secrets long ago. "Everything you say in this room is confidential."

I walk her to the rear exit, where she pauses with her hand on the knob. "If Simon Thibodeau didn't kill Laurel," she says, "then who did?"

That's the one question no one has dared ask me yet this week. Maybe Alice has good reason to be frightened. Maybe we all do.

CHAPTER 2
Farley

Through the blinds in my office, I observe as Alice emerges onto the brick sidewalk below. She puts on huge sunglasses and hurries across the street, waiting for a woman to pass by before enticing Harper into the back of an SUV and speeding away. She's my last client of the day, and even though I should head to the gym before the afternoon gets away from me, I boot up my laptop and check to be sure the bouquet of dahlias and chrysanthemums I ordered has been delivered to Moulton Farm where Alice lives.

I also open her file, where I've questioned before how strong Alice's marriage to Damian might be. Now I type, *Patient reported being frightened. Of what? And whom?*

I should go with the obvious answer: Damian. She'd challenged me to do so during her session, and tonight at the party, I'll observe and piece together what I can, especially if Damian manages to forget that cake. I type *Likely frightened by husband Damian Stone* in the report right as my phone rings.

It's Georgia Fitzhugh, the local Unitarian minister.

"Any chance you could swing by the church?" she asks when I click into the call. "I need someone to pinch hit with Chloe. She messed up. Big time."

Georgia's daughter, Chloe, is thirteen, with fat cheeks and freckles. Up until recently she'd been sweet and kind. Not so much lately. "She's testing boundaries," I say. "It's normal. Healthy even."

"Thanks for the tip, Farley," Georgia says to me. "Why don't you chat with her about healthy boundaries? You can put those fancy degrees to use. I'm stuck here, and Ritchie's at the garage . . . it would be a big help."

Richard, Georgia's soon-to-be-ex, is a mechanic who dabbles in selling classic cars. I haven't a clue what could be so important that he can't stop tinkering with an engine to come help with his own daughter, but I keep the thought to myself. And there's a plea in Georgia's voice I find hard to turn down. Guilt will do that. I've hurt Georgia too many times. "Be there in a few," I say.

After the call ends, I read through the notes in Alice's file one more time and hit *Save*. I leave the office and step out onto Main Street in downtown Monreith, where salty air blows off the harbor. With its jagged beaches and inlets, the town sits on the south coast of Massachusetts, west of Cape Cod and east of Rhode Island. What had once been a community of shipbuilders, whalers, and farmers has given way to commuters and second homes. Here in the harbor, boats line the piers, and a stone jetty juts into the water. We're in the last days of summer, so the street, with its gas lamps and cafes and comfortable restaurants, bustles with people taking in the final warmth of the year. I pass by the shuttered Firefly Bistro. Its wrought-iron namesake hovers over the door and a CLOSED sign hangs in the window next to last week's menu.

Like Alice, I hope Thibodeau's restaurant doesn't close down.

I wear a crisp white shirt and a light navy-blue jacket I know brings out the color in my eyes. As I make my way to the other

end of the downtown, I ignore the glances, the feigned indifference, and the full-on stares. I'm used to people watching
me. I'm handsome. More than handsome. I'm the kind of
good-looking that hurts, the kind that gets me a seat at Firefly
while others wait on the sidewalk, the kind that turns adults
into teenagers. I learned to wield the privilege—and the
power—a long time ago.

Mostly, I learned that it gets me almost anything I want.

I still see myself as a newcomer to tiny Monreith, if living in
a place for two years can be considered new. I grew up in the
middle of nowhere, a childhood I like to forget. I clawed my
way into college in Connecticut and graduated at the top of
my class from med school. Until a few years ago, I'd been hap-
pily living in Boston's South End and jetting around the world
on weekends to chase the next big event. I certainly hadn't
imagined retreating to the country or stepping into a ready-
made family, but now, after living on the ocean, after not having to fight traffic or worry about missing the latest party, I've
grown accustomed to this quieter life. Most days, I can't imagine returning to what was.

On the other end of town, a gaggle of girls perches outside
Cups and Cones, the ice-cream shop. In the very center of the
group, a redhead has what appears to be a shiner developing
over her left cheekbone. These girls must be about Chloe's
age. I wish I'd see Chloe among a group like this one, laughing, probably being mean to the other kids in school. But
Chloe seems determined to be a loner and to forge her own
path. And I suppose that's for the best.

A few blocks later, I come to Georgia's church, classic white,
framed by maples, with a small cemetery of ancient gravestones lining one side. I feel like an interloper when I come
here, to Georgia's territory, where she takes center stage as
Reverend George and plays to her congregation. But I've spent

a lifetime observing, looking in from the outside—it's part of what makes me a successful therapist. I can fit in anywhere, even here.

Ahead, a man and a woman emerge from the church offices. They linger at a family plot where the man traces names engraved in the stone. Up close, I recognize him as the church's treasurer—Everett Irving, a former client. He speaks softly, but as I come into view, his voice catches. Beside him, the woman follows his gaze right to me, her face suddenly flushed. I wonder if that's his wife, Helen, if she's blushing now because she knows I know her secrets.

"Beautiful day," I say.

"Indeed!" Everett says, his voice loud.

The woman tugs at his hand. They hurry out of the churchyard, their heads bent together like those teenage girls I saw in town, whispering the entire time. Maybe Helen Irving just thought I was handsome.

Behind the church, a bike leans against the railing. As I approach, Alice's husband, Damian Stone, emerges from the church offices, clomping down the steps in red-and-blue–striped biking kit. He slips a phone into the pocket at the back of his jersey. He must be verging on fifty, with a trimmed beard just beginning to go gray. His legs are sinewy and shaved clean, not an ounce of fat on his frame. Thin enough to snap in two.

He looks upset and vulnerable, enough so that I wonder what his shadow side hides, but the moment he spots me, his presentation shifts. "Farley Drake!" he says to me, switching on his alpha male. "I was checking in with Georgia about the party. She's doing me a solid. You'll be there tonight, right?"

Seeing him catches me off guard. I take a split second to center myself, to compartmentalize the therapy session with his wife, to categorize anything she mentioned today as off-limits. It's all I can do not to hint at the carrot cake she's expecting, but that would be unethical. "Wouldn't miss it," I say.

Damian gets on the bike and clips his left toe to the pedal. "We should hit the road together sometime."

"I don't own a bike."

"Use one of mine. I can tell you about my film. Would love your psychiatric perspective. How about Sunday?"

Damian's under contract with one of the streaming services for this project, although he's been cagey about the details. I worry he might be seeing me more as an investor than a consultant, and our bike ride might turn into an endless pitch. He's the kind of guy who's impossible to foist off on someone else at a cocktail party, one who talks with a confidence that obscures a lack of substantive success.

"Sunday morning's booked for me," I say.

"Later in the day, then. We'll make it happen."

He pedals off before I can decline, speeding through the cemetery and then onto the street. I wonder what brought him to the church. Lately, I've felt as though Georgia has been keeping something from me, and even though she's close with Alice, it wouldn't be the first affair that broke up a friendship. But that could be my own paranoia. Most of the people I talk to in a day are suffering the repercussions of an affair in one way or another.

Inside the church, the wide-planked floors creak and the air smells of percolated coffee and musty hymnals. At the end of a hallway lined with children's drawings, Chloe slumps in a chair wearing a tie-dyed Greenpeace T-shirt, her gangling legs splayed in front of her. Pink hair falls in her eyes, a new look since last I saw her.

Maggie, the church secretary, plays solitaire on an ancient laptop. She must be close to sixty, with brown skin, hair home-dyed to hide the gray, and an endless supply of pastel-colored sweaters. I cock a hip against the doorjamb and say, "What's the score?"

Maggie minimizes the screen, while Chloe scowls.

"Don't tell on me," Maggie says.

"I'm good with secrets," I say.

She pushes away from her desk, her eyes taking me in. "I've heard about you and secrets, Farley Drake. And that smile of yours is dangerous. Don't forget I'm a married woman."

"My loss."

"I was also supposed to be gone an hour ago," Maggie says.

"I don't need a babysitter," Chloe says. "And where's Dad, anyway?"

I sweep pink hair from her eyes. Chloe bats my hand away, and I nod toward Georgia's office door. "On a scale from one to ten, how bad is it?"

Chloe kicks at her chair. "Like a thirteen? And why don't you tell her to just let me get a freaking phone?"

The phone.

Chloe's phone, or lack thereof, has been the latest battle between mother and daughter. Georgia insists that Chloe wait until she turns fourteen to get one, which is four long months from now. In Chloe's defense, she has to be one of the last kids in her grade to get her own phone. "I'm not stepping into the middle of this," I say.

"I want to know *why* she won't get me one," Chloe says. "She won't tell me, but maybe she'll tell you."

"Now you choose to be nice? When you need something from me? We'll see. No promises, though."

I open the door to Georgia's office, where she sits at her laptop, earbuds in, light-brown curls framing a freckled face. She wears a navy suit, a gauzy scarf, and a pair of wire-rimmed glasses that make her seem older than her forty-one years. Behind her, a rainbow flag hangs beside a peace sign and windows open to views of the cemetery and harbor.

"This will pass," she says into the mic.

For a spiritual leader, Georgia doesn't seem all that spiritual, but she does bring other qualities to her role as a minister. She plays at being financial advisor, best friend, confidante, and counselor, all in one package. As a clinician, I also recognize that her whole life, her very existence, is wrapped up in her career and reputation. She'd be lost without this church and the influence it affords her.

She clicks off the call, adjusts her glasses, and contemplates me for a moment. "Do you have any cash?" she asks. "I need to run an errand before the party."

I check my wallet. "Eighty bucks?"

She holds out a hand. "I'll pay you back."

She never does, but it doesn't matter. I have plenty of money. I press the bills into her palm and kiss her cheek. "What was the call about?"

"Ministering to a parishioner," she says. "And that's all I can tell you."

I wait for the rest. It rarely takes long.

"Fine," she says. "I was talking to Simon Thibodeau. He's stuck inside his house, what with the press hounding him and everything everyone is saying. I need to head over there, and before you try to talk me out of it, he's a member of this community. He needs support from *someone*." She pauses for a breath. "But if I go missing, at least you'll know where to send the cops."

I hold up my hands in surrender. I wouldn't begin to tell Georgia how to do her job. "And what about Chloe?"

Georgia lets her head fall to her desk. "She gave a kid in her class a black eye. She's suspended for three days. Grounded, too. For a month. Not one day less."

I remember the girl sitting outside Cups and Cones on my way here. "Redhead?" I ask.

"That's her." Georgia lowers her voice. "Her name's Taylor Lawson. I'm probably signing up for a week in purgatory for saying this, but I'd bet a million dollars Taylor got what she deserved. Her parents are worse than she is. And don't you dare quote me."

"Not a word."

It takes a moment for me to go through my mental database and place Taylor Lawson's name, but once I do, I realize I know more about the girl than I can reveal. Her mother, Karen, is another of my clients. She spends most of her sessions telling me how much she wishes she'd gone into the Peace Corps after college instead of having children.

Georgia tosses her phone onto the desk. "Chloe won't say what the fight was about. Maybe you can coax it out of her."

I turn to be sure the office door is closed. "You already know what it's about," I say. "It's about the phone. The one you don't want her to have but we all know she'll get eventually. You could let her win once in a while."

"And once she has one, we'll never see her again."

"And if she has a phone, she won't be a kid anymore? Guess what? That's already happened. And everything will be about the phone until you give in."

Georgia bites her lip, and for a moment I think I might have made progress. But she shakes her head. "Chloe punched a classmate. Her punishment can't be a new phone. That's not good parenting. Maybe we can revisit the topic in a few weeks. For now, would you take her home? And make sure she knows she's in trouble. If she won't tell you what the fight was about, lock her in her room. Maybe she can stay there till she turns twenty-one."

"Or at least until dinner," I say. "We have Alice's party tonight. Did I see Damian riding out of here?"

Georgia doesn't answer. "I have to work on my sermon for Sunday," she says. "The whole town is in mourning, so I need to get it right. It's about grief. Is that too on the nose? Should I think of something else? Rumors sure are flying around." She pauses. "Paranoia, too."

That feeling she's keeping something from me returns. What would happen—how would I react—if it turned out Georgia was having an affair?

Maybe I'd snap Damian in two?

CHAPTER 3
Farley

Outside her office, Georgia tells her secretary Maggie to start her weekend. "And you," she adds to Chloe, who still slouches in her chair, "behave and do what Farley says. Don't forget, reputation is everything."

Georgia retreats to her office as Maggie packs up to leave. "Whatever you did, my dear Chloe, it can't be that bad."

"What do you know?" Chloe says with a scowl.

"More than you'd guess," Maggie says. "I have three kids and six grandchildren of my own. And you wouldn't believe what I hear about in this job." She waves over her shoulder as she heads into the hallway and leaves the two of us alone.

Chloe catches my eye. "Don't start with me. You're not my dad, Farley."

"And I'm grateful for that almost every day of my life," I say. I thrust my chin toward Georgia's office. "Should we escape while we can?"

Chloe swings her backpack over her shoulder and lopes off. I run to catch up, following her out of the church and through the cemetery.

"Before you ask," Chloe says, "I'll tell you exactly what I told Georgia: *I don't want to talk about it.*"

"You'll need to tell your mother something. We both know she's relentless. Practice your lines on me. Sound sorry enough to satisfy. And give enough detail so they believe you're telling the whole story, even if you hold some back."

Chloe stops in the middle of the sidewalk. The sea breeze blows pink hair across her face. "You're so weird."

"You're hardly the epitome of normal."

"You're not supposed to say things like that to me. And I'm supposed to be in trouble."

"You are in trouble," I say. "Big trouble. Enough so I don't need to pile on." I glance down the street to where that same group of girls still sits outside Cups and Cones, including Taylor Lawson. "I'll buy you a sundae," I say.

"Ice cream?" Chloe says. "What if my dad finds out?"

"That's easy," I say. "Don't tell him."

I head toward the shop, trusting Chloe will follow. The girls cluster on a bench, spooning frozen yogurt into their mouths and clacking on their phones. Taylor glances up as I approach, red curls framing a round face. Her swollen eye is hard to look at. I stop, pulling Chloe in beside me, but she squirms out from under my arm and escapes into the store, leaving me staring awkwardly at the group of teenage girls.

"Taylor—" I begin.

"You shouldn't talk to us," Taylor says. "We don't know who you are."

"Be kind," I say. "It's a better choice."

Inside, Chloe's face is flushed with rage. "You knew Taylor was there. That's why you tricked me into coming here."

"Which one is Taylor?" I ask.

"Don't play dumb. She's the redhead."

"The ugly one?"

I almost catch her smiling, but she stops herself and says, "You're not supposed to say that, either."

"What should I say?"

Chloe scowls. "Your therapist games won't work with me. I'm immune. Georgia's been using them my whole life."

"Why do you call your mother by her first name?"

"To annoy her. Looks like it works on you, too."

I turn to read the menu. "You could have apologized and been done with it. You know you'll have to in the end."

"I already apologized, like, a thousand times. It doesn't do me any good. And there's sugar in everything here."

"Should we get nips of Fireball instead?"

I've seen Chloe sneaking sips of the whiskey when she thinks no one's watching. Now she stares at me. "I'm telling Dad you said that."

"Better than him finding out I bought you ice cream. Especially when you're supposed to be grounded for the rest of your life."

A burst of giggles erupts from the girls outside. Chloe turns her back on them and orders a sundae. "Large," she says, "with everything on it. Make it as expensive as you can." She jerks a thumb at me. "It's his treat."

I decide to indulge for once, too, although between this and missing the gym, I may need to go on that bike ride with Damian Stone after all. "Small rum raisin."

"That's an old-person flavor," Chloe says.

"How old do you think I am?"

"A hundred."

I'm thirty-six, but I'll give her this one. "Pretty close."

Chloe leads me to a table as far from the window as we can get. She digs into her sundae with gusto, and I see traces of the kid she used to be. I take a single bite of my own ice cream, the sugar tingling on my tongue like a drug. "You'll get that phone," I say. "You just have to be patient."

"And stop getting in fights at school?"

"That might help, too."

Chloe drags her spoon through a melting pool of ice cream and hot fudge. "Do you wear cologne, like body spray?"

"I've aged out of it. I am almost a hundred years old, after all."

"You'd wear it if you were thirteen. Those boys who wear cologne, pretty boys like you, they like girls like Taylor. Not me."

"I am *not* a pretty boy."

"Tell that to your mirror."

"Do you want those boys to like you?" I ask.

"I don't care. I don't like *any* boys. Or girls. And I told you already I'm immune to your therapy games, so quit it."

I take another bite of the ice cream and shove the paper cup away.

"Don't go crazy, Pretty Boy," Chloe says.

I let her score a point by scowling. "Tell me something. Does your mother hang out with Mr. Stone very often? I saw him outside the church."

"They're friends." Chloe takes a huge bite of her sundae. With her mouth full, she says, "But Georgia's not having sex with Mr. Stone, if that's what you're asking."

Blood rushes to my face, and Chloe doesn't try to hide her delight at catching me off guard. Kids often understand more than we realize, but Chloe's perception of the subtlest situations rarely fails to surprise me. Thankfully, the bells over the shop door ring. Chloe glances over my shoulder and smiles as someone approaches. I hope it's not her father, that the grapevine hasn't already found Richard and alerted him to the sundae.

"Hi, Uncle Max," Chloe says.

Max Barbosa, the chief of police, saunters to the table, along with a second man wearing a gray suit who also has the look of a cop. Max takes a seat without being asked. "This is Brock London," he says. "State detective. He's working the Thibodeau case." Max nods at me. "This is Farley Drake. The shrink I told you about."

The detective grabs a chair, too. "Dr. Drake," he says, offering a viselike handshake.

"You gonna finish that?" Max asks Chloe.

She shoves the half-eaten sundae toward him.

Max takes a bite. "Want to tell me what you were thinking, my friend? Punching someone at school? You know better than that."

Chloe stares at the table. Max isn't really her uncle, although he seems to connect to Chloe in a way none of the rest of us can.

"I'm sorry," she says, her voice small.

Max surveys the ice-cream shop. "If this is what it's like to be grounded, then sign me up. I'm sure Ritchie will love hearing about this sundae."

"*Richard* already knows," I say.

"That's right. *Richard*," Max says, staring me down.

Max and Chloe's father have been friends since they were kids, when Richard went by Ritchie. Still, there's no love lost between me and the chief. A voice blares over his radio, something about a loose dog on the town beach. Max stands, his thumbs hanging off his belt. He's tall, at least a few inches taller than I am, and fit from those morning workouts on his back deck. Most days, he does them with his shirt off. And I'm sure most people would find him attractive.

"I should take this call," he says to Detective London. "You okay on your own?"

"All set," the detective says.

"See you around, Chloe," Max says before sauntering out of the store.

The detective must be about my age, with steely gray eyes

and chiseled features highlighted by a blond buzz cut. "I'm working the Thibodeau case," he says, sliding a card across the table.

"Brock London," I say, reading his name. "Sounds made up."

"My wife tells me that all the time."

"Are you looking for a therapist, Detective London?"

"Not yet. But you never know. This job can certainly be stressful enough."

I take another bite of the ice cream. The detective watches me eat. I doubt he touches sugar.

"What can I help you with, Detective?" I ask.

"I'm talking to people in town who have their ears to the ground," he says. "It helps me get the lay of the land, and my guess is you've had an interesting week. I'm sure you've heard things the rest of us haven't. Maybe even some things that give you pause."

I slide the card back toward him. If only Brock London knew how much I yearn to play armchair detective, and how much I'd love to help him find Laurel's killer. "I'm a psychiatrist," I say. "Not a hairdresser. I can't gossip about what I hear on the job. I'm well versed in regulations around disclosure, as I'm sure you are."

"The smallest details can help."

The ethics around disclosure for psychiatrists are clear: if a client reports plans to murder a specific person, then I go to the cops. Anything else stays confidential. "If I hear something I can share, you'll be the first to know. Otherwise, I can't help you."

The detective stares me down with those steely eyes, waiting for me to break.

"You should try the ice cream," I say.

He pats his waist. "Maybe another time. Gotta watch the calories. Especially when I'm on the road." He stands, adding, "Be in touch," before leaving.

Chloe shifts in her seat. "That guy's trying to get Uncle Max to take a job with the state police. They want him to move to Springfield, but Georgia says he'll never do it. She says he's afraid of change."

"Maybe you should be the therapist. Or a cop. You're good at getting to the truth."

"If I was your patient," Chloe says, "what would you ask me? Especially after what I did today."

"You couldn't be my patient."

"But what if I was?"

"I'd assess the situation and figure out your needs. Every time I see a patient, I have a strategy." I think about my conversation with Alice Stone earlier today. "Some patients are pleasers. They want to leave the session knowing I like them, but it doesn't matter what I think of them because my whole job is to be their advocate. Then I have the obfuscators. They talk around the truth. I think that's what you'd be. You'd answer a question with a question."

"What's a question you might ask?"

"Today? I might start with asking why you dyed your hair pink."

"To piss off Georgia," Chloe says. "She can't say anything because she has to be all kumbaya and accepting. Rainbow coalition and all that. But I know she's seething inside. How's that for obfuscation?"

She says *obfuscation* like she'd learned it for the first time, although I doubt that's true.

"I misdiagnosed," I say. "You're a belligerent. Belligerents are pissed off they're in a therapy session talking to a stranger about their problems. Usually, they don't want to be there, even if they made the decision to come on their own."

Chloe swirls the spoon through the dregs of her sundae. A single Reese's Pieces bleeds orange in a pool of white. "My mother must have been a belligerent when she was your patient," she says.

Perceptive. Again. Georgia *was* my patient. That's how we first met, but I didn't realize Chloe knew. It wouldn't do any good to have what happened next scrutinized. I could lose my license.

Or worse.

CHAPTER 4
Farley

Reverend Georgia Fitzhugh's first session with me was on a Monday afternoon a little over a year ago, and it seemed as though she wanted to leave as soon as she arrived at my office. "What do I call you anyway?" she asked me. "Farley? Dr. Drake?"

"Whatever makes you comfortable," I said. "What should I call you?"

Even when Georgia sat still, she kept moving, but the question got her to stop. "We'll see," she said. "I'm used to offering counsel, not getting it. I'm used to people relying on me, to being seen in a certain way."

"We should be well matched, then," I said. "Sometimes helping others stirs things up for ourselves. How do you think you're perceived?"

"Resilient. Unflappable. Certainly not as someone who fails."

"How are you failing?"

She adjusted her glasses. "You'll have to do better than that."

"Meet me halfway," I said. "What do you want to get out of these sessions?"

"I haven't a clue."

"That's okay. This is your time. But try telling me one thing. Anything you want. You never know where it might lead."

Georgia's phone beeped with an incoming text. She banged out a response and hit *Send*. "Today's my day off," she said, "but people need my help. Every moment of every day."

She pushed her curly hair behind her ears and tossed one end of her scarf over her shoulder. "I should go. I'm sorry for wasting your time."

Then she walked out the door.

I assumed that would be the last time she'd come to my office. Maybe in the end that would have been better, although I only have myself to blame for what happened next.

I spent the ensuing week learning what I could about Georgia and her family: she'd been in her ministry for nearly fifteen years; she was married to a local mechanic, Richard Macomber, who spent weekends at classic car shows; she had a daughter. I even went to services that Sunday and sat in the last pew as she delivered a sermon on forgiving and the gift of an apology. "Apologies aren't for the giver," Georgia said. "The gift is to the receiver, who can choose to do whatever they wish with the apology, even reject it."

I meant to slip out at the end of the sermon, but my bad habit of observing clients in the wild took over. I found myself drawn to the coffee hour in the basement, where I watched the reverend interact with her parishioners. She moved with ease from one group to the next, greeting people by name, embracing them. Yet I could see she was both fully present in the interactions and removed at the same time, as though viewing herself from the outside looking in. In a way, it was like watching my own interactions with the world. Maybe that's what drew me to her.

The very next day, she surprised me when she strode into my office right on schedule for our second session. She wore another scarf, this one red and gold. And she sat for a full ten minutes without speaking.

"So—" I finally began.

She waved me off, her face pinched in thought. "You were spying on me," she said.

"I was curious."

"You shouldn't have come to my church. It was intrusive."

She was right. I shouldn't have watched her like that. Not out in the open, for anyone to see. "I'm sorry," I said.

"You're not the only one who can spy," she said. "I know more about you than you'd guess. You're the one trying to build the big house on the cliff. The one everyone hates."

I smiled. I focused on keeping my heart rate low. I'd been trying to build the house for over a year at that point. "I'm building *a* house. And it will be on a cliff. But I don't know that people hate it. At least not *everyone*."

"We do, though. All of us. We talk about it at the coffee shop, at the library, in my church, wherever we gather. But I'd bet a million dollars you already know that. I bet a part of you enjoys having something that makes others jealous. And you should know Max Barbosa is one of my best friends. Your big house will block his view."

I'd bought the land for my house from the chief of police, along with an old ramshackle house that I knocked down the day the sale closed. Max had to have understood I could do whatever I wanted with the land when he sold it, but that hadn't stopped him from using his influence to block construction, which meant I'd had to live in an Airstream while attending zoning board hearings. "You figured all that out about me from the dozen or so sentences we've exchanged?"

"My whole job is reading people," Georgia said. "Knowing who they are at their core. It's the same job you have."

"And you've diagnosed me as a narcissist?"

"Maybe. I know you're highly accomplished and successful. And like most successful people, you expect to get what you want. We have more in common than you may realize."

"What do *you* want?"

"You're playing connect-the-dots."

"Should we play another game?"

"That's the last thing I need." Georgia rested her elbows on her knees. One end of the scarf fell from her shoulder. "I have a thing for Max," she said, as though she'd practiced the line all week long. "And it's not in a romantic way. Or maybe it is, I'm not sure. But when they were kids, Max and my husband, Ritchie, used to spend summers at that house you bought, the one you tore down. And when I moved here, I dated both of them but chose Ritchie because it was the easier choice. When you're young, you don't realize how much you can hurt someone." She closed her eyes. "Max takes care of me like no one else does. He has for as long as I've known him. I like that someone worries about me. Sometimes I want to be the one being saved. It's selfish. And it's sick."

"Sick?" I asked.

Georgia cocked her head. For a moment, I thought she might take the lead and run with it. "That may be all I can give you today," she said. "It was way more than I expected to share. You're better than you realize."

"I didn't do much."

"It's your pretty face. It makes me want to spill my guts." She stood. "You're welcome at services. But only as a parishioner."

At the following session, I took a new tactic and started speaking before Georgia had settled. "So far, you've told me you like to offer counsel more than receive it and that a friend watches out for you. But you haven't told me why you chose to come here. These sessions aren't cheap, and yet you keep returning and only staying for a few minutes. Does your husband know you're here?" When Georgia didn't answer, I added, "How about Max? Does he know?"

"No one knows I'm here. And no one will find out, either."

"Tell me something. Anything. Start with the basics. You're married. I saw your daughter at the service I came to. You mentioned her name. Chloe, right? Do you love her?"

"Of course I do."

"What about your husband?"

"Ritchie? He's always been there. He doesn't mind being at my side or playing a supporting part. That's why I chose him instead of Max. Max couldn't have sat back and watched. He'd have eclipsed me. Does that make sense? I'm a pillar of this community. And most of the time I'm right there in the trenches, lifting others up and keeping their confidences. I counsel people through their worst moments, their worst failures, but God help me if I show weakness. God help me if I make a mistake." Georgia's eyes shone behind her glasses. "It's like I'm two people. There's Georgia who you see right now, the vulnerable one." She shifted in her chair, and something changed in her presentation. The shine left her eyes, and she seemed taller, bigger in every way. Even her voice deepened. "And then there's Reverend George."

"They want to believe you're happy. Even when you're not. They want to believe you've made the right choices, even when you haven't."

Georgia tapped her temple. "This is why they call you a shrink."

"All I'm doing is listening."

"Have you ever done anything that you shouldn't?" she asked.

"Hasn't everyone?"

"Have you ever watched yourself doing that thing and been completely unable to stop yourself?" Georgia stood and paced across the room. "I don't like being introspective. It makes everything worse."

I flipped through my notes. "Remember our game of con-nect-the-dots? Last week you said you wanted to be saved. From what?"

Georgia stopped pacing. "My marriage. It's falling apart."

But I already knew that.

I speed down Main Street in my phantom gray 1962 Tri-umph Spitfire. Taylor and her friends are still hovering out-side Cups and Cones, so I honk the horn.

Chloe sinks into the seat beside me. "Quit it," she whispers.

"Chloe, no one knows it's me."

"You know this car is killing the planet, right? And who else drives a midlife-crisis-mobile like this one?"

Chloe's latest obsession is global warming, and she must have gotten the midlife jab from Georgia. I let it pass as down-town Monreith gives way to winding country roads. A few miles from town, Chloe asks, "What do you think happened to Mrs. Thibodeau?"

"I haven't a clue," I say.

"You must have a guess. And that state detective was right; people must tell you things."

"Why are you asking?"

For a moment, Chloe doesn't speak. Finally, she says, "Jack told me there's a serial killer."

I glance at her out of the corner of my eye. She rests her head against the door, her hair blowing around her face. She catches me watching.

"It could be true," she says.

"Who's Jack?" I ask.

"No one."

I consider my response as I pull onto a lane and edge through grass fields and a grove of trees. Chloe has an active imagination, one I don't want to encourage right now. Still, it could help to learn how these rumors began. "Is Jack some-one from school?"

"He's just a friend, okay?"

"You told me you didn't like *any* boys."

"I don't. And he's probably just trying to scare me, right?"

"Probably. But if he's trying to scare you, he doesn't sound like boyfriend material."

She faces me, her eyes wide with defiance. "I don't have a boyfriend!"

There can be truth to rumors, even ones that begin in the halls of a public middle school, but I don't want this particular rumor to gain a toehold. I say, "There's about as much chance of being killed by a serial killer as there is of being attacked by a shark."

"That surfer was attacked by a shark on the Cape over the summer," Chloe says. "One shark attack. One murder."

"But if there was a serial killer, there'd be more than one murder."

"Unless this is the first," Chloe says. "Or we haven't found the pattern."

"I think you should tell your friend Jack to stop trying to scare you," I say. "Or give him a scare right back. Let him know that if there is a serial killer on the loose, the last thing in the world he'll want is for the serial killer to take notice of him."

Chloe's quiet for a moment. "Hey, Farley," she finally says. "Have you ever had syphilis?"

And here I thought we were bonding. "Why? Does Jack have syphilis?"

"Maybe," Chloe says. "And maybe he gave it to me."

This time when I look at her, she's grinning.

"Don't be such a wiseass," I say, pushing the accelerator to the floor.

Chloe grips the armrest as we speed over the unpaved road, through the trees, and up a hill past Max Barbosa's garden cottage, the one I can see from my kitchen. Right next door, I stop at the wrought-iron gates and wait for them to open. My house sits beyond them, at the end of a peastone drive, perched on the edge of a cliff. Georgia was right about one thing: I get what I want, including this house.

"Dad's here," Chloe says.

I follow her gaze to where her father's gold VW Bug sits outside the six-car garage, probably leaking oil on the gravel. Richard Macomber waits for us on the stone landing by the front door, still wearing his blue coveralls from the garage. As I pull farther into the driveway, one of the garage doors grinds open.

"What's he going to say?" Chloe whispers.

I rev the engine and slide into the garage beside the Range Rover I use for driving longer distances. "That's why we practiced," I say, but Chloe escapes into the house through the side door, abandoning me to face her father on my own. "Thanks a lot!" I shout after her.

Outside in the sun, Richard approaches down the stone steps. He has a new haircut and has slimmed down since I first met him, although I can't help but notice he still has *Ritchie* embroidered on his left-hand pocket. I hover by the VW, my index finger tapping the gold-painted steel.

"Don't worry, I'll move that," Richard says. "Did she escape?"

"You must have heard the door slam."

"What happened, anyway?"

I've made the mistake of getting in the middle of these things before. "Let her tell you."

"Max called. He saw you at Cups and Cones. Are you kidding me? You can't always play the good guy, Farley. Chloe's supposed to be grounded."

I'm too practiced to allow anger to show. "I spent my afternoon dealing with *your* problem," I say, "including your wife."

Richard shoves grease-stained hands into the pockets on

those ugly coveralls. "Sorry. Long day at work. Let's start over. Good to see you."

"Good to see you, too."

"And thanks for watching my delinquent daughter."

"She's hardly a delinquent. But anytime."

Richard takes my hand in his. "She's with me for the weekend."

"She's with us."

As I kiss him, I run my fingers over those embroidered letters and taste peanut butter on his tongue. Until recently, I'd assumed Richard was easy to manipulate, but he's proven to be shrewder than I first believed, something I'll need to deal with eventually.

Like these coveralls.

Tomorrow, I'll take them to the tailor and get the lettering restitched to read *Richard*. It's the least I can do.

CHAPTER 5
Farley

An hour later, I wait in the afternoon sun by the infinity pool, sipping a vodka soda and listening to electronica on the sound system. I've changed into a pair of dark-wash jeans and a blue shirt that, again, brings out my eyes. Even the music can't drown out the shouts between Richard and Chloe emanating from inside. At one point, I swear Chloe screams that she didn't ask to be born.

I turn away and face the water. A fleet of lasers from the local sailing team tack across the placid bay as the sun begins its descent. Max Barbosa, the chief of police, is the only neighbor, the only person close enough to overhear these two going at it. I hope he's still on duty.

"My house, my rules," Richard shouts.

"This isn't your house," Chloe shouts back. "It's *his.*"

Even Chloe doesn't know I signed over half the house to Richard. We are a couple, after all, although I'm not proud of how it began between us. Sometimes, things get out of control before you can stop them.

I noticed Richard at that first sermon of Georgia's I attended. I spoke to him briefly afterward, as he worked his way through a stack of off-brand cookies. "You're the shrink," he said to me. "I've heard about you."

"Farley Drake," I said, shaking his hand. "I can't imagine what you've heard."

"Only good things," he said.

His stomach jutted over his waistband. His dark hair stuck up in every direction and should have been cut weeks earlier, but behind the unkempt façade was a man who could have been attractive if he'd bothered showing up. A project of sorts. That morning, he wore an oversized blazer and relaxed-fit khakis and when I asked him about the sermon, about the gift of an apology, he gave me the once-over and said, "There are some things I wouldn't mind apologizing for."

See, he made the first move.

That next week, I visited his garage. Like today, he had motor oil under his nails and wore blue coveralls. Somehow, he talked me into buying the Triumph. "Mint condition," he said. "Rebuilt engine. Accessorized. You won't need to do a thing."

We took it for a test drive, top down, careening along the coast. "You want to go easy on the gears," Richard said, guiding my hand as I shifted into third.

At least that's how I remember it.

Back at the garage, he drew up the paperwork. "Cash gets a deal," he said.

"Then let's make a deal."

Most men in my position would have dismissed Richard Macomber, who was unkempt and underemployed, not to mention married to a client. But I enjoy a challenge. In him, I saw a man worth shaping. Worth saving. And he seemed willing to come along for the ride.

When Richard moved into my house earlier this summer, Georgia took the news in stride. She even cupped my face in her hands and said, "At least I like you." It was Reverend George speaking, though. I doubt I'll ever see the woman's vulnerable side again, the side she brought to our sessions. And I suppose I deserve that.

One of the floor-to-ceiling glass and steel bifold doors that leads from the house to the terrace opens, and Richard emerges to join me, descending the bluestone stairs through the tiered perennial garden. The conservation commission had tried to block this cantilevered deck, too. Sometimes, it only takes persistence to win. Richard has his own vodka soda. He wears a gauzy green shirt open almost to his navel, and tight white pants that leave little to the imagination. He slides in beside me and snaps a photo with the bay in the background. Later, the photo will show up online with a tag like *#instagay*. After nearly forty years in the closet, Richard has embraced his queerness with a ferocity that makes even me blush.

"Here's to fatherhood," he says.

"Did she tell you what the fight at school was about?"

Richard shakes his head. "Did she tell you?"

"Not in so many words," I say. "But it's not that complicated. You should let her get a phone. Don't you remember being in eighth grade? It sucks. They'll pick on you for anything."

"Try negotiating that with Georgia."

"Chloe may have a boyfriend, too," I say. "Some kid named Jack."

I keep the mention of syphilis to myself. Richard has enough to deal with right now.

"Great," he says. "That's the last thing I need."

I check the time. Alice wanted us at the party by six. "We're late."

As if on cue, Chloe emerges from the house wearing loose-fitting jeans. She's swapped the Greenpeace T-shirt for an orange Burger King one that clashes with her hair. I wonder when father and daughter snuck out for fast food. She shuffles down the steps. "Button your shirt," she says to Richard.

"Don't forget you're grounded," Richard says, as he quietly fastens the two lowest buttons. "I forgot something," he adds, running up the stairs and calling, "I'll meet you at the boat," over his shoulder.

"Like my T-shirt?" Chloe asks me.

I don't take the bait. "You look terrific."

A moment later, we've made our way down steep, weather-worn stairs to a dock. I uncover the Boston Whaler as Richard joins us, and Chloe casts off. I ease out of the protected cove at headway speed, aiming toward a lighthouse on the next point. As soon as I pass beyond the no-wake zone, I rev the engine. "Take the helm," I say to Chloe.

We swap places and give the fleet of lasers a wide berth.

"You're good on the water," I shout over the engine. "You should join the sailing team. I'll get you a boat. And sailing's better for the environment than this old thing."

"Those kids are snobs," Chloe says.

"The snobs are the ones you want to know," I say.

"What are you two whispering about?" Richard shouts from the prow.

"Your gay shirt," Chloe shouts back.

Richard gives her the finger and fastens another button.

After rounding the point, Chloe maneuvers the boat into a cove where steep cliffs rise from a rocky shore. She pulls alongside a deep-water dock sitting at the end of a long gang-way. The gangway crosses over a grassy saltmarsh that will be completely submerged once the tide comes in. A hundred yards down the shore, the marshland ends abruptly where a channel has been cut through the thick peat to a boat launch. I tie off behind a speedboat that belongs to the owners of Moulton Farm, where Alice and Damian are staying. I wonder, briefly, if Damian remembered that carrot cake for Alice's birthday.

At the top of another set of weatherworn stairs, a lush lawn lined with hydrangeas leads to the farmhouse, a motley collection of interconnected rooms and additions. In the middle of the lawn, Alice's teenage son, Noah, smacks a ball with a croquet mallet as the evening sun shines off his mop of blond hair. Chloe glances at her father for permission to join the game.

"Go ahead," he says, and all of Chloe's teenage angst seems to melt as she dashes away.

I take Richard's hand and squeeze it.

"Am I letting her off too easy?" he asks.

"Give her a break," I say. "She's had a rough few months. The separation. You and me. It's a lot for a thirteen-year-old to take, no matter how evolved. She'll behave herself."

"Will you?" Richard asks. "Behave yourself? No baiting Georgia tonight."

"I'm never anything but kind. And you need to watch your carbs. I hear there might be a carrot cake."

Richard drops my hand as we approach a brick patio covered by a pergola. Smoke pours from a cast-iron drum, where Damian Stone sweats over a side of brisket, his slim cyclist's physique clad in the uniform of a Monreith bro: a backwards baseball cap and Nantucket red shorts.

"Dude," Richard says, stepping in for a side hug.

"Nice shirt," Damian says, goosing Richard's nipple.

Richard shoves him, and Damian says, "Grab a drink. You still a Coors Light man?"

Alice emerges from the farmhouse carrying a pitcher filled with something pink. Harper shadows her, as always, trotting along at her heels. I remember our session from earlier today—Alice's confession of being frightened—but I again take a moment to center myself and fully engage with my role here. "You look fabulous," I say.

Alice wears a loose linen dress that billows in the sea breeze, her dark hair tied in a ponytail. "So do you," she says, kissing my cheek. "Though I'd expect nothing less. And thanks for the flowers. They made my day."

The vase of dahlias and chrysanthemums sits in the center of a long teak table.

"It is a birthday party," I say. "Will there be cake?"

Alice meets my eyes and smiles. "There's cake. It's not exactly what I'd hoped for, but it's nothing to be frightened of." She holds up the pitcher. "Cosmo?"

I relent, accepting a plastic martini glass. Over by the fire, Richard pops open a beer can. Damian punches his arm and then lifts the brisket from the fire with a pair of tongs. "Yo!" he says. "Look at that meat!"

"Have I ever mentioned I'm a vegetarian?" Alice says to me.

The door to the farmhouse opens, and Georgia exits with a tray of hors d'oeuvres, her glasses slipping down her nose. She wears the suit and scarf she had on earlier, but at least she survived her meeting with possible murderer Simon Thibodeau.

"Let me help you out there," I say, pushing her glasses up for her and stabbing a cheese-stuffed date with a toothpick. "I'm glad I didn't have to send the cops out looking for you," I add, right as Max Barbosa ducks through the farmhouse door with another tray. "Speak of the devil."

I hadn't expected to see the police chief tonight. I hadn't wanted to, either, and something in my expression must betray me, however briefly, because Alice leans in and whispers, "Last-minute addition. I hope that's okay."

Out on the lawn, Chloe wields a croquet mallet as she chases Noah through the wickets.

"The gang's all here," I say. "What a treat."

CHAPTER 6
Farley

The sun has nearly set and the bay glows in the final light of the evening. We all have a drink in hand, the appetizers have circulated, and the party's underway. Georgia crosses the lawn toward where the kids chase each other with croquet mallets. I wonder if she plans to admonish Chloe for the fight at school or for having too much fun. Instead, Georgia wrests the mallets from the kids, who escape toward the dock.

"Don't forget you're grounded!" Georgia shouts as Chloe's pink hair disappears behind the bluff.

"Farley," Alice asks me as Georgia beckons us into the game, "what happened with Chloe at school today?"

"Let me know if you find out," I say. "Chloe's not talking."

Georgia hands each of us a mallet.

"What rules are we playing?" I ask.

"Cutthroat," Damian says, meaning there's only one winner in the end.

I love games, especially as a therapist. You can learn as much about an adult as you can about a child by observing the role they adopt during a game. Here, tonight, Damian plays the aggressor, striking his ball with confidence and celebrating each wicket with high fives. Alice apologizes when she taps someone else's ball; Richard has to be reminded each time his turn comes up; and Georgia ministers for most of the game. She works to bring everyone together outwardly while, I suspect, plotting a win. Meanwhile, Max avoids any alliances, stays in the middle of the pack, and observes from the outside like a true cop. He and I are more alike than I realize.

Still, that doesn't keep me from knocking him off the course when I have a chance. "Sorry," I say.

"That's the game," Max says, taking a long swig from his IPA.

I bought the property from him over two years ago now, but this is the first time we've been anywhere together socially.

"How'd things go with the free-roaming dog?" I ask him.

"The one on the town beach? Gone by the time I arrived. Not even worth putting in the police blotter."

"A loose dog seems a bit below your pay grade."

"Nothing much is below my pay grade," Max says. "It's a small team. We all pitch in."

Harper runs across the lawn, her tongue hanging from her mouth as she chases after Alice's ball. Damian knocks Georgia off the course, then makes the fifth wicket. He struts around the edge of the lawn, hand out. I let his palm graze across mine.

"Georgia's going to kill Damian when she gets a chance," Max says softly.

"We all might," I say.

"Never bet against Reverend George."

My turn comes up. I opt out of knocking Richard while keeping Damian's ball in sight. Back on the sidelines, Max hands me his beer and takes his own turn. When he returns, we stand quietly for a moment before I say, "I heard you were thinking about a job with the state cops."

Max rocks forward on the balls of his feet. For a moment, I wonder if he might walk away. Instead, he says, "I thought about it for a hot second. Timing isn't right."

"Timing's rarely right for big changes," I say.

Max looks me over. "Now I get it," he says. "You're hoping to buy me out. You could bulldoze the cottage and have the whole point to yourself."

The thought had crossed my mind.

"Maybe another time," Max says. "Word sure does travel fast around here."

"Kind of like a visit to the ice-cream shop. Thanks for telling Richard you saw me with Chloe."

"I look out for all the kids in town," Max says. "It's part of my job, but the ones that get on my radar are the ones who might be in trouble. Chloe's been acting up lately; now she got in a fight at school, so she's on my radar. She's special to me, too, so don't think I'm not watching your every move. I'm not sure how much I trust you."

So much for social time. "You may not like me, Chief," I say, "but you'll have to get used to me. I'm not going anywhere."

From the course, Damian calls my name. "Farley! Keep it moving!" he says.

"Your turn is up," Max says.

I hit his ball as far off the course as I can.

Damian makes it through the final wicket first. He eliminates Richard, then Alice. "Happy birthday to me," Alice says as she takes Richard's arm and the two of them head off to find the kids with Harper sniffing behind them. When Damian turns on Georgia next, she says, "Someone help me out!"

I team up with her to eliminate Damian, who takes the loss with more grace than I'd have expected. Georgia shows her true colors, though, and takes me out next. But Max wins the whole game, as I expected he might. He eliminates Georgia with one final stroke.

After the sun goes down and the kids have been set up by the TV, we gather at the table. Richard and Georgia head to the kitchen to prep dinner. Alice has strung fairy lights through the pergola and lit hurricane lamps. A soft breeze blows off the water, and the sound of gentle waves crashing on the shore fills the night air. Damian grabs the brisket from where it's been resting under foil and brings it to the table. He pops a cork on a bottle of pinot noir and fills glasses, ending with Alice. "Happy birthday, my love," he says, kissing her forehead.

She squeezes his hand. Across from me, Max finishes his wine and fills his glass again.

"Go take care of your dead animal," Alice says to Damian.

Beside me, Damian carves the meat on a bias. Red juices flow onto the white platter with each slice of the knife. I think back to the session with Alice this afternoon when I'd assumed she was frightened of Damian, but here, tonight, the two of them seem comfortable together. Maybe she worked through whatever had been bothering her?

"How did you meet Alice, anyway?" I ask Damian.

Alice already told me their story in her sessions: they met when Alice was an undergrad and Damian was her professor, and he lost his job and his first marriage over the affair. I'm curious to hear his version, and how the public telling might differ from the private one.

"We were work colleagues," Damian says.

"Were you in finance, too?" I ask.

"Not exactly."

"Where, then?" I ask.

"At one of her first jobs," Damian says. "It was before I started making documentaries. Another lifetime, really." He lays the carving knife down. "Meeting Alice was the best thing that ever happened to me. She got me to take chances. Now we go where the story takes us." He nods toward Max, opening up the conversation and steering it away from a topic he'd clearly rather avoid. "Like you, Chief. Tell us, what's the latest with the Thibodeau investigation? I can't imagine there's been a homicide in this town before. Why no arrest? It's been a week."

"Damian, stop," Alice says. "You know Max can't talk about that."

"Let the man speak for himself," Damian says.

"Your wife pretty much got it right," Max says. "I don't talk about open investigations. Certainly not at birthday parties."

"Seems to me," Damian says, "if you haven't arrested the husband by now, you must have other theories. Simon Thibodeau's already been tried and convicted in the court of public opinion."

"Ignore him," Alice says to Max. "He has an MBA in film history from NYU and an advanced degree in *Law & Order* from watching too much TV. He thinks he knows everything there is to know about police procedure. He probably wants to solve the case himself."

Damian returns to carving the meat. "The police must want any help they can get."

"I met the state detective today," I say.

"Brock London," Max says. "He's legit, good at his job. And, Damian, if you have information about the murder, you should talk to him. He lives in Boston, but he's staying local while he works the case. I'm sure he'd love to hear from you."

"Let's spitball," Damian says. "See what we can come up with on our own."

Max makes a locking motion over his lips and tosses the imaginary key over his shoulder.

"Come on," Damian says. "We're all assuming this is a domestic incident, but what if it's something else? We have Simon's gambling debts. Seems like there are plenty of other leads to follow."

"Maybe you should go into fiction instead of documentaries," Alice says. "You might make more money."

Damian rests his elbows on the table and speaks directly to Max. "What if it went beyond this town, and the state cops weren't seeing what they should? Laurel was a beautiful woman. Kind. A member of this community."

"She wasn't that kind," Alice says. "Don't forget, she stole money from old people."

"My guess is she had her reasons," Damian says. "And don't we all deserve to know what happened to her?" He turns to me. "What do you think? You're a psychiatrist. What's the psychology behind a violent murder like this one?"

I shake my head. "I couldn't say."

"Didn't you study abnormal psychology?"

"That was a long time ago."

"But what's your best guess?"

"I'd say whoever killed Laurel Thibodeau hated her enough to want her to suffer."

"That's your answer, Chief," Damian says. "Find someone who hated her guts."

Alice stands. "Stop."

Across from me, Max shifts in his seat. He tosses his napkin on the table. "I should hit the road."

Alice touches his arm. "Stay. And you," she adds to Damian, "quit stirring up trouble. It's my birthday. Make tonight about me for once."

Damian relents. "Fine, but I'll just say this: there's a feeling you get when you start narrowing in on something no one else is seeing. It happened with *Acadian Autumn*, with that priest. And it's happening here, too."

"Try telling your theories to Detective London," Max says. "Not your dinner guests. He'll want to hear what you say, even if it turns out to be nothing."

"Believe me," Alice says. "It'll be nothing."

Max doesn't take his eyes off Damian. "We'll talk to the detective together in the morning."

Right then, Georgia and Richard return and set platters overflowing with food in the center of the table. Georgia has us link hands for a silent prayer.

"What did we miss?" she asks.

"My husband acting like an asshole," Alice says.

"Nothing new there," Damian says. He pauses, staring into a serving bowl filled with a concoction of marshmallows and mandarin oranges. "What's this shit?"

"Ambrosia," Alice says. "Pass it down here and don't make fun of my cooking."

Damian uncorks another bottle of wine and tops us all off. "Who wants meat?" he asks.

I take the platter. But a kernel of doubt has begun to form at the back of my mind. Like Alice, like anyone, I have my own hidden self, a shadow side I try to keep private. I worry Damian Stone may be narrowing in on my truth.

CHAPTER 7
Farley

Alice's dinner, a rich ratatouille, a caprese of late summer tomatoes, and a farro salad, with Damian's brisket on the side, is better than I'd expected it to be. I even let Georgia serve me more ratatouille, though I pass on the marshmallowy ambrosia. Richard piles it onto his plate and mouths ice cream at me when I try to intervene. Damian lets the conversation about the Thibodeau murder drop, while Alice teases him about the film he made in Maine. He hardly seems to care. "*Acadian Autumn* was on its way to being a snooze fest," he says. "The French government hired me to come up with a story about this community, to show how French is spoken outside of France. I just kept filming and hoping something exciting might happen. I almost gave up."

"You think it's cold here?" Alice says. "Try living just south of the Canadian border where the only place to go is the Walmart."

"Then that priest died," Damian says. "And it was like the shit hit the fan. He'd written down every terrible thing he'd done in these journals, and suddenly everyone talked and had a story to tell. Years of awful abuse. From there, the documentary made itself."

"Damian," Alice says. "Dinner conversation. What about the Red Sox? Aren't the playoffs coming up?"

"How did the priest die?" I ask.

Damian catches Alice's eye. "More interested than you care to admit, Dr. Drake," he says to me. "Drowning. In his bathtub. Story was he took a sedative and fell asleep, though God only knows what really happened. The priest wasn't that old. Forty, maybe. Forty-five. Younger than I am. The state detectives didn't try all that hard. There were certainly plenty of suspects."

"And now there's another murder here," I say. "Seems like this kind of thing follows you."

Across from me, Max shifts uncomfortably in his seat. Richard lays a hand of warning on my knee. He wants me to stop talking. "At least Noah learned French!" he says.

"*Bonjour. Salut. Du vin?*" Alice turns over an empty bottle. "One case of wine down. What's a party without a little debauchery?"

"I'll grab some reinforcements," I say.

I excuse myself and escape inside, through a door that leads to a damp dirt cellar, and then up a set of wooden stairs to the level above.

Richard and I come to this house for dinner most Saturday nights. On my first visit, Alice gave me a tour through the warren of interconnected rooms while Damian and Richard watched the Celtics game on TV. She told me about the seven fireplaces and the Glenwood stove and the soapstone sink. I remember her opening a door at the end of a hallway and saying, "This is Damian's office. It's where all his magic happens."

I want to find that room now. I want to see what Damian knows. And what he believes he knows.

I turn a corner, only to stumble on Chloe and Noah sprawled on the floor. Behind them an animated movie plays on the TV, and empty plates cover a coffee table. They both lean over a phone, staring intently at the cracked screen. Chloe inhales when I approach. She shoves the phone behind her. "We're just watching a movie," she says.

I don't care what they're doing. "Where's the bathroom?"

Noah points behind me.

"Don't let your mother see that phone," I say to Chloe.

"What phone?" she asks.

I leave them, heading through the house, down another narrow hallway, and past the bathroom, until I stand outside Damian's office, my hand on the doorknob. I have a feeling this is one of those moments that has a before and an after. Once I turn this knob, once I see what Damian has discovered, I'll be in a position of reacting, one I don't ever care to be in.

I take a deep breath and step into the room.

Even in the dark, I can see the whiteboard hanging on the opposite wall, lit up by the moonlight streaming through the windows. I flip on the overhead light. Crime scene photos hang on the board, surrounded by dates and the names of victims. Names I recognize. Victims I know. *My* victims.

Steve Alabiso lies on a forest floor, with the back of his head shot off. Jeanine Geller sits in a car, her mouth agape, asphyxiated by carbon monoxide in her own garage. Laurel Thibodeau's photo hangs in the center. Her image doesn't come from a crime scene. Instead, she stands against the blue water of the bay, her red hair lifting on a breeze, her eyes creased. She looks happy. Full of life.

My clients led me to both Steve and Jeanine: one client's wife was having an affair with Steve; another client's husband was doing the same with Jeanine. These entanglements enthrall me. They bring out the armchair detective, the one who digs into clients' lives and watches them in the wild. The one who learns as much as he can about all the players involved. Steve was an anesthesiologist who wrote prescriptions to anyone who would pay for them. Jeanine's young daughter had been beset by mysterious ailments her entire life, ailments that disappeared as soon as Jeanine was out of the picture. They were both terrible people.

Steve died first. I followed him into the woods last fall, where we chatted about hunting and prescription drugs. He seemed as ready to hook me up with fentanyl as he was to take down a flock of turkeys pecking at the grass in a meadow. I shot him in the back of the head with his own rifle and carefully placed the gun where it could have landed after he fell face down in the mud. The turkeys took the hint and got out of there fast.

A hiker found Steve the next day. At first glance, the death looked like exactly what it was: a homicide. The police spent an inordinate amount of time focusing on his wife as a suspect, but the medical examiner did her research. She found cases of suicides where the victims had shot themselves in the back of the head, cases that presented exactly like Steve's death, the same cases I'd studied to prepare for the kill.

With Jeanine, I sat in the car beside her wearing an oxygen mask after she'd parked in the garage and closed the door. Tears streamed down her face as the garage filled with carbon monoxide, and I convinced her to unlock her phone with promises of escape. Once she was unconscious, I typed her suicide note myself into a text, where she confessed to everything she'd done to her daughter. In a P.S. I added, *My husband is a good man. He didn't kill me, no matter how it looks.*

I was particularly pleased to learn Jeanine's daughter was the one to discover the body. I imagined the relief the girl must have felt when she learned her years of torment had come to an end. Again, the police spent too much time trying to pin the death on the husband—there's not much that points to guilt more than a P.S. in a suicide note. Lucky for him, he'd been out of town, although rumors have continued to dog him—I do feel bad about that—and the police haven't officially closed the case.

I glance up at the whiteboard. At my victims. At the lines connecting them. Two is enough to prove a trend. And apparently, Damian Stone has taken on that task.

"You found it."

I turn to see Alice standing behind me. I expect her to be annoyed, angry even, at my snooping, but she comes to my side and runs her finger along one of the thick red lines linking the photos. "This is his latest obsession," she says. "Connecting these deaths. Solving Laurel's murder."

"Is this what frightens you?"

Alice touches Laurel's image, and a shadow briefly passes over her face. "What do you do when a patient confesses to murder?" she asks.

This isn't the question I'd expected, but years of practice keep me from showing my surprise. And most of us can do almost anything under the right circumstances. "It depends on whether the patient plans to kill again."

"And if not?"

"Then the confession stays in the room."

Alice turns to me. "I didn't believe Damian in Maine, and he found a monster there. What frightens me is when he gets to the truth, when he finds the evil at the core of his story." Her eyes meet mine, and in that split second, it's as though she sees right to my very core. "That truth," she says, "is usually closer than you'd ever believe."

Harper noses her hand. Alice crouches to pet the dog.

"She's your shadow," I say, scratching the dog's ears.

I imagine the secrets Harper might betray if she could.

"You must think Damian and I hate each other's guts," Alice says. "We've always sniped at each other. It's my birthday, though. I'm supposed to be having fun. But you're off the clock. I'll tell you everything next week. Hold me to it."

"I thought you were finding a new therapist."

"We both know I won't do that. Not now."

I suppose we do.

"We should get out of here," Alice says, "before someone catches us." She ushers me out of the room and turns off the lights. "Promise me you won't say anything out there? I don't want Max to know about this."

Neither do I. "Not a word."

I stop at the bathroom, while she disappears down the hall-way with Harper. I splash water on my face and barely recognize my own reflection in the mirror. Anyone who digs long enough will find other victims, and there are plenty. I killed in Boston. Connecticut. Even back in the Midwest where I grew up. Always staged like possible suicides but with enough doubt to cast suspicion on someone obvious. Enough doubt to distract the police long enough so the trail could grow cold. I'm not one of those people seeking notoriety, but now, here, I imagine my photo caught up in the news cycle, the shots of me entering the courtroom, the stories of how I hid in plain sight. The media will love me. The term for what I am is the one Chloe used in the car today: a serial killer. But they'll probably call me Dr. Death.

Out on the patio, Georgia's telling a story. "It was the both of them!" she says. "I'd barely been in town a week, and they started showing up at services and stopping by the parsonage. This one." She squeezes Max's arm and rests her head on his shoulder. "He invites me out on the boat."

I slide in beside Richard.

"Everything okay?" he asks, softly. "You were gone a while."

"Beautiful night," I say.

Damian sits on my other side. Alice returns from the house and hovers at Damian's shoulder while Georgia gulps her wine and continues. "And this one," she says, pointing to Richard, "he takes me for a drive in an Edsel. An Edsel! I should have known." She smiles. "Maybe I chose wrong, but you certainly knew how to flirt."

"Sometimes," Damian says, "the evidence is staring you right in the face."

Alice lays a phone on the table beside him. I'm the only one close enough to hear her whisper, "You're an idiot," so softly I almost think I may have misunderstood.

Damian slides the phone into his pocket as silence falls over the table. Off in the distance, a foghorn sounds.

Alice takes her seat. I lay a hand over Richard's. "You are a good flirt," I say.

Richard barely shakes his head. He doesn't like when I show affection in front of Georgia, but tonight I don't care.

"And you've had a lot to drink," he says.

I like Richard. I like the family I've fallen into more than I knew I was capable of, but Richard isn't as innocent as he wants the world to believe. He's seen me slipping out at night, and he knows some of my secrets, although I'm not sure he's fully aware of who he's slept next to these last months. I'm not sure he understands how much danger he's exposed his beloved family to.

"He is a good flirt," I say to the table. "You should have seen him that day he drew up the contract for the Triumph. An Edsel has nothing on a Triumph. He flirted over the numbers the whole time. He probably got me to pay an extra ten grand."

Richard nudges my knee. "Please stop," he mutters.

Across from me, the blood has drained from Georgia's face. She glares at the table as the kids approach with a platter of cupcakes, candles lit, singing "Happy Birthday."

Georgia must hate me, in a way, but if only she knew how much she should be afraid. Soon enough, Richard will need to go, and who else but the angry ex-wife will be the suspect?

Noah sets the platter in front of Alice. A buttercream carrot decorates each of the cupcakes, so at least Damian got something right. Alice sweeps hair behind her neck and blows the candles out in a single breath.

"What did you wish for?" Max asks.

"Nothing I'll share," Alice says.

I can feel Damian watching me. I'm used to being the smartest person in the room, and I certainly hadn't expected to be undone by the creator of *Acadian Autumn*. I imagine him adding my photo to the center of his whiteboard and connecting me to each of the three crime scenes to create his narrative. But I'm not *the* killer in Damian's story. That's someone else. Because I didn't kill Laurel Thibodeau.

CHAPTER 8
Farley

LATER THAT NIGHT

Richard takes a shower and leaves his clothes in a pile on the bathroom floor, which he knows annoys me. I consider joining him under the water, but he hasn't spoken to me since dinner. I shove the clothing into the hamper, then undress and wait for him out in the bedroom.

The party broke up soon after Alice blew out the candles. We'd had too much to drink, so we walked home along the carriageway through the woods instead of taking the boat. Georgia opted to come to Mooney Point with us tonight, although Max is putting her up in his bunkhouse, a remnant of when the Point used to house many people over the summer. Chloe should be asleep by now, too, in her own room.

All the players are in one place.

When Richard comes out of the bathroom, he's wearing a pair of boxers I thought I'd gotten rid of. They have smiley faces on them and billow around his thighs. He gets into bed without turning on the light and rolls away from me.

I touch his arm. I run my fingers through his damp hair. He

shrugs me off, but I keep trying, moving my hands down his body, under his waistband. "Watch the sugar," I say. "And the carbs. You don't want to get fat again."

He sits up and faces me, his knees pulled to his chest. "I trusted you, Farley," he says to me. "You're so desperate to insert yourself into my life, but this is *my* family. Not yours."

"I don't know why you're so angry," I say.

"Flirting over the contract for the Triumph?" Richard says. "Did you think Georgia wouldn't pick up on that? No matter what she already knew, she was happy to believe we got together *after* I moved out of the parsonage, but you gave her all the data she needed to figure out what really happened. Georgia knows when you bought that car. Now she knows I lied."

Richard and I met secretly for months before he left Georgia, something we managed to keep between ourselves even after our relationship went public. Now I've hurt Georgia again. "Maybe it's good to have the truth out in the open," I say.

Richard starts to speak but stops. He lies back down and turns away, pulling the blankets up around him.

I lie beside him in the darkness and distract myself by imagining his final moments. Does Richard *deserve* what's coming, the way Steve Alabiso and Jeanine Geller did? No. But my own self-preservation takes precedence over fairness. Maybe the brakes on his gold VW will fail. Maybe Richard will careen off a bridge and into the bay. Maybe this death will appear to be more of an accident than the others, although that will take a different kind of planning.

I like a challenge.

When Richard's breathing finally grows steady, I slip out of bed and kiss him on the forehead before changing into a pair of black sweatpants and a running jersey. I also retrieve the balaclava from my ski bag. The time has come to face the problem at hand.

Outside, the night air has grown heavy. Lightning flashes,

followed seconds later by the rumble of thunder. I set off through the trees toward Moulton Farm. In the distance, Harper barks. I don't like to harm animals or children, but a murder-suicide follows a certain logic, and Alice did confess that her husband frightens her. I even made note of the comment in her patient file.

Tonight will be a bloodbath.

PART II

The Patient

CHAPTER 9

Alice

EARLIER THAT DAY

I sit opposite Dr. Drake as I do every Friday afternoon. He may call me Alice during these sessions, but I won't call him Farley, not in this room. I need a clear distinction between friend and clinician as I contemplate what to reveal. Usually, it's not much, but today I want to give him a tidbit, something to keep him engaged, so I say, "I'm frightened," and watch as he absorbs the statement, turning it over, each of his thoughts betrayed in the tiny, barely perceptible micro-expressions I learned to read almost from the moment I began seeing him.

Right now, hope twitches in the corners of his eyes. He believes we've reached the breakthrough he's been working toward since I started coming to his office. I could give him more. I could admit I have secrets, ones I don't want to share, ones that truly frighten me. But if I tell him what I know about Laurel Thibodeau, he may push me to confess more or go to the police. I'm not ready for that. Not yet.

Dr. Drake waits me out in silence, but I've gone to therapy

my entire adult life. Most of my adolescence, too. For me, these sessions are more of a social call, a guarantee of a positive human exchange at least once a week. I stroke Harper's fur. She sighs and rests her head on my foot, calming me enough so when Dr. Drake reflects my own words, I offer a piece of my secret to see what he might do with it. "I knew Laurel," I say.

Damian and I went to Firefly most Fridays for date night. We'd sit at the bar and watch Simon cook while Laurel worked the front of the house with effortless efficiency. She wore her red hair in a bun and usually comped us a glass of wine. All week, ever since I learned of her death, I've tried not to picture her sightless eyes behind that plastic bag.

"A death like this one leaves a bruise on a community," Dr. Drake says. "One that will take time to heal."

I manage to keep from rolling my eyes. "Believe me, I know. My husband hunts monsters. Now it's like the monster has come to us."

Monsters!

Dr. Drake will appreciate the dramatic flourish, but monsters are everywhere. It's just a matter of looking in the right place. My father was in the military when I was growing up. I went to nine schools in four countries between kindergarten and senior year. I learned how to sweep into a new neighborhood, identify a best friend (and a spare), and begin to share the parts of myself I wanted to be public while holding back the rest.

And I learned to spot the darkness. It's always there.

Life with Damian has followed the same pattern. We've traveled the world, to Romania and Turkey, even the island of St. Helena, where Damian traced Napoleon's final years. Like when I was a kid, I identify a best friend. Here in Monreith, I found Georgia. She hadn't yet split with Richard—who still went by Ritchie—so the friendship was convenient in many ways. My son, Noah, seemed to get along with their daughter, Chloe; Damian could indulge his inner frat boy with Richard; and as a minister, Georgia gave me access to the community as a whole. She connected me with the right yoga studio and introduced us to Simon and Laurel. She also recommended Dr. Drake.

Meanwhile, Georgia's marriage to Richard seemed to disintegrate before our eyes. Within a short time, Richard had moved out of the parsonage and into a little apartment over his garage, and the next thing I knew he'd proposed bringing a boyfriend to the farmhouse.

"We'd love to meet him!" I said.

A few days later, they drove up the lane and into the yard in a tiny gray sports car. The top was down, but it took me a moment to connect the man at the wheel with the Dr. Drake I saw every week in his office. His normally styled hair was tousled from the drive, but his blue eyes were impossible to miss. He held back while Richard, clearly getting used to his new world, introduced him as Farley.

"Alice, right?" Dr. Drake said. "I've heard so much about you."

It was off-putting to see Dr. Drake away from the office, at my house, introducing himself to my husband. Threatening, even. I hadn't had a social interaction with a therapist in a lifetime of therapy, and my first instinct was to claim a sudden headache and retreat. Surely Richard had mentioned my name when we made the plans to get together? Surely Dr. Drake had known he was showing up at a patient's house and ambushing her? I'd talked about Richard and Georgia during my sessions, filling the hour with gossip about new friends, and I'd taken Georgia's side in the split. How many of my confidences had Dr. Drake relayed while the two men lay in bed together at night?

I kept my calm, though, telling Dr. Drake it was nice to meet him. We made our way around the house to the patio, where I'd set up drinks and hors d'oeuvres. "We're having tagine for dinner," I said.

"Alice's specialty," Damian said. "She learned to make it while we were living in Marrakesh."

I handed Dr. Drake a glass of Grüner. "Stunning views," he said, looking out over the bay. "Did you know we're neighbors? I live through the woods on Mooney Point. Maybe I'll take the boat over next time we get together."

"You should see his house," Richard said. "It could be in *Architectural Digest*. And it's totally green."

"Unlike this house," I said. "Which is barely insulated."

"It's a beauty," Dr. Drake said.

"I'll give you a tour," I said, pulling him away from the guys.

By then, I was seething. All this time, he'd been living on the other end of the carriageway. He had to have known that as he pried into my personal life. I walked him through the house, pointing out the fireplaces. I took him by Damian's office. "This is where the magic happens," I said.

In the kitchen, I ran a hand over the green enamel on the Glenwood stove, suddenly at a loss for words. I turned on him. He seemed to anticipate my coming fury. He held his hands out, his body language open.

"You can disclose our professional relationship, or this can be the first time we've ever met. It's up to you."

"You didn't think to give me a heads-up?" I asked.

"I only found out we were coming this afternoon."

"You could have postponed."

"You're right," he said. "I played this one wrong. I should leave."

"That would be for the best," I said.

I led him through the house and down the cellar stairs to where Damian had Richard in a headlock. "Noogie," he said, as they tumbled off the patio and wrestled in the grass.

"Frat boys at play," Dr. Drake said, an eyebrow raised. "Any cause for concern?"

Right there in that moment, he transformed. Dr. Drake was stolid and empathetic. Farley was funny and quick, catty even. "Stay," I said.

"Are you sure?" he asked.

That night, I served a burned tagine. It was terrible, but Richard and Farley stayed for dinner and returned the next week. To his credit, Dr. Drake has encouraged me to find a new therapist ever since. I'm the one who hasn't followed through despite his insistence. It seems like too much of a bother. And besides, I rarely tell him the truth.

"What are your clients saying about Laurel's murder?" I ask.

"What would you guess they're saying?"

That's part of what has me frightened. "That Simon will be charged with obstruction of justice, at the very least," I say.

"Do you think Simon will be charged?"

Most people believe Simon Thibodeau committed the murder or at least arranged for someone else to do it. My husband has another theory. He believes there's a serial killer on the loose here in Monreith and that Laurel Thibodeau was the latest victim. He's been right before, and there are connections between some seemingly unrelated local deaths Damian's been tracking: each of the victims was having an affair and each of the spouses was considered the prime suspect but ultimately produced a solid alibi. Still, that's hardly enough to prove a trend, and now I'd rather the police didn't dig too deep, or connect those deaths back to Laurel. It would expose Damian and me to too much scrutiny.

"You mentioned being frightened," Dr. Drake says. "What were you circling?"

There are only five minutes left in the session. I'll let Dr. Drake believe I've been deflecting all along. "Why not ask what you want to ask? When I say I'm frightened, who would you guess I'm talking about? What do you think I mean?"

A twitch in Dr. Drake's mouth gives him away again. He's been hoping to get a rise out of me all along. He holds his hands open and tells me he can't do the work for me.

So I mention the birthday cake, and that I'll be pissed off if Damian forgets to order one or if he chooses chocolate, his favorite, instead of carrot, mine. I'll be really pissed off if the cake isn't loaded with walnuts, but I don't share that detail, which is for me, and me alone. When the session finally ends, I ask what everyone's been wondering: "If Simon Thibodeau didn't kill Laurel, then who did?"

I hope I don't know the answer.

"Nothing is free," I say to Harper, who awaits her reward for sitting at attention while I fumble for the keys to my ancient SUV. A woman approaches us along the sidewalk. She sports short, graying hair and sneakers, the New England practical look I wish I had the courage to adopt. As the woman walks alongside my car, Harper comes out of her sit and lunges. All she wants is to say hello, but she's a pit bull, and I never know how people will react. Thankfully, this woman doesn't flinch.

"What a sweet girl!" she says. "She'll have to meet my Bonnie."

The vet thinks Harper is four years old. I found her in the woods by the marsh covered in mange and fleas, her swollen nipples betraying a litter of puppies that were never recovered. "I'll call animal control to come get her," Max Barbosa had said to me when I brought her by his cottage.

He filled a bowl with water and cut up some leftover chicken that Harper ate in one giant mouthful. "Beer?" he asked.

"Sure."

He handed me a can of Mighty Squirrel, and said, "No one will want this dog."

I brought her home that evening and gave her a bath. She's rarely left my side since.

Harper knows what it's like to face a hostile world. In spite of that, I haven't ever seen her growl at another dog, let alone a person. She trusts implicitly, while I won't trust my therapist with my most vulnerable thoughts.

I open the back door of the SUV, buckle Harper in, and reward her with a treat. I glance up and see Dr. Drake watching me through the blinds in his office window. In spite of the bright September sun, a chill runs down my back as I think about what truly frightens me.

Damian and I have a good marriage, and we understand each other's faults. He knows I can be rigid and like control, that I don't tolerate suffering. I understand he sometimes has an itch that needs satisfying. It rarely lasts long, but it often seems like he has a homing device that latches onto desperate, unhappy women seeking a temporary reprieve from their troubled marriages.

Here in Monreith, he found Laurel Thibodeau.

CHAPTER 10
Alice

Damian is ten years older than I am. When we met, I was an undergrad at Newburg College where I still went by my maiden name, Alice Starkey, and Damian was married to a rising star in the economics department who'd negotiated a teaching job for him when she was recruited. I majored in finance, so I would see Damian and his wife at department events from time to time. They were a handsome couple: Damian, with his slim cyclist's physique, and his wife with her dark bob and seemingly effortless style. We'd chat, and his wife would tell me I had a bright future in front of me.

On a whim, I decided to take Damian's film history course during my last semester when I needed an easy general ed to meet graduation requirements. It didn't take long for things to progress between us or for his wife to find out. Thankfully, they didn't have children.

At first, the college administration tried to paint me as a victim, but when I wouldn't play along, they wanted me to disappear. So did the other professors in the department, who rallied behind Damian's wife. I quietly finished my coursework, while Damian suffered through a humiliating disciplinary process that resulted in his termination. The morning of my graduation, I ran into Damian's wife in the stairwell at the business school. We both froze in place. I started to apologize, but she raised a hand to stop me and then grabbed my arm, her nails digging into my flesh. For a moment, it seemed as if she might shove me down the stairwell.

"Alice," she said to me. "Why would you do this?"

I knew enough to understand I was in the wrong, and anything I might say would make things worse. When she let me go, I fled.

That summer, Damian and I moved to the mountains of Romania, where Damian worked on the crew for a documentary about Vlad the Impaler. While we traveled, I completed an online MBA, then got a job with an investment firm and began building a client list. His first wife went on to work in the White House. For an economist, she's famous. That's why I haven't mentioned her name.

Damian talks a good game, and he's had enough success over the years that he impresses with his credit list. Most people we meet believe he's the one calling the shots, but I make most of the money we live on as a family. I like being the breadwinner and controlling my own financial future. And Damian would be lost without me.

I haven't regretted a single choice I've made. I was an adult when I met my husband, and there are all kinds of marriages. This is ours. I made my own decisions and knew exactly who he was.

I still know who he is.

I pull away from the curb and drive through town, where shadows of this last week hang over everything. Too many cops come in and out of the police station dressed in smart suits that tell me they don't belong here. A single news truck parks along the street, too, though coverage of the murder has waned since that state detective confirmed Simon's alibi of being at the casinos. The murder hasn't made national news. Not yet at least.

I glance in the rearview mirror, where Harper sits with her nose out the window. I can trust her with my secrets. "First that priest in Maine," I say. "Now your daddy's been sleeping with a dead woman."

Death really does follow us.

A few miles from downtown, a long wooden bridge spans a narrow section of the bay. I roll over the bumpy planks to where a four-mile stretch of sand forms a barrier between the bay and the sound. Only two other cars dot the small, windswept parking lot. A salty breeze lifts my hair as I grab an orange rubber ball and let Harper leap from the car, leash free. A weathered footbridge passes over dunes thick with beach grass. On the other side, an empty lifeguard stand sits at the top of the town beach, overlooking a plane of rocky sand the color of wet cement. Tonight, the moon will be full, so the tides are at their most extreme. By midnight, waves will crash at the shore and the beach will have narrowed to a few hundred yards.

I slip off my shoes and let my feet sink into the warm sand. I toss the ball, and Harper takes off. The ball nearly makes it to the waterline before Harper catches it mid-bounce. After a few hundred yards, we pass an older man walking in the other direction as Harper gallops toward us.

The man nods hello and continues on his way.

I take out my phone.

An hour later, I retrace the mile-long return to the parking lot. By now, the tide has begun to sweep in and cover the rocky shore. Harper pants beside me, her tongue hanging from the side of her mouth. "I have some water in the car," I say. "We're almost there."

I haven't seen anyone else during the walk, and my mind has cleared. At this point, I mostly don't care if Damian remembers the cake.

The sun shines in my eyes, so it's not till I nearly reach the lifeguard stand that I notice the silhouette of a man leaning against the white metal frame. I'm aware of being alone. It's not as if I can't handle myself in tricky situations, but I can't help picturing Laurel's sightless eyes behind that plastic bag and the crime scene photos Damian has pinned to the whiteboard in his office.

I block the sun with my hand, and the pang of fear washes away as the silhouette transforms into Max Barbosa, the police chief. He salutes with two fingers. I wave, but not too eagerly. Then I turn back toward the water and wait to hear the crunch of his footsteps as he approaches across the rocky shore.

"Who ratted us out?" I ask. "No one reports off-leash doodles. It's pit bull discrimination."

I toss the ball and watch Harper's strong legs propelling her forward, her paw prints disappearing in the wet sand.

"You have a good arm," Max says.

Down the beach, the ball bounces into the waves. Harper plunges in after it.

"Muscle memory," I say. "I played softball in college."

Harper leaps from the water with the ball clenched in her jaw. She waits till she's run all the way back to us before shaking the water from her coat. Max shields his face from the spray but laughs. I take the ball and offer it to him. "Give it a try?"

"Come on, Alice," he says. "She needs to be leashed."

"You're afraid I have a better arm than you."

He takes the ball. "You know the rules."

I hold out my wrists. "Cuff me."

"I'll let you off with a warning." He pauses. "Again."

He takes his hat off and sweeps a hand through his thick, prematurely white hair. He's about my age, and solid—broad across the chest, and well over six feet tall, a stoic Great Pyrenees to Damian's wiry terrier.

"Write me the ticket," I say. "I don't want to make any trouble for you."

"Don't worry. I can handle trouble. I'm the chief."

I snap the leash onto Harper's collar. "Rumor has it you won't be the chief much longer," I say, as we make our way toward the parking lot. "I heard you took a job with the state police."

Max shakes his head. "I can't kill that story to save my life. The detective I've been working with on the Thibodeau case wants to recruit me, but I haven't decided what to do yet. I'll probably turn him down. This town is where I belong."

"That's good news," I say. "Or it sounds like it is."

"Pluses and minuses."

"More pluses?"

"We'll see," Max says. "I hope I'm making the decision for the right reasons. I don't know how you and your husband uproot yourselves the way you do."

"Life's an adventure," I say. "That's what I signed up for, at least."

"Don't you sometimes wake up and wonder how you wound up wherever you are?"

"Those are the times I'm glad we keep moving on. At least I know everything is temporary."

We cross to the parking lot, where Max's cruiser sits beside the SUV. I fill Harper's bowl with water and wait for her to lap it up.

Max leans against his cruiser, one foot crossed over the other. "Noah is friends with Chloe Macomber, right?" he asks, casually.

Too casually, and my maternal instincts kick in. There's a

purpose behind the question. "Why would the chief of police care who my son is friends with?" I ask.

"Chloe got in a fight at school today. I haven't heard that Noah was involved, but I'm trying to figure out what happened." Max shrugs. "Chloe's been acting out lately. I caught her sneaking out of the church last night, too. God knows what she was getting into."

I open the back door of the SUV and wait for Harper to jump in. "If you're worried, shouldn't you talk to her parents?"

"I've tried, but they're caught up in their own drama and can't hear what I'm saying." Max kicks a pebble on the asphalt. "Like I said, I've lived here my whole life, and I've known Chloe since she was born. You get a different view of things as a cop that others don't, and the last thing I want is for her to go down a path she can't come back from."

I get in the car and start the engine, then roll the window down. Chloe and Noah hang out all the time. If Chloe's heading in the wrong direction, I'll want to know too. "I'll see what Noah will tell me. He may be thirteen, but he's still sweet if I get him at the right moment."

Max gives Harper one last scratch through the back window. "Keep her on the leash, at least when other people are around." As he turns away, I swear his cheeks flush. "Come by the cottage while the weather's nice. Winter'll be here before we know it."

Damian isn't the only one who engages in extracurricular activities. Max's little cottage is a short walk through the woods from Moulton Farm, and Harper remembers the chicken he fed her the first time they met. Sometimes I send Harper to his door and then follow a few moments later, pretending she ran off. Max fixes Harper a plate and invites me in, where we sit on his back porch, drink hoppy IPAs right out of the can, play cribbage, and talk about nothing and everything. He tells me about growing up on Mooney Point with his father, how much he misses the mother he never knew. I tell him about moving around the world, that I haven't seen my own parents for a few years. "Don't let too much time pass," he said once.

Max has feelings for me, and I like the attention. So far, we haven't gone beyond innocent flirtation, but if he pressed further, I'm not sure if I'd refuse. For the briefest of moments, I allow myself to believe he turned down the job with the state police to stay close to me. But that would be selfish.

"I'm having a party tonight," I say. "You should come. Georgia will be there. Richard, too. So will Chloe and Noah. Maybe you can get the kids to tell you what the fight was about."

"Will the boyfriend be there?"

"Farley? Yeah, he's coming."

"I should pass, then. We're not exactly friends."

"I cooked everything," I say. "There'll be good food and plenty of wine. We might even play croquet. And Farley's not as bad as you think he is."

"Try living next door to him."

"Technically, we're all neighbors. Only the woods separate us. Shouldn't we get along?"

Max shuffles his feet. "What's the occasion?"

"Nothing special," I say, not mentioning it's my birthday. "A friendly get-together. Just come, okay?"

"I'll bring potato salad."

I already have mashed potatoes for tonight, but who cares? "I love potato salad. And I'll see you at six. Drinks on the patio before sunset."

As I drive away, I look in the rearview mirror. Max watches me.

I'm glad he's coming tonight because I'm attracted to him more than I probably should be. I'm also relieved. Max is a professional, and he's good at his job. I know he's worked closely with the state cops to find Laurel's killer. I reach into the back of the SUV and let Harper lick my hand. "Max wouldn't come to the house tonight if he thought it would compromise his investigation," I say to her. "Especially if he thought a person of interest would be at the party, too."

Someone like Damian.

Maybe we're in the clear.

CHAPTER 11
Alice

On the other side of the bridge, I pull over long enough to send a text. *It's me, Alice Stone*, I write. *I'll be there in ten minutes.*

Across town, I turn into a subdivision with a cul-de-sac at the end and park under a canopy of oaks. Five '80s-era colonials stare down at me. I scan the circle for any signs of the media, then feel like a criminal as I put on huge sunglasses and a baseball hat. I get Harper out of the SUV and keep my head down as I hurry across a driveway and around to the back porch. The shrubs at this house are nicely trimmed, like someone cared for them, but the grass hasn't been cut, and the blinds are drawn. It's so quiet, it almost seems as if no one's home, but I know better. I swear someone's watching me as I rap on the door. When no one answers, I pound harder, only to hear tentative footsteps approaching.

"Open up," I say.

A dead bolt clicks. The door opens a crack, and Simon Thibodeau stands on the other side. He scans behind me to be sure I'm alone, slams the door, and slides the chain before ushering me into the darkened house, where the musty air has the stench of—well—death. Laurel Thibodeau was found suffocated in her bed here less than a week ago. Simon steps onto the back porch, absorbing a few rays of sun before closing the door and sliding the dead bolt back into place.

He glowers in the dimly lit hallway, and yes, I'm aware that coming to Simon's house without telling anyone may have been a bad idea. He is the primary suspect in a violent crime. I reach for my phone, only to remember I left it in the car, on the console. At least I have Harper to protect me, though she noses at Simon's knee. He crouches, letting her bat his hands with her paws till she rolls onto her back and offers up her belly. So much for my watchdog.

I haven't seen Simon since Laurel was killed—except in a few brief flashes that showed on the local news. The last week hasn't been kind to him. He must have lost ten pounds. His eyes are red and bloodshot. Every part of him sags with weariness.

"How are you holding up?" I ask.

"Terrific," he says. "I mean, my restaurant is closed, and I can't leave the house without a stranger telling me I'm a monster who put a plastic bag over his wife's head. So I sit here in the dark all day and wonder who's lurking on the other side of the curtains. And I'm waiting for the police to arrest me at any moment. Maybe when that happens, I'll declare bankruptcy."

Harper licks his face.

"Also, my in-laws are preparing a civil suit just in case I avoid being charged. Oh, and I have a gambling addiction. Besides all that, I'm awesome."

The birthday cake my husband may or may not get me doesn't seem like that big of a deal anymore.

Photos cover the wall behind Simon. I focus on one and realize it's of Laurel, who smiles at the misty summit of a mountain, her curly red hair blowing across her face. She's younger here than when I knew her, every part of her brighter, more alive. She seems happy, though photos can lie.

Damian and I began frequenting Firefly soon after we moved to town. The food was great—Simon had trained in

France and worked as a chef in New York for years—and I appreciated that Laurel remembered us and that we soon didn't need to make reservations.

A few months ago, we arrived at the restaurant at our usual time, and I could tell something had changed. Laurel's attention was so focused on Damian she barely remembered to take two menus as she led us to the bar and uncorked a bottle of cabernet.

"On the house," she said.

I knew at once things had begun between her and my husband. It wasn't Laurel who gave away their secret, though. I'd experienced this before: Damian's voice grows louder, his eyes brighter. His confidence surges, and in that moment my heart falls the tiniest bit. I don't take long to recover, and when I do, I'm stronger for it. Remember, I control the money in my house. I'm not a victim. I can leave at any time, and in the end, Damian chooses me.

At least he has so far.

Simon leads me to the kitchen, the one spotless room in the house.

On the counter, a stack of six aluminum trays filled with food awaits me. I hired Simon weeks ago to cater the party and haven't had the heart to cancel. If I were kinder, I'd sneak him into the back of the SUV so he could join us tonight, but I'm not that nice. Besides, if I did, Max wouldn't be able to stay.

"At least I could get food delivered to the house this week," Simon says, "or I wouldn't have filled the order." He hands me a sheet of paper with directions for finishing the prep. "The ratatouille and the puree go in the oven for thirty minutes. Serve the caprese and the farro salad at room temperature. Not cold. Room temperature. You can't mess this up."

I count out five hundred dollars in twenties, then add an

extra. I'd rather not have a paper trail linking me to Simon Thibodeau in any way right now.

"I would help you load the car," he says, "But, well, I don't know who might be lurking out there."

I hand him Harper's leash. "Take a few minutes of canine therapy."

At the SUV, I make room in the back for the food, only to notice a reporter crouched in a minivan snapping photos. I give him the finger and return to the house for the next load. "Do me a favor. Don't tell anyone I hired you." As soon as I say the words, I want to take them back. "Sorry. That didn't sound the way I meant it to. It's just they're always saying I'm a terrible cook. For once, I want them to believe I made something delicious."

Simon laughs. He laughs so hard he can barely breathe. It's contagious, and soon I'm gasping for breath, too.

"Who would I tell?" Simon asks.

He covers his face, presses his back to the wall, and sinks to the floor as his laughter morphs into sobs. I step away from him. I could run. I could escape this prison of a house with its stench of death. Instead, I take Simon's hand. He shakes his head and tries to pull away, but I guide his hand through Harper's fur. She noses her way onto his lap, while I slide down next to him, my legs curled toward my chest. In this moment, I don't believe for a second he killed his wife. "This'll get better," I say.

He rests his head against the wall, his energy spent. "Will it?" he asks.

I follow his gaze. He stares at the same photo I noticed earlier, the one of Laurel on the mountaintop. "We hiked Ben Nevis in Scotland that day," he says. "We were happier then."

I wonder if Simon is looking for an ally, and if he, too, knew all along about Damian and Laurel's affair. Before he can ask, I grab the last of the food and make my escape.

CHAPTER 12
Alice

It's after five o'clock by the time I turn onto the long, tree-lined lane that leads through fields of corn and up to the farmhouse. I pass the red barn with its weathervane and hay-loft and park beneath the ancient beech tree beside Damian's silver Audi. He likes a flashy car, and I'm happy to oblige. A pair of Rhode Island Red hens peck around the compost heap, and the stench of smoking meat greets me as I get out of the car.

"Be good," I whisper to Harper, who dashes after one of the chickens.

It escapes to the coop. When it comes to hens and squirrels, Harper is always hopeful and never successful.

I call Damian's name, but he doesn't answer. He must be out on his bike. In the barn, the mini-goats bleat at the sound of my footsteps. I fill a bucket with feed, and all five of the goats toddle toward me and stick their noses through the wooden slats as I feed them by hand.

Damian seems to have an endless supply of friends willing to lend us housing, and we're staying here rent-free through next summer. Moulton Farm belongs to an old colleague of his from Newburg College who's away on sabbatical, one of the few faculty members who didn't ostracize Damian after we got together. The sole stipulation was that we had to take care of the goats and chickens. "Alice!" Damian had said to me when he'd shown me photos of the farm. "Imagine the cheese! And fresh eggs. We'll have omelets every morning."

As usual, his enthusiasm had been contagious—enough so I'd forgotten that a barn filled with animals smells like a barnyard; and those animals need to be fed and exercised and loved; and to make cheese, goats need to be milked every morning; and many of those responsibilities would fall to me. I mind less than I should, especially in moments like this one when I step into the pen and the goats nuzzle at my legs while I feed them dinner and change their water. Maybe I'll take up goat yoga?

In the chicken coop, I move down the row of nesting boxes and gather the day's eggs in a basket. One hen has been brooding for the last few weeks. I speak to her gently as I slip a hand beneath her soft, warm body and retrieve the egg. "There'll be another one tomorrow," I whisper.

Most of the eggs are brown. A few, like this one, are sky blue. And they do make amazing omelets. *Be grateful,* I tell myself. It's a lesson I have to be reminded of.

Out in the yard, I call to Harper, who trots to my side. At the kitchen door, a bouquet of pink dahlias and chrysanthemums waits in the afternoon sun. Without reading the attached card, I know they're from Dr. Drake. Or Farley, to be more accurate. This is definitely friend territory. I breathe in the blossoms' sweet scent as I step into the kitchen. Dahlias I planted in the spring fill the perennial borders, and Farley's the type who notices those details.

I place the bouquet on the kitchen table along with the serving platters I set out earlier. I add a large ceramic bowl from the hutch and scrawl *Potato salad!* on a Post-it, then almost rewrite it without the exclamation point. Instead, I grab the bouquet and an extra place setting and wend my way toward the back patio through a warren of interconnected rooms. This house has been added onto over the centuries, seemingly with no plan besides increasing square footage. The original farmhouse wasn't much bigger than the kitchen and a few connected rooms surrounding a central fireplace. Since then, the house has grown into a haphazard collection of rooms, each with its own period detail. One wing has high ceilings and ornate Victorian crown molding, another has '70s-era linoleum floors and faux-wood paneling. At the back of the house, I maneuver down a narrow set of wooden stairs, through a damp cellar, and outside to a brick patio, with its sweeping views of the bay.

I place the bouquet in the center of the teak dining table and add a sixth table setting for Max. On the lawn, heat pours from the smoker, and a light coating of ash covers everything on the patio I'd set before leaving for my session with Farley. I gather the plates and glasses and bring them back inside, where I pile them in the soapstone sink and rinse them off right as my phone beeps with a text from Georgia. *Heading over soon. Need anything?*

A carrot cake for the birthday girl? I type, but I delete the message and write *All set!* instead.

Surely Damian remembered the cake.

I dry the plates and glasses and bring them outside. When I return to the kitchen, I start searching for the cake, checking the fridge and then moving onto the cupboards. I open the tiny oven in the gigantic Glenwood stove. It would be just like Damian to hide a bakery box there, forgetting I'd need to light the oven to get ready for the party. Which reminds me, I have to move the food in from the car. I light the oven but head down to the cellar, where I check the shelves by the workbench and the spare fridge.

Still no cake.

Through the TV room and down a hallway, I open Damian's office door. This is the part of the house that was built in the seventies. It has drop ceilings, worn shag carpeting, and smoke-stained walls straight out of a conspiracy film—which fits, since Damian's whiteboard diagrams his own conspiracy theories. A photo of Laurel Thibodeau is taped in the center of it, along with images from the other crime scenes, all connected with thick red lines. Damian's illegible scrawl completes the picture of a man obsessed.

I do a cursory search of the office for the cake, then step closer to the whiteboard. I've seen most of what's here before, though the photo of Laurel is new. She's older than in the Scotland pic, with gray streaking her red hair. This also isn't an image I've seen in the paper or online. I touch her face, tracing the creases around her eyes, taking note that she seems happy here, too. I suspect Damian snapped the photo and it's sitting on his phone, waiting for the cops to discover it. I wonder what other images they might find, what story they'll tell.

Earlier this week, when news of the murder went public, I'd found Damian outside, sitting on the porch swing, drinking a glass of bourbon even though it was before noon. I slid in beside him, and we sat without saying a word. I know he's hurting now. But the thing about secrets in a marriage is if you talk about them, then they're no longer secrets. And it's not as though I don't have my own.

Upstairs, I search in our room, under the bed and in the dressers. I find Damian's pot stash tucked among his socks and count thirteen buds in total.

Across the hallway, I ignore the Do NOT DISTURB sign hanging on Noah's door. I knock and wait a full thirty seconds before entering into a wave of stale air. I yank open a window, then check the closet to see if Noah's hiding. I go through his dresser, too, though his secrets would all be on his phone. I have the right to snoop through Noah's room and electronics whenever I want, and I've made that clear. I have his passwords and have threatened to use them, but I haven't yet wanted to deal with the consequences of what I might find.

I try a drawer in the bedside table, and then sweep a hand beneath his mattress where I brush against something hard and plastic. It's a phone. But it's not the phone we gave Noah on the first day of sixth grade. It's a burner phone. One with a cracked screen. Like something a drug dealer would use.

Footsteps sound in the hall behind me. I shove the phone back where I found it as Harper noses her way into the room, her tail slapping at the doorframe. "Don't tell anyone I was snooping," I say to her.

I take the phone out again, power it up, and enter Noah's passcode, his birthday. It doesn't work, which makes me worry more. He's hiding a burner phone from me. Of course he created a new passcode. I try my birthday and "1234" and "0000," but none of those work either.

Downstairs, a door slams.

I shove the phone under the mattress right as Noah steps onto the landing and points to the Do *Not* Disturb sign. I must look as guilty as I feel. Still, I face him, ready to confront him with the evidence, but he ducks under my arm for a hug.

"*You* can ignore the sign," he says. "That's mostly for Dad."

Unlike Chloe Macomber, Noah's still a kid, still sweet enough to kiss me goodnight. He has his father's slim build and a mop of blond hair he ties in a ponytail. Strangers mistake him for a girl sometimes, but he doesn't care. "Our generation is too fluid to worry about those things," he assures me.

For a while over the summer, he asked us to call him "N," though he switched back to Noah when school began.

"Where have you been?" I ask. "School's been out for a while."

"Down by the dock," he says.

"How was your day?"

He hops onto the bed and lies back. "Fine, I guess."

I remember the promise I made to Max out on the town beach. "Want to tell me about the fight?"

"You already know about that?"

"Mother superpower."

"Chloe didn't do anything, if that's what you're asking. Taylor Lawson picks on her all the time, and I guess Chloe lost it."

"Is she being bullied?"

"Maybe a little."

That's something I can share with Max.

I slide in beside Noah, and he snuggles against me like I hoped he would. I can almost feel the burner digging into my back through the mattress. "Have you ever done drugs?" I ask.

Noah pushes away from me. "I'm in eighth grade!"

I'd smoked plenty of pot by the time I was in eighth grade. Other things, too. "Would you tell me if you did?" I ask.

"Probably not," Noah says. "Because I'd be *doing drugs*. Isn't that something you keep secret from your parents? It's like the way you and Dad smoke the pot he has hidden in his sock drawer. You know it stinks, right?"

I guess I'm not the only one who snoops. I roll off the bed. "The party's starting soon. You can put out the croquet set."

As Noah pulls himself up, I slip the phone from under the mattress and hold it in my palm. He narrows his eyes in a way that doesn't give much away. "What's that?" he asks.

"You tell me," I say.

"It's not mine."

I study his face for a moment, trying to determine if he's being honest. Unlike Chloe, he has his own phone already.

If the burner is his, he's probably using it for something he shouldn't. "Where did it come from?" I ask.

"I've never seen it. I swear."

"Whose is it then?"

"I don't know."

Behind him through the open window, off in the distance, a possible answer appears as a cyclist turns onto the lane. Damian pedals through the trees toward the farm, his sinewy legs straining against the hill. He doesn't have a cake with him, not that I can see anyway. And I doubt he's managed to hide one—carrot or otherwise—in those Spandex shorts.

CHAPTER 13
Alice

"Don't mention this phone to anyone," I say to Noah, leaving the burner on his bedside table and heading outside to meet Damian by the beech tree. He swoops around the barn on his bike, his red-and-blue cycling jersey open on his lean chest. He unclips his shoes and squeaks to a stop.

"Need to check the brakes on this one," he says, tilting his head back and showering his bearded face with water from a plastic bottle. "Took a spill and almost went into a ditch a mile back." He hangs the bike in the barn and kisses my cheek, his every move deliberate. Heat pours off his body, and I'm reminded of what drew me to him when I was a twenty-one-year-old student, even if the packaging masked its flawed contents. I'm attracted to it all over again, momentarily leaving aside the murder and the affair. And the nonexistent carrot cake. Damian can make you believe anything is possible. He can make you forget transgressions, too. I shove him gently. "You're disgusting. And you're lucky I haven't changed my clothes for the party yet."

He pulls me so close that sweat soaks right through to my skin. "Take a shower," I say, extracting myself. "And FYI, I asked Max Barbosa to come tonight."

I study Damian's reaction. He must know the cops might narrow in on him soon. Surely there are DNA traces and a data trail pointing right to the affair, but Damian seems unfazed. He mimes smoking a joint. "The chief of police? Alice, what have you done? Now we can't have any fun."

"We'll have plenty of fun, but you might want to pick a new hiding place for your stash. Your son found it."

"Born snoop," Damian says. "Like his dad. And I'm glad the chief is coming. Now I can quiz him on what's happening with the investigation."

I push Damian toward the kitchen. "Don't embarrass me," I say. "You know he can't talk about an open investigation. Take a shower, and take care of that meat, too. It's leaving ash all over the backyard."

I open the SUV to unload dinner. I'm not completely certain Noah was telling the truth when he said the phone wasn't his, but if it's not his, it has to have come from somewhere. What if the phone does belong to Damian? What if he used it to take the photo of Laurel Thibodeau that's hanging on his whiteboard? How many other photos of her could there be? How many texts? How often did they send the heart emoji to each other? Did they sext? And what will the cops do once they get their hands on that data? What will a defense attorney do, one hired by a spurned husband whose reputation has been dragged through the mud all because his wife's lover didn't come forward with the truth?

What will Max do if he learns I knew about the burner all along?

"Alice?"

Max Barbosa's voice breaks me out of my trance. How long have I been staring at the back of my car? How much of what I've been thinking is apparent to a seasoned cop?

"You're early," I say.

"Sorry," he says. "I'll come back."

I manage to compose myself. "No, of course not. You just surprised me."

Max holds a blue Tupperware container and has changed into a pair of khakis and a white shirt that shows off his summer tan. I could tell him about the phone right now and be done with this. I start to say something but stop as I imagine an army of state cops descending on the farmhouse, followed by a swarm of media, tracking our every move, dissecting our lives. I imagine the police interrogation, and my mother telling me she'd always known Damian was no good. I'm not ready for any of it. Not yet.

From somewhere, I conjure up a smile.

"I was standing beside you for at least a minute," Max says. "What were you thinking about?"

The best lies hone close to the truth. "The murder," I say.

"We're all thinking about it, aren't we?" Max says. "It takes up so much of my day I forget the whole town wants to know what happened."

"Tonight you can leave work behind. We're here to have fun, right?"

"Nothing but," Max says. "Let me help you out." He balances the Tupperware on top of three of the aluminum containers. "You cooked everything, huh?"

"I sweated over the stove all week. That's all you need to know!"

I lead the way into the kitchen, and Max unloads the rest of the food, while I read through Simon's instructions and put the ratatouille and mashed potatoes into the oven to warm.

"I thought Simon closed the restaurant this week," Max says.

The containers are stamped with the Firefly branding. So is the sheet of paper with the instructions.

"I swung by the house," I say.

Max shakes his head. "Stay away from that guy, okay? Even if he didn't kill his wife, he's bad news. And you didn't hear it from me."

"Are there other suspects?"

Max breaks eye contact. "It's not my case. The state cops are handling it."

Harper laps at her empty water bowl. I fill it at the sink while Max organizes the trays. He holds up the Post-it where I'd written *Potato salad!*

"I didn't know you were such a fan," he says. "But I was out of potatoes. I made ambrosia instead. You know, marsh-mallows and mandarin oranges, but you have enough food here to feed an army. I'll take it home. You're too fancy for ambrosia."

"I live in a barnyard," I say. "There's nothing fancy about me." I empty the contents from the Tupperware into a bowl, then retrieve a jar of maraschino cherries from the fridge and sprinkle them over the top. "That's what I call fancy."

"The marshmallows are vegan," Max says. "No gelatin. Aren't you a vegetarian?"

My face turns warm, and this time the pull between us is un-mistakable. I'm standing close to him, close enough to feel his breath on my neck. Upstairs, Damian's footsteps thump through the ceiling. My own husband can't remember a cake, but Max thought to buy vegan marshmallows.

"Beer?" I ask.

"Sure," Max says.

My mouth has gone dry. I inhale Max's musky scent and allow myself to imagine long nights on his back porch, a cen-tury of cribbage, a case of IPA, and nowhere to go. I imagine his lips on mine.

Right then, a car peels into the driveway, and Max steps back. "There's Georgia," he says.

It's 5:59. Georgia is never late for anything, a professional hazard of overseeing the church. For once, I wish she'd managed to hit traffic. But I take two beers from the fridge, twist off the caps, and plant my feet firmly in the business of hosting a party.

Harper noses her way out the screen door and greets Georgia with a friendly *woof*. Georgia gets out of her car with a tote bag hanging from one arm. She finishes banging out a text, makes the dog sit, and offers a treat. When she steps into the kitchen, she says, "This is a nice surprise," to Max. "I didn't know you were friends."

"You're not the only one who gives Harper treats," I say. "She's always sneaking through the woods to his place."

"And everyone knows me," Max says. "I'm the chief of police."

"Has the pink-haired wonder arrived yet?" Georgia asks.

"Chloe's not here," I say. "It's just the two of you, so far."

"Knowing Ritchie," Georgia says, "they'll be here by nine."

"It's *Richard* now," Max says, and Georgia punches his arm.

"Be nice," she says. "And don't start anything with Farley."

"Easy for you to say."

"Are you kidding?" Georgia says. "If anyone gets to have a grudge against Farley Drake, it's me. He stole my husband! But change is good. I get to have my kid half the time and do whatever I want the rest. When Chloe's with Ritchie, I don't think about her. A couple of weeks ago, I watched five hours of *Mad Men* reruns. I spent so much time watching TV, I had to work the show into my sermon. It was about knowing when you have enough."

Georgia's relentless positivity can feel oppressive, and now, with the moment of frisson between Max and me all but evaporated, I'm finding it particularly annoying, especially as I feel myself fading into the background. A part of me regrets inviting Max tonight. I like when we spend time alone, when I can forget I'm married or that he might actually have a dating life. I suspect Georgia wants to be part of that life now that she's free from Richard. Maybe she already is. "Head out to the patio," I say to them. "Take a bottle of wine. I need to mix drinks and finish cooking dinner."

"You're the birthday girl!" Georgia says. "We'll take care of this."

Max meets my eyes. "You didn't mention it was your birthday. I'd have brought a cribbage board."

"Who wants to turn twenty-nine again?" I ask.

"What's the house cocktail?" Georgia asks.

"Cosmopolitans."

"I mix a mean Cosmo. Go get yourself ready, and meet us outside. But remember, it's just us. There's no one here to impress."

Georgia lays the tote bag on the counter and takes out a plastic clamshell of supermarket cupcakes, each one decorated with a buttercream carrot and a splash of walnuts. She holds the clamshell over her head and peers through the liners. "I couldn't tell if they have raisins or not. And if there's already a cake, throw these away. I can't have a dozen cupcakes at the parsonage, especially when I'm there by myself all weekend."

I nearly tell her she shouldn't have bothered, but my voice catches. Instead, I kiss her cheek and head upstairs.

CHAPTER 14
Alice

I change into a loose linen dress, one that will move with the sea breeze. I tie my hair into a ponytail and skip the makeup, because Georgia is right: there's no one coming to the party who I need to impress, no matter what I'd hoped might happen with Max. Still, I check myself in the mirror one last time and put on lipstick. It won't hurt anyone. "Ready?" I say to Harper.

She wags her tail.

Outside, the party's underway. Richard and Farley have arrived, and, out on the lawn, Chloe chases Noah with a croquet mallet raised over her head. I busy myself lighting candles and pouring Cosmos, avoiding looking at Max or the way Georgia hovers by him, her hand clamped on his arm as she leads him to the porch swing. I also ignore the way I feel alone at my own party. I reach for Harper, but she's abandoned me for the smoker, where she sits at attention. Harper should know nothing in life is free, except, maybe, a scrap of brisket.

I feel someone beside me and turn to see Farley.

"Alice," he says, "you look fabulous."

"So do you," I say. "Though I'd expect nothing less. And thanks for sending the dahlias. They made my day."

"It *is* a birthday party," Farley says. He pauses and asks, "Will there be cake?"

Not exactly cake, but something at least.

By the smoker, Damian says, "Yo!" as he flips the brisket. "Look at that meat."

"Dude," Richard says, slapping his palm.

I pour Farley a Cosmo, and he takes a long sip from his martini glass. "*Dude*," he says, adding in an eyeroll that would put Chloe to shame. "Seems like we're the odd ones out tonight. We'll have to stick together." He pauses, adding, "I hope that doesn't frighten you."

For once, his face doesn't betray him with one of his telltale tics.

"The only thing that frightens me," I say, "is an empty glass."

He tops me off from the pitcher. I take him by the hand and lead him to the stone wall at the far edge of the patio where a bed of blue hydrangeas is in full bloom. Behind me, Georgia laughs at something Max says. I rest my elbows on the stone as cool sea air blows in off the water, reminding me of this afternoon. Max flirted with me on the town beach, just as he did in the kitchen earlier. None of that was imagined.

"You look content," Farley says.

"You can do better than content," I say.

"Happy? Pleased? Joyful?"

"Ecstatic," I say.

"Any particular reason?"

With a secret this close to the heart, almost no one can be trusted. I certainly can't tell Georgia. And if I tell Farley, it will get back to Richard, who cannot keep a secret, especially from Damian. Maybe next week I'll work it into my session, when Farley transforms back into Dr. Drake. "It's my birthday," I say. "I'm surrounded by friends. Why wouldn't I be ecstatic?"

Farley rests his back against the stone. "What's going on with Georgia and Max?"

"They're old friends," I say. "Maybe they like each other. My guess is Max has been holding a torch for Georgia for years. Now's his chance. That's why I invited him, anyway. Georgia needed someone to keep her from feeling like a fifth wheel."

The last of the summer sun shimmers pink through Farley's martini glass. "And all this time I thought Max Barbosa had a crush on me," he says. "Why else would he have been such a bitch with the zoning board?"

"You got the house you wanted," I say. "And you should bottle that confidence. I bet you believe all the boys have crushes on you. The girls, too."

"Don't they?" Farley asks.

"Not this girl. And you're ridiculous."

"I like being ridiculous."

"You know what would be ridiculous?" I say, "If Max settled. He's too much of a catch, and Georgia's too easy a solution."

"Now who's the bitch?" Farley asks.

Georgia leaves the patio and heads onto the lawn, with Max trailing behind. She says something to the kids. They drop their mallets and escape toward the dock. "Don't forget you're grounded," Georgia shouts.

As the kids disappear over the bluff, Georgia waves us over. "Let's play croquet before the sun goes down."

Damian doesn't hesitate before knocking Richard out of the game first, then me. He swaggers around the remaining players, while I toss the mallet aside. "Happy birthday to me."

By now, the sun has set, and the fairy lights are shining over the dining table, the whole setting straight out of a magazine spread. I call to Harper and wander toward the dock to find the kids. Richard jogs alongside me. "I'll get them," he says. "Go be with your guests. Have some fun."

What I'd really like is five minutes on my own, but I take Richard's arm in mine anyway. "Let's do it together. I don't think I can bear to see Damian win the game."

We walk in silence for a moment. I manage Richard's money as his financial advisor, but in truth, I barely know him, and it's rare I find myself alone with him. When Damian and I became friends with Richard and Georgia, our alliances formed along gender lines. Later, after the split, Farley took Georgia's place. As we reach the top of the bluff, we both peer down toward the dock where Noah and Chloe sit at the end, their feet dangling over the water, Noah's phone lit up between them. The full moon has risen over the bay and shines brightly against inky black water.

"What's going on with Chloe?" I ask. "I heard she got in a fight today."

Richard shrugs. "I'm hoping this latest event might fade away. Is Noah friends with a boy named Jack?"

There are Jacks and Jacksons in every corner of Monreith Middle School. "At least one," I say.

"Chloe might have a boyfriend," Richard says. "I worry, you know."

I remember my own first boyfriend, Hans, who I met when my father was stationed in Heidelberg. I'd been in eighth grade, too. Hans was dangerous and older, too much older, but he seemed impossibly handsome, especially when we smoked hash on the banks of the Neckar River. I'd never have let my parents know about him, not in a million years, but girls will sometimes confide in an adult they trust. "I could talk to her if you want," I offer to Richard. "Girls like to talk to other women."

"You mean when they're not their own mothers."

He said it, not me. Richard turns toward the house. "Max and Georgia?" he asks, the question hitting me right in the heart. "Is that what Farley was whispering to you about?"

"Maybe," I say. "But aren't you and Max old friends? Ask him yourself."

Richard doesn't say anything at first. To me, Richard appeared lovable if somewhat dim when I first met him. As his financial advisor, a view into his assets gave me a different perspective. He has more money than I'd have expected, enough to earn some respect. Tonight he seems to have something on his mind. He nods toward the dock, where the kids sit. "Max and I used to hang out on his dock for hours. Chloe and Noah, they could be Max and me at the same age." He shoves his hands in his pockets. His pants are so tight, I can see the outline of his knuckles through the white fabric. "I had a crush on him," Richard says. "Max, I mean. And I think he knew."

It seems like it's Max Barbosa who everyone actually has a crush on, not Farley Drake. No wonder Farley hates Max so much.

"He never had a crush on me back," Richard adds, quickly. "But, I don't know. . . . I should stop talking. Let's go get the kids."

In a flash, I remember the hidden burner phone and Laurel's photo pinned to that whiteboard. Damian and Richard are close. They bike together on the weekends. Surely, if there were something to know, Damian might have shared it with Richard. "You'd tell me if Damian was in trouble, wouldn't you?"

"Why would he be in trouble?"

I almost say Laurel's name but don't dare.

"He's not in trouble," Richard says. "Except from Georgia's wrath. She doesn't like to lose—even at croquet." He kicks at a tuft of grass. "Do you like my shirt?"

I'm relieved by the change of topic. I take in Richard's outfit, the form-fitting pants and the barely-there shirt, so different from the baggy jeans and Patriots sweatshirts he'd worn when I'd first met him. "Sexy," I say. "But I bet you'll be cold tonight."

He fastens one of the buttons. It strains over his chest.

"Georgia used to choose everything I wore—and Max; growing up, I was like his shadow. Wherever he went, I followed. Maybe they can focus on each other now, and I can spend some time figuring out who I am."

I squeeze his hand. "We should chat again soon. It's good to have a friend."

A few moments later, the kids run ahead of us, across the lawn and onto the patio where Damian's pouring Max a drink. "You took long enough," Damian says to me. "What were you chatting about?"

"Boys," I say. "Nothing but boys."

"Max won the game. He beat me!" Damian says, and I'll give my husband this: he may love to compete, but he also respects losing. "Stealthy," he adds. "He came out of nowhere! Next thing I know, he'll be betting on the matches."

"Probably not," Max says. "The last thing I need right now are more whispers about gambling."

Damian unwraps the brisket with a pair of tongs. "Is that a reference to our own episode of *Law & Order: Monreith*?" he asks.

"Leave it alone," I say.

"Innocent question," Damian says.

"Carve that meat," I say. "It's time for dinner."

Suddenly, I remember the aluminum trays of ratatouille and potatoes I'd left in the oven probably an hour ago. I swear under my breath and run inside. Max's police instincts must kick in because he follows in hot pursuit, his feet pounding up the stairs right behind me. I rip open the oven door and nearly forget to use mitts to lift the trays onto cooling racks, and maybe it's the relief that dinner didn't burn, or that Max stepped up to play the helper, or that the others are outside and we seem to be alone, or that all day I've wanted everyone to believe I cooked dinner even though it's obvious I didn't, but I tear off the mitts, put my hands to Max's face, and pull him in for a kiss. He doesn't push me away. And the kiss feels like I imagined it might, strong and hopeful. For the first time in my life, I stop fighting.

We break apart. My breath is short, and my heart races.

It's only then the approaching footsteps register. Georgia hovers in the kitchen doorway, watching us, her expression impassive. Like Farley—or Max—there can't be much Georgia hasn't seen in the course of her professional life. How often has she had to push down personal feelings when a parishioner has confessed her heart?

Now she grasps Max's arm in hers like a vise. "Outside," she says, shooing me away. "It's your birthday. Max and I will take care of everything here."

CHAPTER 15
Alice

Max can't retreat from either Georgia or me fast enough. He barrels through the house, down the cellar stairs, and out the back door.

I turn to face Georgia, who stares after him. I brush her hand, and she flinches before conjuring up a smile. "The kids are watching *Finding Nemo*," she says, as she ushers me through the house and toward the cellar stairs. "Nothing to worry about here. I'll finish up dinner."

"Georgia," I begin.

"I mean it, Alice," she says to me, "Enjoy your party. Send Ritchie in. I'll put him to work."

As she escapes to the kitchen, I touch my lips. I can feel Max's body against mine, pressing closer. I've flirted with other men during my marriage. I've gone right up against that line, but this is the first time I've crossed it. Maybe, for once, it's time for Damian to know what it's like to doubt himself.

Outside on the patio, I tell Richard that Georgia needs him. I take my seat at the foot of the table. The sun has gone down, and strings of lights shine over us. Damian stands at the head of the table carving the brisket. Max won't look at me, but the stupid grin he covers with his hand tells me everything I need to know. Damian is too self-involved to notice, but surely Farley senses the spark. Surely he'll carry that feeling over into our session next week. I wonder now how much I'll admit to, or if by then there could be more to confess. Right now, it's all I can do not to take Max's hand and pull him through the dark to his cottage on the other side of the woods.

"How did you meet Alice, anyway?" I hear Farley ask Damian.

This is one topic I've actually touched on in sessions. Farley knows Damian was my professor, that I broke up his marriage, but this isn't a truth I want Max to know. I want Max to see me as the confident, successful forty-year-old woman I've become, not some naïve child taken in by an older man. To his credit, Damian dodges the answer. "We were work colleagues," he says.

"Were you in finance, too?" Farley presses.

"Not exactly," Damian says, then he steers the conversation to the murder. "Tell us the latest with the investigation," he says to Max. "I can't imagine there's been a homicide in this town before. Why no arrest? It's been a week."

I catch Farley's eye and barely shake my head. He smiles like he does in his office, waiting for me to take the lead.

"Damian, stop," I say. "You know Max can't talk about that."

"Let the man speak for himself," Damian says. "Seems to me that if you haven't arrested the husband by now, you must have other theories. Simon Thibodeau's already been tried and convicted in the court of public opinion."

"Ignore him," I say to Max, and then spar with Damian, chiding him for putting Max in an awkward position. Farley sits quietly, absorbing it all. I watch him under the lights, trying to gauge his thoughts. There's something in his expression, something I've seen before, though I don't quite remember where. I'm trying to place it when Richard and Georgia return, and Georgia grasps Max's hand during a silent prayer. The platters make their way around the table. Damian pokes at the ambrosia with a spoon. "What's this shit?"

"Keep it moving," I say, "and don't make fun of my cooking."

When the ambrosia comes to me, I fill half my plate with the marshmallowy goodness.

I reach for a new bottle of wine, but we've finished the whole case. "What's a party without a little debauchery?" I say.

"I'll grab some reinforcements," Farley says. He leaves his plate and walks like someone concentrating to maintain a steady line.

Fifteen minutes later, Richard says, "I should go check on him."

"I'll go," I say.

Harper trails beside me. Inside, I check the kitchen but don't find Farley there. In the TV room, I ask the kids if they've seen him. Noah points toward the other end of the house, where the bathroom is. I edge into the dark hallway and see light spilling from Damian's office. I'm not completely surprised to find Farley standing in front of the whiteboard, running his hand from one crime scene photo to the next. For a moment, I watch him absorbing the images, wondering what he must make of Damian's thought process laid out for anyone to see. "You found it," I say.

Farley turns, unflappable as ever, even when caught snooping. "Is this what frightens you?" he asks.

Damian has pinned his truth to the board, and the truth almost always frightens me. Death has followed us. We've seen it here. We saw it in Maine. I touch Laurel's image, remembering briefly not her but the priest in Maine. Another truth that frightens me. "What do you do when a patient confesses to murder?" I ask.

I don't dare look at him. I don't want to see what his expression betrays, though he takes a moment to answer. "It depends on whether the patient plans to kill again."

"And if not?"

"Then it stays in the room."

"What frightens me is when Damian gets to the truth, when he finds the evil at the core of his story. That truth is usually closer than you'd ever believe."

I crouch to pet Harper.

"She's your shadow," Farley says, scratching the dog's ears.

"Harper knows all my secrets." And maybe I've come too close to sharing my darkest ones tonight. Or maybe I haven't come close enough. Still, I retreat and deflect, like I do in Dr. Drake's office each week. "You must think Damian and I hate each other's guts," I say. "We've always sniped at each other. It's my birthday, though. I'm supposed to be having fun. But you're off the clock. I'll tell you everything next week. Hold me to it."

"I thought you were finding a new therapist."

I finally search Farley's face. He tilts his head, the tip of his tongue finding his front teeth, the corners of his eyes twitching. He's having fun, and I recognize now what I'd missed earlier out on the patio. I see myself in him, a kindred spirit. I wonder if he sees the same thing in me. "We both know I won't do that," I say. "Not now."

As we leave, Farley stops at the bathroom. Around the corner, I press my back to the wall, and breathe for what feels like the first time in a year. Tonight was a first step. Next week in the privacy of Dr. Drake's office, maybe I'll face my truth. Maybe I'll tell him about my time in Maine, where, like here, I'd had a best friend, a spare, and a therapist.

My best friend had an eleven-year-old daughter named Julia who had her own secrets. She told them to me one day on a trip to Walmart, though I had so much trouble understanding her French that I spent most of the conversation trailing two thoughts behind, which I suspect might have

been why she confessed. It was as easy for her to tell her secrets to me as it is for me to tell mine to Harper.

Julia mentioned a *copin* (boyfriend), a *rendezvous*, and something she didn't want her mother to know. As she spoke, I
stopped at a light and waited for the left-hand arrow. I caught
a few more of Julia's words and tried to pin them down. It was
fall, and for a moment I thought she was talking about pears.
Or maybe she meant her father, her *père*. I mumbled something, as though I understood, which made Julia giggle. The
light changed, and I turned into the parking lot, where she
got out of the car and ran inside.

It wasn't till later that my mind relaxed and the fragments
of the conversation snapped into place. Julia hadn't said *pear*
or her *père*.

She'd said *le père*. The priest. Father Jean-Marc.

Down the hall, I open the door to the TV room where the
kids lie sprawled on the floor. *Finding Nemo* plays on the television set, but Noah and Chloe ignore it as they lean over a
phone. Normally, I'd have assumed they were using Noah's
phone, but this time Chloe shoves it under a pillow.

I step into the room. "How's the movie?" I ask.

"Okay, I guess," Noah says.

"Do you want to go shopping sometime?" I ask Chloe.

She doesn't say anything. Her hand is still under the pillow,
and her face has turned bright red. The thing Chloe's parents
can't see is that a kid who gives into guilt this easily will never
slip through the darkened streets of Heidelberg to meet a boy
named Hans on the banks of the Neckar. She'll never be a ju-
venile delinquent.

"Do girls still go shopping?" I ask.

"Sometimes," Chloe says. "Is this about the fight at school?"

"Maybe a little bit. But mostly I want to get to know you better. How about we go shopping next Saturday?"

"Okay."

I snap my fingers and point at the pillow. She hands me the phone without a fight. It's the burner I found under Noah's mattress earlier this afternoon, the one with the cracked screen. "I thought this wasn't yours," I say to him.

"It isn't," he says.

"It certainly isn't anymore," I say. "Where did it come from?"

Noah shrugs. "We found it. We were trying to guess the passcode."

"Is it your father's?"

When Noah doesn't answer, I slip the phone into my pocket and wave them toward the kitchen.

Outside, Farley's rejoined the party. Damian has somehow managed to turn the conversation back to the murder investigation. I want my husband to understand that I know everything: about Laurel, about the affair, about his secret burner phone. I lay it on the table beside him. "You're an idiot," I whisper in his ear.

I touch Harper's head. Max's eyes crease as he smiles. Beside him, Georgia stares at the table, as if she knows she's lost. Max will choose me, maybe later tonight, maybe in a day or a week, but it will happen. I believe that now. Georgia had her chance with him fifteen years ago and blew it when she opted for Richard instead. That's on her.

Behind me, the kids start to sing "Happy Birthday." They make their way to the table with the cupcakes Georgia brought, candles lit, sparklers flaring. A celebration. I sweep hair behind my ear and blow out the candles in one breath.

"What did you wish for?" Max asks.

I hadn't bothered with a wish. I don't need to make one anymore. "Nothing I'll share," I say.

CHAPTER 16
Alice

The party's over. Everyone has left. I help Damian and Noah bring dishes inside, then I sit on the patio and polish off the final bottle of pinot noir. Harper lies at my feet and jolts awake each time thunder rumbles in the distance. I feel her chest, where her heart pounds. "I've been a bad girl," I whisper, pulling her close and snapping a leash onto her collar to keep her from bolting.

Behind me, a Decemberists song plays in the kitchen where Damian and Noah clean up and stow the leftovers in the fridge. We'll be eating ratatouille well into October. What would either of them do if they understood who I really am, if I confessed my missteps?

Like what happened with Hans, my "boyfriend" in Heidelberg, a twenty-seven-year-old teacher at my school. I left him on the banks of the Neckar with a syringe sticking from his front toe.

Or that priest in Maine. Father Jean-Marc.

I went to see him as soon as I knew what he was doing. It took a few visits to earn his trust, to convince him I could be swayed into silence. I told him of a loveless marriage, of being lonely in the world. Eventually, I convinced him to pour us drinks. After that, it didn't take long for him to make his first move, though I resisted. Men like that want to feel as if they've earned their keep.

When his time came, he was easy enough to manipulate once the sedatives in his drink took hold. I told him to undress and get in the water and that I'd join him soon. I stripped naked to keep my clothes from getting wet. Now I picture his face under the water where I held him, his eyes open, a final gasp of breath bubbling from the corner of his mouth.

Like Hans, he'd gotten what he deserved.

Lightning strikes again, and this time, the thunder tells me the storm is getting closer, even as the full moon still shines over the bay. Harper whimpers and curls into a ball, her tail planted firmly between her legs. I could bring her inside, but it doesn't matter where we go or what I do to comfort her. She's terrified, and she'll stay that way till the storm passes. I imagine Harper out on the marsh where she used to live, unloved and facing the elements alone on a night like this one. No wonder she's frightened.

I could be bold. I could walk through the woods to Max's cottage, pound on his front door, and see where the night takes us, though Max isn't alone. Earlier, he'd insisted Georgia come with him rather than drive home drunk. And maybe I'd gone too far this time. Maybe the kiss will push Max away. He doesn't seem like the type who'd relish breaking up a marriage. But my marriage is already broken.

Behind me, the music stops, and the kitchen lights go out. A moment later, footsteps approach. Damian pulls a chair beside mine and holds up a bottle of scotch. I finish my wine. "Just a splash," I say.

Clouds have begun to sweep in and block the stars. I split

the last of the cupcakes in half, then press the stump to the icing. "Cupcake sandwich," I say, holding it toward him.

He takes a bite and washes it down with scotch.

"I wanted a cake tonight," I say.

"The best-laid plans," he says.

"What plans? You didn't do anything. I turned forty and cooked my own dinner."

"Alice," he says, "it's just us, and I know your secrets. You didn't cook dinner."

"So what? And I wanted a cake that was fancy and special."

"What if we have a cake tomorrow? Just us, two forks, and a big fucking cake."

"Three with Noah," I say.

"Three, then."

"What kind?"

"Carrot. Loaded with raisins," he says. "And walnuts."

He rubs my arm, and I feel my anger dissipating. My nerve, too. Am I ready to tear my life down and rebuild it? Am I ready to tell Dr. Drake my truth? Thunder rumbles, followed almost immediately by a flash of lightning. This time, Harper stands and barks.

"The rain's beginning," Damian says. "We should go inside."

I take his hand and hold tight, knowing this conversation, this moment, has a before and after, and I'm not finished with the before yet. Finding that burner phone has caused a low-grade distrust to flare into a full-blown fever because here's another secret I haven't shared: Damian left the house last Saturday night after I'd gone to bed, the night Laurel Thibodeau was killed. I heard him driving away and was wide awake when he returned and went straight into the shower. I assumed then that he was scrubbing away the scent of sex, but could it have been something else? Did he hurt Laurel?

"I know everything," I say, "or at least enough. I know you were with her last Saturday."

Damian sets the bottle of scotch on the brick. He doesn't bother to deny anything. "She was alive when I left that night. I didn't kill her."

"Then you have to tell the police you were there," I say. "We can walk to Max's place right now. We can go together."

"You've seen what's in my office," Damian says. "There *is* a serial killer. And I'm the only one who's figured it out, and he put a plastic bag over Laurel's head and watched her take her last breath."

His voice breaks, as Harper barks again, this time toward the woods.

"Put her inside," Damian says.

"I can't leave her," I say, pulling the dog to my side and running my hands through her coat. Her whole body trembles. "How long were you planning to keep it going with Laurel?" I ask.

Damian hurls his glass against the stone wall. "You invited your little crush to our house tonight and flirted with him the whole time."

"Lower your voice. Noah will hear. And unlike you, I haven't done anything I need to apologize for."

I stare him down until he slumps into his chair.

"Tell me," I say. "Everything. We need to get our stories straight."

Damian takes my glass and finishes the scotch. "This will hurt," he says.

I lift his chin so our eyes meet.

"When we met on Saturday night, we promised . . . *I* promised Laurel I'd ask you for a divorce." He pauses. "Laurel and I loved each other."

I release his hand. I should be angry. I should scream. But I can't yet put a word to how I feel. What I do know is that it's not sad.

Damian covers his face with his hands and stifles a sob.

"The next day, I found out she was dead. I've been in a fog ever since."

I watch him for a moment. Maybe I've been in a fog, too. "Where's the burner phone?" I ask. "The one you hid in your son's room. The one I gave you at dinner."

He takes the phone from his pocket and places it on the arm of the Adirondack chair.

"What will the police find on this?" I ask. "What stupid things did you text to Laurel?"

"It isn't mine," he says. "I've never seen it before."

"Don't lie to me."

I look out toward the bay. Damian touches my arm, but I shrug him off as fat, heavy raindrops begin to fall. Damian has lived with me for almost twenty years. We have a son together. He documented the aftermath of the priest's death on film, and yet he doesn't have a clue who I really am. He swipes at tears with a fist, and I swear if he doesn't stop crying, I might bash his head open.

"Stop talking," I say. "I don't need to hear any more."

"I'm so sorry."

He waits a split second before heading to the farmhouse, but I can't bring myself to follow. For the first time since I was a twenty-one-year-old undergraduate, I hear Damian's first wife's words, the ones she whispered in the business school's stairwell: "Why would you do this?"

For all these years, I've believed she despised me—for self-ishness, for youthful arrogance, for taking what was hers—and maybe that was partly true. But tonight, I remember the touch of someone who'd experienced enough life to spot a mistake. Maybe she'd seen a promising and impressionable young woman about to make a choice she'd spend years ratio-nalizing. Maybe, like me, she'd had her own faults. Now here I am on my fortieth birthday, at the end of one half of my life and the beginning of the next, and I finally understand what I'm feeling tonight: anticipation.

I cannot wait for what's to come.

I lift the burner. I could take this phone to Max right now and tell him everything I know. Or I could throw it as far as I can into the bay. The last thing I need is for the state cops to be looking at Damian too closely. That will lead them to me. And death does follow me wherever I go.

I click the phone's power button. The cracked screen lights up asking for a passcode. A text awaits, too: ***Meet me at the dock.***

I recognize the sender's number, though I have to scroll through my own phone to find who it belongs to. The text came from Richard. He sent it ten minutes ago.

Lightning strikes as another raindrop hits my forehead. Harper presses against my leg. "Stick with me," I whisper.

We cross the lawn to the rickety wooden stairs, where I squint through the rain. Below, the tide surges against the salt-marsh, and boats tug at their lines. Why would Richard know about Damian's secret phone? Why would he ask to meet in the middle of the night?

Clouds pass over the moon, plunging us into darkness. I go down to the gangway as the storm moves directly overhead. In a flash of lightning, I swear I see someone waiting.

"Who's there?" I whisper.

Beside me, Harper growls.

PART III

The Cop

CHAPTER 17
Max

It's after midnight, but I haven't gone to bed since leaving Alice's party. I sit on my deck, beer can in hand, cribbage board waiting. On the cliff, Farley Drake's concrete-and-glass abode looms where the Big House used to be, blocking any view of the bay I once had from the cottage. Mooney Point has been my home for my entire life. It's still my home, no matter the changes.

My phone beeps with a text from Brock London, the state detective working the Thibodeau murder. *Barbosa, you up?*

Brock doesn't seem to sleep. All week, he's called me at any time of night to clarify details of the case that only someone who lives in this community could know. I imagine him now in his hotel room, still wearing a tailored gray suit, sitting at a desk working through evidence while eating a club sandwich from room service. I doubt he drinks on the job. And whatever he wants, it can wait.

I listen to the thunderstorm approach. I grew up in this cottage with my father, when his family owned everything here, including the Big House, the cottage, and the little bunkhouse where Georgia is sleeping off the wine she drank tonight. Aunts and cousins came to visit, and we'd spend summers outside, running up and down the steep stairs to the dock, swimming out into the bay, and playing hide-and-seek till the mosquitos drove us to screened-in porches. At night, the scents of lighter fluid and seafood and grilled linguica would fill the air, while the adults played rounds of *Oh Hell!* and the kids whispered in the bunkhouse long after we were supposed to go to sleep.

Ritchie visited then, too. His parents lived in town, but my father didn't want me going to their place since Ritchie's parents were well known at the police department for their late-night brawls. Back then, my father was the chief of police. I guess this job runs in the family.

To me, Mooney Point was the norm. None of us understood how lucky we were to have it then, because time moves on. Aunts die. And cousins have new priorities. Eventually, only my father and I still came to the Point, the two of us coexisting in the cottage while the Big House mostly sat empty. When my father died, I learned he'd neglected to pay tens of thousands of dollars in taxes, and the property had a lien on it. My cousins voted to sell. I didn't have the money to buy them out, so we put the Big House and most of the Point on the market, though I kept the cottage and the bunkhouse and paid off my cousins for that part of the property.

Farley Drake offered two hundred grand over the asking price, in cash, without contingencies. At the time, the offer seemed like a godsend.

I should have understood he'd do whatever he wanted with the property. Still, I'd convinced myself he'd keep things the way they were. On the day the sale closed, Farley had a wrecking ball on site. He managed to knock down the Big House in a matter of hours and erase decades of memories. After that, I used every connection I had in this town—the zoning board, the conservation commission, the town manager—to thwart his plans to rebuild. I'll admit I haven't always been above-board about it either, though Farley found a way around every obstacle I put in front of him, and now his house sits on the cliff the way he'd planned all along. And yes, I regret selling to an entitled prick, but the only people who can afford properties like this one anymore *are* entitled pricks.

I take a swig of beer, an IPA from a brewery in Maine. It's bitter and hoppy. Next door, the last lights in Farley's house go out. I imagine Ritchie lying in bed in his new home. I still think of Ritchie as my best friend, even if he's a different person since he split with Georgia.

I should take that back. That new person I'm seeing emerge has been hiding there all along, even if most of us refused to recognize him. I can't admit this to Ritchie, or to anyone, but I struggle with the person he is now, the one who obsesses about his weight and clothing. The one who calls that cement monstrosity a home. The one who's happy and no longer has a secret crush on me.

I also understand Ritchie needed to find someone who could help him face his own truth, though I wish it had been someone besides Farley Drake.

Lightning strikes in the distance, followed by a clap of thunder. As the rumbling fades, a noise outside the house catches my attention. I put aside the beer and instinctively reach for my firearm. It's in the safe upstairs in my bedroom where I left it earlier. A twig snaps. Leaves rustle, and I find myself dashing through the living room to the front door.

"Georgia," I whisper into the darkness, "is that you?"

She didn't put up any resistance when I told her she couldn't drive home. In fact, she came willingly and lingered outside the cottage. And I suppose I should have invited her in, if only for a nightcap, though it wouldn't have ended there. It's not like she hasn't joined me in the cottage before. But she was drunk, and Georgia is a mistake I don't want to repeat anymore, especially after what happened with Alice.

The kiss.

The one I'm certain Georgia saw. The one I didn't stop or want to stop.

My phone beeps with another text from Brock London. *There's been a development in the case. Call me.*

I search the darkness outside the cottage one last time but don't see signs of anyone. "Go to bed," I whisper, and then grab another beer, pop the tab, and return to the porch before calling Brock. The state detective answers on the first ring.

"How was the party?" he asks.

"Mostly uneventful," I say.

This town is small, and word about almost anything will spread, so this last week I've made it a habit to inform the detective of my every move. We're all suspects in the Thibodeau murder till there's an arrest.

"Alice Stone's place?" Brock says. "She's the brunette with the dog named Scout."

"Harper," I say. "Close enough."

Last year, Brock made a name for himself when he solved a big missing child case in Boston, and I've been nothing but impressed with what I've seen from him so far. He's focused and professional and doesn't let public opinion sway his actions. After five days in this town, he also seems to know every single one of the twenty-eight hundred residents by name.

"It was a birthday party," I say. "Alice turned forty."

"Big event?" Brock asks.

"Not at all. There were only a few of us there." I take a swig from the beer. "She hired Simon Thibodeau to cook for the party."

On the other end of the phone, Brock pounds at a keyboard. Now he's attached Alice's name to the case. "Did Thibodeau show up?" he asks.

"No, she picked the food up from his place. She and her husband, Damian," I begin, but Brock cuts me off.

"Beard. Filmmaker. Makes documentaries. Always on his bike."

"That's him," I say. "He and Alice went to the Thibodeaus' restaurant most Friday nights."

More typing. "Firefly. You ever go?"

"They have a good beer list."

"Did the Stones go to the restaurant last Friday?"

"I didn't ask. My guess is Alice placed the order with Simon Thibodeau a while ago and felt bad canceling."

"I'll follow up with her," Brock says. He sighs, and I hear him moving through the room. "What was going on between you and the shrink today when we saw him at that ice-cream shop? If I hadn't known better, I'd have thought you were exes. What do you have against the guy?"

"Nothing," I say. "A small-town grievance. Did you get anything out of him?"

"No luck there. But you'd be surprised what people reveal about themselves. Shrinks, hairdressers, ministers—they all hear things that can be helpful when a case hits a dead end."

"You didn't call to talk about a birthday party," I say. "What's going on?"

"We have a problem," Brock says. "Some results came back from the lab. There was semen in the bed, and the DNA didn't belong to Simon Thibodeau. It's not coming up in CODIS, either, which means that between the DNA and the rock-solid alibi, no matter how much we want to pin this on the husband, even the worst lawyer on earth will get this case tossed. There's too much reasonable doubt. So I need your ear to the ground. Find out who was hanging out in Laurel Thibodeau's bed while her husband ran off to the casinos."

The detective has been a good partner this week, keeping me apprised of what he's learned and letting me take the lead with the media. But this is the first I've heard of the DNA evidence, and I could ask Brock how long he's been sitting on it, or why he's sharing it with me now. "This may be nothing," I begin.

Brock waits, and when I don't fill the silence, he adds, "You have good instincts. Tell me what you're thinking, and I'll decide next steps."

"At the party tonight, Damian Stone had a lot of questions about the murder."

"Not surprising," Brock says. "In your position, I doubt you can go anywhere in this town without getting assaulted with questions right now."

"Damian likes to dig into things, though," I say. "He's a story-teller, so you may have an amateur detective on your hands." I try to remember Damian's exact words from dinner, the ones that made me almost leave the party. "He says he's narrowing in on something that no one else is seeing."

Brock's typing stops, and I wish I could pull the words back. Damian talks a good game, but who knows what he's really found. And any questions Brock may have for the Stones will lead right back to me.

"He may just want the attention," Brock says. "But he also knew he was speaking with the chief of police. I'll have to talk with him in the morning, even if it doesn't lead anywhere."

Part of being the chief of police involves a balancing act be-tween always—and I mean *always*—being on duty, while also being a part of the community. People know I watch them. It's only when I get caught that matters turn ugly. This time, Alice will know I linked her family to the homicide, and I doubt she'll forgive me very easily.

I hear Brock moving again. Carbonation releases from a bottle, and ice clinks in a glass. "These nights away are long," he says. "I was hoping to get home to my wife and daughter this weekend, but there's too much to do here. And I don't sleep when I'm working a case, either. My brain doesn't want to shut down." He takes a sip of whatever he's drinking. I toast with my own can and join him. "Have you given any more thought to the job?" he asks.

On Tuesday, after we'd spent nearly seventy-two straight hours working side by side, Brock had told me there was an open position with the state cops.

"Still mulling it over," I say now.

"Barbosa, it's not like you have an actual offer. What's the harm in applying?"

"Have you considered a career in sales?"

"Does that mean you'll think about it?"

"How about it means I'm hanging up at the end of this sentence and going to bed?" I click off the call before Brock can move on to the close.

I grew up in Monreith and went to the local state college, and the idea of leaving town hadn't ever crossed my mind. As soon as Brock planted the seed, though, I began to imagine what it might be like to live someplace else and meet new people. So much had changed lately, with Farley building his house and Ritchie splitting with Georgia, that home didn't feel like home anymore. I wondered if it was my turn to make a change. Later that day, I swung by Ritchie's shop and mentioned the possibility of applying for the job to him. He took a bag of peanut butter M&Ms from a drawer and counted out five, one of each color. He lined them up—yellow, blue, red, green, brown—and ate them in order.

"Do it," he said.

By the next morning, Wednesday, Kennedy, who works the front desk at the station, already had me packing up and leaving. "This town hasn't been without a Chief Barbosa in my whole life!"

"Don't go spreading rumors," I said.

Later that afternoon, the town manager called. "I'll need a time frame," she said. "Finding a new chief will take a while unless you're hiding a spare Barbosa."

"I haven't even applied for the job," I told her.

"And they'd be fools not to hire you."

Maybe they would be.

I put my foot up on the railing and think about leaving again. A move to Springfield would at least help me escape Alice Stone's pull. I close my eyes and finish off the beer. Heavy rain streams off the roof, loud enough that I almost don't notice the sounds coming from the trees. But this time it's unmistakable.

There's someone outside the house.

CHAPTER 18
Max

Lightning flashes, followed by a rumble of thunder. I peer over the edge of the deck and through the rain. Ten feet below, Georgia kneels in the mud.

"You okay there?" I ask.

She turns her head as lightning strikes. Her curly hair is plastered against her pale face. She shoves her glasses up and waves me away. "Leave me alone, Max," she manages to mumble loud enough for me to hear over the rain.

I should go down there and help. Instead, I leave her to her misery.

I like Georgia. I do. We're good friends. And we've scratched an itch for each other from time to time, especially in these last months since Ritchie moved out of the parsonage. I like the way her curly hair cascades over me, the way slipping her glasses off transforms her into a different woman—sexier, less buttoned up. Lately, I've realized she wants more than I can offer, and I've tried to step back. Still, whenever we're together, she clings to me, like she did at the party tonight, as though she has a claim on me.

We did date briefly when she first moved to town to take

over the parish. We were both in our late twenties and ready to settle down, so I started attending services on Sundays and helping her with the endless repairs at the parsonage. A few months in, I bought a ring, but she dumped me before I could give it to her. One day, I was stripping wallpaper at the parsonage and had my whole life with Georgia mapped out. The next day, that future no longer existed.

For a while—a long time, actually—I held a grudge. Back then, my dad was the chief. I was in uniform, and sometimes late at night I'd park by the parsonage. I had every right to be there. Kids would often sit among the cemetery's gravestones, drinking nips or smoking weed. They still do. What I didn't have the right to do was to watch Georgia in her home. Sometimes, she'd come to the window and peer out into the night almost as if she knew I was there, and she was imagining what her life might have been like if she had chosen me.

And then one night, Ritchie stood at the window with her.

Ritchie, who'd seemed like a little brother to me, who I'd watched out for on the playground and in the hallways of the high school, who I'd welcomed to my home. I wonder if he understands how much he betrayed me.

I didn't date again for years, though I've had plenty of women show interest. At the station, Kennedy even tells me I'm Monreith's most eligible bachelor. Still, Georgia had this pull on me that wouldn't let go, and I wasn't sure if it was because I'd played and lost, or if I hadn't met the right woman yet. Then I found Alice, and Georgia faded away almost at once.

Thunder rumbles again.

My imagination travels through the woods, along the rutted carriageway to Moulton Farm. I wonder if the farmhouse is quiet now, or if Alice is lying in bed listening to Damian sleep while she thinks about me. Or maybe the thunder has frightened Harper. Maybe the dog will show up at the cottage, scratching at the door, and Alice will follow a few moments later. I'll invite her inside. I'll get her a beer, and she'll drink it right out of the can.

Tonight I'm not sure we'd stop at cribbage.

Below, Georgia struggles to her feet, then trips in the mud. I watch and can't help laughing.

"You're an asshole, Max," she says.

"Reverend George!" I say. "Watch your mouth."

Georgia swears like a truck driver, but only with certain people. She stumbles to the outdoor shower by the bunkhouse as the rain begins to slow. Upstairs, I grab a towel, T-shirt, and a pair of sweats from my dresser and bring them outside. Wet clothes hang over the edge of the wooden shower stall. I leave the dry clothes behind and take hers into the washer, where I stare at the sudsy water as the tub slowly fills. When I turn, Georgia hovers in the doorway, her damp curls hanging to her shoulders, the T-shirt and sweats swallowing her small frame. I take a bottle of beer from the fridge.

"You want one?" I ask.

"I should pass."

I twist the cap off and toss it across the kitchen. It misses the trash and pings against the wall. "It's late," I say.

Georgia doesn't move. She searches my face. If she asks about what happened between Alice and me earlier tonight, I'll tell her the truth: I wanted it, and I wish it hadn't ended. I don't owe Georgia anything. She should know that. I return to the deck where the cribbage board waits, and the storm has left the air feeling heavy and damp. Georgia follows. "You didn't come to the parsonage last night," she says.

I did, though I didn't go inside. Georgia was talking to Simon Thibodeau in the kitchen, and I watched them from the shadows for a while. I also found Chloe sneaking out of the church, doing God knows what.

"Chloe's getting in a lot of trouble lately," I say.

"She's a teenager," Georgia says.

"Get on top of it before it gets worse."

Georgia shoves my arm, playfully. "Come talk to me when you have your own kids."

Sometimes I think every child in this town is partly mine. Georgia believes she sees it all in her job, but she doesn't know the half of it—the near misses, the tragedy of a late-night visit from the police chief, those parents who can't ever see me without remembering I was the one who changed their lives forever. Yes, Georgia deals with the aftermath but not the front line.

"Ritchie and Damian are close these days," she says. "Closer than I realized." She shuffles the deck of cards. "Ritchie's acting the same way he did when I first met the two of you. He'd have done anything you asked. He had a crush on you back then."

"That was a long time ago," I say.

She rubs my arm. "You'd have saved me some heartache if you'd told me."

Maybe I'd have saved myself some, too, but friends don't betray secrets, even unspoken ones. I turn to face her. "There's something I need to tell you. Brock London, that detective I've been working with, he wants me to apply for a job with the state cops. I'm throwing my hat in."

Word in this town spreads so quickly I can't imagine Georgia hasn't already heard, especially in her position, but her expression remains unreadable.

"It'll mean selling this place," I say, "and moving to Springfield, but maybe the change will do me some good."

She shuffles the cards again. When she speaks, the tremor in her voice betrays her. "I could get a job out there."

"This is your home."

"You need a change from me?"

"Just a change."

Georgia starts to deal the cards. "How many?"

"Six. I thought you knew how to play most games."

"Are you breaking up with me?"

"Are we going out?"

Her expression hardens. "It doesn't matter if you stay here or move to the end of the earth," she says. "Alice won't choose you. Not in the end. You're a distraction for her."

Georgia doesn't have the right to say that, not after all this time. And playing cards out here with anyone but Alice feels like a betrayal. "Maybe we'll play another time," I say.

"You're such a jerk," she says.

She's right. I am. I chug down the last of the beer. The night has grown quiet in the wake of the storm, the only sound being the hum of the washer from inside. "You know where everything is," I say. "Help yourself."

I drop the bottle in the recycling bin and head up the narrow stairs. I'm mostly grateful when the screen door downstairs slams and Georgia returns to the bunkhouse. If I'm lucky, she'll get her car in the morning and head home before I see her.

I lie in bed without bothering to undress, though I doubt I'll sleep. Brock London is probably awake now, too. We could go over the Thibodeau case. I could steer the conversation back toward Damian Stone. I could make him into more than a person of interest.

I imagine Alice here, in this cottage, tending the perennial beds, the sun shining on her face. I even hear Noah down on the dock with Chloe, diving into the bay and swimming away from shore the way Ritchie and I used to. I picture having my own child to raise, one I'd love and protect with all the fierceness I've brought to this job. Maybe, with some happiness, I'll find a way to tolerate Farley Drake.

* * *

My eyes pop open. I sit up, wrenched from a deep sleep. The air is heavy and still. Off in the distance, a seagull cries, followed by the howl of a coyote.

Seconds later, a scream tears through the night.

I don't know how I get my shoes on or make my way downstairs or find the heavy-duty flashlight I suddenly have gripped in my hand. All I know is that my feet pound across the muddy forest floor as I run through the woods toward Moulton Farm.

CHAPTER 19
Max

Ahead, a break opens in the trees as the carriageway ends at a rotted wooden gate. A stone wall marks the tree line and the edge of the farm.

Alice stands at the gate with Harper sitting beside her. I stop a few yards away, gasping for breath. A trickle of sweat drips down my temple. Alice wears the white linen dress from the party. Her hair cascades around her shoulders. She could be a statue, motionless, even as Harper greets me.

I don't quite dare ask yet what's happened. I could take her in my arms. This time, it would be me pressing my lips to hers.

"Max," she says to me. "You came."

"I heard someone scream," I say.

Alice glances behind her, then puts her hands to her face. My training kicks in. No matter my personal feelings, no matter what I'm hoping tonight might be about, I've responded to an incident without backup, without calling in to the station. I've made a mistake that gets cops killed. I dial dispatch. "This is the chief," I say. "Send a car to Moulton Farm on Drift Road. Now."

It's only after I end the call that the details of the scene in front of me begin to take shape. Alice's dress is soaked. So is her hair. She's covered with mud and sand and something else, and a distinct coppery scent hangs in the heavy humid air. I close the distance between us.

"Where's Damian?" I ask.

Alice grips my arm. As I pull away, she clings to me, her nails digging into my flesh. We struggle until I spin her around and pull her close.

"What happened here?" I ask. "What did he do to you? Are you hurt?"

"Oh, God," she says. "I don't know what happened. . . . I was by the water . . ."

Her voice trails off, and I hold tight until her body goes slack. I release her, listening for the sound of approaching sirens. "Don't move," I say, stepping toward the darkened house. Only two patrol cars work during any given shift. They could be miles away. I listen for signs of life as the worst possible scenarios run through my mind.

Behind me, I hear footsteps. I spin to see Alice sprinting toward the dock, her white dress billowing around her, Harper at her heels. I hit *Redial* and wait for dispatch to pick up. "Send anyone on duty," I say. "And an ambulance. Someone's hurt. I don't know how, but let's assume this is a domestic issue, so everyone should proceed with caution. There's a minor child present, and I'm pursuing a female suspect near the Moulton Farm dock. Dark hair, Caucasian, early forties, wearing a white dress. Her name is Alice Stone."

At the top of the stairs, I pause. Below, a narrow gangway crosses over the marsh to the dock, but Alice has climbed onto the grass and is running toward a boat launch a hundred yards down the shoreline. I take the steps two at a time and leap off the wooden planks. The tide has begun to flood the marsh, so my shoes sink into silty mud and release the stench of sulfur.

"Alice," I shout. "Mrs. Stone. Officers will be here any minute. Please stop and let me come to you. Whatever's happened, we can work this out."

I reach for my firearm, realizing too late that I left the cottage without it. I weigh the flashlight in my hand. It's heavy enough to use as a weapon. I move across the grassy plain to where the marsh drops off at a channel. Ahead, Alice wades through shallow water.

"Please stop," I say. "Stay where you are."

She spins toward me. The bottom of her dress swirls in the surf. I steady the flashlight with my forearm and drop from the marsh to the warm, salty water. Horseshoe crabs scurry around my now ruined shoes.

I'm good at my job and know how to respond to a crisis. I've dealt with overdoses and domestic abuse and cars wrapped around trees. This last week, I've had to coordinate the response to a homicide. Now I take in as many details as I can. The scents of sulfur and salt hang on the air. Alice whimpers, her hand trailing along Harper's back. She stands at the edge of the surf beside what, at first, I mistake for a mass of driftwood and seaweed. I focus the beam of the flashlight, and a pile of wet clothing takes shape just over the tide line. Then the contours of a human body materialize.

Alice raises her hands like she's being arrested, as if she's only now realizing what she's done. I take a step closer. I should check for vital signs, but something holds me back. When I turn the corpse over, I suspect I'll see Damian Stone's face.

"Is he dead?" I hear myself ask.

She nods.

I remember the way she and Damian sniped at each other during the party. I hadn't been able to tell if it was the comfort of the familiar or actual marital discord. Maybe I should have intervened. After we all left, she must have told Damian about the kiss. Maybe she confessed feelings for me. I can see her fleeing the house as the storm raged around her. What choice did she have but to defend herself?

"Have you touched anything?" I ask.

"I tried to give him CPR. There was blood. So much blood. I must have gotten it on my dress."

"You have blood on your face."

Alice falls to her knees, scrubbing at her skin with seawater.

"Stop!" I say, wading to her side. She's washing off evidence. "What happened? What did you do?"

"We found him like this."

Off in the distance, a siren sound finally breaks the silence. "Who's we?" I ask.

"Harper and me."

The dog is still on the beach, pawing at the body. I call to her, and she comes to my side. "You panicked," I say to Alice. "That's why you screamed. That's why you didn't call 911."

"I panicked," Alice says.

But Alice Stone doesn't seem the type to panic. She's intentional about everything she does, including reporting free-roaming pit bulls on the town beach when she wants to get me alone, or maybe even when she flirts with a cop who lives next door or steals a kiss or screams into the night and waits for that cop to run to her rescue.

The events of the night unfurl in my mind. Georgia saw Alice kiss me, so our secret isn't our secret. Georgia won't hold back from telling the truth, especially after what I said to her tonight. And what if Alice wanted a witness all along?

I imagine Brock London sitting across from me in the interrogation room, his voice kind, the questions pointed. "You wanted to be the hero," he might say. "You wanted to save her."

And he'd be right.

I should do my job, but now I'm doubting my every move. Will footprints in the sand implicate me? Or will the lack of footprints do the same? A small wave breaks at the shore. Soon the tide will reach the body, sweeping away any evidence the rain didn't already erase.

"What are we going to do?" Alice asks.

I retreat again, running through the steps of what should happen next. "My team will be here momentarily," I say. "They'll secure the scene, and then we'll hand this off to the state cops and the same thing that's been happening to Simon Thibodeau will start happening to you. Law enforcement will descend on this house and your life, and they'll dig into whatever they need to in order to piece together what happened here. This is the last time I can speak to you as a friend. It may be the last time I can speak to you at all. Whatever you're trying to hide, come clean. Why did you kill your husband? Was it because of us?"

The question wakes Alice from her trance. She tilts her head. "Damian's in the house. I assume he's asleep. So is Noah."

"Then who did you kill?"

She steps away from me. "I didn't kill anyone."

I cross the sand to the body and pull a knit cap from the head. It's only then I understand I'm not here on the beach as a cop or a friend or even as a potential lover. I'm entwined in this story as much as Alice is. Maybe more. And like Simon Thibodeau, soon my life may be turned upside down.

Alice joins me. Above us, over the bluff, blue lights flash in the night.

"It's Dr. Drake," Alice says, looking down at the body. "Farley. He's dead. We were with him all evening. Did one of us do this?"

CHAPTER 20
Max

I stare down at Farley's dead body lying on the sand by the boat launch.

"Max," Alice says to me. "What do we do?"

I don't know how to respond. I hated Farley Drake. I've made that clear in public hearings. I live next door to him. My footsteps are here on the sand. None of this looks good for me, but I push away any doubts about working the scene and go right to the basics.

First, I move Alice and Harper into the surf away from the body. My feet sink into the sand as I check for a nonexistent pulse. I snap photos with my phone from every angle I can, and then I scan the shoreline for a murder weapon, anything heavy enough to have caused this much damage. The back of the head is caked with blood, so whoever hit Farley would be covered in splatter.

Like Alice Stone.

I remember her throwing that orange ball to Harper on the beach. She has a strong arm. I should remember that.

When I return to where she waits, we face off as waves lap at our ankles. With each passing moment, the tide inches closer to the crime scene, and I wonder where her loyalties lie, if she's someone I can trust, or if she's already three moves ahead, putting forward alternate theories, establishing motives, creating opportunity.

"Tell me what happened," I say.

"I don't know."

I hit *Redial* on my phone. When dispatch answers, I identify myself and say, "10-54 at Moulton Farm. ID is Dr. Farley Drake of Mooney Point. There's at least one cruiser here already. We'll secure the scene as best we can, but it will be compromised by the incoming tide within the hour. Get the crime techs here ASAP. And alert the state cops."

We go back and forth with a few more details before I click off the call. Alice hasn't stopped staring at me, as though she's trying to decide whom to trust as well. I offer my arm as if we're friends, leading with kindness. It's usually the best strategy to establish trust. Still, she hesitates.

"We need to vacate the crime scene," I say.

She relents, but she doesn't take my arm. Instead, she leads the way across the marsh with Harper as her shadow. When she reaches the stairs, she rests her hands on the railing. "I was outside with Harper after the party when the thunder began. It doesn't matter what I do or where we go during a storm, she gets frightened." She ran off toward the dock. I went to find her. The rain was so heavy, and it was dark, and I couldn't see anything. I heard her barking on the marsh. I tried to follow the sound, but she'd stopped running when she got to the boat launch. That's when I tripped over Farley."

"Where was Damian this whole time?"

"I told you already—in bed. Or I assume he was." She glances down at Harper. "Go ahead," she says.

Harper dashes up the stairs and waits at the top. Alice follows, taking the steps slowly, as if dreading what she'll find on the other side of that bluff. I bring up the rear. As the farmhouse comes into view, both cruisers already sit by the barn, their lights flashing. Damian Stone's voice carries through the night air. "You haven't answered my question," he shouts. "What are you doing here?"

That moment between Alice and me in the kitchen seems as though it happened in another lifetime.

"I shouldn't have gotten you involved," she says.

I'd have been involved no matter how events unfolded tonight, though her phrasing interests me. Could she have known I'd come running to the rescue when she screamed?

"Chief!"

One of the officers calls from the house, where she's blocking Damian from charging toward us.

"Looks like your husband's being a dick," I say. "I should save him from himself."

"Don't try too hard." Alice holds my arm and closes her eyes for a moment. When she opens them, she says, "Farley was my therapist. Dr. Drake. I've been seeing him since I moved to town. I thought I should tell you before you find out some other way."

With each passing moment, I trust Alice Stone less. "Anything else?" I ask. "Because as soon as I cross that lawn, the cops'll know everything I do, and this thing'll start. The state cops will work the investigation. The crime techs will collect evidence, and someone from the medical examiner's office will release the body to the morgue."

Alice shivers. "Is that what we call Farley now? The body?"

"Or the victim." I hear how detached I sound, but stepping outside and looking in is my best defense at this point. What will turn up after the state cops subpoena Farley Drake's records? What might she have said to Farley—to Dr. Drake— about me and our clandestine meetings? "Did you tell the victim anything I should know about?"

"I told him all sorts of things."

I wondered what stays privileged when your psychiatrist's

body shows up on your property. Alice turns toward the house, where her husband is arguing with the officer.

"Barbosa," Damian shouts, "what the fuck is going on?"

We're closer now. Damian's thrown on a pair of jeans and a ratty old Green Day T-shirt. His hair stands on end as though he's just gotten out of bed. Alice crouches beside Harper, and when she speaks, it's as though she's speaking to the dog. "Damian was having an affair," she says. "With Laurel Thibodeau. And I'm frightened about what will happen when it comes out. I don't want the world to see us at our worst."

"That bit of news would have been good to know earlier this week," I say, remembering the conversation with Brock, the DNA the state cops found in Laurel's bed. "Keeping information from the police makes you look guilty."

"I only found out for sure tonight."

"Tell the cops."

Alice shivers. "I just did. And I need to change my clothes. I'm freezing."

On the patio, the hurricane lamps still dot the table where we had dinner earlier, though the candles are extinguished. I click on the strings of lights. Harper sniffs in every corner for a stray scrap of brisket she may have missed. By the house, Noah hovers in the cellar door. Alice calls to him, but he shakes his head.

"Take Mrs. Stone inside," I say to the female officer. "Collect her clothes and shoes for evidence and make sure she doesn't wash her face or hands. Also, let her get her son to bed. It's going to be a long night."

Alice follows the officer. At the cellar door, she holds Noah against her chest and glances toward me one last time before disappearing inside. I wave the second officer over and tell him to cordon off everything from the patio to the water. "Make sure no one sets foot on the marsh or the beach. I took what photos I could, but the tide's coming in fast."

Even as the officer begins to stretch yellow crime tape along the lawn, Damian makes a move toward the beach. I block him, and he puffs out his chest. I must have five inches and fifty pounds on the guy, but he shoves me anyway. The officer drops the tape to intervene, but I wave him off.

"Understand the rules," I say to Damian. "Assaulting an officer gets you arrested."

He lurches. I grab his arm and twist it around his back till he winces. "Had enough?"

He nods curtly. When I release him, he spins, hands clenched. "What's on the beach?"

I pull a chair across the brick and wait for him to sit. "Things seemed strained between you and your wife tonight. Want to tell me why?"

Damian lets out a long, slow breath. "Play your little cop games till the real detectives get here, Chief. I didn't get Alice a birthday cake. She was pissed off and had every right to be. But don't tell me there was a cake down on the dock this whole time. Is that why you're here? To save the day?"

"Does that mean your relationship with Laurel Thibodeau had nothing to do with what was going on between the two of you?"

I should have saved this question for the state cops to use, but I want to be the first to see Damian's reaction. He sits back, arms folded. I've questioned enough guilty teenagers to know whatever he says next will be a lie.

"I only knew Laurel from Firefly. Alice and I went there most Friday nights."

I pull up a chair beside him and straddle it. "Getting access to evidence becomes a whole lot easier with a dead body. By noon, we'll have your phone records, your DNA, anything we need. And then, we'll connect you to Mrs. Thibodeau, and you'll have a whole lot more to worry about than a couple of cruisers sitting in the barnyard."

Damian surveys the farm, from the flashing lights to the

uniformed officers to the crime scene tape bleached white by the moonlight. "Fuck," he says.

Now we're talking. "What happened after the party?" I ask.

"Who's dead?"

"Listen to me," I say. "This is a dress rehearsal for what's about to hit you. You should thank me for the practice session."

Damian closes his eyes. "Alice and I got in a fight. Did she tell you already? Are you checking to see if our stories match up?"

Lights flash from the street. An ambulance pulls up the lane, and two EMTs exit the cab. I don't have much more time alone here.

"I want the truth," I say. "What was the fight about?"

Damian laughs and arches an eyebrow. "She knew about Laurel, but the fight? It was about you, you prick. Alice has the hots for you. And I wouldn't be surprised if you feel the same. She certainly spends enough time over at your place and meeting you out on the town beach."

The EMTs wheel a gurney onto the patio. "There's no rush," I say. "Let's wait for the ME's office."

"Tell me who's dead," Damian says.

This is something else I should save for the state cops, but I watch Damian closely as I say, "Farley Drake."

He tents his fingers in front of his face and nods slowly. He doesn't seem upset. "Why was he here?" he asks.

It's a good question. "You tell me," I say.

An unmarked sedan pulls in alongside the ambulance. Brock London steps out, back rigid, blond hair sheared nearly to the scalp, his flinty eyes flashing under the ambulance lights as he surveys the scene.

"Now the real show begins," I say.

CHAPTER 21
Max

"Chief Barbosa," Brock London says as he strides toward me, "glad you're on this."

Not for much longer, I think. I expect to be shunted off to the sidelines as soon as I brief him on tonight's events.

Brock's swapped out the gray suit for jeans and a slim-fitting flannel shirt, though he's clean-shaven and his handshake is as firm as usual. I introduce Damian. Brock barely acknowledges him before maneuvering me away. "That's the guy you mentioned on the phone tonight," he says. "The one asking about the Thibodeau case."

"He has his reasons," I say, filling him in on what I know about Damian's affair with Laurel.

Brock takes the information in without reaction. "And now there's another body." He waves to Damian. "We'll be with you soon, Mr. Stone."

"Let's not jump to conclusions," I say. "They may not be related."

"Don't worry. I've been doing this for a while, but you picked up on Stone's connection to the Thibodeau case earlier. Shows good instinct. You sure you don't want to apply for the detective job?"

After tonight, I doubt that job will be an option anymore.

"Get me up to speed," Brock says.

"Victim is Dr. Farley Drake," I say.

"The shrink? The one we talked to at the ice-cream shop this afternoon?"

I nod, and Brock listens as I run through the basics, including the location of the body, where we've cordoned off, and photos of the crime scene on my phone. More vehicles begin to arrive and fill the farmyard. Two additional state detectives I recognize from the station confer with Brock for a moment. So does someone from the state medical examiner's office, and a whole slew of crime techs, each changing into white mylar suits before beginning the painstaking task of collecting evidence. Eventually Alice emerges from the house in a fleece jacket and a pair of yoga pants. My officer hands her off to a crime tech, who swabs for DNA and takes fingerprints on a handheld device.

"You live right by here?" Brock says, following my gaze. "And you were at this house for a party tonight. . . ." His voice trails off.

"Glad I told you about that before all this happened," I say.

"Me too," he says.

I take a deep breath. It's best for him to hear all this from me, and besides, cops have a sense for withheld information, and I can see Brock beginning to home in on mine. "There's an old carriageway that connects the two properties." I tell him about hearing the scream and finding Farley's body on the beach.

When I finish, Brock shoves his hands into his pockets. He takes a moment before saying, "Your neighbor finds your other neighbor's body on the beach, and you decide to investigate on your own because . . . ?"

"I wanted to borrow a cup of sugar?" I say, which doesn't earn a hint of a smile. "In my defense, I called it in as soon as

I got to the farm, before I knew about the body. You can check the dispatch records."

This time when Brock speaks, his voice is low enough I have to lean in to hear him. "Mrs. Stone is attractive," he says.

He certainly doesn't beat around the bush. "And she's married," I say.

"You and I both know that doesn't mean a thing. You called into the station *after* you went running into the night to her rescue without backup. That's against protocol, and any rookie cop knows that kind of decision can get you killed."

"I thought she wanted to talk."

"She wanted to *talk?* Come on, Chief. That better not be a euphemism. At best, you're a material witness in a probable homicide. You compromised the investigation simply by being here. If I find out you tampered with evidence or coached the witness, it'll be the last day you wear any badge, let alone on my team. I don't miss the obvious. Only morons assume I will."

He's right on every point. Still, I'm used to being in charge, not getting taken down a peg. "I'll check in with my team and then recuse myself from both your investigations. Give me a few hours, and I'll have someone ready to take my place. And I'll make a formal statement at your earliest convenience."

Brock rocks forward on the balls of his feet. To anyone watching, we'd look like colleagues strategizing on next steps. "Keep talking," he says. "And don't hold back. Not on anything."

"I made some missteps tonight," I say. "And I'll need to be sure you're aware of them all, but unless the murder was committed by someone from the outside, I know each and every one of your suspects very, very well. Consider me one, too."

"And Mrs. Stone?"

I should confess to the kiss. It was a mistake, one that could be easily forgotten under different circumstances, but not now. "We're friends," I say, dodging the truth. "Nothing else, despite what happened tonight. Sometimes we play cards, but that's it."

Brock points to my arms. "Why are there scratches?"

I'd forgotten about the struggle with Alice earlier. "You don't miss much," I say.

"I don't miss anything."

"Mrs. Stone was upset when I found her. I had to restrain her, briefly." I nod toward where the crime tech is taking samples. "You'll find my skin cells under her nails."

Brock steps in close. "Do not make me ask any more questions. Anticipate and tell me what you know. You'll need one of the techs to swab those wounds. But let's get to the crime scene. And understand you're talking as a witness, not the police chief."

As he crosses under the cordon, he confers with one of the crime techs. "Let's get a full-body exam on Mr. and Mrs. Stone."

We both cover our feet before heading along a narrow access avenue and down to the dock. A floodlight bathes the marsh with light where crime techs work quickly to mark, tag, and photograph evidence. Fifty yards away, the coroner kneels over Farley's body, though they've had to move it due to the incoming tide. "Nice property," Brock says. "I didn't know there was so much money in documentaries."

"Mrs. Stone is a financial planner," I say. "She makes a healthy salary."

"My bad," Brock says. "And I should know better. My wife's the one who makes bank in my family, too."

"The house isn't theirs, though. They're housesitting for the year."

"Whose is it?"

"A professor on sabbatical. He used to work with Damian—Mr. Stone."

"We'll have to get in contact with the professor, then. Wait for me here." Brock drops off the gangway and crosses the marsh. He convenes with the coroner and one of the crime techs for a few moments before returning. "Your footprints are in the sand?"

"Mine and the dog's," I say. "Probably Mrs. Stone's, too. And the victim's. My guess is between the rain and the tide, the rest will be washed away."

"We'll need your shoes when we get back to the house. What was Mrs. Stone doing out in the middle of the night?"

"She told me the dog got spooked by the storm and found the body."

"Do you believe her?"

Like confessing to the kiss, here I have to make a choice between Alice and the law. It's not as hard as I thought it might be. "Not really," I say. "Things were strained between Alice and Damian tonight at the party. But she seems protective of him too. Loyal."

"Loyal enough to lie? Even when he's been having an affair?"

I nod.

"Any idea what they were fighting about?" Brock asks.

"She turned forty today. He told me he forgot to order a cake."

For the first time since I met him earlier this week, Brock's face cracks into a smile. I'd assumed those muscles had atrophied.

"Mr. Stone's lucky it's Dr. Drake's body we found on the beach," Brock says. "I doubt I'd be on Planet Earth if I'd forgotten a cake for my wife's fortieth birthday."

Back on the beach, the coroner waves the EMTs over. They lift the body onto a gurney and pull it up and over the boat launch. A moment later, the coroner scales the railing and joins us on the gangway. "Blunt force trauma to the occipital at the back of the head. Death was probably instantaneous, or nearly so."

"Murder weapon?" Brock asks.

"Nothing's been identified yet."

"Any signs of a struggle?" Brock asks.

"Not that I could tell in this light. I'll know more once I get the body on the table. Time of death might be challenging with the water, but I'll see what I can get you."

"That one's easy," I say. "Sometime between eleven p.m. and one a.m." Even under the best of circumstances, we wouldn't get a more accurate time of death than that.

"Noted," the coroner says.

Brock leads her away. They speak softly for a few more minutes before she heads out. "Now for the living," Brock says. "Starting with you. What was your relationship with Dr. Drake? You mentioned a small-town grievance on the phone earlier."

"We weren't exactly friends," I say, summarizing the feud.

"The more you talk, the worse things get," Brock says.

"I could withhold information."

Brock looks up toward the sky. The clouds have cleared, and the stars shine bright. He motions me toward the end of the dock, where he gazes over the inky surface of the water for a moment. "My sister-in-law's a Boston cop," he says. "Last year, she got caught up in a case that hit way too close to home. So did my wife and stepdaughter. So I understand your situation better than you might think. You're in a tough spot, but you have to keep doing what you're doing, which is working with me to find the truth. My best guess is you were in the wrong place at the wrong time tonight. But you know I can't stop with my best guess."

I listen to water lapping around the pilings. Anytime I've needed clarity, I've come to this bay to find it. Tonight is no different. The only way through this will be with honesty. "We drank a lot at the party," I say. "Alice Stone kissed me."

Brock rests his elbows on the railing beside me. "Were you receptive?"

I nod. The threads of trust connecting us fray each time I confess something new. "I could have told you this up by the house—"

"But you chickened out?"

"Pretty much."

"First time kissing each other?" he asks.

"Only time," I say. "And Georgia Fitzhugh saw us, so you'd have found out soon enough anyway."

"The Unitarian minister?" he asks. "Curly hair, glasses, always wearing a scarf?"

"That's her."

"Damian Stone had an affair with our other victim, Laurel Thibodeau, and Alice Stone is lusting after you. Loyal or not, it doesn't sound like a happy marriage. They have a son, right?"

"Noah. He was up earlier but should be in bed now."

"We'll have to talk to him. Kids notice things when you think they aren't paying attention. What else can you tell me about the victim, besides him being a terrible neighbor?"

"Probably thirty-five or thirty-six. He's a psychiatrist and set up a private practice in town when he moved here."

"Shrinks can get themselves in trouble with clients. Did he have a good reputation?"

"As far as I know, though—"

"Just say it," Brock says. "Whatever it is."

"Alice Stone just told me she was one of his clients."

"Are you kidding me?" Brock says. "Alice Stone invited her shrink to her birthday party? The same shrink who lectured me about ethics and disclosure not twelve hours ago?" Brock shakes his head. "This job takes me to tiny towns all over the state, but I'm a city boy. I grew up in Dorchester. I don't understand how any of you do your jobs when you know every single person involved with everything that happens. How can you possibly stay impartial?"

That's easy. I have a choice between making a poor decision to protect a friend or making an enemy. So far, I've mostly chosen enemies. "I try to be professional. In this case, that means telling you what I know and then getting out of your way. Farley Drake lived with his boyfriend, Richard Macomber. You'll need to talk to him, too."

"Mechanic?" Brock asks. "Drives that gold VW. Nice wheels. He's the one who was married to the minister."

"Still is, last I heard. They haven't filed for divorce."

"Who's handling the notification?"

"Under normal circumstances, that would be me, but Ritchie and I grew up together. And we're neighbors. And we were at the same party."

Until now I haven't given much thought to Ritchie or what tonight will mean to him. I imagine him at Farley's house, asleep, unaware his new life is over. Or at least I hope he isn't aware of what's happened, because he'll be a prime suspect now. The partner always is. And for once I won't be able to protect him.

CHAPTER 22
Max

At the farmhouse, more personnel have arrived. Cars fill the front yard and spill over into the fields. Like most crime scenes, there are a lot of people, some who have started to work and others who wait for their roles to take shape. I scan the yard for Alice, but neither she nor Damian are out here anymore.

"We may have a task-force situation on our hands come morning," Brock mumbles as he waves over a crime tech. "Barbosa," he says to me. "What size shoe do you wear? Size 11?"

"Close enough," I say.

He jogs to his sedan and returns with a pair of sneakers. "Take his shoes," he says to the tech. "Record these scratches, and get a DNA sample." He cocks an eyebrow at me. "How about a body exam?"

"Whatever you need," I say, slipping my shoes off and putting on the sneakers.

I lean against a cruiser while the tech swabs the scratches and takes photos of the wounds. Inside the house, I strip to my underwear in the TV room and submit to more poking and prodding and photos. "These better not wind up in *Men's Health*," I say, though no one laughs.

Back outside, my own two officers huddle together by the beech tree, shunted to the sidelines by the arrival of the state cops. They speak softly to each other, and I suspect they're talking about me, something I'll need to get used to over the coming days. My presence has become a hindrance. I suspect I'll be on paid leave by nightfall, which won't play well in the news.

"Barbosa," Brock calls to me from the tree line. When I join him, he says, "Show me the path that runs between the properties, then I'll drop you home on my way to the notification."

I lead him along the stone wall to the gate and shine my flashlight onto the carriageway.

"How far to your place?" Brock asks.

"About a quarter mile."

"And you run that in—?"

"Depends on the situation," I say. "Tonight, maybe ninety seconds."

Brock looks me over. "Let's say three minutes. Is this the path Farley Drake would have taken to get here, too?"

"It's the best bet," I say. "He could have left the Point and walked along the street, and then up the lane to the farm, but that's probably two miles. I suppose he could have come by water, though not likely during the storm. That's how they arrived at the party earlier."

"They came by boat but walked home?"

"We'd all had a lot to drink." I shine the flashlight along the path. "I came through here after the storm ended, and it was muddy. You'll find my footprints. Depending on when people walked the path, there could be others."

"Or they could have washed away," Brock says. "Like on the beach."

Soon the carriageway has been taped off, too.

Brock watches the techs as they move along the path, creating a grid. "Unless Laurel had more than one boyfriend, that

DNA at the Thibodeau crime scene will wind up being Damian Stone's," he says. "I could bring Mr. Stone into the station. See if he'll break. My guess is he'll lawyer up, though."

"He doesn't know we don't have a match for the DNA," I say.

Brock sighs. "If you survive the next few days, you're applying for that job. And I won't take no for an answer." He starts walking toward the house. When I don't follow, he turns. "I'm going in to have a chat with Damian Stone. Come."

I hesitate. "I can't be impartial."

"I'm not asking you to be," Brock says. "But I need the local view on these cases, both of them. Listen, and don't say anything. I mean, not one word."

Inside, we find Damian in the kitchen, eating ambrosia right out of the Tupperware container I brought it in earlier. A crime tech looks on.

"Am I about to get the third degree?" Damian asks.

"We just want to ask some questions," Brock says.

"Well, I need to show you something," Damian says.

"Where's Alice?" I ask.

"Upstairs. Trying to get Noah to sleep." He takes another bite of the ambrosia. "This shit's delicious."

"I'll get you the recipe," I say.

Brock catches my eye. "What did I say outside? Keep your mouth shut." He turns to Damian. "You were sleeping with Laurel Thibodeau," he says, and it's not a question. "Any reason you didn't come forward at any moment this last week when we were investigating her homicide?"

"At least ten," Damian says.

"Start with the primary one," Brock says.

"Why blow up my whole life for no reason?"

Brock takes the Tupperware from him and puts it aside. "We've been trying to chase down stray DNA all week long. So even if you didn't murder anyone, that's time wasted in a homicide, which pisses me off. See how it works?"

"Yeah, I also didn't expect another body to show up. At least not this soon."

"What's that mean?" Brock asks.

"I could get you some of that time back, but when I show you what I show you, you'll think I'm nuts."

"Be nuts, then," Brock says. "I don't really care."

"Fine," Damian says, leading us through the house, down a long hallway to a small room with drop ceilings and faux-wood paneling. He flips on the overhead lights revealing a whiteboard covered in red handwriting and photos, including one of Laurel Thibodeau. "It's all here," he says.

Brock puts a finger to his lips and barely shakes his head, reminding me to keep my mouth shut. Then he approaches the whiteboard. "Lots of crime here," he says. "And lots of notes. Help me make sense of it."

Damian starts with a photo of a man lying face down on a forest floor. "Steve Alabiso was killed in Rhode Island last fall about ten miles from here. His wife was the prime suspect, though she had a solid alibi, and then the ME decided it was a suicide. You probably haven't heard much about the case because it happened over the state line. And here." He moves to a second photo, this one of a woman sitting in her car, her mouth open and her head tilted back. "Jeanine Geller. She died in Westport."

Brock touches the photo. "On May 25. Mrs. Geller's daughter found the body. The death was ruled as accidental, though it was probably a suicide. The victim left her car running in the garage. And the case in Rhode Island happened in October. Steve Alabiso was an avid hunter and died from a self-inflicted gunshot wound. I'm in touch with the Rhode Island State Police on a regular basis, by the way." He moves on to the photo of Laurel at the center of the board. "Now Laurel Thibodeau. What's the connection?"

Damian waves toward the whiteboard. "It took me a while to see it, too. But now, tonight, it makes even more sense."

Brock's jaw is set; the only clue he might not be taking Damian at his word are the white knuckles where he grips the back of a chair. "Get to your theory, Mr. Stone."

"It's a serial killer. The same person killed them all."

"They aren't the same age or sex, and the mode of death is different. What's the connection?"

Damian jabs at the photo of Steve Alabiso. "He was having an affair with a colleague," he says. "And Jeanine Geller had met a man at her synagogue. The affair almost tore apart the community."

Brock says, "That's the connection? They were both having extramarital affairs. We'd wipe out most of the human race if we knocked off everyone who's ever had an affair."

"Then there's Laurel," Damian says.

Brock releases the chair. He approaches Laurel's photo. For the first time, he seems to be truly listening to Damian's theory. "She was having an affair with you."

Damian nods. "And he's been in touch with me. The killer."

Brock turns to face him. "How?"

"Text message. Dozens of them." He fumbles with his phone and pulls up a string of texts. "This one came last week." He holds the screen so I can read the last message: *Sessions with a shrink are confidential*. "And now," Damian says, "our local shrink shows up dead on my property. Don't tell me there isn't a connection."

It's only then I sense someone standing behind me. I turn to see Alice, her face blanched white. I'm not sure how long she's been there, or how much she's overheard, but she steps into Damian's office and takes his hand. "I assume you'll need us to make a statement down at the station," she says.

"When did you get the first message, and who's sending them?" Brock asks, but Alice pulls Damian toward her.

"We'll come down as soon as our lawyer is available," she says.

Damian shakes Alice off and speaks directly to Brock. "If I hadn't been digging into this, Laurel would still be alive."

"Damian, enough," Alice says.

"Would you show me the whole text string?" Brock asks.

"Again," Alice says, "we'll come to the station in the morning. With our lawyer."

Brock starts to say something but stops himself. He takes a card from his wallet and hands it to Damian. "You know where to find me," he says, "And Mr. Stone, not a word of this. To anyone. It's almost six a.m. We have an hour, maybe two, before the story blows up. Don't fan the flames."

"We won't," Alice says.

I follow Brock upstairs and outside. "Did you buy any of that?" I ask.

Brock stands at the edge of the patio, surveying the crime scene. The team has brought in more floodlights, and the grid search has progressed from the marsh to the front lawn, where the croquet set sits with five of the mallets in place. "I worked that case in Westport," Brock says. "Jeanine Geller, the woman who died of carbon monoxide poisoning. We thought the husband was good for it, but he had a rock-solid alibi."

"Like Simon Thibodeau."

"Exactly," Brock says. "I'll go through the file again and see if anything stands out."

"Was Jeanine Geller really having an affair?"

Brock nods. "We talked to the guy she was sleeping with."

"And you found him . . ."

"Through DNA," Brock says. "His name is Zach Lawson. He lives here in Monreith."

I know Zach Lawson. His daughter Taylor is the girl Chloe punched at school yesterday afternoon, but I keep that information to myself for now.

"We'll get Damian Stone's phone records," Brock says. "All

his electronics. We'll know soon enough who he's been talking to, if anyone."

Again, I scrutinize the croquet set sitting on the lawn. "Did your team find a murder weapon?" I ask.

"Not that I know of," Brock says. "But I can check."

"One of the croquet mallets is missing," I say. "There should be six there, but there are only five."

Brock crosses the lawn and examines the set right as my phone buzzes. It's Georgia. *What's going on?* she texts. *I can see the lights through the trees.*

I'll be back in a few minutes. Will explain then.

Is Chloe okay?

I'd be with you already if she wasn't, I respond, as Brock joins me on the patio. I show him Georgia's message. "Word's already spreading," I say. "You should make the notification soon."

He nods. "It was a nice night," he says. "Did you play croquet?"

"We all did."

"Which mallet did you use?"

"Green."

"Not your lucky day," he says. "That's the missing one. I assume your fingerprints will be all over it."

Of course they are.

I picture the crime scene, the blood caked on the back of Farley's skull, the wool cap hiding his sandy-colored hair. The wound could easily have been caused by a croquet mallet, but another thought crosses my mind. "It was warm tonight," I say. "Humid."

"What about it?" Brock asks.

"Farley Drake was wearing a hat."

"To be exact," Brock says, "he wore a ski mask. A balaclava. And he brought a hunting knife with him."

That's what the ME must have whispered on the beach, and the fact that Brock withheld the information serves to remind me how much I'm wrapped up in this case. I lower my voice. "Are you telling me Damian Stone's theory might have merit? And Farley Drake is a suspect?"

"I'm not saying anything. I'm presenting the evidence. But no matter what, Dr. Drake was up to something, or else he wouldn't have worn all black and snuck onto the neighbor's beach with a knife. And if it turns out he actually was a serial killer, the feds will be all over this soon, and we really will have a task-force situation on our hands. But it doesn't matter if we connect Dr. Drake to a hundred murders on the south coast. Someone killed *him.* My job is to find out who."

CHAPTER 23
Max

Brock calls another detective over to join us. I've seen her around the station this week. She's young, with thick black hair and dark eyes. "Iris Parke," she says, with a curt nod.

"Max Barbosa," I say.

"I know," she says. "You're the chief of police. I wouldn't be much of a detective if I didn't know that."

"We're taking the chief home," Brock says, "and making a notification. Why don't you come?"

We get in the car, the two detectives up front, and me riding in the back like a perp. As Brock drives away along the lane, I turn from where I sit in the back seat to watch Moulton Farm recede. Every light in the house is ablaze, and I wonder what Alice is doing right now, whether she and Damian are strategizing their next moves. Guilty or not, they'd be fools not to.

Brock updates the second detective on everything I've told him, though he doesn't mention Damian's serial killer theory. He'll want to confirm that one before it gets any air. I lean my head against the cool glass, feeling the weight of the night fully descend. I don't like the position I'm in, or that I'll need to step away from my job later. More than I realized, everything I have, everything I am, is wrapped up in being the chief of police, and I don't like not being in control.

My head knocks the glass as the car rumbles along rough terrain, and I realize I've briefly fallen asleep. Brock pulls through grass fields, into a grove of trees, and then up the little hill, where he stops beside the cottage. My own cruiser sits along the cutting garden. "You live here," Detective Parke says, "on a cop's salary?"

To me, the cottage feels one step above a shack, especially beside Farley's new house. But it's beautiful. Special. Something I should remember. And Detective Parke is right, most cops could never afford it. "It's complicated," I say, before remembering any statement I make could be dissected for a hidden meaning. I get out of the car and talk through the open window. "And I'll make sure you have access to my financials."

"Tell us now," Brock says. "We'll confirm later."

"My great-grandparents bought all this land in the thirties for almost nothing right after they emigrated here from the Azores. The family kept the Point till we had to sell most of it." I nod toward where Farley's house looms on the cliff. "That's who we sold it to."

Brock points through the windshield to the top of the front gate. "I see the cameras. What's the security situation out here?"

Farley's house is like Fort Knox, with sound- and motion-activated cameras covering every inch of the property. He'd wanted to install cameras along the lane, too, but I'd drawn the line at anything pointing toward my cottage. "There'll be plenty of footage you can use," I say.

"Good to know," Brock says, putting the car in gear. "If we need anything, I'll call you."

I rest a hand on the car door. "There's a teenage kid at the house. Chloe. Richard Macomber's daughter."

"The one I met at the ice-cream shop," Brock says. "Pink

hair. She was with the victim. She's the same age as my step-daughter."

Right then, Georgia steps out of the shadows where she must have been listening to our whole conversation. "What's going on with Chloe?" she asks, an edge of panic to her voice. "Max, I thought you told me this had nothing to do with her."

"Chloe's fine," I say quickly.

I wish I could take back some of the things I said to Georgia earlier tonight, because she needs all the support she can get right now. As much as I want to move on, I'll always have a small place reserved in my heart for Georgia.

"Reverend," Brock says. "You're here, too."

"Georgia's staying with me," I say.

"Not with your husband?" Brock says.

"We're separated," Georgia says.

Brock looks me up and down, and I suddenly wish I'd mentioned Georgia's presence earlier.

"I'll leave you to get her up to speed, then, Chief," he says, pulling away.

"Come in for a sec," I say to Georgia.

She starts moving toward Farley's driveway, where the detectives exit the sedan and head up the stone stairs toward the house.

I put a hand on her arm to stop her.

She shakes me off. "What's a detective doing here in the middle of the night? Why does he need to talk to Ritchie?"

"You can't get in the middle of this."

"What happened?"

I turn to Farley's house, where the door opens, and the detectives step inside. Maybe it's best if I let Georgia insert herself in the investigation. She'll want to be there to support Chloe. And she'll be able to stay close to Ritchie and protect him in ways I can't. "It's Farley," I say. "He's dead."

She takes a step backward, stumbling.

"Go," I say.

She turns and runs up the driveway. At the house, Detective Parke steps out of the doorway and lets her inside.

Back at the cottage, I check my own phone and find dozens of unanswered calls and text messages, including one from the town manager. I tap in a text to Ritchie, telling him he can stay in my spare bedroom after he finishes with the police. I take a quick shower and change my clothes. I strap on my holster and retrieve my firearm from the safe. On the horizon, the sky turns gray. I've barely slept, but morning has arrived. I need to get ahead of these events before they consume me.

The town has only begun to wake up as I drive along Main Street, then pull into the lot behind the station. It's right before eight o'clock, when shifts will be changing over and the two officers who responded to last night's call will be heading home. Even though only a few people dot the street, I can't help but feel as if all eyes are on me as I walk the short block to the local coffee shop. The owner greets me as I come through the door and waves away my money when I try to pay. For once, I insist. Everything I do will be scrutinized now, including accepting free coffee.

At the station, Kennedy has taken her seat at the front desk as her computer boots up. She has jet-black hair cut in a severe bob and must get up at the crack of dawn to apply her eye makeup. She's also a gossip, which I've used to my advantage before. She glances away as soon as she sees me coming, meaning the whispers have already reached her.

"My office," I say.

She scurries after me, down a hallway and past a conference room the state cops have commandeered for the Thibodeau case. Later this morning, they'll be talking about me in there.

I close the office door and wait for Kennedy to sit.

"You look like you got hit by a garbage truck," she says.

Kennedy's parents named her after the famous Massachu-setts family, and her accent reflects the state—*gahbage* instead of *garbage*—something that's becoming rarer, especially among younger people.

"Pretty much feel that way," I say. "Now spill."

Kennedy crosses one leg over the other. She wears silver stilettos and an ankle bracelet. I wouldn't be surprised if she wore heels to the gym. "Those people out at Moulton Farm found a body," she says. "It was the shrink. The one who looks like a movie star."

"That part I know. I want public opinion. Where's it headed?"

"Everyone gets that you hated your neighbor," Kennedy says, knowing not to hold back. "But no one's saying you did it—not yet. And I'd tell you if they did because I'm not putting up with that shit." She uncrosses her legs and leans forward, her voice lower. "The husband, that guy who makes documentaries, he has some crazy shit on his walls about a se-rial killer."

So that's out already.

"And then there's Ritchie. It's early, but if I were to place bets, I'd say folks'll pin it on him or the nut with the conspir-acy theory by the end of the day."

That would be my bet, too. Though maybe I can help turn the focus on Damian. Besides, this town protects its locals. "Anything else about Damian Stone?" I ask.

Kennedy shakes her head, which means word hasn't spread yet about the affair with Laurel Thibodeau. I could get that going easily enough—right here, right now—but that's a line I won't cross. Yet. Still, I say, "This is the second murder in a week."

"Oh, yeah," Kennedy says. "It don't take a brain surgeon to know they're connected."

Or they're not. That's still a possibility.

I turn on my computer. "I probably won't be around much for a few days, but you know where I am, right?"

Kennedy winks at me. "I got you covered, Chief."

After she leaves, I call the town manager and tell her I'm taking a leave of absence before she can suggest it herself. "I'll be out of here by noon," I say.

I get online next. Monreith has begun to trend, and the local TV stations have preliminary reports posted about last night's events, complete with a rehash of the Thibodeau case. The news cycle had begun to move on, but now it will be back in full force.

Someone taps at my door. Brock London sticks his head in. "You're already here," he says.

"Tying up loose ends. I'll be out of your hair later today and will stand by for any formal interview you might need."

"Help me out before you leave," Brock says, leading me into the conference room.

"How did things go with Ritchie?" I ask.

Brock considers the question for a moment. "People deal with this kind of news in all different ways. I would say he seemed surprised enough, but then he didn't ask many details about the incident."

Like he already knew what had happened. "He must have been in shock," I say.

"Sure," Brock says, turning to a whiteboard and writing *Motive*, *Means*, and *Opportunity* across the top in red marker. "We're trying to identify the means," he says. "But with the right swing, anyone could have used a croquet mallet as the murder weapon. And anyone who was on Mooney Point or at Moulton Farm last night had opportunity."

He lists names down the side of the whiteboard, starting with Alice, followed by Damian, Ritchie, and Georgia. The marker hovers over the whiteboard for a second before I say, "Do it," and he adds my name too.

"Motive?" Brock asks. "I need your help understanding how the suspects fit together."

"Farley was armed," I say. "Couldn't it have been self-defense?"

"That's a possibility. And it's one we could hint at with the suspects, but no one's come forward to say that yet." He jots *Self-defense?* under motivation. "Let's start with Alice Stone. She's the one covered with the victim's blood."

"Let's start with me instead," I say. "Farley paid three million dollars for my family home and tore it down in an afternoon, and then he built an ugly house and tried to deny my right-of-way to the dock we share. He was an asshole, and I hated his guts."

Brock writes *Property dispute* next to my name. "Anything else?"

"That covers it."

"The reverend is pretty straightforward, too," Brock says, writing *Jealousy?* next to Georgia's name. "How's the split been between Georgia and Richard? Amicable?"

"More than amicable," I say.

"Amicable for real or more public-facing? She has a high-profile job and probably has to maintain her public image."

"As far as I've seen, it's mostly genuine."

"What's your relationship with the reverend, anyway?" Brock asks. "She spent the night at your house last night. Are you sleeping with her?"

"You're obsessed with sex," I say.

"Sex is one of the things that leads to jealousy. And then to murder. And avoiding the answers won't help you. Besides, I can add two and two."

I puff my cheeks out. "We get together once in a while."

"Before or after she split with her husband?"

"Definitely after. And it's not serious."

"Does the reverend know that?" Brock asks.

I'm not sure what she knows, but I made myself pretty clear last night. "We have an understanding."

"So, back to Mrs. Stone, who certainly had opportunity," Brock says. "She found the body, and she was covered with the victim's blood splatter, which makes her a prime candidate. What's the motive? She was seeing Dr. Drake as a patient."

I force myself to stay detached. "Did she tell him something in a session?" I ask. "Did he know a secret she didn't want revealed? Maybe she told him she hated Laurel Thibodeau."

"Or maybe," Brock says, "Alice Stone confessed to murder during a session and had second thoughts. Mrs. Stone certainly didn't want us to see her husband's phone, or any of those messages he claims to have received. Do you remember the exact wording of that text?"

"Sessions with a shrink are confidential."

Brock writes *Text messages?* on the whiteboard along with *Laurel Thibodeau.* He also adds Simon Thibodeau's name to the list of suspects. "We should find out what Mrs. Stone and the chef talked about yesterday when she went to his house," he says. "And we should find out what the chef was doing last night when Dr. Drake was killed. And we need to take a look at the rest of the text messages Damian Stone received."

"*We're* not doing anything," I remind Brock. "Not as long as my name is on that list."

"Let's finish working through these names," Brock says. "What about Richard Macomber? What's the motive?"

Here I really don't have an answer. Ritchie's seemed happy recently, but Brock points at Farley's name. "Farley Drake had a knife with him and was wearing a ski mask. Why? What was he hiding? And what might Richard Macomber have known? Can you live with someone and not know their secrets?"

"Ritchie," I start to say, and then catch myself. "He's a good friend, but I can't see him pulling something like this off."

"Why not?"

"He can be . . . obtuse."

"Most murderers are pretty dumb," Brock says, writing *Dumb mistake?* next to Ritchie's name. "It's a weak motive, but we can come back to it. That just leaves Damian Stone," he says. "He's gotta be a suspect in the Thibodeau case now. What's the tie between the two crimes?"

I study the whiteboard for a moment. "Alice is the connection from Farley to Damian. The answer could be in the records of her therapy sessions."

"We'll need a court order for those," Brock says.

"Don't lose sight of the Thibodeaus," I say. "Neither of them was an angel. Laurel stole from parishioners at Georgia's church to pay off Simon's gambling debts."

Brock draws a line connecting Georgia's name to Laurel's.

"And let's not forget about Simon, either," I add. "Simon Thibodeau killed his wife. It's not complicated. He wanted that insurance money. I'm sure of it."

Right then, Kennedy knocks on the conference-room door and comes in. Brock flips the whiteboard over so she can't see what he's written.

"I know you're recusing yourself," Kennedy says to me, "but you wanted me to tell you if there's ever a loose dog on the beach."

"Let me guess," Brock says. "A pit bull?"

Kennedy bites her lip and nods, then ducks out of the room. Free-roaming dogs really are below my pay grade, and it hasn't taken Brock long to put together Alice's code.

"I'll need your electronics," he says, his voice clipped. "Your phone. Your laptop, too."

I lay the phone on the table and jot down the passcode. "You can use my office while I'm out. Kennedy can get you access to the laptop."

I feel those steely eyes following me as I leave the building.

CHAPTER 24

Max

Max, don't be paranoid, I tell myself.

But paranoia might be for the best right now. Outside the police station, I get in the cruiser—the chief's cruiser—and pull through town. A call comes in over dispatch about a speeding car on Route 42. It's something I can ignore for now. Besides, it won't be mine to respond to for much longer.

A few people along Main Street wave. They all think they know who I am. My entire identity is wrapped up in the police chief's public face. What would they say if they had a view into my inner world, those darker thoughts that hope this case will turn on Damian Stone so Alice can choose me in the end?

I follow the coastline, wending along the narrow, sandy road. A peloton of cyclists hugs the curves ahead of me, and I give them a wide berth as I pass by. In my rearview mirror, I search their faces for Damian but don't see him.

I stop at the foot of the wooden bridge. Like yesterday, a handful of cars dot the parking lot on the other side of the bay. It's early, and the tide is coming in, but unlike yesterday, the beach will be packed within the next few hours. Here's where I could leave. Maybe I should. Instead, I ease onto the bridge and park right next to Alice's SUV, which has a smashed-in front headlight. If I hadn't left my phone at the station, I'd take photos of the damage.

On the other side of the dunes, Alice waits by the lifeguard stand, her dark hair tucked into a baseball cap and a pair of sneakers dangling from one hand. Despite the dark circles under her eyes and all the questions I should be asking her, she looks beautiful as she tosses an orange rubber ball down the sand for Harper to retrieve. She does have a good arm, strong enough to wield a croquet mallet. Strong enough to hurl it far out into the bay where the changing tide could have swept it out to sea before the sun rose. Still, it's all I can do not to take the initiative this time and kiss her myself. But there are too many people here. Too many witnesses.

Alice doesn't acknowledge me. She walks along the stony shore, tossing the ball at intervals as I trail behind her. Plenty of other free-roaming dogs dash along the sand this morning, though the owners leash them up when they see me coming. Many of them offer exaggerated waves, too, as if I can't see what they're doing. Today they get free passes.

Once the lifeguard stand is no longer in sight, I say, "Harper should be on a leash."

We don't want the attention.

Alice calls to the dog and clips the leash to her collar. "The news trucks are lined up alongside the farm," she says. "Damian took off on his bike already. I had to get out of there, too. Did you see my car? I hit a post trying to get away from them. It's already feeling like a prison."

"You called dispatch," I say.

She turns her head. A strand of hair blows across her face. "I needed to see a friendly face."

My hand brushes hers.

"I shouldn't have done what I did last night," she says. "I shouldn't have gotten you involved. I'm sorry."

A little voice reminds me not to trust her. But if I don't trust Alice, how can I trust Georgia or Ritchie? They're wrapped up in this as much as she is. Soon enough, we'll turn on each other, our treaties breaking down as alliances shift.

"They record your number when you call the station," I say. "There's a data trail connecting us. Every call. It was fine before, but now . . . I'll need to write you a ticket."

Alice takes my hand. Despite my better inclination, I move closer.

"I have to tell you something," she says, "before I lose my nerve. I should have told you last night."

"If you tell me," I say, "you'll need to tell the detective."

Alice takes the cap off. Her hair blows across her face. Behind me, waves crash on the shore. "I found a burner phone," she says. "I'm almost certain it belongs to Damian, and that he used it to contact Laurel. My guess is there are texts and photos and God knows what else on it. Honestly, I don't want to know, but I'm sure you can use it."

"I can't take evidence," I say. "It'll compromise the case. You'll have to leave it at the police station."

Alice shakes her head. "I don't have the burner anymore. Damian took it on his ride this morning."

"Call him," I say. "Tell him to drop it by the station."

Alice pulls out her phone and sends Damian a text. "There's something else you should know too," she says.

More people are filtering onto the beach. I write out a citation and hold it toward her, my hand shaking. "You should leave," I say.

Alice takes the slip of paper and slides it into her sneaker. "Last night after the party, Richard texted Damian."

"So what? They're friends."

"The text came to the burner. Richard asked Damian to meet him on the dock."

Right where Farley's body was found.

"I'm sorry to be the one to tell you," Alice says. "I know you and Richard are close."

She heads toward the lifeguard stand on her own. I wait for her to turn before disappearing into the dunes, but she doesn't.

When I get back to the parking lot, Alice's SUV is gone, but Brock is waiting for me.

"She wanted to explain what happened last night," I tell him. "You know, the kiss. She doesn't want it getting out." I duck into my cruiser.

"Did you see her headlight?" Brock asks. "It was smashed in."

"She told me she hit a post avoiding the news trucks. It should be easy enough to verify, especially if they had the cameras running."

"Okay," Brock says. "And thanks for keeping me in the loop. Here's something to chew on. The warrant came in on Dr. Drake's office. There was a note in Mrs. Stone's file from her session yesterday. It said she reported being frightened of her husband. Any idea why?"

I shake my head.

"Also," Brock says, "there was a third set of DNA found at the Thibodeau crime scene, and I'll give you one guess who it belongs to."

"Farley Drake," I say.

"You got it." Brock gets into his car and rolls down the window. "Keep your head down. This'll seem unbearable, but then it'll be over."

I sit in my cruiser long after he drives away, replaying the last few hours over and over while the lot fills around me. Why didn't Alice tell me about the phone last night? And what possible explanation could there be for Ritchie to ask Damian to meet him on the dock? I'm so lost in thought I almost miss the call coming in over the radio.

There's been an accident out on Drift Road, not more than a mile from here. "Send a bus," the voice on the radio says, "though it won't do much good. When it's cyclist against guardrail, the guardrail almost always wins."

PART IV

The Boyfriend

CHAPTER 25
Richard

THE PREVIOUS DAY

Most people think I'm a happy idiot in coveralls, someone who needs protecting and who's easy to manipulate. Certainly, Max and Georgia believe that. Farley, too, at least till recently. And I guess I have spent most of my thirty-nine years hiding behind masks: the chief's best friend, the reverend's husband, that guy who'll fix your car. Even now, I'm Richard Macomber, the handsome doctor's new boyfriend. But let's just say still waters run deep.

Yeah, I have some secrets, and I can't admit to everything I've done, but I'll start with the money.

I work with rich people. And I'm not talking Farley-and-a-mint-condition-phantom-gray-Triumph-Spitfire kind of rich. I'm talking the kind of rich that you can't imagine unless you see it for yourself, the kind where every whim is satisfied, and none of the rules apply. Those guys—and they're all guys—like their fancy cars.

Today, I brokered a sale for a 1952 Aston Martin DB 2/4

Mark I to some asshole who lives on Long Island and wants to enter the Mille Miglia Classic Auto Race in Italy. He paid cash for whatever reason he had—probably laundering or drugs or plain old tax evasion, I never ask—which means I have twenty grand of pure profit in a paper bag sitting here in my office at the garage. I open the bottom drawer of my desk and dump it in. Later, I'll move it all into the offshore account Georgia doesn't know about—something Alice, my financial advisor, suggested. "Keep a little for yourself," she said after we met a few times. "Just enough so you don't get caught. It's all about risk."

At the time, Alice didn't know I was about to leave Georgia. If she had known, I wonder if she'd have given me the same advice.

I could feel bad about hiding money, but honestly, Georgia would never believe I'd hide anything from her. Except an affair with her therapist. *Oops.*

To celebrate the sale, I dig out the orange bag of peanut butter M&Ms—another secret—from under the wads of cash and count out five, one of each color, and then eat them in order: yellow, blue, red, green, brown. I save brown for last because it's the one everyone overlooks.

How's that for symbolism?

I'm not so dumb after all. I did take English 101!

Out in the garage, I pop open the hood on a blue '64 Ford Falcon that needs a rebuilt engine to come back to life. Soon I've positioned the hoist and removed the hood, and I'm in my happy place, which makes answering Georgia's phone call that much harder. These days, Georgia only calls with bad news. But I'm a good person.

"Chloe got in a fight," Georgia says.

Get ready, because this next part won't reflect well on me. I get that. But I *really* need to finish this engine, and if I miss a step once the engine is in pieces, it can cost me days. Plus I have the garage to myself for the afternoon, and Chloe will be with me all weekend. I can talk to her about whatever happened then. Also, sometimes it's better to let things cool off before you deal with them, right? That's why I lie to Georgia. "I have to get through three more cars before I can leave," I say. "People are waiting. And it's the weekend, you know?"

Maybe I'm not such a good person.

The long silence on the other end of the phone makes me dread what's coming next. "I'll figure something out," Georgia says. "Do you want Chloe to stay with me tonight?"

"That's not what I said."

"Fine. But make sure she stays out of trouble for the *whole* weekend. She's grounded for the next month."

Georgia clicks off the call, and I'm sure she would have slammed the receiver down if we still did things like that. Fifteen years of marriage to her has taught me how to make sure she believes she has that control, but Georgia hasn't figured out there's nothing that can be controlled about a thirteen-year-old girl.

I start draining fluids from the engine, but it's not like I'm *enjoying* myself after a call like that. Soon motor oil covers my hands, and a line of parts snakes across the cement floor. Really, Chloe's the center of my world, and the split with Georgia has been hard on her—harder, probably, than I even realize, because till recently Chloe hasn't been the type to get into fights. She also wasn't the type to dye her hair pink or sass her mother, and I suspect more mother-daughter time won't help the situation.

I should close early, go to the church, and pick her up. The Falcon can wait till Monday.

See, I get there. Eventually.

I make notes of where I am with the engine and head to the office to change out of my coveralls right as my phone rings again. I couldn't be more relieved when Max's name flashes across the screen instead of Georgia's. That is, until I answer. "Do you know what your boyfriend's doing right now?" Max asks.

Boyfriend. I've wanted a boyfriend literally for my entire life, but I'm not used to hearing the word, even now that the truth is out there. Sometimes I jot the word down and trace the letters with my finger, then scratch it out before anyone else can see.

"How's life on the streets?" I ask.

Max and I have been friends since before I can remember, back when my father was the town dentist and my mother ran his front office. Now my parents are divorced and live next door to each other in Florida. Growing up, I'd been that sensitive kid, sensitive enough so my father walloped me pretty much every day while my mother smoked cigarettes in the next room. At least I was safe at school, where Max made it clear anyone who messed with me would have to go through him. I guess I'll always be grateful for that.

"Chloe gave Taylor Lawson a black eye this afternoon," Max says.

"Georgia told me. Is she with you? I'll come get her as soon as I'm done here."

"Ritchie, do you understand this is serious? I had to do a song and dance to keep the Lawsons from blowing it way out of proportion."

"Okay, okay," I say. "I'm leaving right now."

"I just left Cups and Cones," Max says. "Your boyfriend bought her the biggest sundae I've ever seen in my life. And Taylor's sitting right outside documenting the whole thing on her phone. It's probably already posted somewhere."

My stomach clenches. "What was Farley doing?"

"What do you think he was doing? He was eating ice cream." Max sighs. "Listen, Ritchie. You need to watch out for your kid. I caught her sneaking around the church last night.

And now she's starting fights? Take care of this. In case you forgot, I have a homicide to focus on."

I click off the call and shove a fistful of M&Ms into my mouth with no regard for color. A moment later, when I leave the garage in my 1975 gold VW, I haven't brushed the peanut butter from my breath or changed out of my coveralls.

I consider stopping downtown at the ice-cream shop but opt against a public confrontation. Instead, I head home and practice what I'll say to Farley, because I'm pissed off. Really pissed off. And my ire isn't directed toward Chloe. Farley's not the parent, and he shouldn't try to play one, and Chloe is supposed to be in trouble, and now I'll be in trouble with Georgia, because Max will tell Georgia about the sundae if only because Max can't stand Farley.

But what I'm mad about is the ice cream.

Farley calls sugar *death crystals* and bans it from the house along with dairy and gluten and soda, even diet Mountain Dew, and if he ever knew about that bag of M&Ms in my drawer it would be the only thing he'd talk about until I agreed to get rid of them and never have another M&M again in my entire life. He's controlling. Like Georgia. So I guess I have a type.

And I love ice cream.

And I don't like hypocrisy.

I pull off the road, through the fields, and up onto the Point. Max's cottage sits in the trees, with its window boxes and perennials, dwarfed by the new house where the gates glide open, and I eye one of the cameras that watch every move on and off the property. Farley probably pulls up the footage to make sure I don't eat ice cream when he's not here. I park in the driveway and run up the steps to the front door, only to hear the distinct purr of the Triumph approaching. As the car pulls along the peastone, Farley catches my eye before coming to a stop and whispering something to Chloe.

He's coaching her on what to say. He drives past my car and into the garage, and I'm hardly surprised when Chloe escapes inside through the side door.

Farley emerges from the garage. He taps the gold paint on the VW with his index finger.

"I'll move that," I say, already apologizing. That's not the way I want this to go.

Farley checks the driveway, probably for oil stains. I almost remind him I'm a mechanic. My own cars don't leak oil.

"Max called," I say. "He saw you at Cups and Cones."

"And I gave up my afternoon taking care of your problem," Farley says.

I could press further. I could turn this into a full-scale argument, and I would if Farley weren't so easy on the eyes, preppy and fit, a splash of outdoorsy freckles across the cheeks. So out of my league I spend most of my time wondering what he sees in me. Handsome and rich makes it so much easier to overlook someone's faults.

I kiss him.

Peanut butter lingers on my breath like a smoker trying to hide his last cigarette. I can tell he tastes it. He also traces the stitching on my coveralls that reads *Ritchie*. I should get those redone because here's another secret: I hate being called Ritchie.

Inside, I hurry upstairs, slip out of the coveralls, brush my teeth twice, and scrub at the motor oil built up under my nails. The party tonight will be small and with close friends. I won't have to worry about what I wear. I grab a pair of loose jeans and a long-sleeved T-shirt, still appreciating how the fabric hugs my newly trim body.

Maybe death crystals aren't so great after all.

I take a deep breath and tap on Chloe's door. She doesn't answer. I turn the knob. She's standing in her closet hiding something behind a stack of sweaters, something I'll have to come back later to find. God help me if it's condoms. We face off. She crosses to her bed and lies down beneath a poster of a polar bear, a book propped up in front of her. She doesn't bother to acknowledge me as I sit beside her and wait. Finally, she lets the book fall and says, "It wouldn't have happened if you got me a phone."

Everything comes back to the phone. I'd get Chloe a phone in a second if Georgia would give in, but they're both stubborn and for now Georgia has the upper hand.

"You know you can't punch people, right?" I ask.

"What do you think?"

"And you'll apologize to Taylor?"

"I already did. Like, five times."

"And I hear you're not going to tell us what the fight was about."

"I told you already. It was about the phone." She lifts the book and pretends to read.

"Was Uncle Max pissed off when he saw you getting ice cream?" I ask.

Chloe sighs. Loudly. "He was with that state detective. You know Uncle Max, he's like two people: the chief is all business, and Uncle Max is more goofy. He was playing the chief."

Max wears his masks, too.

I cross the room and open one of the windows. "Yell," I say. "Loud enough that your voice carries all the way to Uncle Max's cottage. Say things like *Shut up* and *You're not the boss of me*. Sound really angry."

"No one says *You're not the boss of me*."

"What would you say instead?"

Chloe puts the book aside, her brow creased in thought. "Can I ask you something first?" she says, softly.

"Anything."

"Will you and Mom get back together?"

The question hits me right in the chest. Too often, I forget

Chloe's in the eighth grade, and even though she seems wise beyond her years, she's a child, one I need to protect at any cost. Really, she's my whole life, which I should have remembered earlier when Georgia called.

I run my fingers through Chloe's pink hair. "That's not going to happen," I say.

I swear Chloe ages the tiniest bit right before my very eyes.

"I was just checking," she says. "I like to know what to expect."

She steps to the window and shouts, "Shut the fuck up!" then slaps her palm over her mouth.

"Perfect," I say, before shouting. "Don't talk to me like that, young lady."

"I didn't ask to be born. And I'm tired of you."

"My house, my rules!"

Chloe lowers her voice. "It's *his* house," she says.

Not completely, not anymore, but no one knows that yet, not even Chloe. That's another one of my secrets, but I'll get to that later.

I promise.

CHAPTER 26
Richard

"Dad, do I have to go to the party?" Chloe asks me after we finish pretending to fight. She sits on the side of her bed. "I thought I was grounded."

I ruffle her hair. I'm the only one she still allows to do that, which is a win in my book. "You are grounded," I say. "That's why you have to spend the night with a bunch of boring old people instead of eating pizza by yourself. Besides, Noah will be there. It'll be more fun than you deserve."

And I'll run interference with Georgia for her.

In my own room, I step into the marble-lined shower, turning on the massage jets. This shower, the bathroom, everything in the house is top-of-the-line, way fancier than I knew existed, let alone imagined having. I'm not used to how much nicer Farley's shampoo makes my hair feel and smell. We're running late, which might send him over the edge, but I haven't forgiven him for the ice cream yet and I plan to eat and drink anything that comes my way at the party. I take a few extra minutes to spite him.

Out in the bedroom, a light green shirt and a pair of white pants lie folded on the bed under a note with my name,

RICHARD, spelled out in neat script. This is the outfit Farley wants me to swap out for the jeans and sweatshirt I'd already chosen. He's even attached a safety pin to one of the button-holes to show me how to wear the shirt. I refold the clothing I'd chosen and squeeze into this new outfit. I fasten the shirt to where Farley indicated. It opens nearly to my belly button, and I'm grateful I got my chest waxed yesterday because Far-ley likes smooth skin.

I choose my battles. And besides, I do look kind of cute.

Out on the patio, Farley waits. I snap a photo with the bay in the background to post online.

"I think Chloe has a boyfriend," Farley says. "Some kid named Jack."

A boyfriend. Great. That's the last thing I need. When Chloe emerges from the house, I picture her writing *Jack* on a notepad and scratching it out. I also remember her hiding a stash in her closet earlier when I walked into her room. "I for-got something," I say. "I'll meet you at the boat."

I dash into the house and disarm the alarm system. Up-stairs, in Chloe's room, I shove aside a pile of sweaters expect-ing the worst: drugs, condoms, cigarettes. Instead, the blue cellophane of a package of Chips Ahoy greets me. And it's open. I shove three of the cookies into my mouth before heading out to the boat.

"Nice shirt," Damian says when we arrive at the party.

He tweaks my nipple, and I shove him, but I don't mind, even as I catch Alice shooting me a glare. She hates the whole bromance thing. But here's another secret: I wouldn't mind if Damian tackled me to the ground—or went even further—because he's kind of hot. Instead, he grabs a Coors Light from the cooler as I fasten a button on my shirt. Georgia emerges from the house carrying a tray. She wears one of the endless scarves that fill her dresser at home. Her curly hair is mussed, her expression strained, and a pang of guilt hits me. I should have been a better partner to her this afternoon. Max follows and raises a hand in greeting. "Surprise guest," Damian says, softly.

"Try not to get into it with him," I say.

I stick with Damian by the smoker. Farley pours himself a Cosmo, which, by the way, is loaded with *death crystals*.

I finish my beer and grab another.

"Dude," Damian says.

He's ten years older than the rest of us and is one of the few people who doesn't treat me like a happy idiot. Maybe that's why I'm attracted to him. Since we haven't been friends forever, Damian only knows *this* me, not the one who was pretending to be someone else, so I trust him in a way I haven't ever trusted anyone—not my parents, not Georgia or Farley, not even Max.

Damian was the first person I confessed to about Farley. We'd stopped for coffee on a bike ride, and I hadn't planned to tell him anything, but I wound up sobbing enough that snot streamed onto the sidewalk along with all that pent-up guilt. I mean, it's not like Farley was the first man I ever slept with—I am thirty-nine years old *and* was in the high-school drama club—but this is a small town, and we all have the roles we play, the ones people get uncomfortable with if you deviate from them. And no matter how many rainbow flags come out in June, no matter how many Aunt Dianes bring their "friend" Kathy to backyard barbecues, some of the people I see every day cling to values they tuck away unless they know they're in a safe enough place to share them. Certainly my parents do. I worried about losing friends and my business. I worried about losing Chloe. So don't think for one second that coming out to Damian wasn't a big step.

"Bro," Damian had said. "The heart wants what the heart wants."

And maybe it's because Damian's made every mistake in the book—he's broke, he slept with a student, my guess is he doesn't even have a 401(k) or an IRA, let alone an offshore account—he doesn't judge. Even when I crack open a third beer.

"Yo!" he says, turning the brisket in the smoker. "Look at that meat."

"Dude," I say, slapping his palm.

He nearly shoves me off the patio, then relents. "You're in good shape now," he says, a palm to my chest, his fingers brushing my skin.

I'm in better shape than I've ever been in. And it's nice when people notice. Even my straight married friends.

We stand quietly, the way men do. Out on the lawn in the fading light, Chloe chases Noah with a croquet mallet, her face set somewhere halfway between rage and glee. Across the patio, Georgia hovers beside Max, too distracted by him to be concerned with discipline. Georgia took the news about Farley in stride, and now she seems like she's getting closer with Max. But here's one more secret: seeing them together makes me jealous.

Listen, if I know one thing, it's that I have no right to interfere in Georgia's happiness. She's been supportive and understanding and nothing but kind in these last months. I knew from the start we shouldn't be married, but all those years ago when she moved to town to take over the parish and started dating Max, somehow I turned it into a competition, one I was determined to win at any cost.

Growing up, Max had been better at everything than I was. And I mean everything. He played soccer and made the National Honor Society and was elected class president. In my junior year, the drama club put on a production of *Oliver!* and I bought tapes to practice my Cockney accent and auditioned by singing "You've Got to Pick a Pocket or Two." Max tagged along to the audition, did one reading on a lark, and got cast as Fagin, the lead.

So I made winning Georgia into a game where no one knew the rules but me. On our first date, I took her for a drive in a '55 Chevy Bel Air. We made it all the way to Newport, where we stopped at the beach and lay in the sand, talking till the sun went down. A few days later, she told Max they wanted different things. It was the one time ever I came out on top, even though I didn't want the prize.

Now, as I watch the two of them together, I'm not sure I want Max to win, even after all these years. That makes me a selfish jerk. But only if I say it aloud.

The kids flee toward the dock as the sun sets behind us. Georgia whacks a blue croquet ball across the grass and waves us onto the lawn.

I grab another beer. "I'll help you win if you help me," I say to Damian.

"Whatever you need, bro."

"Knock me out of this game as soon as possible."

Playing games with Georgia is the worst.

On the croquet field, Damien sasses the rest of us as he takes the lead. He also keeps his promise and takes me out of the match as soon as his ball turns poison. I head off to find the kids before Georgia remembers Chloe's supposed to be grounded, only to have Alice follow.

"Damian knocked me out of the game, too," she says. "On my birthday!"

"I can get the kids," I say. "Go be with your guests."

Instead, she takes my arm in hers, walking uncomfortably close as her ponytail whacks the side of my face, and we make our way to the bluff. Below, the kids sit at the end of the dock, their feet in the water, a phone lit between them. It's dark now, and the full moon shines over the bay. Alice asks about the incident between Chloe and Taylor Lawson at school, which is the last thing I want to think about. "We've put her through a lot these last months," I say. "I'm hoping this latest event might fade away. Is Noah friends with a boy named Jack?"

"At least one," Alice says.

"Chloe might have a boyfriend," I say. "I worry, you know."

What if Jack is charming, like Farley, or a cad, like Damian? What if he's a senior in high school? Or worse.

Alice squeezes my arm. "I could talk to her if you want. Girls like to talk to other women."

I turn toward the house, where Georgia's voice echoes across the lawn. "You mean when they're not their own mothers," I say.

Alice follows my gaze. "Max and Georgia?" she says.

"Is that what you and Farley were whispering about?" I ask.

"Maybe," Alice says. "But aren't you and Max old friends? Ask him yourself. He'll tell you what's going on."

I nod toward the kids and tell her about growing up with Max, about sitting side by side just like our own children are doing now. "I had a crush on him," I admit, before catching myself.

"Everyone has a crush on Max Barbosa," Alice says.

True, but saying certain things out loud gives them power, and I'd rather have kept this secret to myself. I call to the kids. Alice puts a hand to my arm.

"You and Damian are close," she begins. "You'd tell me if he was in trouble, wouldn't you?"

I wouldn't. "Of course," I say.

"Is he?"

Not that he's mentioned to me. "Only from Georgia's wrath. She doesn't like to lose." I change the topic. "Do you like my shirt?"

Alice steps away and looks me over. "Sexy," she says. "But you'll be cold tonight."

"Georgia used to choose everything I wore."

Now Farley plays that role. I suddenly feel completely exposed in these clothes and fasten another button. "Max," I add. "Growing up, I was like his shadow. Wherever he went, I followed. Maybe Max and Georgia can focus on each other now, and I can spend some time figuring out who I am."

The kids run up the stairs and across the lawn. As we follow, Alice says, "We should chat again soon. It's good to have a friend."

Back at the farmhouse, she runs inside. Max follows her as I pop open another beer. That's my fifth, but who's counting?

Farley, apparently, who pats my belly, and says, "Watch the carbs."

"Alice shouldn't be working so hard on her birthday," Georgia says, heading inside, too.

A moment later, I find myself dragged into the kitchen where Georgia fills bowls and platters from enormous aluminum tubs labeled with the Firefly logo. After fifteen years of marriage, I can read Georgia's every emotion. She's pissed off about something.

"The birthday girl wants us to believe she cooked this herself," she says, "so don't blow it."

At least we won't have to spend the evening pushing Alice's terrible food around our plates.

"Do you like ambrosia?" Georgia asks. "Max made it." She shoves a spoonful of it into her mouth. "*Mmm. Yum.* Only your finest marshmallows and mandarin oranges."

"I'll take these outside?" I ask.

"Do whatever you want."

Georgia lifts an aluminum tub filled with ratatouille from the counter. Almost as if in slow motion, it starts to fall. I lunge and send it spinning across the floor where the tomatoey stew lands in a gloppy mess.

We both freeze for a moment. Then we fly into action, working in tandem like we had so many times as a couple as we

192 / EDWIN HILL

scoop the ratatouille back into the tub and clean the mess as best we can. Georgia collapses against one of the counters and slides to the floor, her legs splayed in front of her. "You better not say one word."

I slide down beside her. She takes my hand. "We should get out there," she says.

"Or we could stay for another minute."

She rests her head on my shoulder. "I'm lonely," she says.

With everything that's happened between us, I forget I loved Georgia for a long time. I still love her in my own way. I kiss her forehead. "I'm sorry," I say.

"I know," she says. "I've had the worst week of my life. And the cherry on top was today. I could have used a co-parent this afternoon instead of having to rely on your boyfriend to take care of our daughter. And now, tonight. . . . Max can be such a prick."

If I were a good person, I'd own up to flubbing things with Chloe this afternoon. I'd also ask what Max has done and whether there was anything I could do to help. But I guess I'm not a good person. "You're upset about the ratatouille?" I ask.

She pulls herself up and offers me a hand. "Exactly," she says. "It's all about the ratatouille."

CHAPTER 27
Richard

Outside on the patio, Georgia and I serve dinner as Alice talks about living in Maine. "When Damian was shooting *Acadian Autumn*," Alice says, "we would set the cameras up in this couple's house and leave. Their names were Bernard and Micheline. And then, later, Damian would have to go through ten hours of footage that was either an empty room or Bernard and Micheline watching TV, because guess what? They had other rooms in the house, and who wants to have their every move videotaped? If they wanted to talk, they left the room with the camera. The documentary was supposed to be about the French diaspora, and we couldn't get them to say *croissant* on camera."

It feels as though Alice is belittling Damian's documentary, even as she pretends to be supportive of his work. People underestimate Damian, just like they underestimate me, and maybe that's one of the reasons I want to come to his defense. Instead, I say, "Dinner is delicious. You must have been in the kitchen all day."

"All week," Alice says.

"Ritchie," Georgia says to me, her eyes twinkle in the light.

"There's a *je ne sais quoi* about the ratatouille. Something extra."

Like dirt from the kitchen floor. Or dog hair.

"I learned how to make it in Maine," Alice says. "One benefit to *Acadian Autumn*."

"*Acadian Autumn* was on its way to being a snooze fest," Damian says. "The French government hired me to come up with a story about this community, to show how French is spoken outside of France. I just kept filming and hoping something exciting might happen. I almost gave up."

"You think it's cold here?" Alice says. "Try living just south of the Canadian border where the only place to go is the Walmart. We froze our asses off."

"Then that priest died," Damian says. "And it was like the shit hit the fan. He'd written down everything he'd done in these journals, and suddenly people talked and had stories to tell. Years of awful abuse. From there, the documentary made itself."

"Damian," Alice says. "Dinner conversation. Shouldn't we talk about the Red Sox? Aren't the playoffs coming up?"

Beside me, Farley says, "How did the priest die?"

"He drowned in a bathtub," Damian says. "Story was that he took a sedative and fell asleep, though God only knows what really happened. The police didn't try all that hard, if you ask me."

"And now there's another murder here," Farley says. "Seems like this kind of thing follows you."

I touch his knee. He shouldn't even hint at something like that, not with Max sitting right across from me. "At least Noah learned French," I say.

"*Bonjour. Salut. Du vin?*" Alice uncaps the wine bottle, but it's empty. "One case down. What's a party without a little debauchery?"

Beside me, Farley pushes away from the table. "I'll grab

some reinforcements," he says, stumbling inside without waiting for a response.

Farley's barely said a word during dinner, and now he's so drunk he can't walk straight. "I'll check on him in a minute," I say.

Damian swirls his wine, turning his attention to Georgia. "How many sermons do you write a year? Thirty? Forty? Some have to be better than others, right? If you mess one up, you move on."

Georgia stabs at a slice of brisket. "Mostly."

"What did you talk about last Sunday?"

"Let's not do this," Georgia says.

"Come on. Tell me."

"My sermons are all recorded and posted online. Go listen to it for yourself."

Georgia's pissed off at something, and if Damian doesn't watch out, she'll direct her anger at him.

"This whole town is grieving," Damian says. "It's like the priest in Maine, an incident like that one infects everyone, even those who weren't impacted directly. How did you address the murder?"

Georgia drops her fork with a clatter. "My sermon last week was called *Informed by Death*. It was about appreciating those around you while you're living." She shoots a glare at Max. "No one told me someone had *actually* died a horrible death not twelve hours earlier. Let's just say it wasn't a good look. I came off a little unaware."

"Cops can't talk about open investigations," Max says. "Even when the minister has a sermon to deliver. Help me out here. Ritchie? Alice? Anyone? Don't we all know this from watching TV?"

Georgia leans forward and speaks to Max as though they're the only two at the table. "You could have whispered it in my ear. A little hint would have helped. I'm an adult. And we've known each other long enough we don't need to keep secrets from each other."

Max rests his head against the trellis. "You're right. I should have told you sooner," though it feels as if they're talking about something else.

"Fine." Georgia finishes off the last of her wine. "Farley better get out here with the reinforcements soon. I'm parched. And I have to make up for that blunder this week—which is probably why I haven't managed to write a word for Sunday's sermon and it's already Friday night." She lifts her glass. "Tomorrow's hangover won't help, either."

Damian sits up. "I'll come on Sunday!"

From the other end of the table, Alice shakes her head, but Damian continues, "I'll record the sermon. We'll capture the whole thing on tape!"

"Not in a million years," Georgia says. "People will be upset. We can't have a film crew there."

"How about this?" Damian says. "I can sit in the loft with the choir and use a handheld camera. You won't know I'm there. We'll just need everyone to sign a release on their way out so I can use the footage."

"That's a definite no," Georgia says.

"She doesn't want you there," I say, but I say it so softly I'm not sure anyone hears me. And honestly, I don't want Damian to think I'm not on his side, even if he is pushing this one too hard.

Damian strokes his bearded jaw. "How about I only record you? A really tight shot with no one else in the frame." He stands and paces across the patio. "I can see it right now, and I know you'll be incredible. The sermon could be a centerpiece in this project I'm working on. Jesus, this is awesome!" He catches himself. "Sorry. I don't mean to be blasphemous."

"Then don't be," Georgia says, though she's hardly above taking the Lord's name in vain.

"Damian!" Max says. "Read the room. No means no. Give it up."

This is usually where I jump in to play the happy idiot, injecting something dumb into the conversation to defuse the tension. It's a skill that comes from growing up with two alcoholics bent on destroying each other. "How about charades?" I ask.

"Shut up," Georgia says.

"I could use some of that wine your boyfriend went to get," Damian says.

"I should check on him," I say, but Alice folds her napkin and tosses it on the table. "I'll go."

"Sorry to be an asshole," Damian says, after she leaves. "I get excited about things."

Georgia holds her fork over Farley's plate. "Is he going to eat any of this?"

"I doubt it," I say.

"Waste not, want not." She stabs at another slice of brisket. "Nice job on the meat," she says to Damian. "We dropped the ratatouille all over the floor when we were getting ready. Sorry."

Damian laughs.

"Thanks a lot!" Max says. "I had thirds."

"Well, don't tell Alice, Mr. Ambrosia."

Max shrugs. "I promised potato salad but didn't go to the market."

Georgia rests her head against his shoulder. "You don't have potatoes in the house, but you have marshmallows and mandarin oranges. Someone needs to do your shopping for you."

"What is your sermon about this week?" I ask her.

Georgia rolls her eyes. "Ritchie, I told you I don't want to talk about it. It's stressing me out."

Whenever Georgia used to struggle with a sermon, I'd

spend the week nudging her along, asking questions that helped her think through whatever ideas she wrestled. Now I say, "I mean, the town's mourning, but Simon's mourning the most, though we all know he probably killed his wife. It's like a . . ."

It's a *conflict*, by the way. I do know the word. But I let Georgia complete my thought.

"It's a *conflict*," she says. "That's the challenge. And, also, there can't be one single moment of levity. There's nothing to laugh at. Not right now. The theme is grief. It was the only thing I could think of."

Damian drinks down the last of his wine. "I *will* come on Sunday, if you don't mind."

"No cameras," Georgia says. "Not a single one. And I'm not signing a release."

Damian takes a deep breath. He stands and walks out of the circle of light and down toward the water.

Georgia watches him leave. "Grief works in strange ways," she says. "It's been walking into my office all week. Maybe that's why I don't have my sermon finished."

" 'Grief has been walking into my office all week,' " I say. "That's a pretty good first line. Jot it down."

Georgia fumbles in her bag for a pen, while I take off after Damian.

I find him sitting at the end of the dock, where the kids were earlier. His feet dangle in the darkened water. He turns at the sound of my footsteps and wipes at his eyes with a fist. "You caught me. Crying like a baby."

I don't say anything, not at first. I sit beside him and pull my shoes off. The water's warm from the long summer. Beside me, Damian sniffles and fights to get the tears to stop till, finally, he punches his fist into one of the pilings. "I messed up," he says. "Big time. Laurel and I . . . we had an affair."

I can hardly judge. I had my own affair this year, and Damian was the one person I confided in.

"I was with her on Saturday, the night she was killed," he continues. "When I left, she was alive. And happy. We were both happy. And now I need to figure out what to do."

"How long had it been going on?" I ask.

"A few months."

Damian slouches forward. For a moment, I wonder if he might launch off the dock into the water. "It was different this time," he says. "Serious."

I remember Alice's question from earlier this evening when she asked if Damian was in trouble. At the time, I hadn't quite understood what she meant, but now it's clear. "Alice knows about the affair. She's worried."

Damian exhales.

"If Laurel was having an affair," I say, "that gives her husband even more of a motive."

"It also gives me a motive," Damian says. "Maybe she tried to break things off, and I got angry."

I don't believe that. Not for a second. "If you were there on Saturday," I say, "you must have left fingerprints."

"I left more than fingerprints. I'm surprised the cops haven't hauled me into the station by now. I've been waiting for it to happen all week."

"Tell them," I say, "before they come to you."

Damian turns to me, his face lit up by the moon. "You want me to confess? To Max?"

"He's a good cop. He'll listen."

"If he's a good cop," Damian says, "then he'll treat me like a suspect. I've been acting like one. Whatever I decide, it won't happen till morning. For now, keep this to yourself. And I should go play the happy husband."

Back at the patio, Max and Georgia sit quietly. Damian seems to turn a switch, hiding the grief he showed on the dock and returning to the role of host. He looks from Georgia to Max, and then to me, and says, "How did the three of you meet, anyway? And don't tell me there wasn't a love triangle. Who asked whom out first?"

I don't want to listen to this story again. Not tonight. Not ever. I try to catch Georgia's eye, but she ignores me. "It was the both of them," she says. "I'd barely been in town for a week, and they were showing up at services, coming to the parsonage. This one," she says, nodding toward Max, "invites me to the Point and takes me out on the boat."

Beside me, Farley returns from the house. He pulls the cork from the wine we've all been waiting for and fills everyone's glasses. "Beautiful night," he says.

Alice follows a moment later, hovering at Damian's shoulder.

"And this one," Georgia says, waving toward me, "takes me for a drive in an Edsel. An Edsel! I should have known."

It wasn't an Edsel. It was a Bel Air—a pristine, white Bel Air—but Georgia's told this story so many times she no longer knows what's true and what's not. She smiles at me. "Maybe I chose wrong, but you certainly knew how to flirt."

I don't think of our marriage as something anyone got wrong. We loved each other. We have Chloe. Isn't that enough? Alice lays something next to Damian and returns to her seat.

Beside me, Farley says, "You are a good flirt."

"And you've had a lot to drink," I say.

Farley holds my hand. "An Edsel has nothing on a Triumph! You should have seen Richard the day he drew up the contract for that car."

I kick him under the table to get him to stop, but his grip on my hand tightens. Farley bought the Triumph months before I left Georgia. "He flirted over the numbers," Farley continues, "and he probably got me to pay an extra ten grand. Then we drove that thing all the way to Newport. Best drive of my life."

The door to the house opens, and the kids join us with a platter of cupcakes. It's not till we've begun to sing "Happy Birthday" that I dare look at my wife. She's had at least a bottle of wine, if not more, but one glance at her tells me she heard every word Farley said. She stares at the table, her face pale. I wonder how much of what Georgia chose not to see during our marriage has become reality with Farley's slip of the tongue.

We finish singing, and Alice blows out the candles.

"What did you wish for?" Max asks.

"Nothing I'll share," Alice says.

Georgia reaches across the table and touches my hand the way she used to when we loved each other. She should be so angry at me right now, but it's as though she's crying out for help.

CHAPTER 28
Richard

As the party breaks up, Chloe tugs at my sleeve. "Dad," she says. "Can I stay here at the farmhouse tonight?"

"You're grounded," I remind her, though it's not as if either Georgia or I have enforced that tonight.

"Please," she says.

Her fingers dig into my arm, and I almost give in. Right now, I'm pissed off at Farley, and it might be better if Chloe was away from the house for the evening. Besides, it's hard for me to say no to her, but I give in to my parental duties. "Sorry," I say.

"Fine. I'm leaving." Chloe skulks off.

Georgia slides from behind the table. At the edge of the patio, she does a little dance. "I'm not gonna fall. I'm not gonna fall," she says, and then plunges off the edge. I dash to where she lies in a shrub. She rolls onto the ground, her glasses askew, laughing even as blood trickles from her forehead. "Don't look so concerned," she says to me, turning onto her hands and knees.

"Are you okay?" I ask, touching her arm.

She shakes me off as Farley joins us. "Let's get out of here," he says.

He snakes an arm around my waist, standing too close, his lips on my cheek, drunkenly affectionate. I edge away from him. If Georgia wants to be pissed off at me—which I deserve—I'll pay it forward by being pissed at Farley. He had no right to reveal how our affair had actually begun.

Max hauls Georgia to her feet. "Do you know what will get the chief of police fired?" he asks. "Letting intoxicated people leave a party and drive home. We're all walking tonight. No boats. No cars. Georgia, you can sleep it off in the bunkhouse."

"Fuck you all," Georgia says, stumbling toward the carriageway and disappearing into the trees.

Max watches her retreat. "I'm not taking the hit on this one," he says to me.

I kiss Alice on the cheek and thank her for a wonderful night. "You're a great cook. The food was amazing."

"So was the company," Alice says.

I shake Damian's hand. "We'll ride tomorrow," he says.

And we'll finish the conversation we started on the dock about his affair with Laurel.

I jog into the woods. Georgia hasn't made it very far over the uneven ground. I catch up and take her arm, but she swats at my hand.

"I'll just walk behind you, then," I say, "in case you fall."

She almost trips.

"I'm sorry," I say, which is all I seem to have said to her for the last few months. Maybe she's as sick of hearing it as I am of saying it. "I felt lost for a long time. I mean years. And things started with Farley before I knew what was happening, and I could have slowed it down, but . . ."

But I didn't want to. That's the truth.

"Slowed it down?" Georgia puts a hand to my arm to steady herself. Her words are slurred. "You live in a mansion with Prince Charming, but it feels like you attended the ball last night. You haven't slowed anything down. What do you even know about Farley?"

I don't answer. I've said I'm sorry. There's nothing I can do to change what happened.

"I'll tell you," Georgia says. "You don't know anything about Farley except that he has a pretty face and a big bank account."

We reach the end of the path. Here the trees open above us, and light from the full moon filters through the leaves. I touch Georgia's face. Behind us, I hear Max and Farley on the path, and I wonder if Georgia's waiting for my permission to move on. She should be happy, too, even if it is with Max. "You know you can tell me anything, right? Just like I can tell you anything."

Max and Farley emerge from the trees.

"Your name's Ritchie," Georgia says. "Don't lose yourself in becoming Richard."

Max clamps an arm through hers. "And that's a wrap," he says. "Have a good night."

I watch him lead her toward the cottage. I don't have a right to be jealous, but I am.

Farley and I walk in silence up his driveway, the peastone crunching beneath our feet. Inside the foyer, I duck away as he tries to plant a sloppy kiss on my lips. "Suit yourself," he says, dropping his keys on the front table and heading to the great room.

I head upstairs. Chloe's bedroom door is closed. Even Chloe's angry at me.

I get in the shower to wash away the night. When I step out a few moments later, the green shirt and white pants I left piled on the bathroom floor have been moved to the hamper. Farley lies on his side of the bed, his skin smooth, his chest bare. I'm reminded now of what I saw in him all those months ago when he came into the garage. Still, he went too far tonight.

I pull on a pair of my old boxers. In bed, Farley clicks off the light and touches my chest. I'm tempted to go with it. I even kiss him before shaking my head. "I trusted you," I say.

He rolls off and sits up with his back against the bed frame. "Watch the sugar and the carbs. You don't want to get fat again," he says, while turning a page.

Georgia was right about one thing just now: I don't know Farley that well. I haven't met his parents or his friends, if he even has any. And I didn't know him the day he signed the contract for the Triumph, or that same night when we tore at each other's clothing by the water after driving to Newport, or when I undid my whole life and moved into this house. He says he grew up in the middle of nowhere and escaped as soon as he could, but I haven't a clue what existed in that nowhere or who he escaped from. What I have figured out, though, is he wants to control me, and that control only begins with what I eat and how I dress. "You're so desperate to insert yourself into my life," I say, "but this is *my* family. Not yours."

"I don't know why you're so angry," he says.

He seems so at ease that for a moment I doubt my anger. Maybe I misunderstood what he said at the party. Or maybe he had too much to drink and forgot himself. But Farley's a pro. He doesn't disclose secrets without a purpose. "Flirting over the contract?" I say. "Did you think Georgia wouldn't pick up on that? No matter what she already knew, she was happy to believe we got together *after* I moved out of the parsonage, but you gave her all the data she needed to figure out what happened. Georgia knows you bought that car long before she and I split up. Now she knows I lied. And don't think for a second she won't hold it over my head next time I have to negotiate something with her."

"Maybe it's good to have the truth out in the open," Farley says.

I don't want to have this conversation tonight. I'm not sure what I want anymore, and I can tell I'm on the verge of doing something I'll regret. Instead, I turn off my light and roll away from him. Off in the distance, thunder rumbles.

I lie in the dark, listening to myself breathe as the thunderstorm sweeps in over the bay. Eventually, Farley slips out of bed, changes, and leaves the room. A few moments later, the front door opens and closes. I move over to the bedroom window and peek through the drapes. Outside, a lightning bolt strikes. For an instant, I see Farley slinking around Max's cottage and into the trees toward Moulton Farm.

I get back in bed, but there's no way I'll sleep, not now. An hour later, I put on a robe. On the landing, I peer out over Farley's dream house, with its open plan and fine finishes. Rain lashes at the floor-to-ceiling windows. I search for my phone but can't find it and try to remember if I brought it home from the party. I check upstairs in the hamper. It's not there either. In the great room, I take the orange bag of peanut butter M&Ms from where I've hidden it in a vase. I count out five and eat the brown one last. I open the door and squint into the storm.

Remember the secret I promised to share? This isn't the first time Farley's snuck out of the house at night. For a while, I imagined where he went and what he got into: drugs, sex. Maybe he joined Simon Thibodeau at the casinos. The truth is, I don't know where he goes or what he does, but I'm almost certain it's not something good. I lied and told him I'd followed him one night when he left. It was a test to see how he'd react.

"What did you see?" he'd asked me.

"Enough," I said.

Then he put my name on the deed to the house. And he changed his will. Now I'm rich, too.

See, I'm not so stupid after all.

CHAPTER 29
Richard

Outside, the sky has begun to turn gray, and the storm has ended. I've made it through the entire bag of M&Ms, not that eating them has made Farley return or helped me find my phone. I check all the places I've already searched, including the clothes I left on top of the hamper. I pull the bed apart to see if the phone slipped in among the sheets. I peer out the window through the blinds, hoping Farley might return through the woods.

Across the hall, I stand at Chloe's door. She knows the passcode to my phone. She might have taken it upstairs and fallen asleep with it beside her. I tap gently, but she doesn't answer. I open the door a few inches. A faint glow filters in through the blinds.

Her bed is empty.

I step back into the hall and close the door with a gentle click. *Richard*, I tell myself. *Don't panic.* And I don't panic. Not at first. I check the media room and Farley's office. I wonder if maybe Chloe slipped next door to stay with Georgia. I remember being her age and sneaking out of the bunkhouse with Max. We didn't tell his father where we were going, either. I could check the security footage to see when she left.

If I had my phone.

But this is the kind of thing kids do: they break the rules. Chloe and Noah probably had something planned, some kind of trouble they wanted to get into. That's why she'd asked to stay over at Moulton Farm last night. That's why she snuck out in the middle of a thunderstorm. Or did she leave to meet the mysterious Jack, her possible boyfriend? Is Noah in on this plan? Is that what they whispered about down on the dock this evening? Could Jack be an older boy, a man even? Has he been grooming Chloe now for months, preparing for this very evening?

See, I get where I'm supposed to. Eventually. This time, judging by the pit forming in my stomach, I might be too late. Oh God, my daughter could be in deep, deep trouble, and I've totally messed everything up. I get dressed. Max will know what to do. I'll tell him everything. About the house. About Farley's late-night jaunts. I'll even tell him about the cash hidden at the garage if I have to.

A fist pounds on the front door.

The world seems to slow as I dash down the stairs, the whole time clinging to the hope that I'll find Chloe waiting on the stoop, drenched from head to foot, her house keys missing, even though we don't use keys. The locks on this house open with a six-digit code.

I yank open the door.

A man and a woman wait, detective badges out. My worst fear. I recognize the man from the Thibodeau case. The woman must be his partner. "Detective London," the man says. "This is Detective Parke. Can we come in for a moment?"

I try to say something, but no words form. Detective London steps past me and into the foyer. When he speaks, I don't hear what he says. The other detective stops him. "Mr. Macomber?" she asks. "We're so sorry. Can you tell us the last time you saw Dr. Drake?"

Nothing makes sense to me. Behind them, the door is open onto the driveway. In the dawning light, Georgia hurries toward us, her feet slipping on the stones, and suddenly she's beside me, holding my arm, her glasses fogged over from the damp night air. "It's okay," she says. "I'm so sorry."

And with that, the words and phrases the detectives have been using start to piece together.

"Farley's not here," I say.

"Ritchie," Georgia says, putting her hands on my shoulders and facing me, "Farley's dead."

"Farley's dead," I repeat.

I hope my reaction is one of shock, not relief. And it's not that I wanted Farley dead; it's just that I want Chloe to be safe so much more. "Was there an accident?"

The detectives glance at each other. "Why don't we chat for a moment?" Detective London says.

I nod but don't move. Georgia presses on my arm and guides me through to the great room. I take in the loose T-shirt and sweats that hang off her body. She's wearing Max's clothes. Outside, the sky has turned from gray to pink. "Do you want coffee?" I ask.

"Coffee would be great," Detective London says. "I've been up all night."

"Me too," I say, which is probably a misstep judging from the way the detectives again exchange glances.

Farley had a coffeemaker from Italy installed under one of the kitchen counters that might as well roast the beans for you. "I could make you a latte," I say. "But there's no milk."

Not in this house. No sugar either. That'll change soon enough.

"Black would be great," Detective London says.

I rest my hands on the edge of the counter. I can't quite figure out what my next step should be.

"I'll make the coffee," Georgia says. "Talk to the detectives." She lowers her voice. "And be careful what you say."

The warning wakes me from my trance. The detectives stand by the windows, looking out over the water, waiting for me to take the lead. I wave to a sofa and sit across from them. Detective London reiterates their condolences. "How long have you and Dr. Drake been a couple?" he asks.

"A few months," I say. "Since my wife and I split."

In the kitchen, Georgia clears her throat. "But you met before that," she says. "Farley bought the Triumph from you."

So she had heard what Farley revealed at the party.

"That's right," I say, which elicits another exchange between the detectives. They aren't very skilled at hiding their tells. "I deal in antique cars. Farley bought one. It's in the garage here. Or it should be."

"But you didn't date each other till later," Detective London says.

I shouldn't lie to the police, but if I correct myself, it'll make me look worse. I start a mental list of lies to track. This one is easy because I've been telling it since last year, and I have the timeline down pat. "I moved out of the parsonage in the spring. We started dating soon after that, but I met him for the first time last fall when I sold him the car."

"And you live here full-time?" Detective Parke asks. She can't be more than twenty-five years old, too young to be picking apart my life. Her wavy black hair has a streak of pink. Like Chloe's hair.

Chloe.

I need to find her. "Could you excuse me?" I ask.

"Just a few more questions," Detective London says. "We're trying to piece together what might have happened."

"What did happen?" I ask.

"We're hoping you can help us with that," Detective London says. "When was the last time you saw Dr. Drake?"

"When I went to sleep," I say.

"So when you went to sleep, he was in bed with you?"

I nod. Another lie to remember.

"But didn't you tell us you've been up all night?" Detective Parke asks.

Georgia brings the first mug of coffee over and puts it on a coaster. "It's one cup at a time," she says.

Neither of the detectives touch the coffee.

"I must have woken when he left," I say. "Because he wasn't there. And I got worried."

"Did you try calling him?" Detective London asks.

"I couldn't find my phone."

"Any idea why Dr. Drake left? He's a physician, right? Was he on call?"

I shake my head. "No, you go first. What happened? You have to tell me." I'm shouting, I realize, because I need an answer, but mostly because I don't know where Chloe is. And it's probably good for the detectives to see me upset.

"Ritchie," Georgia says from the kitchen, "cool it."

Detective London picks up the mug of coffee. He blows on it and then takes a long sip. "We found Dr. Drake's body. And judging from what we saw, it's a probable homicide."

"Who killed him?" I ask.

Detective London rests his elbows on his knees and speaks slowly. Like I'm an idiot. "That's why we're here, Mr. Macomber. We're trying to find out. You'd probably know better than anyone, right?"

And I'm probably the prime suspect. "Farley leaves the house some nights," I say. "Not often. Maybe once every few weeks."

"Did you ask where he went, what he was doing, who he might be seeing?" Detective Parke asks.

"Are you married?" I ask.

She shakes her head.

"I am," Detective London says. "For about a year now."

"Do you keep things from your wife?" I pause, taking in his steely gray eyes. "Or husband?"

"Wife. And everyone has their secrets, ones we hope don't matter in the end. But everything matters with this."

The second mug of coffee finishes brewing. Georgia brings it over. "Does he need a lawyer?" she asks.

"Does he?" Detective London asks, though he turns to me for the answer.

I don't want Georgia to make me seem guilty. "I haven't done anything."

"Then being straight with us is your best course of action."

"He's not that skilled at being straight," Georgia says, "if you know what I mean. Trust me."

This time when the detectives glance at each other, it's about Georgia, not me.

"Dr. Drake leaves and heads off into the night," Detective Parke says. "You must have had a guess where your husband was headed."

"They're not married," Georgia says.

I'm still Georgia's husband, at least legally.

Detective London points to the untouched mug of coffee. "Thanks for the coffee," he says, trying to dismiss Georgia. She doesn't take the hint. She's not one to take orders from anyone, not even a state detective.

"Boyfriend, then," Detective Parke says.

"Last I saw him," I say, "he was walking toward Moulton Farm." This must be the right answer because the detectives show their tells all over again. "It was midnight," I continue. "Maybe a little after. It was before the rain started, if that's any help."

"So you did see him after you went to sleep," Detective Parke says.

"Very helpful." Detective London cuts her off and makes a

note. "I noticed the cameras on the gates. Can we access the system? That'll help us with the timeline. And if you're looking for an alibi, the footage will help. We can go back a few nights, too. See if we can figure out what other times Dr. Drake left. Any chance he knew Simon and Laurel Thibodeau?"

I take a moment to answer. I haven't given Laurel Thibodeau's murder a single thought tonight, but the detectives must believe the deaths are connected. Why wouldn't they? "I couldn't tell you."

"This is a small town," Georgia says. "Most people know each other. You and Farley went to Firefly, didn't you? He must have met the Thibodeaus there."

I nod.

Detective London stands and crosses to the windows. "Tell me about your relationship with Dr. Drake? Positive? Caring?"

Now I can feel Georgia at my shoulder. The last thing in the world I want to do is to talk about my relationship with Farley in front of her. "It was new," I say, "in all sorts of ways."

Detective London picks up a photo of Farley. It was taken on a beach before we met. He has his shirt off and his sandy-colored hair is tousled from the wind, and I used to wonder who'd stood behind the camera. "Good-looking guy. Successful, too. Must be nice living in this house."

I glance toward Georgia.

"Would you give us a moment, Reverend?" Detective London says.

"I'll check on Chloe," Georgia says. "We'll need to tell her what happened, anyway."

"No," I say, quickly.

Quickly enough for Detective London to slide his hands into his pockets and stroll toward us. "I met Chloe yesterday," he says. "She was having ice cream with Dr. Drake. They seemed close. I'm sure she'll be upset. Chief Barbosa told me she was staying here tonight. She *is* here, right?"

"Where else would she be?" I ask.

Detective Parke stands. I swear, her hand is poised over her holster. "Go get your daughter," she says to Georgia.

"Why would you need to talk to Chloe?" I ask.

"Where is she, Mr. Macomber?"

"Asleep."

"Get her up. It's not that early anymore."

"I'll take care of it," Georgia says.

I shove past her and run, even as I hear Detective Parke shouting my name, and the pounding of footsteps following me up the stairs and down the hallway. I barge through Chloe's door.

She's in bed, stretching. "Can you knock already?" she asks.

CHAPTER 30
Richard

I cross Chloe's bedroom floor in three giant strides and pull my daughter to me right as the detectives appear at the door.

Chloe twists out of my grasp. "What are *they* doing here?"

Detective Parke has her hand over her holster. She stops, frozen in place. Even Detective London has the decency to seem chagrined. He says, "Sorry. We'll give you a minute."

I cling to Chloe as the detectives leave. Georgia joins us on the bed. In a small way, this feels right, the three of us together again. We can be a family, even if we don't look the way we used to.

"Dad," Chloe says, "what's wrong with you? And why are those detectives here?" She gives Georgia the once-over. "And what are you doing here?"

Georgia takes Chloe's hand.

"What?" Chloe says. "You look like someone died."

She glances from my face to Georgia's, and then gasps as if she already knows what happened. Georgia takes a deep breath and starts to speak, and I'm happy to let her take the lead on this one, especially after Chloe starts to sob. Georgia delivers bad news practically every day of her life. What's one more time?

I try to picture the room earlier when I thought Chloe's bed had been empty. Maybe I missed her in some way. The room had been dark. Maybe Chloe had disappeared beneath the pile of stuffed animals, and I spent the last hour in a panic for no reason.

Well, no reason except that Farley's dead.

Beside me, Chloe's sobs have begun to subside. She rests her head against her mother's chest, wiping at her nose with the back of a fist. "Ritchie," Georgia says to me. "We should probably head over to the parsonage. And my car's at the farmhouse."

"I can take you over there," I say.

"Let's grab your school things," Georgia says, moving around the room and gathering books and notepads and stuffing them into Chloe's pink backpack while Chloe watches in a daze. She leans against her mother as we make our way downstairs.

Detective Parke nods at the bag. "Mind if I take a look?"

"Do you have to do that?" Georgia asks.

"Afraid so," Detective Parke says.

Georgia hands the bag over, and the detective pulls out the contents. "Do you have any electronics? A phone?"

"Don't ask," Georgia says.

I open the door and step outside into the fresh air. Last night's humidity has been replaced by crisp hints of autumn. Down in the driveway, two cruisers have pulled through the gate, and Detective London speaks with the officers, both of whom bring their cars to my garage to be serviced. They turn to stare.

"Can you move the cruisers?" I ask. "I have to get past. My wife needs a ride home."

"Why don't you stick around?" Detective London says. "Parke, give them a ride, okay? Where's your car?" he asks Georgia.

"At Moulton Farm."

"It's part of the crime scene then," Detective London says. "So you'll have to get it later. The news trucks have shown up over there already. They're having to coordinate traffic control. Leave your keys, and I'll have someone bring it by the parsonage."

"You have to be kidding me," Georgia says, but she hands over her keys anyway and then pulls me in for a hug. It's not the kind of hug we gave each other when we were married. It's the kind she reserves for people at church who have received devastating news, big and somehow insincere at the same time. Still, I let her hold me tight.

"You're wearing Max's clothes," I mumble into her ear.

"Mine got wet," she says. "And come to the parsonage if you need to."

"I can stay here with you," Chloe says. "You shouldn't be alone."

"You go," I say to her. "We'll see each other soon enough."

As they head toward where Detective Parke waits in the driveway, Chloe says, "Imagine if I had been the one to find the body. I wouldn't have had a phone to call for help."

"You don't have your own phone?" Detective Parke asks. "How old are you anyway?"

"See?" Chloe says to Georgia.

At last, Georgia gives in. "We'll get you a phone this weekend," she says. "I promise."

They get into Detective Parke's car and pull away.

"She's a good kid," Detective London says. "Reminds me of my stepdaughter, Mavis. I bet they'd be friends."

Maybe. If circumstances were different. But right now, I can't trust a single thing the detective does or says.

"She's a rock," I say.

"It's tough being a stepparent. I've certainly made a mess of things with Mavis more than once. I saw Chloe with Farley yesterday. They seemed to get along. That must have been nice."

I wait for a question, but one doesn't come.

The detective picks up a phone from the front table. "I thought you said you couldn't find your phone."

I take the phone from him. I know I looked for it on that front table earlier. I had to have. That's where I put it anytime I get home. I click the power button. There's a text from Max telling me to come over to the cottage if I need a place to stay. I quickly check the browser history to see if Chloe's been on the phone, but there's nothing out of the ordinary. She could have erased the history, though. "I must have missed it," I say.

"Happens to me all the time," the detective says. "I search everywhere except where the damn thing is supposed to be."

I doubt that ever really happens to the detective.

"Let's pull up that surveillance footage," he says. "Is it motion activated? Sound?"

"Both," I say. Nothing but the best for Farley Drake.

I open the app for the security system and click through to the last recordings. I click again, but there's nothing there from last night. Not even a raccoon. I turn the screen to show the detective. "Someone turned off the system."

Detective London takes the phone and taps the screen. "Who has access?" he asks.

"Just Farley and me."

"What about Chloe?"

"If she did, it would be off all the time."

"Does she like to sneak out of the house, too?"

I shake my head. The detective is getting too close to the truth. "Does your daughter sneak out at night?" I ask.

"Not yet. But it's coming soon enough."

"Probably for us, too," I say. "The cameras creep Chloe out. But she doesn't have a phone, so she wouldn't be able to get to the security system anyway."

Except I couldn't find my phone earlier.

And Chloe knows my passcode.

Detective London taps the screen a few more times.

"What are you doing?" I ask.

"Checking to see if anything interesting happened here last Saturday night."

"We were at Moulton Farm," I say. "Like last night. Farley and I went over there almost every Saturday night for dinner."

"You and Dr. Drake were at the farm last Saturday with the Stones. Was the reverend there? Chloe?"

"Just the four of us. Noah, too. And Harper, the dog."

"What time did you get home?"

"Probably around ten. Check the footage."

"Did your husband sneak out that night?"

"He's not my husband."

"Boyfriend."

"Not that I remember."

Detective London gets on his phone and steps outside. When he returns, he says, "We'll need to search this house. And I can get a warrant if you want me to, but I'm telling you right now it'll be here within the hour no matter what. I have a team on their way over. You can either cooperate or not. It's up to you."

At least I polished off the M&Ms before anyone could find them. I slide my phone into my pocket.

"I'll need that, too," Detective London says, "and tell me now if there's anything you don't want me to find. It's better if I hear it from you."

"Sometimes I watch porn."

"You and everyone on the planet."

"Get the phone back to me soon," I say. "My daughter's been traumatized. I'll need to stay in touch with her and my wife." I take one step up the stairs. "I'll be next door at Max's cottage if you want to talk to me. I have to grab some clothes first."

The detective follows me upstairs, where I throw a few things into an overnight bag. In the walk-in closet, my hand brushes against one of Farley's dress shirts. It must seem like I didn't like Farley that much. We moved too fast, but relationships are complicated. Just ask Georgia. Most of my life I've been invisible, and being seen by him, by someone successful and attractive, had been more than I'd ever hoped for.

"Grief works its magic all different ways," Detective London says. "Sometime soon, you might be in the grocery store or out jogging, and all of this will hit at the same time. Watch yourself."

I turn away from the shirt. "All good," I say.

In the bathroom, I toss my toiletries on top of the clothing and glance toward the hamper where Farley put my green shirt last night, and where I searched for my phone early this morning. A swatch of bright orange pokes out.

Chloe's Burger King T-shirt.

I lay my hand on it. It's damp to the touch. Like Chloe was in the rain.

Where did you go last night, Chloe? What were you doing in that storm?

"Can I put these in the wash?" I ask.

Detective London shakes his head. "You never know, right?" He eyes the finishes in the bathroom. "I wouldn't say no to this house," he says. "What'll happen to the estate now? You're not married, so who's the next of kin? We'll have to get ahold of his will. Money's a good motive for murder."

I look in the mirror. The blood's drained from my face. I'm in big trouble.

CHAPTER 31
Richard

An hour later, I lie in Max's spare room trying to get some sleep. Through the open window, the morning sun shines bright, and I can hear the crime techs coming in and out of Farley's house.

My house.

Though no one knows that but me. And the registrar at the county office where we filed the deed. Maybe, if I'm lucky, Farley didn't get around to creating the new will, though the cops will probably find a draft of it on his computer. It's there. I stood over his shoulder while he wrote it.

Downstairs, someone pounds on Max's front door.

The detectives must be here already. They probably have their handcuffs out, and I imagine myself in the back of a cruiser, riding into town past the news trucks, cameras pointed my way.

I did nothing more than a little emotional blackmail, and there's no way to prove that anyway. Farley and I loved each other. That's what I'll tell them. We loved each other whole-heartedly and unconditionally, and I was never happier in my entire life, and I'm devastated, and Farley insisted on signing the house over to me even when I protested and told him it was too early in our relationship. The will was his idea, too. He wanted to be sure I was protected in case something happened to him.

And the cops can charge me with whatever they want. But they can't come near Chloe, no matter where she disappeared to last night. Or what she did.

The pounding continues.

I make my way down the narrow stairs. At the front door, I stand for a moment with my hand on the knob. "I loved Farley," I mumble under my breath.

"I can hear you, Richard," a voice calls. "Let's go!"

I yank the door open and find Damian on the stoop wearing a black cycling jersey and matching shorts. "How you holding up, bro?" he asks.

I practice my lines. "I'm devastated."

He pulls me into a hug, his beard bristling against my cheek. "I get it, man," he says. "We're here for you. The whole clan."

For the first time since I found Chloe's empty bed, the numbness begins to wear off. "Careful," I say, extracting myself from the embrace. "You'll get the rumor mill started."

"Who gives a shit?" Damian says. "And let's get out of here. I brought over one of my bikes for you to ride."

"I should stay here. The cops want to talk to me again."

"Join the club," Damian says. "And they can find you when the time comes. Get changed and let's ride."

This won't look good. "But—"

He tosses me a pair of pink shorts and a matching pink jersey. "I've got a target on my back," he says. "Maybe even bigger than the one on yours. Remember what I told you last night on the dock? Laurel and me? Our little affair? Those detectives aren't idiots, so this could be my last ride for a long time. Don't make me do it by myself."

I hold up the jersey. "Pink? On today of all days? I should be in black, like you."

"Don't bitch," Damian says. "It's from the Giro Race in Italy. It means you're the leader."

Fifteen minutes later, my legs burn as we pedal along the coast, riding side by side, taking turns falling back as we let cars pass in the outside lane. Sweat pours down my face, and the events of last night begin to fade away.

We leave Monreith and head inland. Ten miles out of town, at the base of a steep incline, Damian brakes. "We can go back," he says, nodding at the hill and gulping down water. "But there's a great coffee shop on the other side."

"Up and over?" I say.

"Last one there buys the coffee."

Damian takes off up the hill, his sinewy legs bearing down on the pedals as he leans into the climb. I follow, taking the hill at my own pace but keeping Damian in sight. I'm sucking air by the time I hit the crest. A hundred yards ahead, Damian cruises into the turns. Today, I have no interest in losing. I lean into the descent, not letting up on the pedals till I close the gap between us, sweeping past Damian as the road flattens and we coast into town. I skid to a stop in front of the café.

"Well played," Damian says, unclipping his shoes and congratulating me with a touch of the hand.

I'm not used to winning. At anything. And certainly not sports.

Inside the shop, a few people wait in line while the baristas steam milk and a group of friends meet at a small table. "Pumpkin spice latte," Damian says, when our turn comes.

"Are you kidding me?" I ask.

"I love me some PS," Damian says.

I order a straight coffee and wait for the order while Damian goes outside to watch the bikes. One of the baristas catches my eye. He's probably thirty, handsome. "Nice shorts," he says, handing me the coffees. "Your boyfriend's cute."

"He's not my boyfriend," I say.

"Good to hear." The barista fills a card with ten stamps. "Next coffee's on me. I work most mornings. Come again."

Am I a terrible person for enjoying the attention? Probably. But it feels good, even though I know I should be mourning. I add four sugars and plenty of cream to my coffee and feel the barista watching me the whole time. I steal a glance his way. He smiles and gets back to work.

Outside, Damian has sprawled across a bench, his helmet beside him saving my spot. We sit quietly for a moment till Damian pulls the lid from his cup and inhales. "Tomorrow's the first official day of autumn. Pumpkin spice everything until Halloween." He takes a long sip of the coffee. "I saw you in there talking to that guy. It looked like you were flirting. Watch yourself, okay? Someone else could have seen you, too. It's early, but this thing will blow up soon. You might even wind up on the news. Don't give them ammunition."

He's right, of course. Perception is everything. Sad people don't flirt or wear pink jerseys. They also don't go for bike rides. Now's not the time to be noticed for anything.

"What did the cops tell you, anyway?" Damian asks.

"They had a lot of questions I couldn't answer," I say. "They wanted to know why Farley left the house in the middle of the night."

"Did you have a guess?" Damian asks.

"I doubt it was anything good."

Damian tells me about Alice finding the body on the beach, how Farley had been hit on the back of the head, and about waking up to cruisers speeding onto the farm. "Your good friend Max Barbosa was there from the start," he says. "The state cops showed up eventually. They set up a perimeter and access avenues. Asked a million questions. Focused on scratches on my legs I got yesterday when I fell off my bike. They know I was schtupping Laurel, too. It sure doesn't help to have a second body. So I had to come clean about everything, especially that I was at her house on the night she was killed."

I sip my own coffee. Damian makes a pretty good case for his own guilt.

"Let's hope they don't waste too much time on me," Damian says, "no matter what the chief is whispering in their ears."

"What would Max have against you?" I ask.

"Don't play dumb," Damian says. "I realize the two of you go way back, but he's got the hots for Alice."

"That's not true," I say.

"Believe me," Damian says. "It's true. Alice sneaks off to that cottage all the time. She claims they play cribbage, but does she think I'm an idiot? Max would be thrilled to see me hauled off to jail so he could ride to the rescue. I mean, how well do you know him?"

I've known Max my whole life, but my version of Max defends others and wouldn't betray Georgia, no matter where his heart pulls him. My version certainly wouldn't make a move on someone else's wife.

Damian continues, "And don't forget what Max lost when he sold that property to Farley. He probably sits on that back deck and stews. Listen," he adds, "you don't know this yet but consider yourself lucky. Farley wasn't who you thought he was."

I stare at the ground. I think about how Damian confided his darkest secrets to me last night on the dock, the way he'd guarded my own secrets when I confessed to the affair with Farley.

"What's going on?" Damian asks. "You'll feel better if you get it off your chest."

I tell him about how Farley would leave at night. About the deed to the house and the will, too. And the money that Alice has been hiding for me in that offshore account.

When I finish, he cracks his knuckles and takes a last swig of his coffee. "Have you fessed up to the cops?"

"Not yet."

"Did you kill Farley?"

"No."

"Right now, one of the things each of us needs to determine is who's a friend and who's a foe. I'm hoping I can trust you."

"I just told you everything," I say.

"What about last night?"

"At the party?"

"No, I mean later." Damian takes a phone from his jersey. "Why did you want to meet? Did it have something to do with what I told you about Laurel?"

He clicks the phone's power button, and a text message appears on a cracked screen. *Meet me by the dock*. While I recognize my own phone number, I didn't send that text. But I also couldn't find my phone last night.

"It's a burner," Damian says. "And I don't have the passcode, so all I can access is the last text that came in. And the last text is from you asking someone to meet you twenty yards from where your boyfriend's body was found. Seems kind of suspicious."

I reach for my own phone, then remember I gave it to Detective London. Whether I sent this text message or not, they'll find it when they search my data. They'll link the text message to this phone.

"Listen," Damian says, "you're a pal, and I want to believe you, but none of this adds up. And it doesn't leave me with a good feeling, either. And now you tell me you're set to inherit a shit-ton of money from someone you've known for a few months. What's the deal, bro?"

"You're the one who has a burner phone," I say, my voice rising enough that a woman across the street turns to stare. I don't care who overhears me. "How would I even know that number?"

Damian gets onto his bike. "Alice found Chloe and Noah with the phone last night. Noah insists it belongs to Chloe. You can tell the cops you were texting her. Maybe they'll believe you. Maybe you can convince them you wanted to meet her on your own dock."

But Chloe doesn't have a phone.

Damian clips in one of his shoes. "It's everyone for themselves now," he says. "And if you're trying to cast blame for something you did, don't believe I won't come for you." He hands me the phone. "Alice wanted to turn this in last night, but I got her to hold off. Bring it to the cops and tell them whatever you need to tell them. But don't get my family involved. Whatever's on that phone, I don't want anything to do with it. As far as I'm concerned, I've never seen that thing in my life."

I watch him pedal away till he disappears around a corner. I'm not sure how long I sit there, but when I sip my coffee, it's grown cold. I feel someone join me on the bench. The barista holds out a paper cup. "Four sugars, right?" he says. "And cream."

I stare at the coffee.

"Are you sure the two of you aren't boyfriends?" the barista adds. "That seemed like quite a fight."

He really is cute, but I stand and hand him the coffee card he gave me earlier. "Thanks anyway, but I won't be back," I say, as I get on my bike and pedal away.

CHAPTER 32
Richard

I feel like an idiot as I steer the bike into downtown Monreith. Damian played me. He knew I trusted him. And now he knows every one of my secrets.

The streets are filling with pedestrians. I'm not giving the impression of someone in mourning in these pink shorts and jersey that make me look like a lozenge. Damian has an entire closet filled with biking gear. He probably chose these ones on purpose to be sure I'd be noticed. I imagine the whispers, but I also feel the burner in the back pocket of my jersey, the phone Damian claims belongs to Chloe. The whispers could work in my favor. Whatever the cops do, I need to be sure to keep the spotlight away from my daughter, even if the focus turns on me.

At the station, Detective Parke sits on the front steps smoking a cigarette. I glide in and twist my foot to detach the shoe but somehow get tangled and crash to the pavement right in front of her. I swear to myself as she helps me up, the cigarette dangling from the side of her mouth. She's changed into a boxy, navy-blue suit and rubber-soled shoes.

"You out for a ride?" she says.

"I needed to clear my head. It was a long night."

"How's your daughter doing?"

"Why?" I ask and regret it at once. Of course the detective's asking after Chloe. "She's with her mother at the parsonage. I'll head over there after I talk to Detective London."

"He's following up on something over by the beach," she says. "But you have me to chat with. Let's head inside."

I inhale her secondhand smoke. I'm not a smoker. Farley wouldn't have allowed it in the house, or anywhere, really. Neither would Georgia. But for the first time in my life, I can do whatever I want. "Could I have one of those?"

"Anytime," Detective Parke says, placing two cigarettes between her lips, lighting them both, and handing one to me. "Most people just glare at smokers."

I inhale and cough. Almost at once, my head feels light. Between the bike ride, the lack of sleep, and the cigarette, I'll probably tell Detective Parke anything she wants to hear.

"Sit," she says. "We can go in when we're done."

"I don't think we can smoke on municipal property," I say.

"You're a little rule follower," she says, but she moves over to a bench anyway.

After two inhales, I've had enough of the cigarette. I leave it tucked between my fingers and let it burn down to ash to avoid having to go into the station.

"I'm Iris," the detective says. "Iris Parke. We can go on first names if you like. Ritchie, right?"

"Richard," I say.

"Got it. Richard Macomber. And again, I'm sorry about everything. This must be hard."

"Devastating," I say. "Farley and I loved each other."

"I need a diagram to keep all the relationships straight, so bear with me. You're the victim's boyfriend and the reverend's ex-husband?"

"Current husband," I say. "We're not divorced yet."

Which means Georgia owns half of everything I own. Including half of Farley's house.

"And the police chief, Max Barbosa . . ."

"We're friends. We both grew up here and went to school together. I've known him my whole life."

"He's been dating your wife? The reverend?" Iris says.

Now the interrogation has begun, and I've already been played once today. "I'd ask them," I say. "I'm not sure what's going on."

"The chief's been talking about taking a job in Springfield," Iris says.

"Again, you should ask him about that."

Iris exhales a long plume of smoke. "I'll tell you one thing. Folks are losing it."

She pulls out her phone and shows me a video of an SUV crashing into a pole. "That's Mrs. Stone trying to escape the press parked on the street in front of the farm. It's been posted everywhere. My guess is this story goes national pretty soon and we'll be in task-force territory. London hates task forces. He says they're where good ideas go to die, but, I mean, there hasn't been a suspicious death in this town since . . . probably since forever."

"Sounds more than 'suspicious' to me. I thought someone hit Farley on the back of the head," I say, which, of course, the cops haven't told me yet. Damian told me, but I don't trust him to back me up. Still Iris lets my words hang in the air, like she wants me to know I betrayed myself.

"We don't know the cause of death, not officially," she finally says. "We're waiting for word from the coroner's office. Could have been an accident. Could have been something else."

"Like Farley bashed his own head in?"

"You played croquet last night?"

"We all did."

"What color mallet did you use?"

"Orange," I say. "I got knocked out early in the game."

"What about the other mallets? Did you touch them?"

"Maybe? Why, is it Farley Drake on the beach with the croquet mallet?"

I don't sound like I'm grieving. I sound defensive and
angry. The detective lets her cigarette fall to the pavement
and grinds it out with her heel. "Rumors spread before we can
get on top of anything. Brock—Detective London—he goes
berserk when false information gets out there. That kind of
thing can lead to lawsuits, especially when there's money involved."

"Who has any money?" I ask. I should stop talking. It won't
take a rookie forensic accountant long to unwind my finances.

Iris shrugs. "Your husband had plenty of money."

"Everyone keeps calling him my husband. We weren't married. Honestly, we barely knew each other." I catch myself.
"But I'm devastated."

Iris hits her forehead with her palm. "You told us you
weren't married last night. And just now, you told me you're
still married to the reverend. Sorry. Like I said, I need a flow
chart. What's it been like, anyway, living with Dr. Drake while
you were still married? Must have been tense with your ex-
wife—sorry, your wife."

My cigarette burns to the filter. I drop it to the ground and
rub my nose. My fingers smell of tobacco. "Georgia's supportive, especially under the circumstances."

"I wonder if she had much of a choice," Iris says. "She has
such a public job."

"Leave Georgia out of this. My daughter, too. My choices
have nothing to do with them."

Iris's phone vibrates from where it sits on her knee. "Just a
sec," she says, answering the phone with her last name. She lis-

tens for a moment. "He's right here," she says, glancing at me. "Yeah, he's on his bike."

"Who is that?" I ask. "Where's Detective London?"

Iris stands and walks down the street. She lights another cigarette and exhales. When she returns, her demeanor has changed. "Did you bike out on Drift Road?" she asks. "Were you with Damian Stone?"

"Are you looking for him? Did he kill Farley?"

"We should move this inside," the detective says. "Make it official."

"What is happening?"

An officer comes to the door of the station. "You all set?" he asks.

Iris waves him away. "Mr. Macomber, come inside and make a statement. We've searched your house. Now we have a search warrant to go through your garage. Do you have any secrets hidden there?"

Just an orange bag of peanut butter M&Ms.

And a drawer full of illicit cash.

"I need a lawyer," I say.

"You sure about that?"

More than I've ever been about anything in my life. I get on the bike and ride away as the detective watches me the whole time.

In fact, it feels as though every single person in town is watching me.

I pedal to the other side of town, through the cemetery, and right up to the parsonage, the house I called home for so many years. I need to be close to Chloe. I need to ask Georgia what to do. She'll know. Georgia invites the world into this house and offers healing and solace. Surely she can do that for me now.

I step through the front door and into the tiny mudroom.

Georgia's office is to the left, a sitting room is to the right, and a narrow set of stairs leads to the second-floor landing. I move through the house as though I've never left, instinctively knowing when to duck my head, where to avoid the nails that shimmy their way out of the wide floorboards. I call out Georgia's name, but she doesn't answer.

In the kitchen, a cat sits on the counter. Black, with white paws.

I'm allergic to cats, so no matter how much Chloe had begged for one, I'd had to say no. Still, I'm surprised this home could have changed so much already and that no one's bothered to tell me. The cat leaps to the floor and snakes its way through my legs. I retreat and head up the back stairs, where I tap on Chloe's bedroom door. When she doesn't answer, I ease the door open, only to see her lying on the bed, headphones on. I catch her eye and touch my ears. She pulls the headphones off and sweeps pink hair from her eyes. "When did you get a cat?" I ask.

"Like, two months ago. Her name is Tippi."

"Good name. Where's your mother?"

"I don't know. She went out."

I come into the room and sit on the side of her bed. Chloe's lying about something, and I need to get to the bottom of it. "Who's Jack?" I ask.

Chloe sniffs the air. "Have you been smoking?"

"Tell me about Jack."

"He's no one," Chloe says.

I think of stories of older men manipulating children and convincing them to do things they shouldn't. Could Jack have persuaded Chloe to kill Farley? "Did Jack get you to do something you didn't want to?"

"God, no."

"What's his last name?"

"I don't want to talk about Jack."

"Chloe, you can tell me anything," I say. "You know that, right? But you don't need to."

Chloe puts the book back up in front of her face, though her eyes aren't following the words.

"Whatever they ask," I say, "you were in bed all night."

"Dad, I didn't . . ."

I put my fingers to her lips. "You were home all night. You loved Farley like a second father. We were happy."

I lay the burner phone on the bed.

"Where did you get that?" she asks.

"It's not important, but the police will find out about this soon," I say. "What's on it? Tell me so I know what to say to them."

Chloe sits up and faces me, and in that moment, I get a glimpse of her in forty years, when our roles will have reversed, and she'll care for me. Right now, though, it's my job to protect her. At any cost.

Behind me, floorboards creak. I turn as Max appears in the doorway, his head stooped beneath the low ceiling.

"Where have you been?" he asks me.

"I went to your place," I say. "Like you said I should."

"After that, though."

"What does it look like? Damian came over. We went for a ride."

"Out by the beach?"

"We started there," I say.

"I thought so," Max says. "I just saw Damian."

"Didn't he tell you the same thing?"

Max doesn't speak for a moment, and when he does, he's speaking as my protector. "You could have talked to me," he says. "You didn't need to do any of this."

I don't dare respond. I'm not sure what he knows, or what he thinks he knows. Max taps the screen on his cell phone. A second later, the burner rings from where I'd left it on Chloe's bed.

"We recovered the text you sent to that phone last night and tried to delete." Max takes out a pair of handcuffs. "Ritchie, you're under arrest for the murder of Farley Drake. And Damian Stone."

PART V

The Daughter

CHAPTER 33
Chloe

TWO DAYS EARLIER

It's Thursday evening, and more than anything in the world, I need to see Jack.

Georgia sits at the kitchen table, her curly hair pulled into a knot at the back of her head. She stares at the blank screen on her laptop while Tippi walks over the keyboard. I slip past them both and have nearly made it onto the stoop before Georgia says, "Where are you going, Chloe?"

"I'll be back."

Georgia lifts the cat off the computer. "I was hoping Tippi might write this sermon for me. Only gibberish, though."

I wait. These days, I never know when Georgia will decide to act like a mother and demand to see my homework. "Don't be long," she says, turning back to the screen.

Outside, night has fallen and the air's heavy with late summer humidity. I wait in the darkened graveyard beside the church with my back to a lichen-coated gravestone. Maybe I should be frightened. There *is* an actual killer on the loose in this stupid town. And if this were a movie, the first place the killer would go would be this creepy graveyard. But I'm not alone. A few people walk by on Main Street. And voices from this week's choir rehearsal filter into the night. Above me the stars blanket the sky. And I have John Ricketson.

Jack—that's what I call John Ricketson—is buried here. He died in 1792 at the age of thirty-eight, which I used to think was really, really old, but now Mrs. Stone is turning forty tomorrow and Mr. Stone might as well be a hundred and still rides his bike, and I suppose thirty-eight is actually kind of young to die. I started learning about Jack and his family in sixth grade when I had to do research on something about Monreith for history class and decided to discover what I could about one of the families in the cemetery. There were some papers to go through at the church, and the librarian helped, too, but ever since I've come out here to Jack's grave and tried to imagine him and fill in the missing details of his life on my own.

I bet he had bushy sideburns and floppy hair and tiny glasses, and that he wore wool even on the hottest summer days. The part I don't imagine is the smell, which was probably worse than the boys at school, even when they douse themselves in cologne. I hope Jack didn't wear a powdered wig, though I know for a fact he drank beer from morning to night, because that's what everyone did in 1792.

The church records showed Jack was the local apothecary. I bet he spent his days mixing tinctures and salves that were supposed to ease suffering but that—let's face it—probably didn't work. They certainly didn't save him at age thirty-eight. The Ricketson family went to this church, too, though I bet they had to go every day, not just on Sunday, and they certainly didn't have a ukulele ensemble, and they burned gay people at the stake instead of waving rainbow flags. In the winter, they huddled in the pews to stay warm, and the sermons were all written to make them feel terrible about ever wanting anything, so I like to imagine the secrets Jack kept to himself. The dreams he hid, even from Hortensia, his wife, who died two months earlier than he did.

In a way, Jack is my best friend. I tell him secrets, like that I want to move to California. For Jack, the equivalent of California would have been Hartford, maybe, or Albany. I bet he wanted to join the circus, though I suppose there wasn't much circus life, not in this Puritan corner of the world. Still, he knew he wanted something bigger, something with spectacle.

Jack had other secrets, too, like what killed him. If I had to guess, I would say he died of syphilis. We learned about syphilis last year in Human Sexuality where Ms. Blake, who spent her weeks traveling from one school to another teaching units on STIs, told us the disease used to be a painful and humiliating death sentence, but it could now easily be cured with antibiotics. "As long as you catch it early. Don't let shame be your own undoing." She paused and waited for us to stop tittering at the slideshow.

"Watch it, kids," Mr. Shea, the gym teacher who co-taught the course, said from the side of the room.

Jack probably mixed one of his useless tinctures when the lesions first appeared, but that same shame Ms. Blake warned us against kept him from confessing to his wife, which is why I imagine Hortensia succumbed to the same unspoken illness. My bet is there was much more to the story than a simple dalliance on Jack's part. I can't believe for one second he would ever do anything to hurt Hortensia. My theory is Hortensia brought the disease into the house herself—a tryst with a farmer, maybe, or a whale hunter, or maybe even the minister at this very church—and she let the town gossips take the story wherever it went as long as she came out in a positive light.

Jack and Hortensia had eight children, though only one of

them, a girl named Silence, survived infancy. She was thirteen, exactly my age, when her parents died, and had probably spent the year begging for the eighteenth-century equivalent of a cell phone—a hairpin, maybe, or a thimble—something her mother could deny. Unlike her parents, Silence lived a long life, never marrying and dying at age ninety-seven, and I hope she spent every one of those years rebelling against that terrible name. How much of her parents' story did Silence figure out in that sad, sad year or the many years that followed?

Probably all of it.

I peek around the gravestone. A light shines from the kitchen window in the parsonage where Georgia still sits at the table pretending to work on the sermon for Sunday. She's already chosen the theme—grief—and she'll finish it in a flurry on Saturday before standing at the pulpit and practicing all afternoon. She used to make me sit through the rehearsals. Now I refuse. And this weekend I'll be with Dad, anyway.

Thank God.

I lie back on the cool grass and gaze up through the maple leaves toward the moon. It's one day away from being full. Jack is beneath me, along with Hortensia and Silence, and those seven tiny little unnamed skeletons. What did Silence want for herself? Did she dream of putting on pants, sailing off to sea, and never returning? She didn't have to worry about global warming washing Monreith away, but she did have to face rigid gender norms, though I suspect she decided to slay the patriarchy and go to the tavern with the men. Did she ever stumble to this same graveyard and fantasize about a different life?

I want a different life. One where I'm not being watched all the time.

Georgia thinks I'm obsessed with getting a cell phone, and that as soon as she gives in, I'll develop an eating disorder or something. But what I'm obsessed with is fairness and equity and trust. And living in the twenty-first century, and no matter how many times I ask Georgia why I can't have a phone, she doesn't have an adequate answer. Everyone in the eighth grade has a phone (except Connor C, Connor H, Drew, Mackenzie, and Mona, but they're all freaks. I don't want to be mean; it's just true. Even the teachers know it). Also, Georgia wants me to be popular like she was when she played field hockey and was a National Merit Scholar.

Memo to Georgia: *You cannot be popular in eighth grade without a phone.* You can't text. You can't participate in group threads. You can't get on social media or have any clue about what's going on. When girls like Taylor Lawson mention hanging out, they don't mean at a specific time and in a specific place. At best, they mean a vague future everyone learns about on social media when the plans suddenly become real.

I am trustworthy. I've proven this way more than Georgia could ever know because I keep *everyone's* secrets, like that my mother's secretary, Maggie, doesn't only play solitaire at work but also spends most of her day drafting a manuscript for a romance novel called *The Earl's Pearl Dagger,* and that Mr. McEvoy, the music director, has a plastic bottle of Fireball whiskey hidden behind the organ pipes. I've only tried it four times. Tiny little sips that Mr. McEvoy will never miss. It's delicious.

But mostly, I have a superpower I suspect Jack had, too. I have a sixth sense for when people are into each other, especially when they're not supposed to be. I've had it ever since last year when I showed up early to that same Human Sexuality class where we learned about syphilis. The classroom door was closed, and when I opened it, Ms. Blake and Mr. Shea were standing at the computer, probably going over the day's lesson, and it could have been nothing and it could have been something, but they spent a nanosecond too long focused on each other—and when they split apart, they were way too happy for people about to talk about sexually transmitted infections. Six months later, Ms. Blake went on maternity leave. And now, she's Mrs. Shea.

Talk about human sexuality.

But I kept their secret, just like I did for Dad and Farley when that whole thing started and they thought I didn't notice when Farley came by the garage one too many times, or when he teased Dad about eating too much candy. And now I'm keeping my mouth shut about Georgia and Uncle Max, too, even though some mornings he's still at the parsonage when I have breakfast.

Inside the church, the singing ends. A moment later, the back door to the church opens, and the members of the choir stream out into the night. Some head off in pairs. Others linger. Georgia must hear them, because she comes to the parsonage's kitchen door and calls to Mr. McEvoy, the music director. She's probably doubting herself and wants to change the music for the service on Sunday. Mr. McEvoy probably gives in, if only to keep her from smelling the scent of cinnamon on his breath from that hidden Fireball.

After the choir disperses, Georgia hovers on the back step, peering into the dark. I wonder if she's searching for me, or if she even remembers I left. Maybe she's waiting for Uncle Max. Tippi comes to the door. Georgia picks her up and holds her over her head so she splays her white feet.

I check my watch. It's almost nine. The church should be empty soon. I have a French test tomorrow and should go over the vocabulary one more time. I also have to read two chapters from *The Outsiders* that I haven't finished yet, and the teacher, Mrs. Fernandez, likes to call me out in class. In fact, I'm behind in all my schoolwork, and it's only a few weeks into the semester. After tomorrow, I'll have the whole weekend to catch up.

A moment later, the last meeting of the night breaks up as a group, mostly men, shuffles into the churchyard. Some light up cigarettes. One turns the key to lock the door to the meeting hall. I roll onto my stomach and watch them from behind Jack's grave.

This is the local chapter of Gamblers Anonymous. The group is more subdued than the choir, though a few of them linger too, standing in a loose circle. Mr. Thibodeau is here, hovering on the outside, as if he doesn't know whether he's welcome or not, even at a meeting like this one. I'm surprised he's left his house, with what people are saying about him. Eventually, this group disperses, too, though Mr. Thibodeau stays, hands in his pockets. He probably doesn't know where to go.

My mother comes to the door again, watching for a moment before opening the screen. "Simon," she calls.

He takes a tentative step toward her, and she waves him inside.

A cloud sweeps over the moon, and a chill runs down my back. Even with Jack here, I feel alone. In the warm light of the parsonage's kitchen, Georgia talks to Mr. Thibodeau, her hand resting over his hand as she offers counsel.

I know it's her job. But now I really don't want to go home.

CHAPTER 34
Chloe

It's easy enough to break into the church. There's no real security or cameras of any sort. I remember a few years ago when some money went missing from the offering and Georgia installed a system where Maggie had to tear herself away from writing her romance novel long enough to buzz people into the offices. That lasted for about a week. The doors that lead into the church are two hundred years old and so warped that snow blows through the gaps in the winter. There's also a key to the church hall hanging by the door with a sign next to it that reads key.

But the easiest way to get in, and what I do now, is to shimmy through an open window into the basement. I drop to the floor and listen. I'm almost certain I'm alone, but it doesn't hurt to be cautious. The basement is pitch black. I make my way across the floor and trip on one random chair. Out in the hallway, a light glows over the fish tank by the little preschool I attended when I was a kid. I watch the fish move in and out of the ceramic castle for a moment, before heading up to the choir loft and taking my fifth sip from Mr. McEvoy's Fireball. It burns at the back of my throat.

By now, my eyes have adjusted to the dark enough to see the rows of pews below. I'm sure they've been replaced since Jack came here with his family, but I know for a fact the Ricketsons sat in the fourth row, close to the front but not all the way. Silence Ricketson might have sat in that pew by herself after her parents died, but I imagine, like Taylor Lawson, that Silence didn't go anywhere without a group of friends, even to church.

I check the time. It's been fifteen minutes since Mr. Thibodeau went into the parsonage. Visits like his can take five minutes or hours. He has a lot going on, so my guess is he's still there. I make my way down from the choir loft, out of the nave, and into the offices. I could have used the flashlight on a phone right about now, but I manage without one. In the third drawer of Maggie's desk, I feel around under hanging files till my fingers brush along a set of keys.

Bingo.

In the basement, I stop at the fish tank again before using the keys to open the pantry door at the rear of the kitchenette. The church may be easy enough to access, but the one thing Maggie insists on keeping under lock and key are snacks. "People come and go all week," she says. "And the snacks have a habit of walking off with them."

I take a risk and turn on the bulb with the pull string. Packages of cookies line an entire wall. I take a box of Chips Ahoy from where I hope Maggie's eagle eye won't notice it missing, though she usually has my back when it comes to this kind of thing. I yank the light off, shove the cookies under my coat, and get out of there before anyone can catch me. This weekend, at Farley's house, Dad and I will shove the cookies into our mouths when Farley's not paying attention.

Yes, I could have bought my own cookies. I have plenty of my own money stashed away, and there's a convenience store right in the middle of town that sells Chips Ahoy, but I'm not lying when I say I can't make one single move in this town without it getting reported back to Georgia or Uncle Max or even my dad. If Georgia finds out I bought cookies, she'll want to know why, and then she'll use it to get me to talk about Farley. She'll probably ask why Dad can't have the cookies at the house, and then want me to delve into all the weird things Farley does, which she'll store up to use as weapons when she needs them. Public Georgia is cool and happy with my dad and Farley. Private Georgia, not so much.

I replace the key in Maggie's desk and then step into Georgia's office, where I peer through the window toward the parsonage. Mr. Thibodeau still sits at the kitchen table, his black hair shining under the lights. If I had a phone, I could study for my French test tomorrow. Instead, I'm stuck here in the dark. I sit at Georgia's desk and spin around on the chair. Outside the window, the moon emerges from behind clouds, and enough light shines into the office to make out the contours of the room. A rainbow flag hangs behind my mother's desk.

Of course it does.

Georgia hosts the regional PFLAG chapter here at the church and sponsors the LGBTQ+ Alliance at school, which means I have to duck into a classroom when I see her parading down the school hallways. One of these days, I'll record some of the things she says about Farley. Let's just say they aren't very nice. Or all that supportive. Or anything she'd want the world to hear.

I ease open a drawer in the desk. Farley calls me a snoop.

Whatever.

I slide my hand into the drawer. It's filled with files, probably financial records or old sermons. Nothing worth bothering with. The next drawer holds a metal strongbox, the cash from the weekly collection. I shake the box. The key to open it is out in Maggie's desk with the one I used to break into the pantry, but when I need money, I go to Dad's office. He has a drawer filled with cash, and he hasn't ever noticed when a few twenties have gone missing. Besides, I'd have to be more than a snoop to steal from a church.

In the bottom drawer, I find a collection of miscellany—a pair of mittens, an old hat, an empty handbag. Someone's sweater. Georgia keeps the Lost and Found here and puts it out on Sunday to see what's claimed, then sells some of the unclaimed items at the church fair every October. Once in a while, I find something I want. And if it doesn't get claimed after a few weeks, I take it.

These items have all been here since last spring. I nearly shut the drawer and give in to going home when my fingers brush something hard and plastic. From beneath the pile of cloth and knitting, I unfurl a power cord. People are always leaving power cords plugged into the few sockets around the church, but this time, the cord has a phone attached to it.

I rest the phone on the desk. The screen has a crack running through it, but someone will probably be looking for it on Sunday.

I click on the power button and am surprised when the screen lights up and casts a blue glow through the room. I flip the phone over to block the light. I slip under the desk and click the power button again. The phone has a passcode. I try 1234 and 0000, but neither work. I try two more before the phone locks for the next minute.

How many four-digit passcodes could there be?

Only 9,999.

It's Thursday night. If someone had left the phone behind on Sunday, they'd have asked about it by now. They might have even posted on the local message boards to see if it had been found. In fact, when important things get left behind at the church, Maggie posts about them in the church bulletin, so even if, say, someone on the flower committee left the phone behind during the week, it should have been claimed by now.

So I don't feel that bad when I slip the phone and the

power cord into my coat pocket, hug the cookies to my chest, and make my way through the church, down to the basement, and out the window I came in earlier. My foot catches on the sill, and I sprawl across the ground, only to see a pair of shoes in front of me. I remember, suddenly, that there's a murderer on the loose in this town. I scramble backwards and almost start to run, but the shoes are attached to Uncle Max, who seems to have his own superpower. He finds me whenever I do something I'm not supposed to.

"Chloe," he says to me. "It's late."

I pick myself up.

"What are you doing out here?" he asks.

"What are *you* doing out here?" I ask, even though he's the chief of police and can be wherever he wants to be.

"Where's your mother?"

"Working on her sermon."

"It's almost ten," Uncle Max says. "I thought I saw a light in her office."

"I go there to be by myself. To think. Isn't that what church is for? Sometimes I need a place to work things out." I pause before adding the last bit. "Especially lately."

The adults in my life are easy to manipulate, even Uncle Max. He hates Farley, probably more than my mom does. I move toward the parsonage. I stop, my hand on the front gate, the cookies against my chest, the phone burning in my pocket. I pray no one decides to call it right now. "Are you coming inside?" I ask.

Uncle Max doesn't move to follow.

"Georgia could use some company," I say. "It's a big deal this week, you know, with everything going on."

"I'm heading to my own place tonight," Uncle Max says. "Keep out of trouble." He melts away into the dark.

I stand there for a moment, hoping he might return, hoping I might be reading this wrong. See, my superpower goes both ways. I have a sense for when people are into each other, but I also have one for when they start to cool off, and lately, I've had that sense around Uncle Max and Georgia.

I run inside. Thankfully, Mr. Thibodeau has left, but Georgia still sits at the kitchen table surrounded by notes. She lifts her glasses off and swipes tears from her eyes in a way she only does when she's by herself. I freeze in place. We stare at each other. She conjures up a smile and blows her nose. "I'm never going to get this sermon done."

"I have a French test in the morning."

"You should get a good night's sleep."

"I could practice vocabulary on my phone if I had one."

"I used index cards when I took French. They work just as well."

Upstairs, I stash the cookies in my backpack and lie in the dark. I try four more passcodes and the phone locks for another minute. I wonder how many times I can do this before the phone locks permanently. I glance out the window toward the church, to where Mr. McEvoy's Fireball sits in the dust behind the organ. I wouldn't put it past Uncle Max to stake out the parsonage to make sure I don't sneak out again, but I could use another shot of that whiskey.

CHAPTER 35
Chloe

The next day at school, the bell rings to mark the end of fifth period. I hand in my French test, which I probably bombed since I got about three hours of sleep last night and didn't ever make those flash cards Georgia suggested. Out in the hallway, Noah waits for me, his curly blond hair tied into a man bun. He speaks some weird archaic version of French after living in northern Maine the last two years, so he never studies and always gets an A, which feels like cheating to me. Couldn't he take Mandarin or something?

"My mother's birthday party will be an intimate affair," he says, imitating his mother's voice as he spins away from me. "Meaning no one's coming."

"I get it," I say.

"We can ditch the adults and hang out on the dock."

To Noah, that means smoking his dad's pot, but if Georgia gets even a whiff of the stuff, I'll be grounded for the rest of the year.

The phone I found last night sits in my pocket now. After Georgia finally went to bed, I logged onto her laptop and researched the hundred most common passcodes, though I haven't tried any of them yet because I also managed to wake up Georgia.

"Chloe," she said to me. "What are you doing?"

"Studying," I said, without looking away from the laptop screen.

"Bed," Georgia said, checking the search history.

Thankfully, I'd already erased it.

I haven't told anyone about the phone since I did technically steal it, but Noah knows a lot about computers and programming. "How do you figure out a passcode?" I ask.

"Are you trying to hack someone?"

I pull him into an empty classroom. "Look at this," I say.

He takes the phone from me.

"I already tried 1234," I say.

"It's a burner," he says. "Whose is it?"

"Mine."

"Why don't you know the passcode, then?"

"Fine. I found it."

"It probably belongs to a drug dealer, so put it back and pretend you never saw it."

"Don't you want to see what's on it?"

The bell rings again, meaning I'm late for my English class.

"How many passcodes have you tried?" Noah asks.

"Eight," I say. "It keeps locking."

"Careful," Noah says. "It might lock permanently. But figure out who owns it. Social security numbers, birthdays, anniversaries, old phone numbers—the answer's usually there somewhere. See what you can learn, and we'll try more tonight."

He dashes down the hall toward the science wing. I start to head toward English but try one more passcode: my own birthday. Four months from now. When Georgia promises I'll get my own phone.

The passcode doesn't work.

Mrs. Fernandez, the English teacher, uses a seating plan, which unfortunately means I have to sit next to Taylor Lawson. Taylor and I used to be friends in elementary school, but now she's a bully, though not the kind you see on TV. She isn't blonde or rich or even all that pretty, but she loves to create drama and place herself at the very center of it by pitting friends against each other. I learned my lesson in sixth grade when she managed to get the entire class to believe I'd left a pair of bloodstained underwear in the girls' bathroom. To this day, I believe Taylor planted them herself. The whole incident meant I spent almost all of seventh grade eating lunch alone till Noah moved to town and befriended me. Now I try not to give Taylor any power, though she still sometimes calls me "Flowy Chloe."

"Thank you for joining us, Ms. Macomber," Mrs. Fernandez says as I try to slip into the room.

I keep my head down, phone clutched in my hand, and slide into the seat beside Taylor. As soon as Mrs. Fernandez returns to her lesson, Taylor whispers out of the side of her mouth, "Mack's got a crush on you," loud enough for Mack Davis, who sits two rows ahead, to hear.

Mack used to go by Emily, but now they're trying out a different name. I don't have crushes on anyone besides Jack, and he's been dead for over two hundred years. And who knows if Taylor's even telling the truth or just trying to stir up trouble?

"Shut up," I say.

"Chloe," Mrs. Fernandez says, "is there something you want to share with the class?"

I shake my head. Last year, in the seventh grade, the world at school had seemed defined. There were good kids and bad kids, and I was solidly in the good-kid camp, and Taylor wasn't. I got all As and came to class on time and certainly didn't whisper while the teacher was giving her lesson. This year, I seem to be slipping over to the other side, or at least into some murky gray area. I didn't finish *The Outsiders,* so all I want is to make it through to the end of class without getting called on.

"Does Mack scare you?" Taylor whispers.

Don't engage, I remind myself. That's the only way to neutralize Taylor. But she nudges my foot with hers. She touches the phone, which I forgot to stow away. I move it under a notebook, but Taylor takes it back out. *Nice,* she mouths to me.

Mrs. Lawson works in Boston, and Taylor's had her own phone since fifth grade. She keeps a running list of who has one and who doesn't.

"Give it to me," I whisper, trying to take it back.

"603-5589," Mrs. Fernandez says, reciting my mother's phone number by heart, which she does anytime she's a final warning away from calling a parent.

"Chloe's phone was vibrating," Taylor says.

Mrs. Fernandez takes a few steps through the desks. "It's Friday afternoon, Taylor. Could you make it through the end of the day without stirring up trouble?" As she turns away, she adds, "No phones in this class, Chloe. Put it away."

I shove the phone into my bag.

"While you're at it," Mrs. Fernandez adds, "tell us what you thought of chapter 9 in the reading. Why do you think the boys fought? What about Pony?"

Is Pony a boy? Or a horse? I have no idea. "They're angry?" I say, and even I can hear the question mark at the end of my statement.

"Why?"

Mrs. Fernandez waits for me to respond. Mack Davis turns. "Pony's sensitive," they say. "He's smart, too."

Mrs. Fernandez thanks Mack for answering and seems to give up trying to catch me out. At the end of class I escape, but Taylor clearly has me in her sights today. "Give me your new number," she says, following me through the hall. "I'll text you. Then we can hang out."

The very idea of hanging out with Taylor makes me nauseous. "My mother doesn't want me texting anyone but her."

"But that's what a phone is for," Taylor says. "And how will she even know?"

"She checks it. She has my passwords. She'll take it away if I break any of her rules."

I keep walking. My last class of the day is history, just a few doors away. All I have to do is make it there, keep my head down for the next fifty minutes, and get off campus. I don't even have to deal with Georgia's crying this weekend because I'm staying with Dad. I'll walk to his garage and hang out while he finishes work for the day. I may even help myself to the stash of M&Ms he hides under the money.

"You told me your mother said you couldn't have a phone till you turned fourteen," Taylor says. "You're not fourteen. Not till January."

"I convinced her to get me one," I say. "And don't you have someone else to terrorize?"

Taylor steps in my path. She holds out her hand. When I don't give her the phone, she tries to open my bag and get it herself. I tear the bag away from her. "What's your problem?" I ask.

"You're lying. I bet that phone doesn't even work."

"You got me," I say. "I brought a fake phone to school so you'd believe I had one and want to be my friend. I've been planning it for weeks because I'm so desperate to have you like me."

I maneuver around her. Ahead, Noah waits. Our history teacher stands outside the classroom too, talking to another teacher, and Taylor's not in my history class, so I won't need to see her again till Monday, and maybe by then we'll have figured out the passcode and the phone won't feel fake anymore. Maybe I'll let Taylor text me so I can block her number.

Taylor grabs my arm. I don't break my stride.

"What if I asked your mother if we could text each other?" she says. "I bet she'd say yes. I mean, you're totally out of it, Chloe. You can't be on a group thread. How can you even know what's going on?"

Does Taylor really believe I don't already know that? "I don't like you," I say. "And you don't seem to like me either, so why don't we agree to leave each other alone? Forever."

Taylor's tall and gangling. She leans over me and whispers, "At least my father's not a fag."

I shove past her, weighing my options. Taylor sits at the LGBTQ+ table during lunch. I could out her as a homophobe right here and now, but I wonder who'd believe me and who she'd manipulate against me. No one was around to hear what she said but me.

"Everything okay?" Noah asks.

"All good," I say.

"Your dad is a total inspiration," Taylor calls after me. "We all admire him. Your mom, too."

I press the phone into Noah's hand. "Hide this for me," I whisper.

Then I turn, cock my fist, and punch Taylor right between the eyes. Even as I hear a shout from where the teachers had been gossiping, even as I see my weekend disappearing behind a wall of my mother's disappointment, even as blood starts dripping off Taylor's chin, I'm not the slightest bit sorry. In fact, I hope I broke her nose.

CHAPTER 36
Chloe

Taylor sobs like a baby from where she's splayed on the floor, blood pooling across the white-and-gray tile, while a teacher holds a paper towel to her nose and tells her to lean her head forward. Another one holds me by the shoulders like I might go at Taylor again. I wouldn't mind. But I've made my point. And I'm definitely the one in the wrong in both public opinion and in actuality. Plus at least a half dozen students have phones out, recording the whole thing.

Great.

Taylor tries to say something but only manages a gurgling sound. I shouldn't, but I say I'm sorry. If I don't, it'll come back to bite me later.

One teacher tells students to put their phones away and get to class. Another one hauls me down to the office, mumbling that this is the last thing in the world she needs on a Friday afternoon.

Welcome to my world.

In the office, the teacher parks me on a hard plastic chair and tells me not to move, then confers with the school secretary before heading back to class. This row of chairs is meant for delinquents, and I have never been seated in one before, and I certainly have never been spoken to like I'm a problem. The bell for seventh period rings. Classes have begun, and the whispering will have started. Forty-five minutes from now, the whole school will know what I did. With the video evidence, they probably already do.

Outside the glass walls, Taylor appears, leaning on the school nurse. The secretary clucks her tongue, then shakes her head, and the shake could be about me or it could be about—I don't know—maybe she can't get Twelve Down on the daily crossword puzzle. Or maybe she just wants her weekend to start, too.

I wonder if the principal's office is like prison, where you get one phone call. If so, I'll have to choose between Georgia and Dad, and then deal with the aftermath from whomever I don't choose. Maybe I'll call Uncle Max, if he doesn't already know what happened. I mean, I did technically assault Taylor. Isn't that a criminal offense?

Mr. Omani, the assistant principal, comes to his office door. "Ms. Macomber," he says.

"How do you know what pronouns I use?"

"I don't," he says. "But if you want me to call you something else, let me know."

"Chloe's fine."

"Works for me."

He leaves the door propped open and indicates another hard plastic chair. Normally Mr. Omani smiles when he sees me, but now he's all business. Whatever's coming my way will be something to endure, then it'll be over. I already know punching Taylor was a poor decision, but I'll let Mr. Omani feel as though he did his job.

"Tell me what happened," he says.

"I said I was sorry," I say.

Mr. Omani's old, around Farley's age, and he has a goatee

he probably thinks makes him seem cool but approachable. Noah told me he saw Mr. Omani kite surfing in the bay.

"This isn't like you, Chloe," he says, and I almost ask him what, exactly, is like me, because I'm not sure I know the answer anymore.

He rifles through some papers. "You got all As last year," he says. "We're few weeks into the year, and you're already missing homework assignments and coming to class unprepared. Now this."

I slouch forward and focus on a bobblehead by his laptop. It takes me a moment to realize it's of him. "My wife got me that for my birthday," he says.

"What else did she get you?" I ask.

"A wet suit."

Maybe he does kite surf after all, like Noah said. I'll need to confirm. That's something I can do while I'm grounded this weekend. After all, I have a view of the entire bay from Farley's deck.

"You know if you're upset, you can tell me," Mr. Omani says. "Or someone else. And there are two sides to every story. Tell me yours."

I wonder what he'd do if I told him what Taylor had said, if he'd keep it between the two of us. I could make him promise not to punish Taylor in any way. "My dad," I begin.

Mr. Omani leans forward as my words begin to form, his eyes shining, ready to jump into action with whatever plan he wants to initiate. He must live for this. But right then, out the window, behind where he sits, Georgia hurries across the schoolyard, her curly hair blowing in the breeze. Georgia rarely hurries in public. Usually, she moves deliberately, engaging with anyone she encounters. I suppose this is an extraordinary event. "My mom's here," I say.

Even if I wanted to tell my side of the story, the opportunity has passed.

A few minutes later, Georgia breezes into the office. She must have taken a moment to collect herself because she's in full-on Reverend George mode. She greets the secretary by name while tossing one end of her scarf over a shoulder. Georgia wears a scarf nearly everywhere, using it as a prop. The more anxious, the more dire the situation, the more she tosses. Funerals are the worst.

"Reverend," Mr. Omani says when she comes to the office door.

"Give us a minute, Chloe," Georgia says.

I leave without a word, and she closes the door behind me. I imagine her on that hard plastic chair, her legs casually crossed, asking about Mr. Omani's wife, getting him to tell her about his weekend plans for kite surfing in the bay, putting him at ease so he can deliver his bad news. That's how my mother works with everyone except a select few, mostly me. And my dad.

The door to the office opens. "Let's go," Georgia says, waiting for me to follow.

She heads out of the office, her exit as grand as her entrance. I scurry after her, and it's not till we're well away from the school that she drops the act. "Tell me Mr. Omani got part of this wrong," she says.

What can I say? There were too many witnesses for me to deny anything. "There are videos. They're probably already online."

"You're suspended for three days," Georgia says. "But you're grounded for a month. And you'll get your grades back up, too. And that hair—" She catches herself and stops. I dyed my hair pink on Monday and have been waiting for her to comment on it. I guess she doesn't like it.

"He asked if you need to go into therapy," Georgia continues. "Is that what you want?"

I can't tell if she likes the idea or if it pisses her off. She's been to therapy. She went to Farley for a while a year ago when she and my dad started having trouble with their marriage, though none of them—Farley included—realizes that I know. "Why can't I have a phone?" I ask. "It's not fair."

"Because you just got suspended. That's why."

"But I didn't get suspended until today, and you wouldn't let me have a phone before, either."

"Listen, sweetie," Georgia says. "You'll meet dozens of Taylor Lawsons in your life. But every day she has to wake up and be herself, and you are lucky enough to be you. Do me a favor and ignore her."

That's exactly what I tried to do, but if I say that to Georgia, she'd tell me to try harder next time. Georgia plans everything, even her emotions. She doesn't understand that emotions can't be planned. When my dad told her he was moving in with Farley, Georgia lit a candle of gratitude at that week's service. "For honesty and bravery," she'd said, her eyes closed, knowing her whole flock was looking to her for guidance.

"I'm supposed to go to Dad's place this weekend," I say. "Can I walk to the garage?"

"It's not your father's place. It's Farley's," Georgia says, turning away and offering a hand as if I were still in elementary school. I don't even consider taking it. "You're with me for now."

We walk through the wrought-iron gates and past Jack's grave. Jack knew it was important to keep quiet to protect others. Georgia doesn't need to know what Taylor said about my father. She'd tell him I was getting bullied because of what he'd done.

As we get to the church, Georgia says, "Listen, we can't appear as if we're coming apart at the seams. Some people spend their lives breaking rules and getting away with it. You're not that kind of person."

She doesn't know about the cookies. Or the phone. Or the Fireball. I get away with more than she'll ever know.

Upstairs, Maggie minimizes the game of solitaire on her computer as we pass her desk. She tells Georgia that Mr. Stone is waiting in her office. "Did he have an appointment?" Georgia asks.

Maggie shakes her head. She's probably waiting for this damn week to end, too. Georgia points to a chair. "Don't move," she says to me, then she opens her office door and says, "Damian!" with a toss of her scarf.

Mr. Stone has a bike helmet tucked under his arm and biking gear on. My mother kisses his cheek. As she goes to close the door, I check my superpower, but there's nothing there, which is good because I don't need any more relationship drama. And even though I like Noah, I'd rather not have a stepbrother, either.

Maggie returns to her game. She clicks on the three of hearts, and the board clears. "Whatever you did," she says, "no one will remember in a week."

"I punched Taylor Lawson."

Maggie starts another game and moves the queen of diamonds over the king of clubs. "She's kind of a pill. I bet she deserved it."

A moment later, Mr. Stone clomps out of Georgia's office. "I got in fights all the time when I was your age," he whispers, as he passes by and heads down the hallway.

Maggie watches him leave. "He could bike to *my* house any-time."

If Mr. Stone is old, then Maggie is prehistoric. "Aren't you married?" I ask.

"It doesn't hurt to look."

I stare at the computer screen where her game of solitaire waits. She follows my gaze and I say, "I don't care what you do."

Maggie nods toward Georgia's office. "Don't mention it to her. You'll get me in trouble."

CHAPTER 37
Chloe

I hear Farley's voice before I see him. There he is, haloed in pink through my bangs, hip cocked against the doorjamb. Farley reminds me of the hat boys at school who play lacrosse, all popularity and hair. Like them, Farley thinks he's all that, but really he's full of himself, and sometimes after he leaves, Maggie will try to make Georgia feel better by calling him a peacock, and Georgia will tell Maggie to stop even though it's clear she wants her to keep going.

Still, I'd expected my dad to show up. "Why'd she call *you*?" I ask without thinking. The question gives Farley power. He loves power.

Maggie flirts with him for a moment, which he doesn't seem to mind, though Maggie flirts with anyone over twenty-one. "Don't forget I'm a married woman," she says.

"My loss," Farley says, crossing the office and sweeping hair from my eyes. I slap his hand away.

"On a scale from one to ten," he asks, "how bad is it?"

He's trying to bond with me, and if Farley takes my side, it will piss Georgia off so much maybe she'll forget about what happened at school. "Like a thirteen? And why don't you tell her to just let me get a freaking phone?"

"No promises," Farley says as he disappears into the office.

Maggie starts shutting down her computer. "One of these days, Reverend George'll have to write a sermon on humility."

She doesn't look at me, but the edges of her mouth tip into a grin. Maggie understands there's a line she can't cross, but that's enough for me to remember some people are on my team and always will be.

I hate Farley. I hate him for being a snob and ostentatious and for trying to insert himself into my life like he's my stepfather, but mostly I hate him for coming between my parents. One thing I can't admit to anyone, ever, because it would do nothing but create trouble and it would also be totally selfish to say it out loud, is that I wish my parents were still together and it makes me sad all the time that they're not. I liked it when we lived at the parsonage, and even though my dad is allergic to cats and Tippi wouldn't live with us now, I wish nothing had changed. All of us were happier before Farley Drake showed up.

"You want an almond?" Maggie asks.

I shake my head.

She lines almonds up along the edge of her desk and eats them one at a time, just like my dad.

"My dad does that with M&Ms," I say. "But don't tell. He's not supposed to eat sugar anymore."

Maggie pops an almond into her mouth and jerks her head toward the door. "Because of the peacock?"

"Farley says sugar is poison."

"Your grandmother and I are friends," Maggie says. "I've known your dad my whole life. He loves his sweets. When he was little, he'd come to my house while your grandmother was working. We'd bake cookies, and he'd eat about ten of them." She pops another almond into her mouth. "Want to tell me what happened at school?"

"Taylor said something mean," I say.

"About you?"

I shake my head.

"Kids can be little shits," Maggie says.

A few moments later, Farley emerges from the office.

"Behave," Georgia says to me. "Don't forget, reputation is everything."

She's lucky she disappears into her office because I nearly tell her to fuck off.

Instead, I stomp out of the church to the cemetery and stop by Jack's grave. By the time Jack was thirteen, he was already apprenticed to another apothecary, his whole life mapped out in front of him. I wonder if he'd met Hortensia by then, if they knew their future, or if there was some awful girl like Taylor who terrorized those eighteenth-century teenagers too.

Farley catches up, and I hurry away. The last thing I want is for him to latch onto Jack. "I don't want to talk about what happened today in school," I say.

He follows along, coaching me through defending myself later. "Practice your lines on me. Sound sorry enough to satisfy."

What Farley doesn't understand is that Dad will take my side no matter what I did. We're a team. "You're so weird," I say.

"You're hardly the epitome of normal."

"You're not supposed to say things like that to me. And I'm supposed to be in trouble."

"You are in trouble," Farley says. "Big trouble. Enough so I don't need to pile on. Come on. I'll buy you a sundae."

"Ice cream?" I say. "What if my dad finds out?"

"That's easy," Farley says. "Don't tell him."

Don't worry, Farley, it'll be the first thing I mention when I see him later.

He takes off down the sidewalk, and I consider heading in the opposite direction to my dad's garage, but I'm in enough trouble at this point. It's not till we get closer to the shop that I figure out Farley's real motivation. Taylor Lawson sits out front with her minions and a black eye. Farley wraps an arm around my shoulders and tries to pull me in to talk to her, but I duck away and dash into the shop as Taylor says something about texting me.

"You knew Taylor was here," I say, when he follows.

"Which one is Taylor?"

"Don't play dumb. She's the redhead."

"The ugly one?"

I laugh before catching myself. Then I find myself rising to Taylor's defense. What is ugly anyway, especially from someone like Farley? "You're not supposed to say that, either."

"What should I say?"

This constant reflection is one of the things that drives me the craziest about Farley. "Your therapist games won't work with me. I'm immune. Georgia's been using them my whole life."

When Farley saw Georgia as a patient, I imagine them sparring with endless open-ended questions, neither of them answering the other. Georgia's secret sessions with Farley, and Dad's affair, the whole mess, every part of it, makes Farley, like, a *total* creep, one who probably shouldn't be allowed to ever treat another patient or be alone with a thirteen-year-old girl, but sometimes I think I'm the only one in the world who sees that.

I turn to the counter and study the menu.

"There's sugar in everything here," I say.

"Should we sneak Fireball instead?"

I had a sip of the whiskey at Moulton Farm a few weeks ago while my dad and Farley had dinner with Mr. and Mrs. Stone on the patio and I thought I was alone. Farley must have seen me. But again, only creeps offer alcohol to kids. "I'm telling my dad you said that."

"Better than him finding out I bought you ice cream. Especially when you're supposed to be grounded for the rest of your life."

I order the most expensive sundae on the menu.

At a table in the back of the shop, I shovel ice cream into my mouth till my stomach starts to hurt. I also tell Farley he's a pretty boy, which is a mistake because that's the kind of thing he likes to hear. It stokes his ego, even as he denies it. "I am *not* a pretty boy."

"Tell that to your mirror."

He dabs his spoon into his own ice cream, licks a tiny droplet off the end, then shoves the ice cream across the table.

"Don't go crazy, Pretty Boy," I say.

"Tell me something," he says. "Does your mother hang out with Mr. Stone very often? I saw him outside the church."

"They're friends," I say. "My parents and the Stones hung out all the time, you know . . . before."

Since my parents split up, Georgia doesn't go over to the farm as much as she used to.

"I mean, do they hang out alone?" Farley asks. "Just the two of them."

It's all I can do not to roll my eyes. Farley of all people has no right to comment on my mother's personal life, no matter what she does with it. "Georgia's not having sex with Mr. Stone, if that's what you're asking."

I suck ice cream off the plastic spoon and grin into the paper cup while Farley actually squirms. Behind him, the door to the store opens and Uncle Max walks in, followed by that state detective he's worked with all week. "This is Brock London," Uncle Max says to Farley as he pulls up a chair. "He's working the Thibodeau case. This is Farley Drake. The shrink I told you about."

The detective grabs a chair, too. "Dr. Drake," he says.

The detective is trying to convince Uncle Max to join the state police, though it's still a secret, one Georgia's not supposed to know, even though she does. "He'll never do it," she'd said to me. "Max is afraid of change."

She said it as if trying to convince herself, and I suppose this might be why she was crying last night when I came in for the night. I guess I could have been nicer. I hope he doesn't take the job, but I would if I were him.

Here Uncle Max is in full-on chief mode, serious and focused on impressing the detective. But I'm grateful when he asks if he can finish my sundae. I don't think I could have eaten much more of it.

"Want to tell me what you were thinking?" he says to me.

Unlike Farley or Georgia or even my dad, Uncle Max can make me feel really, really bad when I do something I'm not supposed to, so between the breaking into the church last night and stealing the Chips Ahoy and the Fireball and punching Taylor today, he has plenty of material to work with. I'm not sure which infraction he's talking about, but I apologize anyway.

CHAPTER 38
Chloe

Farley toots the horn as we speed down Main Street.

I sink into my seat. "Quit it," I say.

"Chloe," Farley says. "No one knows it's me."

"You know this car is killing the planet, right? And who else drives a midlife-crisis-mobile like this one?"

Farley revs the engine and peels out of town. I grab the door handle and shriek. Driving in the Triumph is more fun than I ever want to admit. It doesn't even have seat belts.

Back at the ice-cream shop, Detective London asked Farley what his patients were saying about Mrs. Thibodeau's murder. Farley didn't answer the question, but my guess is the murder has been the single topic of conversation all week in his office. It certainly was at school, at least till I started the fight today. Most of the kids believe Mr. Thibodeau is guilty, but Taylor's convinced Mrs. Thibodeau was killed as part of a mob hit. "They used a plastic bag!" she said the other day, as though she were some expert on mob hits. "It was meant to send a message."

Noah told me his father's working on a documentary about the murder. "He has crime scene photos taped all over the whiteboard in his office," he said. "There's a serial killer."

"There is not," I said.

"Next time you're over, I'll show you," he said. "You'll see. And he could be coming for you next."

Now I ask Farley, "Are you going to help that detective find Mrs. Thibodeau's murderer?"

He shifts gears and turns onto the lane. "Why are you asking?"

I test out Noah's theory, though I keep his name out of the discussion. "Jack told me there's a serial killer." I watch as Farley glances at me out of the corner of his eye. I can see him mulling over his response. "It could be true," he says. "But who's Jack?"

Oh, God, I never should have brought Jack into this. Now Farley will think I have a secret friend and won't let it go till he queries me into submission. I really don't want my father's psychiatrist boyfriend to know my best friend has been dead for two hundred years. "No one," I say.

"Is Jack someone from school?"

"Jack is a friend, okay?"

"I think you should tell your friend Jack to stop trying to scare you," Farley says. "Or give him a scare right back. Let him know that if there is a serial killer on the loose, the last thing in the world he'll want is for that serial killer to take notice of him."

Whatever, Farley. Thanks for the advice. "Have you ever had syphilis?" I ask.

Even ever-unflappable Farley seems taken aback by that one. "Why?" he asks. "Does Jack have syphilis?"

Yeah, he probably did. And so did his wife. But now Farley will tell my dad I asked, and Dad will probably think I'm having sex. I need to learn to keep my mouth shut.

When we get to Farley's house, Dad's waiting for me on the front steps. I escape through the garage. Upstairs, I slam my door and scan the room for hidden cameras. Farley's obsessed with security and control and has cameras all over the property that mostly record raccoons going through the trash. I'm convinced he'll start spying on me soon, especially if I keep getting suspended at school. Before my dad can come lecture me about starting fights, I retrieve the box of Chips Ahoy from my bag, rip it open, shove a cookie into my mouth, and stash the package behind a pile of sweaters in the closet right as the bedroom door opens.

I spin around and face off with Dad.

He comes into the room. I lie down, lift a book in front of my face, and pretend to read while I manage to swallow the cookie. He sits on the side of the bed and waits for me to talk first, but there's no way I'm doing that, though I really can tell my dad anything. But if I told him why I hit Taylor, he'd feel like it was his fault, and Georgia would get involved, and the school would need to do damage control, which might mean an assembly with, like, singing or something and a fake apology from Taylor. And no matter what, I'd still be suspended because the school has a zero-tolerance policy for violence, even against bullies. But my dad is good at waiting me out, so I let the book fall and say, "It wouldn't have happened if you got me a phone."

"You know you can't punch people, right?"

I do know. But my dad makes me feel worse about it than anyone else has. And I shouldn't ask him this, but I do anyway, because I need to hear the answer. "Will you and Mom get back together again?"

In my heart, I already know what he'll say, but it hurts when he tells me the truth. "That's not going to happen," he says.

After Dad leaves, I hear the shower running in his bathroom. I change into a pair of loose jeans and a Burger King T-shirt that will make Farley obsess over when Dad might have eaten a Whopper. The orange clashes with my hair, which will drive Georgia crazy.

Outside, Farley and Dad wait by the pool. My dad has changed

out of the jeans and T-shirt he wore earlier and into a new outfit that's way too tight and that I'm pretty certain Farley chose.
If I ever started doing things because a boy wanted me to, Dad
would lecture me for a week about standing up for myself.

"Button your shirt," I say to him.

"Don't be fresh," he says, though he seems grateful as he
fastens the two lowest buttons.

CHAPTER 39
Chloe

"Poison!" Noah says, knocking his red ball at my green one.

He misses by a mile, and in return I knock him out of the game with a careful tap.

"Thanks a lot, Chloe," he says.

Then I chase him around the lawn, the mallet raised over my head until Georgia comes charging toward us.

"We're all going to play," she says. "Join us!"

The last thing I want is to play croquet as Georgia, Dad, Farley, and Uncle Max find ways to annoy each other. I drop my mallet, take Noah's hand, and flee over the bluff and down the steps to the dock. Somehow, Georgia has put my infractions aside and forgotten I'm grounded, at least temporarily. Maybe it's because only a few people are here, ones she trusts not to gossip. I don't care what the reason is as long as she doesn't follow us.

Noah and I sit at the end of the dock and dangle our feet in the water. The sun sets behind us, and the moon, full and bright, hovers over the bay. I lie down. The wooden slats are warm from the day's sun. Above us, the first stars of the evening twinkle in the sky.

"You should see the stars in Maine," Noah says. "There isn't as much light pollution there, and there are, like, millions of them."

"Do you miss Maine?" I ask.

"Some of it. There was a lake for swimming. And I had a friend named Pierre."

"Will you visit him?"

"Why?" Noah asks. "We're here now. And next year, we'll be somewhere else. You get used to making a new life everywhere you go."

I've gotten used to having Noah as a friend. I guess I'd hoped he felt the same way.

He asks, "What happened between you and Taylor at school today, anyway?"

I don't even trust Noah enough to tell him the awful word Taylor called my dad in the hallway at school. He'll tell his mother, and his mother will tell his father, and his father will tell my dad when they're out on one of their bike rides. "Taylor was just being herself."

"Meaning she deserved it."

No one deserves to get hit, which I know, even if I don't want to admit it out loud.

Above us, on the other side of the bluff, laughter from the adults rings through the night air. Noah fishes a joint from his pocket and lights it. He inhales and offers the joint to me as the skunky scent hangs on the humid air around us. I shake my head. Some of the kids at school vape, but Noah's the only one I know so far who's crossed this line, and I'm definitely not ready for pot yet. Maybe when I'm fourteen. "It stinks," I say. "And when they smell it, I'll be grounded for two months instead of one."

Noah takes another hit and stubs out the end of the joint. "Why did you give me that phone at school today?" he asks.

"I didn't want the principal to take it from me," I say. "What did you do with it, anyway?"

"I hid it under my bed, then my mother found it. Now she thinks I'm a drug dealer."

I sit up. "Did you tell her it was mine?"

"Relax. It's in my room. Where'd you get it, anyway?"

"I found it. It's a burner, so the minutes are already paid for. If we can figure out the passcode, I can use it till I turn fourteen and get my own phone."

"Or until your mother takes it away."

"Let's keep that from happening."

I lie back. To me, there seem to be an awful lot of stars, no matter how much light pollution we have here. Sometimes, Uncle Max will take me down to his dock to show me the constellations. It seems as if he has a new one to point out each time.

"Does your father still think there's a serial killer?" I ask.

"It's all he talks about," Noah says. "That and his next bike ride."

Up on the lawn, someone howls in triumph. The croquet match must be coming to an end. On the stairs behind us, two people appear, silhouetted against the night sky. A dog, too.

"It's your mom," I say.

"We should go meet her," Noah says. "If she comes down here, she might smell the pot."

"I can get my own dinner," I say to Georgia, who's in efficiency mode, hovering over the food in the kitchen while Noah and I fill plates and my dad delivers platters to the patio.

"You might skip the ratatouille," Georgia says.

I hadn't planned on taking any of the ratatouille, but now I load my plate with it.

In the TV room, Georgia puts on *Finding Nemo* without asking what we want to watch.

"Back in a sec," Noah says, dashing out of the room, his feet pounding up the front stairs.

I sit on the floor in front of the coffee table, while Georgia hovers. "Are you having fun tonight?" she asks.

"Mostly," I say.

"You're grounded, so *mostly* is a good answer." Georgia stares at the TV screen. "Do you want to watch *Ratatouille* instead? It goes with the meal."

"Then I'd have to listen to Noah speak French."

Georgia runs her fingers through my hair. She seems like she doesn't want to return to the party, so for once I don't shake her hand away. "I like the pink," she says.

"You don't."

"What do you know? I was a Goth in high school. For a little while at least. I dyed my hair black and wore tons of eye makeup and big, heavy skirts."

"I thought you played field hockey," I say.

"You can be a Goth and play field hockey at the same time." She lies back on the sofa and watches the movie for a moment. Both of us have seen *Finding Nemo* twenty times and can recite most of the dialogue. "When you're at Farley's place, does Uncle Max come over?" she asks.

I shake my head. "Only to go to the dock or the beach."

"Does Alice come over?"

I've seen Mrs. Stone sitting on Uncle Max's deck. But Georgia doesn't need to hear that from me. "Only when Harper is on the loose," I say. "But when that happens, we put together a search party."

"You all live out here in the same place," Georgia says. "You, your father, Farley, Uncle Max. Even Alice and Damian. Everyone but me. It makes me wonder what I miss out on."

"It's pretty boring. And none of them get to hang with Tippi at the parsonage."

"Maybe we're the lucky ones," Georgia says, kissing my

cheek. "You can still be sweet every once in a while. Try to remember that. And some things you don't outgrow, like being jealous when you're kept in the dark about something that matters. I should get back out there." She stands to leave. "I know you won't watch *Finding Nemo* tonight. Promise me you won't choose anything too scary."

"I promise," I say.

A moment later, Noah returns, and we actually do watch the movie while we eat dinner. When the credits roll, I ask, "Can you help me figure out the passcode to the phone?"

Noah pulls the burner from his pocket. "What do you think I was getting from my room earlier? Do you know anything about where the phone came from?"

"Not much. I found it in the Lost and Found at the church. It was in Georgia's desk. In her office."

"Then it's probably hers."

Or maybe it really did just land in the Lost and Found last week, and my mother will be searching for it tomorrow.

"Go with the obvious," Noah says. "That's my dad's philosophy."

"I already tried my mother's password and her birthday."

I try my grandparents' birthdays. I even try the last four digits of my grandparents' landline, the number Georgia grew up using. None of those work either, and the phone locks again.

"You probably have one or two more attempts before it locks permanently," Noah says.

"I don't think it's my mom's. Besides, the obvious is that Mr. Thibodeau killed his wife for the insurance money and there's no serial killer. You should tell your dad that."

Noah hits me with a sofa pillow. I hit him back, and we wrestle across the floor till I have him pinned beneath me, hitting him with the pillow while he covers his face and laughs.

"Say uncle," I say.

"Uncle!"

I roll off him onto the rug. He takes out his tablet, and we troll through social media to see what other kids in school have to say about the fight with Taylor. Public opinion seems split down the middle, which doesn't seem fair since, well, I shouldn't have hit anyone.

"Post something nice about her," I say.

"About Taylor?" Noah says. "Why?"

"Just because. Write that she's smart or pretty or something like that."

"Taylor's not smart or pretty," Noah says, "and everyone knows you and I are friends. They'll think I'm being sarcastic."

"Then write that *I* say that I was a jerk today. And that Taylor's awesome. And her hair is really nice."

Noah types a few lines into the tablet and hits *Send*. "I didn't add the part about her hair. It would have sounded mean."

I glance at the burner phone. If I found the phone in Georgia's desk, isn't it probably hers? And if it is Georgia's, what else would she use as a passcode?

Harper noses her way into the room, tail wagging, and licks the plates we left on the coffee table.

"Stop," Noah says, pushing her away.

I suddenly have an idea.

I enter a four-digit code. The screen clears and opens right as the floorboards squeak behind me. I shove the phone under a pillow and turn to face Alice Stone.

"Do you want to go shopping sometime?" she asks me. "Do girls still go shopping?"

All I want is to see what's on that phone, and who it belongs to. "Sometimes. Is this about the fight at school?"

"Maybe a little bit. But mostly I want to get to know you better. How about next Saturday?"

"Okay."

For a split second, it seems as if she might leave us alone.

But she snaps her fingers and points at the pillow, and I hand over the phone without a fight. "I thought this wasn't yours," Mrs. Stone says to Noah.

"It isn't," he says.

"It certainly isn't anymore." She slips the phone into her pocket, though she doesn't seem upset, or even angry. "Time to sing 'Happy Birthday.' Come help me out."

CHAPTER 40
Chloe

Later that night, after I've watched Mrs. Stone pass the burner to Mr. Stone out on the patio, after he's slipped it into his coat pocket, after we've sung "Happy Birthday," and I've tried to negotiate staying at the farmhouse for the night only to have my father of all people thwart me, and after I've run through the woods to Farley's house, I lurk in my room and formulate a plan.

Across the hall, Farley and Dad argue about something, their fierce whispers piercing the quiet night through their bedroom door. Outside, a thunderstorm makes its way across the bay, the time between lightning flashes and rumbles of thunder still long enough to tell me the storm is far off. If I'm lucky, the phone is in Mr. Stone's coat pocket, and his coat will be hanging in their foyer with all their other coats. It will be easy to get in and out without being caught.

I slip along the downstairs hallway and then into the garage, where I ease open the window at the back. Somehow, Farley missed this window when he had the security system installed. This is the one blind spot where I can sneak into Uncle Max's yard without being captured on video.

I fall onto the ground and crawl through the trees. The night air is thick, waiting for the coming rain to release the humidity. When I reach the edge of Uncle Max's garden, I nearly stand, but a flash of lightning captures him in a freeze frame, sitting on his back deck, one foot up on the rail, a can of beer to his lips. I keep still, barely daring to breathe. When the thunder rumbles, I use the noise as cover to ease around the cottage. Still, Uncle Max must hear me. In the moonlight, his silhouetted form stands. He whispers Georgia's name as lightning fills the sky again and I finish my retreat.

Out on the lane, I keep to the shadows before plunging onto the carriageway and through the trees toward Moulton Farm. Here the canopy of leaves blocks out any light. When a twig snaps a bit too close, my feet start pounding the forest floor. I crash to the ground, sliding across leaves and pine needles. My hands grasp a tree branch. I brandish it, swinging at the dark.

"Who's there?" I whisper to silence.

I pick myself up and tell the voices in my head to shut up as I make my way to the stone wall. Here the lawn swoops up toward the farmhouse, where Mrs. Stone sits looking out over the bay with Harper at her side while music blasts from the house. Lightning strikes, and this time the thunder tells me the storm is getting closer. The moon still provides enough light that I don't dare move. Instead, I hunker down and wait.

Mrs. Stone squints into the dark, as though she senses my presence. A few moments later, the music stops mid-song, and then Mr. Stone comes outside to join her. He's changed out of the coat he wore earlier and into rain gear. He sits beside Mrs. Stone, and they speak in voices too low for me to overhear. A cloud rolls over the moon. As I edge from behind the stone wall and into the shadows, Harper rises and barks toward me. I will myself to fade into the night, but I'm close enough now to hear Mr. Stone say, "The rain's beginning. We should go inside."

Mrs. Stone holds Harper's collar. "I know everything," she says.

I wonder what she knows. Of course I do. But I can't risk being caught, so I keep moving, out of the dog's line of sight. When I reach the other side of the farmhouse, I press my back to the wall. Before I can lose my nerve, I ease open the kitchen door, patter through into the next room, and then to the foyer. I find Mr. Stone's coat hanging on a hook, but the pockets are empty.

"You won't find it."

I turn. Noah hovers in the doorway. I stare at him.

"My dad has the phone," Noah says. "It's his."

It's not, though. I know who it belongs to now. The passcode gave it away.

"You shouldn't break into people's houses," Noah says.

"And you shouldn't smoke pot," I say. "Keep my secret, and I'll keep yours."

Noah squelches a grin. "Want another cupcake?"

"I'm good," I say, retreating back through the kitchen and escaping into the yard.

Outside, fat raindrops smack the ground and soak my Burger King T-shirt. I backtrack along the stone wall. Mr. and Mrs. Stone have left the patio along with Harper. I nearly reach the carriageway when a figure appears in front of me, stepping out of the trees. I freeze in place, hoping not to be seen.

I'm in so much trouble.

Now, hours later at the parsonage, after that detective gave my mother and me a ride home, I lie in bed in my room, going over the events of last night, trying to make sense of them, trying to make them mean something they don't. But you can't twist lies into truth. What did Alice Stone know about? Why did one of my parents have a burner phone? And why had one of them snuck through the woods to Moulton Farm in the middle of the night? What do any of them know about Farley's death?

I'm here by myself. Georgia's gone. She left the parsonage as soon as the cops brought her car back this morning. Now, downstairs, the door opens, and someone makes their way through the house. Footsteps approach up the creaky old stairs. I suppose I could be frightened. But I'm not.

My bedroom door opens. Dad steps in. He's wearing pink cycling clothes and holds a helmet under one arm. He doesn't need to say anything for me to understand he knows about the phone, about my midnight jaunt next door, that I'd been gone last night when Farley was killed. Maybe he knows what I saw, too.

"When did you get a cat?" he asks.

I wish the cat was here, that I could let her walk across me and knead my chest. I swallow and can barely find the words to respond. "Like, two months ago. Her name is Tippi."

"Good name." He glances over his shoulder. "Where's your mother?"

"I don't know. She went out."

He approaches the side of my bed and sits, and I remember the way he came into my room at Farley's house yesterday, the way we hurled insults at each other, the way he understood what I needed at that moment. My dad's always been that way, but every problem I've ever faced till now has been so simple. He can't offer an easy fix this time.

"Who's Jack?" he asks.

His breath smells like smoke. "Have you been smoking?"

"Tell me about Jack."

Even Jack can't help me with this. "He's no one."

"Did he get you to do something you didn't want to?"

I should never have mentioned syphilis to Farley. "God, no."

"What's Jack's last name?"

"I don't want to talk about Jack."

"Chloe, you can tell me anything. You know that, right? But you don't need to. Whatever they ask, you were in bed all night."

I start to tell him everything, but he puts a finger to my lips. He lays the burner phone on the mattress between us. I run my finger along the crack in the screen.

"Where did you get that?" I ask.

"It's not important," he says. "You were home all night. You loved Farley like a second father. We were happy."

I hear footsteps in the hallway. Uncle Max appears at my door.

Out in the cemetery, after Uncle Max takes my father away in handcuffs, I sit by Jack's grave and trace his name. "I don't know what to do," I whisper. "What should I do? Tell me what to do, Jack."

Tears sting my eyes, but I swipe them away. This isn't the time for that.

Jack thought he knew everyone's secrets, but he missed his own wife's. Hortensia was the type, I'm sure, who believed we have to be all good or all bad and there can't be a middle ground, so she denied her own truth even as syphilis lesions flamed across her groin, even as the disease brought her own death. For her, it was easier simply to lie.

The wind blows, and I shiver. It's grown cold out, the humidity from last night swept away with the storm. I lie on the grass. Above, blue sky shows through maple leaves blushing red from the first hint of fall. When footsteps approach, I want to sink into the ground and disappear, but Georgia stops, her curls blowing across her face. She adjusts her glasses, and says, "We have to stick together. They'll be coming soon. For all of us."

Uncle Max has the phone now. The passcode connects the phone to Dad. To Georgia, too. And soon enough, I'll need to choose between them.

PART VI

The Minister

CHAPTER 41
Georgia

I suppose my story begins the day I moved into the parsonage fifteen years ago. The day I started to become Reverend George.

I'd never lived anywhere by myself in my entire life, and I wanted nothing more than to welcome people into my little home in this little town I'd stumbled upon. But the parsonage was in complete disrepair. To start, it needed a new roof, then plumbing and electrical work, and I doubted the chimney would draw much smoke. In the kitchen, the faucet dripped. Upstairs, a water stain had spread across the bedroom ceiling, and I swore I heard squirrels in the eaves. Add it to the list, right? Or don't. I was only supposed to stay for the year, a lucky last-minute placement when the prior minister dropped dead.

Or not so lucky for him, I suppose.

But the post was on an interim basis while the committee conducted a thorough ministerial search. I never thought I'd be asked to stay. I was twenty-six and felt way too young to offer guidance to anyone, but, I reminded myself, plenty of ministers younger than I was had risen to the occasion and led congregations. Now was my chance to prove myself!

On that first day, a steady stream of people stopped by to introduce themselves and deliver casserole dishes and plates of sweets, enough meals to get me through the new year. The faces and names blurred so I already knew that by the following Sunday, when I delivered my first sermon, I would have to make a joke about meeting them all again for the first time.

I was sure they'd understand.

In the kitchen, I lit sage and opened windows to air out any ghosts the last minister might have left behind.

"Don't burn the place down."

I turned to see a police officer standing at one of the open windows. He had a thatch of thick dark hair and wore a uniform that hugged his lean frame. "This house," he said. "It's one lost shingle away from collapse, but I'm good with my hands. I'm like your unofficial handyman. Max Barbosa."

I dropped the smoking sage into the kitchen sink and doused it with water. The faucet dripped when I turned it off.

"I've been meaning to fix that," Max said. "Call with anything you need. I'm easy to find. Everyone knows me."

He saluted, heading off through the cemetery in what could only be described as a strut, passing two women surrounded by a bevy of children. I hoped he might stop and look back.

He did.

"Knock, knock," one of the women said, poking her head through the kitchen door.

She had short dark hair and thick glasses. Behind her, the whole troupe of children dashed through the garden and around the gravestones. She said her name and introduced the other woman, along with the roster of children's names.

The woman offered a paper plate covered in foil. "We made brownies."

"I love brownies!"

I should have asked them in. Made tea. Offered them brownies or cookies or cake or any of the other sweets that covered the kitchen table. "Where does your family live?" I asked.

"My husband and I live on Peter's Hill," the woman said.

"And I'm her neighbor," the other woman said.

I'd assumed the two women were a couple, that they raised the brood together.

"We'll let you get settled," one of them said while the other gathered the children.

As they headed out, they turned to assess me, framed by the gravestones behind them.

I imagined them walking home and reviewing their impressions of the new minister. They'd talk about my age or my marital status or my lack of lipstick. By the following week, I tried to spot them in the congregation, but by then their features had merged into the sea of faces that had streamed in and out of the parsonage that day. If I did meet them again, they were kind enough not to hold my lack of recognition against me, so I never made the connection.

Even now, I wonder who they were. They always know who I am.

CHAPTER 42
Georgia

LAST OCTOBER

"My marriage," I said to Farley. "It's falling apart."

I paced across the carpeted floor. This was my fourth session with him, and probably my last, and I wasn't sure why I started coming to see him in the first place, but as soon as those words crossed my lips, I understood Farley had been waiting for me to say them since the moment I'd stepped into his office. Or maybe I'd been the one waiting, but now that I had, I wished I hadn't.

"Falling apart," he said, hands tented. "What's changed?"

Nothing had actually changed between Ritchie and me. At least nothing I could point to.

"Why did you move to this town?" I asked Farley.

"Georgia," he said to me. "Don't change the subject."

"I'm curious. You're young. Single. Rich. Why here of all places?"

"Why don't you tell me why *you* moved here," he said.

I didn't answer. I could wait anyone out.

Farley jotted something on his legal pad. "You're right. I'm rich. And I suppose I wanted a change, and this was a place I could reinvent myself. It seemed like a good decision at the time."

"Was it?"

"Mostly. And if it turns out I made a bad decision, I'll make another one. Now it's your turn. Why did you move here?"

"The job," I said. "They needed an interim minister. I thought the move was temporary, but the next year, the committee offered me the permanent position, and now I'm married and have a kid and I'm still wondering if it's temporary."

"It can be," Farley said.

"Not at this point," I said. "And I should go."

"You have five minutes," Farley said. "Three hundred seconds. Make the most of it. What's going on with the marriage?" He flipped back through his legal pad. "Richard, right?"

"Ritchie," I said.

"Ritchie, then," Farley said.

"And you know him. I've seen you driving the Triumph around town. You bought the car from him."

"The mechanic. Of course." Farley jotted something else on the legal pad. "Why did you say your marriage was falling apart?"

I laughed. Now that I'd said it out loud, now that Farley had reflected those words back to me, I heard the hyperbole. "I didn't mean anything," I said.

Farley crossed one leg over the other. He glanced over my shoulder. "Tick, tick, tick," he said.

"That's 1 percent of my three hundred seconds," I said.

"You're good at math. You just told me you chose Ritchie over . . ." He checked through his notes again. "Max, right?"

"Yes, Max," I said. "And you look through your notes for show. It's part of your act. You know exactly who Max is. He's your neighbor."

Farley nodded. "Sure," he said. "I know him outside of this room as my neighbor, but here, in these sessions, he's someone important to you. Why is he important? What place does he hold?"

"A different choice," I said. "A different life."

Ritchie had been the easy choice, the one I could control, the one I could shape to match the image I wanted to project as Reverend George. He was happy to come to church every week and watch my sermon from the front pew. He was happy to fade into the background and let me shine bright.

"How would that life have been different?" Farley asked.

"I guess I'll never know."

"Never say never," Farley said. "Life is full of surprises."

I left Farley's office through the rear entrance and made my way down the stairs to Main Street. I checked to see that no one was watching and stepped out of the building onto the sidewalk where I transformed into Reverend George—out for a walk, shoulders back, head high, greeting anyone I saw. I spent so much time playing Reverend George, I wasn't sure I could recognize myself anymore.

A BMW swerved into a parking space on the street. Karen Lawson got out, an orange bag slung over her shoulder, aviator glasses blocking the sun. Karen wasn't part of my congregation, but I knew her from the birthday party circuit. Her daughter, Taylor, was a twit.

"Reverend," she said.

"Nice to see you," I said.

She headed inside the building. She must be Farley's next patient.

At home, Ritchie greeted me from the kitchen, where he chopped vegetables, and the scents of garlic and ginger hung in the air. "What's for dinner?" I asked.

"Curry," he said. "With cauliflower rice."

I kissed him. He felt comfortable. The session with Farley seemed as though it had happened to someone else. "I have a little work to do," I said.

"I'll call you when dinner's ready."

I found Chloe in her room lying next to a stuffed polar bear, her schoolbooks spread out around her. "Math test tomorrow," she said.

"What's 1 percent of three hundred?" I asked.

"Too easy," she said, letting me slide onto the bed beside her. She rested her silky brown hair against my chest while she told me about her day. When my phone rang, she went back to studying. "That thing rules your life," she said.

I clicked into the call anyway, greeting Everett Irving, the church treasurer. Everett told me he had something to talk about even though it was Monday, my day off. "Can you send me an e-mail?" I asked.

"This is more personal."

Everett kept everything close to the chest, so whatever he wanted to say must be important. And he often had a line on things I wouldn't necessarily have known on my own. Last year, a parishioner had stolen over a thousand dollars from the reserve fund, and Everett had been the one to uncover it. We'd managed to replace the funds and keep the incident quiet. The parishioner still even came to services as though nothing had happened. "Meet me tomorrow," I said. "By the town forest. I take a walk there most afternoons."

Downstairs, Ritchie finished cooking dinner. I set the table. "Wine?" I asked.

"Not tonight," he said.

I glanced at him. "Have you lost some weight?"

"Maybe a little bit," he said.

I filled my own glass, all the way to the rim.

* * *

The next afternoon, I drove to the western part of Monreith, which was sparsely populated and dotted with crimson cranberry bogs flooded for the harvest. As I pulled into a small parking lot at the edge of the forest, I noticed for the first time that the maples had begun to turn for the season. Everett waited beside his black Mercedes. He must have been verging on sixty, with thinning silver hair and sloped shoulders from years of hunching over ledgers at one of the area's top accounting firms. He had two grown kids, and I'd been to his house, right over the state line in Rhode Island, which was enormous and on the water. From the outside, he didn't seem like someone with much to complain about, but if working as a minister had taught me anything, it was that we all have our inner demons.

We greeted each other and walked along a well-maintained path. Everett tried to make small talk, though with him, small talk involved the church finances. We scaled one of the many old stone walls that crisscrossed the forest and leapt over a swollen stream. Finally, he told me he was upset and didn't know who to talk to.

"Try me," I said.

Everett's wife, Helen, was a doctor. She'd been having an affair with an anesthesiologist in her practice, and from what Everett had been able to ascertain, it seemed like it had been going on for a while. "This guy's been to our house. I took him fishing on the boat."

Helen was an agnostic and didn't attend weekly services with her husband. According to Everett, she often scheduled her trysts for when he was at church. "I could kill him," Everett said, smacking his fist into his palm.

"You don't want to do that," I said.

"I do," Everett said. "Or I did. Someone may have beaten

me to it. His name's Steve Alabiso. And he's dead. He was hunting turkeys last week and got shot. It was in the news. Honestly, I already suspected the affair, but Helen was so upset by Steve's death that she confessed the whole thing to me."

Everett walked me through more details of the death. I wondered if the police had questioned him, and I briefly considered that I was alone with him in the woods where anything could happen. Maybe Everett had already known about the affair. Maybe he'd snuck up on this man and then staged the shooting to look like an accident. If Steve Alabiso had been sleeping with Everett's wife, it seemed that Everett had a motive to kill him, too.

"The police were focusing on the wife, Penny," Everett said, "though she was out of town on the day he was killed. Even so, she's retained a lawyer."

"Sounds like she has an alibi," I said.

"Or she hired someone to kill her husband." Everett shook his head. "But I suppose it's not any of that. When the body was found, it looked like a homicide. Now forensics is saying it may have been self-inflicted. Steve may have committed suicide."

"How would you know any of this?" I asked. "That's not public knowledge. It's still an open investigation."

Everett had the decency to blush. "Gossip," he said.

"Let's ignore the whispers."

"Helen says Steve would never kill himself."

"It's hard to know what someone else is feeling," I said.

As we made our way to our cars, Everett told me he hoped to rebuild trust with his wife, though he couldn't see a path there yet. "I've been talking to Farley Drake," he said. "He's a therapist here in town."

I almost confessed I'd been seeing Farley, too, but decided

to keep that piece of information from becoming a permanent part of Reverend George's story. "I've heard good things about Dr. Drake," I said.

At the time, Everett's sessions with Farley seemed like the least important part of our conversation.

CHAPTER 43
Georgia

YESTERDAY

I stare at the blank screen on my computer, my fingers poised over the keyboard refusing to move. It's Friday afternoon, a few hours before Alice's birthday party is set to begin, and I'd hoped to have the sermon written before the end of the day so I could refine and practice it tomorrow afternoon. So much is riding on every word that I'll say on Sunday morning, but no one can plan for a week like the one I've had. Murder. A community in mourning. A member of my own flock dead, one who'd spent her days off selflessly driving parishioners to doctors' appointments, all of which should be at the forefront of everything I say, every beat in this sermon. Too bad none of those beats want to show themselves right now.

Still, I tell myself, *I can do this*. If I type one word, the screen won't be blank anymore.

My fingers finally move. *Grief* appears at the top of the page. I even manage to hit the return key twice.

How's that for a win?

Some sermons come easier than others. Two weeks ago, right after Labor Day, I used the sermon to reminisce about playing field hockey. I focused on the teamwork necessary to guide our community toward larger goals. I brought in the opportunities field hockey had offered me, how I'd earned a scholarship to college and how the scholarship had paved my way right to this parish. "Sometimes," I said, "it felt as if the path had been forged for me, but when I look back, I see a whole team guiding me along the way."

Not everyone plays sports, and I wanted the sermon to be as inclusive as possible, so I brought in a member of the ukulele ensemble to talk about playing music. I also asked Laurel Thibodeau to speak.

She wore a pink summer dress and had her red hair loose. Her husband, Simon, sat in the front pew as she talked about managing a restaurant. "Each night," she said, "is opening night. If one customer leaves unsatisfied, we all fail, but it's the successes we focus on. If someone falls behind, we pull together to make sure our audience doesn't sense that absence."

Afterwards, at the coffee hour, I could tell the parishioners had left the service ready to tackle the week. People clustered in groups around the basement, though Laurel stood by herself, coffee in hand, a shoulder against the wall. "Simon went back to the restaurant," she said. "We have to serve Sunday brunch this morning. It's a team, you know."

"And you're sitting on the bench?" I asked.

"What was your favorite part of playing field hockey?"

I liked the strategy of moving the ball down the field, of dismantling the opposing team one player at a time until they couldn't work as a unit anymore. I liked winning at any cost. "I was the captain," I said. "It's where I learned to be a leader."

Laurel bit a cookie in half. "My guess is you don't like to lose."

* * *

"Georgia?"

I look up from the screen, where I've still only managed to type *Grief.* Maggie rolls her chair to my office door. "There's someone here to see you."

I close the laptop. The state detective who's been working with Max strides into my office. "Brock London," he says, flashing his badge. "Do you have a minute to chat?"

I'm practiced enough to welcome him warmly, though I have to admit to some trepidation. It's not as if I haven't been expecting this conversation. I may have even rehearsed some of what I plan to say. "Coffee?" I ask. "Tea?"

Maggie hovers in the doorway, not even trying to pretend indifference.

"I'll only be a minute," Brock says.

"Thank you, Maggie," I say, and wait for her to close the office door. "You're here about Laurel?" It's best to cut to the chase. "She was a member of our community. We're devastated."

"I can only imagine," Brock says. "It was tragic what happened."

"I mentioned this to Chief Barbosa, but I was at the Thibodeaus' house last Friday, the day before Laurel was killed."

Brock nods. "He may have said something about that. How long have you been at this church?"

"Fifteen years," I say. "Time flies."

Brock crosses his legs. "You must hear things. People must confide in you."

"All the time, Detective. Listening to others is 90 percent of my job. Just like yours."

"Has anyone said anything recently that gave you pause? Anything that might be connected to what happened at the Thibodeaus' house? With a case like this, I'm interested in the whispers."

"The whispers don't always reach me," I say.

"My understanding is Laurel Thibodeau volunteered for the parish on her days off."

"For ten years now. Ever since she and Simon opened Firefly."

Brock lays a folder on my desk and turns back the cover. A screenshot from an online auction site sits on top. "We found a number of stolen items in Mrs. Thibodeau's possession, most of which seem to have come from older members of your community, the ones she was purporting to help. She'd been selling the items online."

I pick up the screenshot. I suspect the detective will want to draw out some of what I have to say. He'll want to work for the information I share. "Simon Thibodeau has a gambling problem," I say.

"Did Mrs. Thibodeau ever talk to you about it?"

"Not in so many words," I say. "But she suggested it here and there."

The detective tents his hands, waiting, like Farley used to do during our sessions. I make a show of shuffling papers on my desk. "My guess is that the Thibodeaus are in a lot of debt."

"You've heard about the insurance policy, too," Brock says. "The one that Simon Thibodeau took out on his wife."

I nod.

"If Simon's lucky, there won't be so much debt anymore." Brock tilts his head. "This job brings me to a lot of small communities. You watch out for each other. When people make mistakes, you help them make amends. Especially if there's a reason for the mistakes, one you can understand." He taps the screenshot. "Any chance this came up during your visit to the house last Friday?"

"If I had known what Laurel was doing," I say, "I'd have tried to stop it."

That part is true.

The office door opens. "Sorry," Maggie says. "It's the school calling. It's about Chloe."

"You'll have to excuse me, Detective," I say.

He slides a card onto my desk as I pick up the phone. "Call if you think of anything," he says. "Anytime."

I hurry the few blocks to the school, cell phone to my ear. A part of me is grateful for the distraction from the sermon and the detective's visit. I half expect Ritchie to ignore the call, but he picks up. "Chloe got in a fight," I say.

He grunts on the other end of the phone, and I imagine him rolling out from underneath one of his classic cars and wiping motor oil from his hands. "I have to get through three more cars before I can leave," he says. "People are waiting. And it's the weekend, you know?"

I can't trust Ritchie to deal with the school, even if it is his weekend to have Chloe. He lets her off the hook all the time. And, does he think I spend my afternoons waiting to deal with my teenage daughter by myself? I tell him I'll figure something out and call Farley next. Appearances are everything. With Farley, it's best that I appear to trust him. "Any chance you could swing by the church?" I ask him when he answers. "It's Chloe. She got in trouble. And I need someone to pinch hit."

He agrees right away.

At the edge of the schoolyard, I pause. The building looms, dozens of windows facing me. In my years serving this town, I've learned that my every public action can be observed, consumed, and regurgitated. Going out without lipstick, scowling at poor service, drinking, it can all come back to me. Now I slow my pace and adjust the blue-and-green scarf draped around my shoulders. I lift my chin. It won't do to come across as a panicked mother. At the door, I greet the security guard by name but don't bother with ID. Everyone in this town knows Reverend George. In the school office, the secretary sits up as I enter the room. I ask about her grandson, and she shows me a photo on her phone.

"Adorable," I say.

Chloe slumps on a hard plastic chair in the assistant principal's office, the pink hair falling in her eyes. She doesn't acknowledge me as I greet Vince Omani.

"Reverend," he says, going for formal.

What do I know about Vince? What can I use if I need to? He lives here in town with his wife and two small children. His family attends services at the mosque in New Bedford. He's maintained a mostly squeaky-clean reputation since moving here two years ago, though Max did once mention pulling him over and smelling liquor on his breath. "A DUI would sink him," Max said as he lay beside me in the parsonage. "I let him off with a warning."

I catch Chloe's eye and nod toward the lobby. "Wait for us outside," I say.

She moves as though her limbs are filled with sand as she gets up and slumps to the outer office. I close the door behind her, while Vince shuffles through a file and scratches at his goatee. I wait for him to start his lecture. I counsel myself to remain calm, to avoid getting defensive, to speak to him as a minister, not a mother.

"Five minutes?" he says.

"For what?" I ask.

"To make her sweat it out?"

I can't help but smile.

"You know how this works as well as I do," Vince says. "Chloe's a good kid going through a rough patch. She'll punish herself more than we can. Still, she's suspended for three days. There's nothing I can do about that, not in a zero-tolerance world."

"Any idea what happened?"

"Taylor Lawson's a bully, but she's been going through her own things at home. Do you know her parents? Zach and Karen Lawson?"

My guess is I'll get a call from one of them tonight.

"Zach Lawson's a piece of work," Vince says. "I'm not surprised Taylor lashes out, but Chloe won't say a word about what happened." He leans back in his chair. "Reverend, is everything okay at home? I know there's been a lot of changes. Chloe could visit the school counselor."

It hasn't been close to five minutes, but it's time to leave anyway. "Thank you, Mr. Omani," I say, in full Reverend George mode.

I breeze out of the office, knowing Chloe will follow in my wake. As we make our way toward the church, it feels like every person we pass is watching us as I try to play mother and talk Chloe through this, but she keeps asking why I won't let her get a phone, and I'm exhausted from the endless debate, knowing the moment I let her get the phone she'll drift further from me. At the church, I tell her she's grounded for a month. "And you'll get your grades back up, too. And that hair—"

I catch myself before I say anything else. The last thing I need is for Chloe to know how much the pink hair bothers me. Upstairs, Maggie tells me Damian Stone is waiting in my office.

"Sit," I say to Chloe. Farley should be here soon to pick her up. "And don't move."

I step into my office, where Damian turns from reading the spines on a shelf of books. He clutches a bike helmet under his arm and clomps across the floor to give me a sweaty hug, his beard brushing against my cheek. "I was in the neighborhood."

I'm not completely surprised to see him. Damian has a

habit of swinging by the office to chat when he's out on his bike. If I weren't a minister, I'd think he was making a move on me.

I wave toward a chair. He perches on the very edge, his jersey open on his lean chest. Damian has a public persona, too, confident and bold. That's who he presents right now, as if he's forgotten I've seen the real him plenty of times. "Big night," he says, his voice too loud. "Alice's four-oh. Do me a favor; tell her the food is great. She's been cooking all week."

"Of course," I say.

Damian fishes a wallet from the back of his jersey and counts out four twenties. "And could you swing by Mirabella's? I ordered a cake but can't carry it on my bike. I have to get home and help get ready."

"Happy to do it."

I take the twenties and knock my mouse. My laptop lights up with that single word, *Grief*. I wait for Damian to speak, to tell me the real reason for his visit this afternoon, and it's not to ask me to run an errand for him. Finally, he closes his eyes. "It's been a long week," he says.

"I'm sure," I say.

Damian's grieving. More than most. He confessed his affair with Laurel to me during one of his visits to this office, and now I suppose I'm one of the few people he can confide that grief to. Maybe the only one.

I nearly mention Detective London's visit but decide to keep it to myself for now.

"I can't stop thinking it's my fault," he says. "What if Laurel's dead because I got too close to the truth?"

"You can't think that way," I say.

Soon, that's exactly what the police will believe happened. At least I hope they will.

CHAPTER 44
Georgia

EARLIER THIS YEAR

In January, Alice and Damian moved into Moulton Farm. At the church, I was transitioning from the warmth of the holiday season into the depths of winter, when enticing people into the pews becomes more challenging. I'd also ended my sessions with Farley. Ritchie was still living in the parsonage. Chloe hadn't dyed her hair pink, and she certainly wouldn't have started a fight at school.

And me? I was comfortable. Content. Happier than I realized. I hadn't imagined anything would change.

Alice brought Noah to the church for services right after they moved to town. I noticed her at once, sitting close to the front of the church, wearing a cashmere scarf and a light green sweater set. She was the kind of woman who drew attention, the kind who I had to remind myself not to spend the entire service speaking directly to. During the coffee hour, she worked the room, introducing herself as she moved from one small group to the next, till she sidled up beside me and launched into conversation as if we'd already met. "Harper's had it rough. That police chief said no one would want her, but he got that one wrong. Now she's rolling in kibble."

"I take it Harper's a dog," I said.

"A pit bull."

"Max Barbosa gets a lot wrong," I said.

"What's his deal, anyway?" Alice asked. "He lives near me. Harper's always running through the woods to his place and hanging out on his deck."

"Knowing Max," I said, "he's leaving treats out for her. But Max is single."

Alice held up her hand, where a wedding band flashed on her ring finger. "Thanks, Reverend, but my husband Damian's out on his bike. Maybe I'll get him to come next week. When's the blessing of the animals, anyway?"

"Not till October," I said. "But we'll make Harper's extra special."

Alice turned to face the room. "I have recommendations for a yoga studio and a restaurant for date nights. Now I just need a therapist. Also, a friend for my kid. Yours seems available."

Chloe and Noah were talking by the snacks. "Looks like they found each other already," I said.

"How about dinner at our place next Saturday?"

Part of my job was to welcome new families to town, though I usually hosted at the parsonage. It felt almost conspiratorial to accept the invitation, but I did anyway. "And I can recommend a therapist, too."

Back then, I still trusted Farley.

Alice pulled me in for a hug. "Please. I'll take all the recommendations I can get!"

That Saturday, we went to the farm for the first time. Chloe and Noah disappeared upstairs to Noah's room. The four of us paired off at once along gender lines—Ritchie and Damian, Alice and me. The boys drank beer and played video games; the girls gossiped and sipped chardonnay in the kitchen, not my usual thing, but I loved every moment of it. Alice served a dry lasagna with undercooked noodles, a salad drenched in Ken's Italian, and banana cream pie that refused to set. "Delicious," I said.

"If you say so," Alice said.

After dinner, Damian told us about his latest project with a streaming service, the one that brought them to Monreith. "I signed a nondisclosure agreement," he said, "so I can't say much more."

Then he screened *Acadian Autumn* for us beside a roaring fire. It was better than I'd expected it to be.

Soon Saturday night dinners became a regular occurrence, and Alice and I were going to yoga together like we'd been friends since childhood. She shared the most intimate aspects of her personal life. She told me about her marriage, her sex life, how Damian had lost his job teaching at the college when she was an undergraduate and they'd started sleeping together. She understood that if I wanted a second glass of wine without being bothered by someone, we had to drive two towns over, where they had their own Unitarian church and no one knew me. She felt like a real friend.

So when Damian swung by my office for the first time, my guard went up. Ritchie and I hung out with the Stones as a foursome, but my friendship was with Alice. Damian was attractive and had the vibe of someone who didn't think twice about stepping out on his wife. She'd hinted that much already over a glass of chardonnay.

"I was biking in the neighborhood," he said.

He wore long sleeves and black leggings and had frozen snot caked in his beard. I handed him a tissue, and he asked what I'd thought of *Acadian Autumn*.

"Fascinating," I said. "I love seeing micro-cultures in action, and you captured the power dynamic really well in a faith-based community. There's a whole cottage industry out there on ministerial boundary training."

"Did it make you want to visit northern Maine?" he asked. "That's what they wanted me to make, sort of a travel piece."

I smiled. "There are so many places to visit."

"I guess I made it look kind of bleak." He rubbed his beard. The snot had thawed. "But at least I got paid."

He returned over the coming weeks, each time stopping by unannounced, claiming to be riding near the church. He began to share details about his life. His first confession was about meeting Alice when she was his student, something I had to pretend to not already know.

"Not my finest moment," he said.

He admitted Alice was the family's breadwinner, and he felt threatened by her at times. And in late March, he asked if I had to keep his secrets. It was the week of Easter, and I was distracted by my sermon, one of the most important ones of the year. "Mostly," I said. "Except if you commit a crime."

"You're friends with Alice. Isn't that a conflict of interest? What if I told you something you thought she should know?"

I hadn't mentioned Damian's visits to Alice, even as I'd grown closer to her. That was Damian's place, though I had begun keeping track of what he told me in private, and what was said during our weekly dinners.

"I couldn't survive this job without compartmentalizing," I said. "You can tell me whatever you want. Or keep it to yourself. It's up to you."

He hunched forward, the arms on the leather chair seeming to swallow his slim frame. "I'll be fifty this year," he said. "And I don't know what I'm doing. I don't know if I ever did. I've been working on these documentaries for twenty years now. *Acadian Autumn*'s the best thing I've done, and even that's not getting the traction I thought it would. I can't even get financing anymore."

"What about the project here?" I asked. "You told us it was for a streaming service."

"There's no project," he said. "We're only here because I could get the farm for free from a former colleague. His sabbatical ends next year. After that, I don't know what we'll do." He shook his head. "I go into my office and pretend to work most mornings. Then I spend the afternoon biking. But I have a lead. We'll see if it turns into anything."

I folded my hands and smiled. As much as I enjoyed Damian's visits, as much as I wanted to help, I needed to get back to my sermon.

He took out his phone and pulled up a website. "Have you heard of this case?" he asked, passing the phone to me.

It was the same case Everett Irving had mentioned to me in the fall: Steve Alabiso, the man who'd shot himself hunting turkeys. "What about it?" I asked.

Damian shrugged. "Could be nothing," he said. "But something about it seems suspicious."

"Keep digging," I said. "Who knows what you might find?"

At the time, I was just trying to help.

CHAPTER 45
Georgia

YESTERDAY

My cell phone rings. I answer right as Farley strides into my office and sits without being asked. I should be grateful he dropped whatever he was doing to take Chloe off my hands, but Farley's entitlement annoys me. I've learned to mask my true feelings about him most of the time, though.

"I might as well be in prison, Georgia," Simon Thibodeau says on the other end of the phone.

I can see Farley pretending not to listen. "This will pass," I say in my softest voice.

"When?" Simon asks. "Right now, it's unbearable."

The call disconnects. I stay on the line for a moment, watching Farley from the corner of my eye. Maggie calls him the peacock to show solidarity, though I also know she loves it when he showers her with attention.

I set the phone on my desk, face down. "Do you have any cash? I need to run an errand before the party."

He checks his wallet. "Eighty bucks?"

"I'll pay you back."

I won't, though, and Farley won't dare ask, either. This is one of the little ways I get back at him for what he did.

"What was that call about?" he asks.

"It was Simon Thibodeau. He's stuck inside his house, what with the press hounding him and everything everyone is saying. I need to head over there, and before you try to talk me out of it, he's a member of this community. He needs support from someone. But if I go missing, at least you'll know where to send the cops."

He nods toward the outer office. "And what about Chloe? What happened at school?"

My head falls to the desk as I tell Farley what I know about Chloe's fight with Taylor Lawson. He makes a half-hearted attempt to play therapist and take Chloe's side about the phone but gives up soon enough.

"Take her home," I say, "and make sure she knows she's in trouble. I have to work on my sermon. This whole town is in mourning, so I need to get it right. It's about grief. Is that too on the nose? Rumors are flying around." I pause. "Paranoia, too."

Farley should be paranoid, though I doubt he's figured that out yet. He's not as smart or shrewd as he believes. Honestly, he's earned everything he has coming.

I pull into the cul-de-sac and park my silver Camry on the street beside Simon's house. As I get out of the sedan, I take a moment to adjust my scarf. I turn to each of the other four houses on the circle to see who might be watching. Some of these neighbors have appeared on TV this week, talking through Laurel's best qualities and avoiding implicating Simon in her death. No one's mentioned her affair with Damian or seems to know about it yet, though I suspect the whispers will begin soon, the kind the detective came looking for.

A single reporter lurks in a beige minivan, his camera already poised to snap a photo. I make sure he captures my good side. I'm here to minister to someone in need. Report away.

At Simon's front door, I ring the bell and hear footsteps in the hallway. "It's Reverend George," I say.

The dead bolt clicks, and the door opens an inch. Simon squints into the afternoon sun. He's almost unrecognizable nearly a week after his wife's death. On a good day, Simon's more rakish than handsome, with a hook of a nose and a belly that juts over his belt. Usually, he makes up for what he lacks in looks with confidence, but now his eyes are bloodshot, and his skin is drawn and pale as though he's been trapped in a cave for weeks. He wears jeans and a yellowed T-shirt stained with what I hope is tomato. He opens the door further to usher me inside, but I pull him close for a supportive embrace, my arms wide and inviting. I can almost hear the shutter clicking on that reporter's camera.

As soon as I step inside, Simon slams the door and locks it. The aroma of onions and tomatoes can't mask the stale stench of Simon's unwashed hair and clothes. He waves me through the house to the kitchen, where a Dutch oven simmers with ratatouille. Six aluminum tubs labeled with Sharpies wait. "Who's this for?" I ask.

"Alice Stone," he says. "She's having a party."

So much for doing her own cooking.

Simon scoops a spoonful of ratatouille from the pot and blows on it. "What's it need?" he asks.

I taste the stew. It's rich, infused with earthy eggplant and grassy zucchini, just like when Simon makes it for the restaurant. "Summer in a pot," I say.

He tastes it himself and adds a pinch of salt and a few cracks of pepper before turning off the burner.

"So," he says.

I push myself up onto one of the counters, my legs dangling in the air. "You tell me."

He rests his hip against the stove and eyes me from head to foot before breaking away and ladling the ratatouille into an aluminum container.

"There'll only be seven of us at the party," I say. "Eight, if you count Harper. You made enough to feed the whole town."

"You're going?" he asks.

I nod.

"My invitation must have been lost in the mail."

A part of me was surprised to be invited tonight. Alice doesn't ask me over very often these days, not since Farley replaced me in the foursome. "You don't want the world to see you at a party," I say. "Are the police still questioning you?"

"The chief is relentless," Simon says. "He doesn't buy my alibi."

Max is a good cop, even if he lets the assistant principal off with a warning instead of issuing a DUI. Earlier this week, he said to me, "Simon Thibodeau's up to his ears in gambling debts. He defaulted on every loan he has but kept paying the insurance premium?"

I ran my fingers along his chest. If Max wanted to focus on Simon, that was fine with me.

"It's greed," Max said. "Plain and simple."

Now, to Simon, I say, "Be patient. They'll have other leads soon."

"When?"

When they find the right evidence. "What about the state cops?"

"They had me at the station from Sunday almost through Monday afternoon trying to get me to confess. And I can't leave the house without one of my friendly neighbors posting a photo online. I look like shit in every single one of them."

"You could take a shower. Change your clothes." I nod to the waiting food. "Alice won't want to serve what you made if she sees you like this."

He sniffs under his arm.

"You're pretty ripe," I say. "But come to the service on Sunday."

"Are you kidding me?" Simon says. "If I show up, the whole town will be talking about me."

"And what will they say if you don't come?"

He seals the top of the container, writes *Ratatouille* across the top with a Sharpie, and adds it to the other food. As he brings the Dutch oven to the sink, his hand brushes my thigh. Desperate men can take the wrong cues from any woman, even a minister. I push off the counter and land on my feet. "I'll wash. You dry. I don't know where things go. And you should get a lawyer."

"With what money?" he asks. "The restaurant's closed. This house is mortgaged to the hilt."

I slide the eighty bucks Farley gave me into his shirt pocket. "There's a start," I say.

It's the least I can do.

CHAPTER 46
Georgia

LAST MAY

In the spring, after Ritchie moved out of the parsonage and into the little office at the garage, Saturday dinners at Moulton Farm ended without notice. We were a foursome, and the foursome didn't exist anymore. Soon after that, I noticed Ritchie driving around town with Farley in the Triumph. Others noticed, too. The car is a convertible, after all. On May 31, Ritchie fumbled around trying to tell me the truth. "I'm so sorry, Georgia," he said.

I let him off the hook. "Go be yourself," I said.

Or really, Reverend George said that while I listened. In fact, she rose above it all. She understood reputation and appearance come before anything else and that I, Georgia, would be lost without my job. The next Sunday, she lit a candle of gratitude at the end of the service. She attended committee meetings and waved off anyone who tried to gossip or offer condolences. She even told Farley he was lucky she liked him. She may have said it as a gentle threat, one meant to remind Farley she could lodge a formal complaint against him at any time.

I, on the other hand, felt betrayed. Angry, even. I spent most nights watching endless hours of television on my phone. Therapists shouldn't sleep with their clients' husbands, no matter what's going on in the client's marriage. But I pushed that all down and kept it to myself.

Alice started canceling on me, too—not all the time, but enough that I noticed. The Saturday dinners, as it turned out, hadn't ended. They'd gone on without missing a beat, though I'd been replaced by Farley, something I figured out when Chloe mentioned being at Moulton Farm during one of her father's weekends.

"How long have you known about Ritchie and Farley?" I asked Damian the next time he came by my office.

He had the decency not to lie, though he didn't tell the full truth, either. "We all have to compartmentalize sometimes," he said, reflecting my own words back to me.

I gave Damian a pass. Or Reverend George did. As a minister, I'd witnessed enough divorces to know people expected me to move on, and that the bitter ex-wife didn't win in the end.

"How's the true crime?" I asked. "Anything ever come of that hunting accident? The one in Rhode Island? What was the guy's name?"

"Steve Alabiso," Damian said.

It had been a month or two since Damian had first mentioned the Alabiso case. He seemed relieved by the change of topic, and why wouldn't he be? Who wants to be caught out on betraying a friend? "The case is still open," he added. "I talked to the cops, but they didn't tell me much. The wife, too. She's shaken by the whole thing, and claims some of her former friends think she had something to do with her husband's death. The first time I went by her house, she thought I might be a drug dealer. Turns out Steve had a heavy hand with the prescription pad. Besides that, there's nothing much to go on. It's probably a dead end."

"Probably," I said.

Later that week, I drove to Fall River to meet with the Interfaith Council. It was almost the end of the school year, and this was our last session of the season. We reported on the year's initiatives, elected a new chair for the fall, and adjourned. As I headed out to the parking lot, one of the members, Ben Fisher, caught up with me. "Any chance I could bend your ear?" he asked, sweeping dark hair from his eyes.

Ben probably wasn't even thirty years old and was new to his position at a local temple. We'd hit it off earlier that year, and I'd been mentoring him. "How can I help?"

"We had a suicide a few weeks back," he said. "A woman named Jeanine Geller. She died of carbon monoxide poisoning. I can't help thinking I could have done more. And that I should be doing more."

As he spoke, I remembered the first time someone in my parish had taken their own life, and how helpless it had left everyone feeling, including me. During the eulogy, I'd talked about the temptation to blame ourselves when something like that happens. "Don't look for answers where there aren't any," I said to Ben.

"Try telling that to the police," Ben said. "They're making things worse."

I leaned against the car. The early summer sun felt good on my face after a long winter. "Focus on helping each individual heal in their own way."

"It's messy. Jeanine was having an affair with another member of the temple. Now some people are choosing sides, and it's hard to stay neutral."

I almost told Ben about the end of my own marriage, how people gossiped even about me, but it was important to rise over a community, to be part of it but separate at the same time. Reverend George was good at that. "That's your job," I said.

"The man she was seeing lives in your town," Ben said. "Zach Lawson. His wife's name is Karen. They have a daughter, Taylor. Karen keeps coming to talk to me, but there's only so much I can say."

"Don't say anything. Just listen." I gave him a hug. "You've got this."

On my way home, something about what Ben had told me niggled at the back of my mind. I stopped at Target. As I rolled my cart into the electronics aisle, a memory flashed through my mind of leaving Farley's office and seeing Karen Lawson pulling to the curb in her BMW and then heading inside. Karen was Farley's patient, just like Everett Irving. Karen's husband had betrayed her with Jeanine Geller. Everett's wife had betrayed him with Steve Alabiso. Two betrayed spouses linked to the same therapist. Two lovers dead. Two makes a series.

I'm not sure how long I stood there in that aisle, my fists gripping the shopping cart. I wonder now whether I'd have made different choices if events had unfolded in a different sequence. What if Everett and I hadn't gone for that walk in the town forest, and he'd shared his wife's betrayal with someone else? What if I'd left my session with Farley two minutes earlier and hadn't seen Karen pulling up in her BMW? What if I hadn't been standing right in the Target electronics department as all these pieces formed a whole?

"Excuse me."

Someone jostled me with their cart. I focused. A burner phone hung on a display in front of me. I paid for it with cash.

When I got to the parsonage, I left my own phone behind and walked to the other end of town where I tore at the burner phone's plastic clamshell packaging. When the plastic ripped apart, the phone fell to the concrete and the screen cracked. I swore under my breath, but the phone still worked. I created a passcode, 0531—May 31, the day I told Ritchie to go be himself. *Keep digging*, I wrote in a text to Damian, along with a link to a news story about Jeanine Geller's death. It was June 14, three full months before Laurel Thibodeau died.

Maybe Damian would establish that link between Farley and each of the murders. And maybe he'd see that two made a series. Or maybe Damian would dismiss the text as a prank, because, really, I meant the whole thing to be harmless. I didn't believe Farley had anything to do with the murders. I just wanted him to squirm, to have to explain himself for once, to get a tiny piece of what he had coming, my own sliver of revenge. Didn't Farley deserve to pay a small price for betraying my trust?

I didn't mean for the rest to happen.

CHAPTER 47
Georgia

YESTERDAY

I'm halfway to Moulton Farm before I remember the cake Damian asked me to pick up or that the bakery closes at five. Instead, I buy a dozen cupcakes at the supermarket. "Carrot," I say. "All of them," and at six o'clock on the dot, I pull in alongside the barn.

I cut the engine and step out under the beech tree right as Harper charges from the kitchen. A hen retreats to the coop, but I stand my ground. Long ago, I learned there was no easier way to someone's heart, or to their shit list, than through their dog, so Reverend George carries treats everywhere she goes. Besides, Harper's a good girl. I make her sit.

I inhale the funky smells of the farm. Behind me, the sun hovers near the horizon. As I head inside, I'm so focused on my excuse for forgetting the cake that it takes a moment for me to notice Max hovering by the soapstone sink while Alice fusses with something on the table.

"This is a nice surprise," I say. "I didn't know the two of you were friends."

"You're not the only one who gives Harper treats," Alice says. "She's always sneaking through the woods to Max's place."

"And everyone knows me," Max says. "I'm the chief of police."

I give Alice the cupcakes. She hugs me way longer than I deserve. "Go get changed," I say. "We'll finish up down here. Remember, it's your birthday!"

After she leaves, I kiss Max, clinging to him. I expected him to come by last night, but he didn't show. There was a time not that long ago when I truly believed something might come of things between Max and me. Maybe I still hope for that. Mostly, though, I keep him close enough to hear what's going on in the investigation.

"That detective came to my office this afternoon," I say.

"Brock London?" Max says. "He's expanding the investigation and talking to people who have a line into the community. He spoke with Farley, too."

A heads-up would have been nice.

"Brock's wondering if the murder may have something to do with those items Laurel stole."

"Those were trinkets," I say.

"Tens of thousands of dollars' worth of trinkets. No one ever said anything to you about missing jewelry? Most of Laurel's targets were members of your parish."

"Now I'm getting the third degree."

I touch his hand, and he flinches and takes a step away. "Sorry. I have a lot on my mind."

I push down how hurt I feel and let Reverend George take over for a moment. "Anything you want to share?" she asks.

"Later," he says. "After the party, maybe."

We stick with each other as we finish the prep, and the party begins. Damian takes the news about the cake in stride. "I'll pick it up tomorrow," he says.

Ritchie arrives by boat with Farley and Chloe in tow. Damian teases Ritchie about his barely-there shirt, which keeps me from having to say anything about it. Max and I sit closer than we should on the porch swing while the others pair off: Ritchie and Damian by the smoker; Alice and Farley gossiping over Cosmos; Chloe and Noah out on the lawn playing croquet. "Did Chloe wear that Burger King T-shirt to annoy me?" I ask Max.

"Probably," he says. "It goes with the hair."

Chloe thinks of Max as a second father. When he comes by the parsonage, when he stays till breakfast, I see her hopes growing. More than anyone, she wants me to be happy. I catch Ritchie watching us, too. Him, I care less about. He should be supportive of any choice I make, especially after the sacrifices I've made.

Out on the lawn, Chloe chases Noah, a croquet mallet raised over her head. These days, most of the time she acts like a sullen teenager. I cling to these carefree moments that offer a tiny window onto what she was like when she was younger.

"Should I break them up?" Max asks. "She might crack his head open."

I extract myself from under Max's arm. "I'll take care of it."

As soon as the kids see me coming, they drop their mallets and flee to the dock.

Max wins the croquet match. At least he apologizes before knocking me out.

Afterwards, Alice runs into the house and Max follows. Damian tosses Ritchie a can of Coors Light.

"Watch the carbs," Farley says.

I have to bite my tongue to keep from saying anything. Farley probably chose that shirt Ritchie's wearing, like I used to choose Ritchie's clothes. Farley catches my eye, and something in my expression must give me away because he raises his Cosmo glass and takes a sip. For a fleeting moment, I don't regret anything I've done.

"Alice shouldn't be working so hard on her birthday," I say, and excuse myself.

Inside, I hear Alice and Max talking in the kitchen. I hurry down a narrow hallway, past the bathroom, to Damian's office, where I peek through the doorway at his whiteboard. A photo of Laurel Thibodeau hangs in the center, right where it should be.

Back in June, Damian responded almost at once when I used the burner phone to anonymously send him information on Jeanine Geller's death.

Who is this? he demanded.

You already know, I wrote.

Don't contact me again, Damian replied a moment later.

Despite his protests, I imagined him here in this very office, staring at the three dots on his phone, hoping for more. I imagined him pulling up a browser on his laptop and searching Jeanine Geller. Her death was still an open investigation then.

Don't you want to catch me? I wrote. *I'm right here. Watching you're every move.*

I misspelled *your* on purpose, thinking Damian would like that, imagining him trying to find a hidden meaning in the mistake.

After that, I was careful with the phone. I kept it turned off whenever I was within a mile of the church, and when I did use it, I left behind anything that tracked my whereabouts and could link me to it, like my own phone, my FitBit, even my car. When Damian stopped by my office, I wondered if he'd mention the texts, if he'd ask me what I thought of them. But he kept them to himself.

Last week, I biked over to Mooney Point and sent a text

from outside Max's cottage that read, ***Sessions with a shrink are confidential***.

I study Damian's scrawl on the whiteboard. He hasn't made the connection between Farley and the deaths yet, though it's only a matter of time and giving him the right clues. Damian believes he's found his own Jack the Ripper or Son of Sam, a serial killer who's teasing out hints to his identity. Damian also believes his investigation brought the killer to this town, and that he's responsible for Laurel's death.

I leave the room and close the door.

The next time Damian comes to my office, I'll suggest again that he go to the police with what he knows. Max is used to fielding useless tips, to parsing through the helpful and the insane. But the state cops must have found the random hair at the Thibodeau crime scene. It's sandy in color. And even if it doesn't match DNA in the national crime database, it won't be long before they connect it to a local psychiatrist. In a way, planting the hair was a step too far, much further than the gentle revenge I'd originally planned, but by the time I'd planted it, I'd already reached a point of no return.

As I enter the kitchen, Max and Alice step away from each other. They stare at me, and it takes me a moment to parse what's happening between them. Max swipes at his mouth with the back of his hand. "Georgia," he begins to say.

Reverend George steps right in and takes over for me.

She shoos Alice away and watches as Max retreats, too. She recruits Ritchie to help with dinner, and when the ratatouille starts to fall from her grasp, she doesn't try hard enough to keep it from spilling across the floor. She sets the kids up in front of the TV and manages to have a warm moment with her daughter. "I like the pink," she says.

"You don't," Chloe says.

"What do you know?" Reverend George says.

Outside, she slides in beside Max at the table and rests her hand on his knee as though nothing has happened. He seems relieved as we link hands for a silent prayer.

Later, she tells Damian he can't come to the service on Sunday with a camera crew. When he suggests filming her using a tight shot, a seed of doubt lodges itself at the back of her mind. She begins to wonder if Damian knows more than he's let on, if maybe he's begun to suspect her of sending the texts—or worse. She thinks about *Acadian Autumn*, the way the mystery surrounding the priest seemed to emerge from the narrative, tiny threads there all along for anyone to pull at. She wonders if Damian plans something similar for her.

Farley disappears into the house to get more wine. Alice follows. When Damian and Ritchie leave to go to the dock, Reverend George finds herself alone on the patio with Max. She rests her head on his shoulder, if only to feel him close. If only to feel safe. "Do you want to talk about what you saw in the kitchen?" he asks.

"Not really," she says.

So they sit quietly. When the others return, I listen as Reverend George tells the story of meeting Ritchie for the first time. In a way, she tells it to hurt Max, to remind him he wasn't her first choice. "This one took me for a ride in an Edsel," Reverend George says. "An Edsel!"

Across the table, Farley lays a protective hand over Ritchie's. "An Edsel has nothing on a Triumph," he says.

It's only when Reverend George sees Alice standing beside Damian that I begin to settle back into myself.

Alice whispers in Damian's ear and lays a phone beside him. It's the burner that should be hidden in my drawer at the church office. I recognize the crack running across the screen from when it fell onto the concrete sidewalk.

Across the table, Farley's talking about a contract and a drive in the country, but all I can focus on is that phone—the one I used to send texts to Damian connecting three unrelated murders. Damian moves it from the table to his pocket.

Earlier this afternoon, at the church, Maggie let Damian into my office while I was at the school dealing with Chloe. He was in there by himself for God knows how long before I got back. Tonight, he asked about filming at the church as though he wanted me to take a central role in his documentary. As though I might be his secret killer.

For the first time, I start to panic.

CHAPTER 48
Georgia

ONE WEEK EARLIER

Last Friday, Maggie knocked on my office door right as I finished writing my sermon for Sunday. "Georgia," she said to me. "Do you have a minute."

I waved her in, on a high from finishing the writing so early. "*Informed by Death*," I said. "That's what I'm calling my sermon. It sounds like a murder mystery."

"They'll love it," Maggie said.

She took a seat but looked ready to bolt out of the room. Maggie has spent her whole life in Monreith. She and her husband live in the same house they bought right after they married, and her children have settled nearby. We get along, though I maintain a professional distance with her, even when she mocks Farley.

"My mother has a new boyfriend," she said.

I closed the laptop and gave her my full attention. Maggie's parents had moved into an independent living facility a year earlier, but her father died a few months later, and Maggie's mother recently began to show signs of dementia.

"What's her boyfriend's name?" I asked.

"Russ," Maggie said. "He seems nice enough. Harmless. They go to meals together and walk around the facility. The staff tells me this kind of thing happens all the time. I suppose they should have some fun while they can." She picked at imaginary lint on her pastel-green sweater. "He's got the same thing going on as my mother. You know, he's forgetful, so seeing them, it's kind of like you hear the same stories over and over. The same complaints. Sometimes I tune them out and let my mind wander."

My own mind was wandering now that I'd finished the sermon. I wondered whether Max would come by tonight, whether we'd do something with Chloe or go out for the evening. More than anything, I wanted Maggie to get to the point so I could send her home early, and I could get some time to myself before school ended for the weekend. "Understandable," I said.

"My mother had this charm bracelet she lost years ago," Maggie continued. "My father gave it to her. I don't think it was worth much of anything, but lately she's been obsessed with it. Every time I go over there, she tells me one of the staff members stole it, and Russ will be sitting beside her, and it's like the first time he's ever heard the story, too. He gets all indignant and can't believe anything like that would happen, and half the time I have to run interference before they go accusing someone. I mean, I don't need a fuss right now."

The independent living facility was already putting a strain on Maggie's finances. If her mother needed more services, Maggie had told me she doubted she'd be able to pay for them.

"That's why I didn't take it seriously at first," Maggie said. "I thought she was talking about the stupid charm bracelet. But then I found it online."

I pushed my chair away from my desk. "I'm not following. What did you find online?"

"Sorry," Maggie said. "I'm getting ahead of myself. The last few times I went over there, my mother mentioned something was missing, but she wasn't talking about the charm bracelet anymore. She was talking about a diamond ring, and I didn't believe her and now I feel like I'm the worst person on the face of the planet because it really was missing. I mean, it's not the Hope Diamond or anything, but the ring has to be worth a couple thousand bucks. And honestly, if we're going to sell it, I could use the money myself."

I put a hand on Maggie's arm. "Why don't you start at the beginning?"

An hour later, I parked on the circle by the Thibodeaus' house. I adjusted my scarf before heading up the driveway and ringing the bell. I heard footsteps in the hallway, and the door swung open. "Reverend George!" Laurel Thibodeau said. "I'm getting ready for work. But come in! I have fifteen minutes before I have to leave."

She'd already changed into black pants and a white Oxford. Her red hair spilled from a messy bun at the back of her neck. I stepped over the threshold. I'd been to the Thibodeaus' house a few times, and it always smelled of garlic and baking bread. It smelled of home.

Laurel led me into the kitchen and offered iced tea when I could have used a shot of vodka. She'd been an integral part of the parish since the Thibodeaus moved to town and opened Firefly a decade earlier. She spent her days off helping older parishioners get to appointments or do their shopping.

Parishioners like Maggie's mother.

Lately, more than one person had mentioned missing valuables, not enough for anyone beyond me to notice, but more than enough for me to have narrowed my focus to a handful of suspects. It wasn't till Maggie showed me the photo of her mother's ring for sale online that I found my culprit.

I glanced at Laurel as I took a sip of the iced tea. I'd had to speak to parishioners about crimes before. Sticky fingers in the collection box. Handsy men at the coffee hour. It was never easy to point out someone's failings, but I tried to work with them to maintain dignity and make restitution. I tried to keep reputations intact. I'd also learned early in this job to face difficult conversations directly, so I pulled up the photo of the ring on my phone.

"Nice ring," Laurel said. Her smile didn't touch her eyes. "You in the market?"

"Maggie's in the market," I said. "My secretary at the church."

"Why show me, then?"

I zoomed in on the photo, where the wing of an embroidered firefly poked into the very corner of the image. The ring was lying on a napkin from Laurel's restaurant. "You took the photo," I said. "You posted the ring for sale."

I expected her to deny everything before apologizing and offering up excuses—to cry, even. I'd have found a way to keep what happened quiet.

Instead, her face hardened. "What about it?" she said.

"Why do this?" I asked.

She opened a cabinet and took out a bottle of vodka. She poured a shot into an empty teacup and drank it down. She held the bottle up, and I shook my head. "Last week when I left the restaurant," she said, "some guy was waiting outside in the dark. He told me Simon owed him fifty grand and that he'd be back to collect another time. I thought he was going to kill me. I don't have that kind of money."

"There has to be a better solution," I said.

"Let me know when you figure it out." Laurel rested her forehead on her palms. "If your boyfriend finds out about this, he'll arrest me." She caught my eye. "See, we all have secrets. You've been sleeping with Max Barbosa. I've been sleeping with Damian Stone."

"If you know, then I suppose it's not a secret anymore."

"I suppose not," Laurel said. "Damian tells me you're a friend. That you have his back. And you're good with secrets."

She was bargaining, but this wasn't a secret I could keep. "I can help you tell your story your own way."

She faced me, her brow furrowed in thought. "Has Damian told you about the texts he's been getting?"

"Texts?" I asked.

"Some asshole has been sending him anonymous messages, trying to get him riled up, trying to convince him we have our own Son of Sam working the area."

As Laurel reflected my actions, for the first time I saw my own pettiness. I shivered at what I'd become capable of. "What are the texts about?" I asked.

"That's not really important," she said. "The more interesting question is who's sending them. And why. It's the kind of behavior that could ruin a reputation. A career even, especially these days. Imagine having that kind of thing follow you for the rest of your life anytime someone searched your name online. You'd be completely unemployable. A laughingstock." She nodded at my empty glass. "You done? I have to get to work."

I slid the glass toward her, my fingertips trailing down the damp surface.

Laurel folded her arms. "Damian showed me the texts. All of them. The last one said, *Sessions with a shrink are confidential.* Can you think of someone with a grudge against a shrink? Someone who Damian might trust enough to believe?"

I stood. I ran my hands through my hair. I adjusted my glasses. She was threatening me, and it should have been my turn to bargain. Instead, I put my phone away and said, "Max is the one with the grudge against a psychiatrist."

"I'll make sure to tell him you said that if he stops by to ask about a few missing trinkets. Who knows what rumors might take hold?"

I didn't trust myself to say anything else, so I headed toward the front door. By then, I'd left my fingerprints all over the house. Skin cells and hair, too. Out by my car, I faced the five other houses on the circle so their doorbell cameras could record my presence, a visit that was easy to explain away. Laurel, after all, was a valuable member of my parish.

The next afternoon, Damian came to my office at the church. I could tell right away Laurel hadn't revealed her suspicions, not yet at least. He trusted me too much, especially when he told me Simon Thibodeau had a wedding to cater that evening. "I shouldn't," he said, "but I'm heading over to see Laurel tonight after the restaurant closes. I'll slip out of the house once Alice goes to bed." He blushed. "I feel like a teenager again."

After he rode his bike away, I took my car to Farley's place for a quick visit. "Could I use your bathroom?" I asked as I was leaving.

"Of course," Farley said.

"You don't have cameras in here, do you?"

"Not yet."

That night, I returned to Laurel's house, slipping in through the woods to avoid any security cameras on the street. I hid in the dark, watching, till Damian appeared, and Laurel let him in the back. A few moments later, I slipped through the unlocked door and lurked in the shadows. Upstairs, they tore at each other's clothing. When they finished, they opened a bottle of wine and lounged on the sofa in the front room. "I'll tell Alice tomorrow," Damian said. "I promise."

I could hear them kissing from where I hid. "I should go," Damian said a few moments later, his breath heavy.

"You should go," Laurel said.

"Simon may be home soon."

"Have you heard from your friend?" Laurel asked. "Any more texts?"

"Not for a few days."

"My guess is you won't hear from him again, but you'll tell me if you do, right?"

"No secrets," Damian said.

"No secrets," Laurel said. "Not anymore."

Eventually, Damian left to go back to Alice, and Laurel was alone. She washed Damian's glass and put it away but filled her own with more wine. Upstairs, she took a shower, which gave me a chance to move to the next room without being heard. I waited till she'd turned the light off and her breathing grew steady before slipping into the room and standing over her.

By then, my eyes had adjusted enough to the darkness so I could see the steady rise and fall of her chest. It wasn't as though I didn't tell myself to leave, or that this particular mistake couldn't ever be undone. I simply chose not to listen to those voices.

No secrets.

I imagined Laurel telling Damian exactly what I'd done and how I'd abused his trust. She might do it in this bed, and soon enough the whole world would know, my career would be over, and my reputation gone. Laurel had said as much herself.

So I placed the plastic bag over her nose and mouth and held it there even after she woke up and tried to fight me off. I held it till her sightless eyes stared at me. I also left behind the hair I'd taken from Farley's bathroom. My final touch was to snap a photo of the crime scene to send to Damian. If he needed more proof he'd found a serial killer, this was it. That photo is still on the burner phone. The one Damian has now.

CHAPTER 49
Georgia

YESTERDAY

I stare at the table while the others sing "Happy Birthday" to Alice. Ritchie catches my eye. I touch his hand, and he squeezes my fingers. He mouths, "I'm sorry," and I say, "It's okay."

Alice blows out the candles on the cupcakes.

"What did you wish for?" Max asks.

"Nothing I'll share," Alice says.

Damian watches his wife, his eyes glistening. He must be thinking about Laurel and the life they could have lived. I wonder whether he's found his way into the burner phone yet, whether he's read through the texts and seen the photo of Laurel with a plastic bag over her face. If he's planning to turn the phone over to the police, how long will it take to trace it right back to me?

The others have begun to move away from the table. Now that the cupcakes have come out, the party is breaking up. At the edge of the patio, Ritchie whispers to Chloe till she dashes across the lawn and onto the carriageway. I wish I could run with her.

Ritchie's phone sits on the table, beside his half-eaten cupcake. I palm it and slide it into my pocket.

Unlike the others, I haven't had much to drink tonight,
though I doubt any of them have kept track, and I need an excuse to stay on the point tonight. At the edge of the patio, I
wave my arms. "I'm not gonna fall. I'm not gonna fall," I say,
and then I tumble off the side and into the shrubs. To
Ritchie's credit, he's the first one to my side. He finds my
glasses in the grass and apologizes again.

I touch his cheek. "Come on," I say. "Don't look so concerned."

Max helps me up. "Do you know what will get the chief of
police fired?" he asks. "Letting intoxicated people leave a
party and drive home. We're all walking tonight. No boats. No
cars. Georgia, you can sleep it off in the bunkhouse."

It's Ritchie who walks with me through the woods, who
checks to be sure I make it along the carriageway in one piece,
who apologizes the whole way. Ritchie was the person I
trusted most in the world. Now I don't trust anyone. Still, my
hand finds Ritchie's phone where it sits in my pocket, and I
feel a flash of remorse for what I plan to do to him.

In the end, someone needs to take the fall for what I've
done.

The bunkhouse sits in a grove of trees a few yards from
Max's cottage. It's rustic, built from pine with a single bare
bulb that hangs in the middle of the room. I make up one of
the beds with blankets and sheets stored in plastic tubs. Then
I take Ritchie's phone from my pocket and sit on the edge of
the mattress. When Ritchie and I were together, we shared
our passwords. I told him it was a matter of trust, though I
changed all of my passwords the day Ritchie moved out of the
parsonage. Thankfully, he didn't update his.

Once the first clap of thunder rumbles through the night, I
slip outside. At the farm, Alice and Damian are bringing

dishes up to the house. I wait till they're both inside and then edge onto the lawn and take one of the croquet mallets from the set before making my way down the rickety wooden stairs. I swing off the gangway, onto the marsh, and huddle under the wooden planks. I pull up a blank text on Ritchie's phone and add the burner's phone number. *Meet me at the dock.*

Damian will recognize Ritchie's number when the text appears on the burner phone. He'll want to know how Ritchie knows about that phone. He'll begin to suspect Ritchie sent him texts about two unsolved murders. He'll want to give Ritchie the benefit of the doubt, but he'll also demand to know what any of this has to do with Laurel's death.

I grip the croquet mallet with both fists.

I don't plan to give Damian the chance to find the answers.

Footsteps sound on the boards above me, followed by the patter of paws. I catch my breath, not daring to move.

"Who's there?" someone says, but it's Alice who's come. Not Damian.

Thunder rumbles. Harper leaps off the gangway and onto the marsh. "Harper," Alice whispers. "Come back."

The dog must smell me. She wags her tail, her haunches halfway to a sit as she tries guessing what might earn her a treat.

"Harper," Alice says, "don't make me go chasing you down."

I slide my hand into my pocket as quietly as I can and retrieve a plastic baggie. I hold a treat in my palm and Harper gobbles it up, chomping loudly.

"What did you find?" Alice asks.

She swings a leg over the railing and jumps to the ground, her back to me. I hold the mallet, ready to swing. Above us, thunder claps loud enough that the world seems to shake. Harper takes off, dashing across the marsh, her tail tucked between her legs. Alice runs after her as lightning fills the sky. I scramble to escape onto the gangway as the skies open and rain lashes my face.

I retreat up the stairs. I swing the mallet. I stride across the lawn. Damian must be inside. I'll finish this there.

But as I approach the farmhouse, Chloe materializes out of the rain and breaks through my focus. I freeze, staring at her Burger King T-shirt soaked through, her pink hair plastered to her face. Chloe starts to say something. She takes in the croquet mallet gripped in my fists.

"What are you doing here?" I ask.

I'm the mother, right? I went out into the storm searching for my daughter.

Lightning strikes, and I wonder what she sees in my face as she turns and flees onto the carriageway, back toward Mooney Point.

I stare after her, my body drained. Then I drop the croquet mallet and follow. Tomorrow, I'll find Damian and get the phone from him. I'll talk my way out of this. Now that Chloe's seen me here, I have no other choice. Besides, what else could happen before morning?

It's not till hours later, after Max tells me he doesn't love me, after Farley's body has been found, after the police question Ritchie and we've packed Chloe's bag and headed out to Detective Parke's car to return to the parsonage, that Chloe plays her hand.

"Imagine if I had been the one to find the body," she says to me. "I wouldn't have had a phone to call for help."

"You don't have your own phone?" Detective Parke asks. "How old are you anyway?"

Chloe turns to me. "See?" she says.

"I'll get you a phone this weekend," I say.

It's a small enough price to pay for silence.

CHAPTER 50
Georgia

When the detective drops Chloe and me at the parsonage, I tell Chloe to get some sleep, and I head over to the church office where I tear through the Lost and Found. The burner's gone, the way I knew it would be. I'm not sure how long I sit there, staring into the drawer, my laptop open to that single word, *Grief*. We're all grieving in our own ways.

Alice is grieving the end of her thirties and the beginning of middle age. Max is grieving what Mooney Point once was and will never be again. Simon Thibodeau is grieving his choices and asking if he had made different ones whether his wife would still be alive. Ritchie is grieving, too. He found a new life with Farley, one that's now lost forever. And then there's Damian. I wonder if in the end he'd have left Alice and chosen Laurel, if he'd have followed through on his promises to her, or whether he and Alice would have left Monreith for a new adventure when that professor returned to claim Moulton Farm. Even Chloe's grieving the end of her childhood, an end I assured.

Outside, an officer pulls up beside the parsonage in my car and leaves the keys on the dashboard before walking the two blocks back to the station. This was once the kind of town where people left their doors unlocked, their keys in their cars. It probably won't be anymore. I suppose the town is grieving, too.

Someone taps at my door. I turn from the window to see Damian in his black cycling jersey. "Maggie's not here standing guard," he says.

"Just me," I say. "Reverend George, at your service."

Normally, Damian would come into the office, sit in a chair, and rest one of his biking shoes on my desk. Today, he hovers in the doorway and won't meet my eyes.

"I thought you'd be talking to the cops," I say.

"They're at the house," Damian says. "They can come find me when they need me."

"You'll need to tell them about Laurel now," I say. "The rest of it, too."

I could ask him for the burner phone right now. He probably has it with him, tucked in the pocket of that black jersey.

"You mean the texts?" Damian asks. "I told the police about them last night. About Laurel, too. That's one of the reasons they're searching the farmhouse."

I nod toward my laptop. "I'm working on my sermon, though it's still only one word."

"*Grief*, right?" Damian asks. I nod.

"What have you been grieving?" he asks.

No one ever asks the minister how she feels. "The end of who I was," I say.

"Now you can be someone new. Isn't that something we all hope for?"

I'll never again be anyone but who I am now. I assured myself of that when I killed Laurel Thibodeau.

"Ritchie came with me on my ride this morning," Damian says. "I thought he'd be grieving more."

"He's in shock," I say.

"Maybe."

Suddenly the last thing in the world I want is to face this nearly blank screen or my own grief. "Why'd you come by, anyway?" I ask.

Damian kicks at the doorframe with the toe of his cycling shoe. "I have a friend who has made some bad decisions. Someone who should own up to them. I'm hoping they do so before anyone else finds out."

I try to keep my voice light as I say, "Are you playing amateur sleuth?"

"Isn't that what I've been playing all along with those text messages?"

I stand and cross to the other side of my desk. A part of me still believes I can talk my way out of this. "You could just give me the phone," I say.

Damian tilts his head, eyes squinted. "How do you know about Richard's burner phone?"

"He called me. He told me about it."

"When?"

"Just now."

Damian doesn't answer for a moment. "The cops took Richard's phone this morning." he says. "How would he have called you?"

I start to speak and stop. Then Damian comes at me, shoving me against the wall, his hand twisting at the scarf around my neck. I claw at his skin, fighting to breathe. His face red, so close I can feel his short gasps against my skin. "Please," I manage to say.

He rams his forearm into my throat and then suddenly releases the scarf and steps away. I slump to the floor, gasping at air as he stares down at me with a mixture of horror and loathing. He's the first person to see me for who I've become. It's a look I suspect I'll have to get used to. "You're lucky I don't kill you," Damian says.

He leaves. I listen as the clomp of his shoes fades down the hall. I struggle to my feet, touching the bruises on my neck. At the window, I watch as he pedals through the cemetery and up to Main Street. I half expect him to stop at the police station to turn me in, but he keeps pedaling through town.

Out in my car, I take the keys from the dashboard and drive till I see Damian ahead of me on Drift Road. I slow behind him till we reach a turn. He waves an arm for me to pass. I grip the steering wheel. We're the only ones out here, and Damian knows too much, and I've made nothing but bad decisions. What's one more?

I floor the gas. Damian slams headfirst into a guardrail with a thud. I glide to a stop, careful not to hit the brakes too hard. It won't do to leave tire treads for the police to find.

When I reach him, Damian's unconscious but still breathing. Barely. He won't last long enough for anyone to find him here alive, let alone for an ambulance to transport him to the hospital. I have to act quickly before someone drives by.

My heart pounds as I search his jersey. I comb through sand and clumps of beach grass, too, as Damian takes his last breath, and panic begins to rise in my throat.

He doesn't have the burner phone with him. If Damian doesn't have it, where could it possibly be?

Chloe's in the cemetery when I return to the church an hour later. She traces the names etched in a gravestone. I watch her for a moment and wonder if she'll ever comprehend how much I truly love her. "We have to stick together," I say. "They'll be coming soon. For all of us."

"Dad was here," Chloe says.

"When?" I ask.

"Just now. Uncle Max arrested him."

The police must have found the text I sent using Ritchie's phone.

"Why were you out in the storm last night?" Chloe asks. "Why did you go to the farm?"

"I was looking for you."

Chloe shakes her head. "That phone is yours," she says. "I found it in your office. Whatever's on it belongs to you."

I run my fingers through her hair, knowing in my heart it will be the last time. Chloe won't trust me again, no matter what happens. "I love the pink," I say. "And I love you. Don't ever forget that."

Chloe puts a hand over mine as though to brush me away. Instead, she squeezes tight.

"Where's the phone now?" I ask.

Chloe swallows. Her voice shakes when she says, "I gave it to Uncle Max."

I leave her and don't dare look back as I head upstairs and into my office. The sermon waits on my laptop, but I've had the theme wrong all week. It shouldn't be grief but choice: stay or leave, hate or love, lie or confess. It would have been so easy to write.

I swivel in my chair. The late summer sun shines through the glass and onto my face. Outside, Chloe stands in the cemetery, looking up toward my window. A few early autumn leaves fall around her. I raise a hand to wave. She waves back. I smile and nod to send her on her way. Then she turns and takes a tentative step, followed by another. Soon she's running onto Main Street, up the concrete steps, and into the police station where I hope Max is waiting. Chloe's made her choice. And it's for the best. In truth, it's almost a relief.

But remember this: I didn't kill Farley Drake.

PART VII

The Dog

CHAPTER 51
Harper

THREE MONTHS LATER

Here's my secret: I like treats. And I don't care what shape they come in or how I get them. I've even eaten trash.

Max isn't stingy with the treats, and he doesn't make me perform for them, either—unlike Alice, whose constant refrain is, "Nothing is free."

Lately, Max and Alice pretend they don't live together, but they spend every night in the same bed, sometimes at the cottage, sometimes here at the farm. No matter where they are, I lie between them when they're sleeping, then stand up, turn around, maybe stick my nose under one of their chins, then lie down again. I really like it when Max presses his palm to my chest and says, "Quiet there, girl."

It's nice to know he's there.

Now the sun has begun to come up, so I let them know it's time to go out. I stretch, first upward, then downward, then I walk across them, leaning all my weight on each paw. They're both wide awake but don't want me to know. I stand over Alice first and stare at her with my nose as close to her face as possible. She put on perfume three days ago when she and Max went to Firefly for dinner, but to me, the scent is intoxicating, almost overwhelming. When she squeezes her eyes shut, I shove my nose into her ear. "Harper, stop," she says, pulling the comforter over her head.

Max comes next. Even though he only smells like man, he gets the same treatment. Plus he's easier to manipulate. When we're alone, he tells me he can't believe Alice is his and he's terrified she'll find an excuse to leave even though they've decided to stay here in Monreith instead of moving to "Springfield." I have no idea what "Springfield" is. "She's too good for me, Harper," he'll say. "Can't she see that for herself?"

Now he swings out of bed and pulls on a pair of jeans. "Come on, girl," he says.

My paws thump to the floor.

I patter down the stairs. I don't like that black and white thing over there, the one that hisses, and I let it know. "Leave Tippi alone," Max says.

Tippi.

"You two, you'll need to be friends. We'll all be living in the cottage soon, and there's not as much space there."

I'll never be friends with awful *Tippi.*

But *Tippi* doesn't get to go outside, unlike me.

Max takes the leash from where it hangs in the foyer but doesn't connect it to my collar. He rarely does, not even at the town beach. We head down the cellar stairs and through the back door, and I dash across the patio and onto the lawn, where I squat, then I take off toward the bluff. A light rain falls, and everything is brown, and there's so much mud and so many scents, and if I had to choose, I'd take sniffing over treats.

"Harper!" Max calls, and I have the decency to let him catch up and give me another treat. "Ritchie's coming for dinner tonight with Chloe," he says. "Richard, I mean. I'm trying to get that right."

When we reach the top of the stairs, I see Chloe waiting way out on the end of the dock, where the gray water of the bay has receded with the tide. She wears a red rain jacket and has her back to us.

"You need to be extra sweet," Max says. "Let Chloe rub your belly. She's sad and misses Georgia. And despite everything Georgia did, I guess I do, too."

Georgia used to carry treats in her pocket, but I haven't seen her for a while, and most of the time when her name comes up in conversation, the subject gets changed almost at once.

"Don't tell Alice I said that, okay?" Max says. "She won't understand, and I can't expect her to."

He shouldn't worry. I keep everyone's secrets.

I take a step toward Chloe and look to Max for permission. "Go ahead," he says.

I run down the stairs and along the gangway, my tongue hanging out one side of my mouth. When I reach Chloe, it's all I can do to skid to a stop before we both tumble off the edge of the dock and into the water. She gets right down on the boards beside me and lets me lick her face, which is wet and tastes of salt. Chloe's hair used to be pink. Now it's just brown. Part of the reason Max isn't moving to Springfield is because of Chloe, who he says he can't leave right now. Behind me, he approaches. "What's got you up so early?" he asks.

"Couldn't sleep," Chloe says.

I wriggle onto her lap and submit to that belly rub, my eyes squeezed shut, my lips flapping open to reveal my canines. Max sits beside her. Sometimes when we find Chloe here in the morning, we'll watch the sun rise, and neither of them will say anything to each other. Afterwards, Max will slam his car door and drive off toward work at a million miles an hour, and Alice will say, "He wishes he could make it better for her."

This feels like it may be one of those mornings, at least until Chloe says, "How long will it be till this dock washes away? How long till global warming floods this whole shoreline?"

"Hopefully never," Max says.

"Hope isn't a strategy." Chloe kicks at the pilings. "Is my dad going to jail?"

"Where are you getting that from?"

"Someone at school."

"Is Taylor Lawson bothering you again?"

Chloe shakes her head. "Taylor's been kind of nice, at least since her parents got divorced. She wants to be a marine biologist, and I guess we're friends now. She and Noah run interference for me."

Chloe's friends with *Taylor Lawson?* Maybe I could give *Tippi* a chance.

"That's good to hear," Max says. "And the DA didn't press any charges against your dad. That was part of the deal your mother struck. It's part of the reason she confessed, and the case didn't have to go to trial."

"But if there was a deal, didn't Dad do something?" Chloe asks. "Doesn't a deal mean guilt?"

"After the murders, I had to go through that internal investigation before I could get my job back. It was humiliating and nerve-racking, and there are certain people in town who won't ever believe I didn't know something, but it doesn't mean I did anything. I just have to know that in my own heart." Max takes a deep breath. "Your mother killed Laurel Thibodeau and Mr. Stone. She confessed, and she's in jail."

"But she didn't confess to killing Farley," Chloe says. "And the case is still open. What if they come for my dad?"

"Damian Stone was right about one thing," Max says. "Farley Drake was a serial killer. The feds have connected him to murders in four states, and who knows what else they'll find. So the state cops won't invest any more time or money in closing Farley's homicide. They have better things to focus on."

Max doesn't mention that Chloe was the one who ran into the police station and told him she'd seen Georgia at Moulton Farm on the night Farley was killed, nor does he remind Chloe that she used the passcode 0531, the date Georgia discovered Farley's betrayal, to unlock the burner phone's secrets. Max believes Georgia killed Farley, and so do the state cops. Instead, he says, "You can ask yourself *why* for the rest of your life. No matter how many times you find part of the answer, it won't be enough. I know that's awful to hear, but it's the whole story. Your dad isn't guilty of anything besides falling for the wrong person."

And for being an idiot, and for taking dirty money, and probably for blackmailing Farley into signing over the deed to the house, but Max only tells me those parts when we're alone.

"Well," Chloe says, "he might be falling for the wrong person all over again. That barista's at the house right now, and Dad's bringing him for dinner tonight."

"He seems nice enough. What's his name? Bruce? Scott?"

"Duncan. Like the doughnut. No wonder he drinks so much coffee."

It's the first joke I've heard Chloe make in months. And it gives me a ray of hope. I nudge her elbow with my nose, and she scratches right at the base of my tail as it thumps softly on the dock.

"You should tell me who's been picking on you at school," Max says.

"Maybe I should," Chloe says. "But I won't."

"Why not?"

"Because I don't want you showing up at school as the chief

of police. It'll make things worse. Just be my Uncle Max, okay? And besides, I have to fight my own fights." She kisses Max on the cheek and scratches me behind the ears. "Don't worry about me. I'll see you tonight."

"Stay," Max says. "I'll make you breakfast. You can hang out with Tippi."

Tippi.

"I should go," Chloe says. "Duncan likes to make me a latte in the morning. And besides, my dad'll wonder where I went."

"You drink coffee now?"

"Don't worry. It's decaf."

Max watches as she runs along the gangway and up the stairs until she disappears beyond the bluff. He shoves his hands into his pockets. "You did a good job with her," he says to me.

Instead of returning to the farmhouse, we head to the salt-marsh, where I lose it because the bay is empty, really empty, and the mud flats stretch for what seems like miles. Max says, "Don't go too far," and tosses a stick.

I take off. Every time one of my paws sinks into the mud, I'm enveloped in what heaven must smell like. I find the stick and bring it back. I drop it at Max's feet. He makes me wait, then offers a treat before tossing the stick into the marsh again. This time, once I get going, I forget about the stick and keep running until the marsh ends and the thick mud of the bay begins. Max might be calling my name, but I pretend not to hear. I find a dead horseshoe crab and roll along it. I find another stick, one that's slick and shiny, with green stripes on the end. I grip it with my teeth and yank it from the mud. I remember this stick, because even after all this time, it reminds me of the night of the thunder. The night Alice got in a fight with Damian. The night I ran.

I remember how Alice stood on the edge of the patio as rain fell around us. "Who's there?" she called into the dark.

When no one answered, she glanced toward the house where Damian had retreated not five minutes earlier. Then she slipped that phone with the cracked screen into her pocket and stepped across the lawn to the wooden stairs. By the time we reached the gangway, I could smell Georgia waiting beneath us. Her scent was stronger than normal, as though she were sweating. Georgia always had treats, so the moment Alice released my leash, I leapt onto the marsh.

"Harper," Alice said. "Come back."

Georgia lurked in the shadows beneath the gangway, gripping this same stick, the one I just found in the mud. I wondered if she might throw it for me. Instead, she offered a treat. I gobbled it up and waited for another.

Alice called to me again. I could tell she wanted to put the leash on my collar. "Don't make me go chasing you down," she said, as she clambered over the edge of the gangway.

Right then, thunder rumbled, and I remembered being on this marsh by myself before I knew Alice. I remembered being hungry and cold and searching for something, anything, to eat. All I wanted was to get as far from the noise as I could. I forgot all about Alice and Georgia and the treats, and I ran. But the noise wouldn't stop. It didn't matter where I went or how I dodged, I couldn't escape. I reached the channel right as the night lit up. It was enough to make me stop in my tracks, if only for a moment.

Alice tackled me.

We splashed into the shallow water as another rumble began and I struggled to escape. But Alice was strong. She held me to her chest as my heart pounded, and water lapped around us. "This will pass," she whispered.

When I gave in and stopped fighting, Alice attached the leash to my collar. She rolled onto her hands and knees and stood slowly. We made our way over the marsh and to the stairs. Alice limped a little from where she'd banged her knee

354 / EDWIN HILL

in the fall. By now, the rain was coming down heavily, and the thunder and lightning had moved right overhead. As we crossed the lawn, Alice tripped over the stick Georgia had been holding under the gangway. Alice picked it up right as an unsettling scent wafted over me. I couldn't help it. A growl formed at the back of my throat.

"It's probably just a raccoon," Alice said as she peered into the trees.

I heard a twig snap, then someone stepped out of the shadows.

"Farley?" Alice said.

"You're awake," Farley said.

I barked, and he took a step backward.

Alice rested a hand on my head, but she didn't tell me to be quiet like she normally did. I know a threat when I smell one. Maybe she smelled it, too.

"Did you forget something?" Alice asked.

"I was out for a walk," Farley said.

"Harper doesn't like the thunder."

"It frightens her," Farley said.

"Let's walk together. The storm will pass soon enough, then we can all go to bed."

Farley glanced toward the farmhouse.

"Not that way," Alice said, taking his arm and steering him away from the house, the stick still gripped in her hand. "We'll go down to the water."

When we reached the stairs, Farley said, "After you."

Alice took the stairs quickly, pulling me along, even as I did my best to keep Farley in sight and make sure he followed. Alice swung onto the marsh and waited for me to leap after her. When thunder rumbled, she whispered, "Don't run, sweetie," but I wouldn't run now. Not when every fiber of my being howled that Alice was in danger.

Farley landed on the grass beside us. It took all I had not to snarl again. He lifted a wool hat off and swept his hand through his wet hair. "Where are we going?" he asked.

"Toward the boat launch. We'll walk along the shore." Alice swung the stick beside her as we made our way across the marsh. "You came back for a reason, though. Tell me why."

"Earlier tonight," Farley said. "You asked what I do when a patient confesses to murder."

Alice twisted the leash around her wrist. "Is that why you came back? To ask if I had something to confess? Are we in a session now?"

"We could be," Farley said. "Like I told you earlier, the confession stays in the room. And it feels good to let it go. I saw the way you looked at Laurel Thibodeau's photo tonight."

He stopped. Rain poured down around us. I strained at the leash, but Alice held tight.

"You should get your dog under control," Farley said.

"She is under control."

"I suppose she is," Farley said, reaching toward me until I snapped at his hand.

Alice kicked at a tuft of marsh grass. "I didn't kill Laurel Thibodeau, if that's what you're asking."

She jumped from the marsh and into the channel, pulling me with her. As we crossed the shallow water to the boat launch, Farley caught up with us. "That weight you're carrying," he said, "that tightness in your chest, it all dissipates when you tell the truth. You can tell that truth to me. You can trust me."

Alice faced him. "Okay," she said. "What if some men deserve to die?"

It took a moment, but Farley's eyes lit up as the realization dawned on his face. "That priest in Maine?"

"Maybe. He'd hurt too many people, destroyed too many lives. So maybe I destroyed him."

"Others, too?" Farley asked.

"Like I said, maybe."

Farley let the words hang in the damp night air like he did whenever Alice spoke during their sessions.

"It's your turn now," Alice said. "Tell me why you came back tonight. Tell me why you're wearing that hat?"

"I thought it might be cold," Farley said.

"But it's not. It's humid."

"I try to be prepared."

"I saw you tonight, too," Alice said, "when we were talking in Damian's office, when you were looking at his whiteboard. You don't realize it, but you're not as impassive as you think you are. Your face gives you away, all those twitches and tics. They tell your truth. We're the same, you and me. I've told my story. Now tell me yours."

Farley ran a hand along his leg, where the hilt of a knife stuck out from a sheath. I growled deep in my throat and hoped Alice could see the knife, too.

"Confessions don't work both ways," Farley said. "If you know my truth, you can disclose to anyone you want. Besides, your husband's gotten a little too close on his own."

"Those people on Damian's whiteboard?" Alice asked.

"Most of them," Farley said. "And like you, others as well."

Now I could smell Alice's sweat. Her fear, too. "What if I plan to kill again?" she asked.

"Someone specific?"

Alice nodded.

"Then I'd have to disclose."

"That's what I assumed."

Lightning struck right over us. Steel flashed in Farley's hand. The tightness at my throat released as Alice dropped the leash. I lunged, but Alice swung the mallet once, then again. And then once more, until Farley slumped to the sand, the knife still clutched in his fist.

The thunder faded. Alice froze in place, her eyes wide, the

mallet raised over her head. I forgot to bark, as Alice fell to her knees. I came to her side. I licked blood splatter from her face. "I had to do it," she whispered as she held me close. "He was coming for me. For Damian and Noah, too. I didn't have any other choice."

For once, she didn't need to rationalize. And I wished I could tell her that. But instead, we huddled on the sand until the storm passed and the incoming tide inched closer to Farley's body. Finally, Alice waded into the water and hurled the mallet as far as she could into the bay where I suppose she hoped it would be swept out to sea when the tide turned.

She has a much better arm than Max.

"Harper!"

Max calls to me now from the shoreline. He's come as far as he can without wading into the mud. "Let's go, girl. I have to get to work. And leave whatever you found there. I'm sure it's disgusting."

I don't care what he says. I'm bringing him this mallet. Or maybe I should bring him the dead horseshoe crab instead.

Yes, I bet he'd prefer that. It smells so good. I'll bring him the mallet another time.

ACKNOWLEDGMENTS

For anyone who'd like to visit Monreith, you can find parts of it in three Massachusetts towns: Plymouth, Westport, and my home town of Duxbury. The rest, particularly the residents, I made up.

So many thanks to all the people who helped make this novel a reality:

To Lynne Griffin and Joseph Moldover, who advised me on the details of counseling ethics, particularly around disclosure. To Gwendolyn Lowrance and Lydia Scharer, who gave me tips on making Chloe's voice authentically 13 years old. To Katherine Ramsland who gave me ideas for authentic crime scenes, especially that *P.S.* Also, to the two ministers who guided me through the daily tasks of running a congregation. As always, any errors are mine.

To Trisha Blanchet, Dana Isaacson, Kate Kinast, Kimberly Hensle Lowrance, August Norman, Karen Odden, and Whitney Scharer, for being tough editors and readers and making this novel so much better.

To Ryunosuke Akutagawa, Akira Kurosawa, and anyone involved with the TV shows *The Affair* or *Clickbait* for inspiring the structure of this story. It was much harder to pull off than I ever could have imagined!

To Nancy Blaire for that charm bracelet.

To the teams at Kensington Books and Sterling Lord Literistic: Robin Cook, Lynn Cully, Jackie Dinas, Vida Engstrand, Darla Freeman, Lou Malcangi, Tracy Marx, Alexandra Nicolajsen, Steve Zacharius, and especially Larissa Ackerman, Robert Guinsler, Lauren Jernigan, and John Scognamiglio.

To Michael Starr, Edith Ann, Jack and Betty Hill, Christine Hill, Chester, and all the Hills, Rowells, Starrs, Miraldas, and Sullivans.

To librarians and booksellers everywhere.

To friends and the whole writing community. Here are just a few of the folks and organizations who helped make this novel happen: Samantha M. Bailey, Maggie Barbieri, Jenna Blum, Peter Cannon, Hillary Cassavant, Mark Cecil, Bruce Robert Coffin, Oline Cogdill, John Copenhaver, Crime Bake, Karen Dionne, Sara DiVelo, Charlie Donlea, Emerson College, Daniel Ford, Stephanie Ford, Charles Garabedian, Julie Gerstenblatt, Mario Giordano, Connie Johnson Hambley, Julie Hennrikus, Alex Hoopes, Femi Kayode, John Keyse-Walker, Dru Ann Love, Bracken MacLeod, Malice Domestic, Hannah Mary McKinnon, Louise Miller, Scott Montgomery, Paula Munier, Mystery Writers of America, Carla Neggers, Hank Phillippi Ryan, Sisters in Crime, Joanna Schaffhausen, Shawn Reilly Simmons, Missy Stockwell Martin, Adam Stumacher, Peter Swanson, Jessica Treadway, John Valeri, Gabriel Valjan, Tessa Wegert, Kristopher Zgorski.

And most of all, thanks to you for taking a chance on this novel. Please stay in touch!

edwin-hill.com

Facebook, Twitter, and Instagram: ***@edwinhillauthor***

Visit our website at
KensingtonBooks.com
to sign up for our newsletters, read
more from your favorite authors, see
books by series, view reading group
guides, and more!

BOOK CLUB

BETWEEN THE CHAPTERS

Become a Part of Our
Between the Chapters Book Club
Community and Join the Conversation

Betweenthechapters.net

Submit your book review for a chance to win exclusive
Between the Chapters swag you can't get anywhere else!
https://www.kensingtonbooks.com/pages/review/